OUT OF LOVE,
DESPERATION
EMPIRE. . . .

RAPHAEL—A penniless Sicilian immigrant, he made his way across America, living on dreams of love, of making fine wine, of the ripe new land he would call his own.

ANGELICA—Beautiful, stubborn, courageous, she defied her father's pride to marry Raphael. Together, they would found a dynasty.

RIVERA—A man of pride and passion, he was Raphael's brother in blood—until La Causa separated them . . . violently and forever.

ALICIA—She lived in the nightmare cocoon of a terrible secret. Only Rivera could lead her back to life—and even then, the past reached out to claim her.

A SAGA AS RICH AND LUSH AS THE VINEYARDS OF CALIFORNIA. A NOVEL AS RICH AND EXHILARATING AS . . .

BLOOD
RED WINE

BLOOD
RED WINE

LAURENCE DELANEY

A DELL BOOK

Published by
Dell Publishing Co., Inc.
1 Dag Hammarskjold Plaza
New York, New York 10017

Dell ® TM 681510, Dell Publishing Co., Inc.

ISBN: 0-440-10714-8

Printed in the United States of America
First printing—July 1981

Especially for
My Mother—Evelyn
My Father—Charlie
and
Mary Louise—
For the ultimate gift . . . and surprise.

The author would like to express his appreciation and respect to Jeanne F. Bernkopf for her counseling, consoling, hand-holding, and most of all—her editing. The author would especially like to express his thanks to her for rekindling the desire to finish the unfinishable.

Thanks also to the winemakers of Sonoma County, California. Their warmth, graciousness, willingness to share gave the author moments and memories to draw from to tell this story.

BLOOD
RED WINE

BOOK
ONE

BOOK
ONE

CHAPTER ONE

She had a wide-eyed girlish charm about her. Yet Alicia Orsini's fawn-brown eyes hinted of a womanly sexuality. She was barely into her teens and looked—and was—innocent. But most men who saw her for the first time assumed, or at least hoped, she wasn't.

She was being watched now as she made her way through the throng of Sunday strollers parading along Montepulciano's main avenue.

Dressed in a flowing, virginal white dress, with a lace handkerchief still pinned in her hair from Mass, she followed a half block behind her mother down the wide, parklike avenue, away from the three-hundred-year-old, spired cathedral.

Falling in behind two handsome couples, Alicia was reveling in the joy of just being alive. The bright sunlight that filtered down between the overhanging chestnut trees felt luxurious against her body. She loved Sundays. The crowded streets. The strollers. The endless parade of pushcart vendors selling frozen ices and spicy sausages cooked over the wood coals of black braziers. The men hawking trinkets.

She even enjoyed the musky smoke from the Turkish tobacco cigarettes that hung from the mouths of the dark-headed young men who passed dressed in their rough, hand-woven Sunday pants.

Unlike the two elegantly clothed couples she walked behind, most of the citizens of this small city on Italy's eastern coast halfway between the Po River and the heel of the boot were poor peasants struggling just to survive.

But on Sundays Alicia felt as though a spell had been cast over them all, and she imagined they were all rich, important, and without worries.

Every Sunday Alicia was up before dawn to bathe and put on her Communion dress for the six-mile walk into Montepulciano along the narrow, windy road above the cliffs that fell into the sea. After Mass, she and her mother would rush back through the crowded streets to the outskirts of the small city, hoping to catch a ride home on the back of a cart. Once home, she would take off her dress, fold it carefully, and spend half the afternoon pounding laundry on rocks next to the well near their dirt-floored hovel.

Sundays were a whirlwind—a blur for Alicia. She wished there was some way to draw out their visit to Montepulciano a little longer and that her mother could enjoy standing around after Mass talking and visiting with other families who lived near them.

But there was little in her mother's life to enjoy. They were poor and she had to worry about their survival. For more than half of every day, Maria Orsini sat in a dimly lit room with a dozen other black-shawled women making delicate lace for a broker who got rich from it in Rome. Her eyes were already growing weak from the terrible lighting. And her fingers were showing the arthritic effects of the day in and day out needlework.

Alicia worked also. She was younger so her work was harder. In the fields . . . the vineyards . . . the orchards. In town she was a girl-child ravaged by hundreds of eyes. In the fields she was merely one of a hundred faceless figures hidden from the sun or cold by scarves and worn clothing that were almost a natural part of the landscape in this primitive part of Italy.

Yet Alicia and her mother survived a little better than most, for Alicia had two older brothers who also contributed to their subsistence.

Pietro Orsini, the oldest at nineteen, was a shepherd for the Padrone on whose land their hovel sat. He received no pay, but his work gave them the right to live on the Padrone's land.

Rafael, a year younger than Pietro, lived in Milan where he was an apprentice in the prestigious Bugatti Motor Car Works. He lived meagerly and sent most of his salary home for them every month.

The thought of Rafael brought a smile to Alicia's face as

14

she followed after her mother, whose determined pace had now taken her almost a full block ahead. She would never forget how Rafael had looked that delirious, joy-filled day he had returned from the army. He was gaunt . . . tired looking. But the years of war hadn't dimmed his sparkling eyes or wiped the disarming smile from the face of her favorite brother.

In many ways the army had proved a blessing for Rafael and them. It had taken him out of the small province of his birth and exposed him to the once mysterious world.

Shortly after returning, Rafael had left them once again and headed back north. The industrialized cities were suffering from the manpower lost to the war. And within a month, Rafael's mechanical talents were recognized by a foreman at the Bugatti Motor Car Works. The man remembered the young man from the army. And remembered his reputation for being able to keep things running when no one else could. The foreman had Rafael signed to a long-term apprenticeship which included teaching him to read and write, then technical school. And the Orsinis had celebrated. Rafael's good fortune would lead them out of their poverty.

Approaching The Montepulciano, the city's most elegant hotel, which was near the fountain-filled main plaza, a melodic laugh drew Alicia's attention back to the two couples she'd been walking beside. She'd first seen them during Mass in the ornate cathedral. Now she was lost in a fantasy of what it would be like to have clothes like the two young women were wearing.

The taller of the two had large breasts outlined by a glossy silk blouse under her blue velvet jacket. The other young woman was petite, with sharp aristocratic features and ivory-colored skin. She was wearing a delicate peach-colored dress covered with embroidered brocade. As they moved down the avenue, their two companions occasionally had to dodge the ladies' broadbrimmed hats as they looked around.

Alicia saw that a circle of people had stopped to visit in the middle of the sidewalk. She hurried so she could pass the two couples before they reached the logjam She smiled as she too had to duck one of the ladies' hats as she passed.

Suddenly, Alicia felt her face flush a bright red. The skinny man with the drooping waxed mustache had his hand casually around the woman with the huge breasts. It seemed that he was guiding her down the sidewalk. But when Alicia had to dodge the woman's hat, she could see that neatly hidden by the folds of the velvet jacket the man's hand was brazenly cupped around the woman's breast.

As the flush in her face started to pale, the shock she momentarily felt was replaced by a strange sensation. It was a warmth she had never experienced before. She looked to see if her mother had noticed. Fortunately, her mother had walked on, concentrating only on her destination, not even aware that Alicia was falling farther behind.

As Alicia hurried to catch up, the rays from the bright sun outlined her long, fawnlike legs through the delicate material of her dress.

From his table at the cafe on the veranda of the hotel, Pasquale Gianini caught sight of Alicia's legs silhouetted through her dress.

Bellissima! he thought as she seemed to glide toward him.

As she sauntered past his table, he was mesmerized. His imagination sent his blood pounding as it traced her figure upward, past her long, flowing legs, her flat stomach, to her blossoming young breasts with their tiny, immature pink nipples.

Every Sunday Pasquale Gianini sat like a reigning monarch in the shade of festively colored umbrellas at the cafe where he could be seen, admired, and envied as the wealthiest man in the province. The widower owned all the important agricultural lands, controlled the city's leading bank, and the province's leading industries. Directly or indirectly, this grandfatherly looking man ruled the lives of every man, woman, and child in his part of Italy.

As he crushed his dry, black cigar into the ceramic ashtray, his hand trembled slightly. The ashtray rang against the marble tabletop attracting a harried waiter.

"Signore?" The waiter asked rushing to him and bowing slightly. *"Un altro espresso?"*

"No." Gianini said shaking his head impatiently. He waved his hand for the waiter to clear his table.

The waiter bowed again as he picked up the empty demitasse and twisted lemon peel.

"An interesting young woman," Gianini said to the waiter, nodding in Alicia's direction.

The waiter looked up, searching the passing strollers for a young woman.

"The child?" The waiter asked as his eyes fell on Alicia. He was secretly amused. The old Padrone's passion for young girls was legendary.

"*Sì*," Gianini said almost to himself as he watched Alicia disappear among the Sunday strollers. "Do you know her?"

"No, *signore*." He shrugged. "But I think I have seen her pass this way a few times after Sunday Mass."

The following Sunday, standing next to her mother waiting for Mass, Alicia watched as Pasquale Gianini's new Bugatti convertible glided to a stop in front of the crowd of parishioners waiting to enter the cathedral. His sparkling new car was one of the finest available in all Europe. The bright oak wheel spokes glistened from heavy coats of lacquer and the brass straps circling the bonnet looked like bands of gold. Alicia felt a tug at her heart when she saw the name of the car emblazoned across the grill. Bugatti! Rafael probably worked on that very automobile, she thought.

As Gianini swung out of the pleated leather seat to the running board, the gaping peasants stepped back, their hats in their hands, to form a cordonlike pathway toward the cathedral doors.

Gianini made his way regally through the throng of favor seekers, smiling at his subjects, those already indebted to him and the black-shawled widows shading themselves under their parasols. Briefly his eyes rested on Alicia standing respectfully on the steps above him. He'd taken note of how the girl's eyes widened at the sight of the gleaming, hand-constructed automobile.

Alicia watched as the Padrone made his way up the steps slipping silver coins to the peasant children who surrounded him so they would have something to drop in the collection plate.

She knew Pasquale Gianini, of course. The Padrone!

Who in this part of Italy didn't? Her own brother tended some of his endless flocks of sheep. She had seen him on occasion from a distance. But this was the first time she'd seen him this close.

He looked old to her, his soft white skin sagging over the starched collar of his suit. But there was something pleasant about his smile.

"Signorina?" he said stopping in front of her and offering her a coin for the collection.

"No, *signore. Molto grazie."* Alicia answered, embarrassed that he should think of her the same as the other peasant children. She felt her mother's fingertips pushing sharply on her back, a warning not to offend the Padrone.

Gianini smiled at the girl's pride and at the apparent uneasiness of the old crone behind her.

"Come si chiama, signorina?" He lifted her chin in a fatherly manner while relishing the feel of her skin on his fingertips.

"Alicia . . . Alicia Orsini, Padrone."

"And this lovely woman with you?" he asked smiling at Alicia's mother.

"This is my mother, Maria Orsini," she said, stepping away from her mother's warning hand.

"Orsini . . . Orsini?" He thought aloud. "Ah! *Sì . . . sì!* Now I remember. One of your sons . . . I forget his name . . . abandoned my service for the military."

Maria paled. Did the Padrone think a member of her family would dare offend him? "Pardon, *signore.* My younger son went to the war, that is true. But he had no choice, Padrone. The army, they came for him. But my older son, Pietro, still serves you as a shepherd."

"I see," Gianini said. "Then please accept my apology for voicing such a misinformed opinion."

"Oh no, Padrone! *Prego.* No apology is needed." Maria was embarrassed that a man as powerful as Gianini should apologize in public to someone as unimportant as she.

"No. I was wrong." Gianini interrupted. "And I am a man who willingly acknowledges his mistakes. So to show my penitence, I insist that you occupy the seat next to me during Mass."

There was a murmur from the crowd standing near them. Black-clad matrons nodded their approval at the

Padrone's charity. They were unaware that the Padrone's usually quiet conversation was louder than normal. Just loud enough to make them all a party to his generosity.

Gianini's private box was the most conspicuous in the whole cathedral. It had been bestowed on him by a grateful bishop as a reward for his many generous contributions to the Mother Church. Rarely did he share it with anyone other than his family, visiting church leaders from the Vatican, or royalty.

Alicia's knees felt weak as Gianini took her elbow and guided her past the curious faces down an aisle that suddenly seemed a hundred miles long to her.

For Gianini the aisle seemed shorter than he remembered it to be. Nodding politely as he guided Alicia and her mother past two portly matrons, he was mesmerized by the possibility that because of her age, Alicia might not be wearing anything under her dress other than underpants. The thought of tracing her flat hips up to her sweet young breasts brought perspiration to his forehead.

Throughout Mass, Alicia was aware of the hundreds of eyes staring at the back of her head. When the collection plate passed, Gianini handed Alicia a thick wad of folded bills. Her hand trembled as she put the money on the gleaming silver tray engraved with a picture of the crucified Christ. It was more money than she had seen in her entire life.

"*Mille grazie* for this honor, Padrone," Maria mumbled as Gianini guided them back through the crowd toward his car after the service.

"*Prego, signorina.*" He smiled graciously. "The pleasure was indeed mine. But now may I ask you a favor of your daughter in return."

"*Sì*, Padrone. Of course. Anything!"

"I need someone to sit in my automobile and depress the throttle linkage," he said, explaining something he knew was absolutely beyond her comprehension. "It will inject petrol into the cylinders and ignite the engine when I crank it."

"But, Padrone. My daughter is a child. She knows nothing about automobiles."

"It doesn't require experience." He put his arm around Alicia's waist and lifted her into the seat behind the ebony

19

wheel. "Besides . . ." He leaned back and whispered to Maria, "It is just a little treat . . . a reward."

Maria smiled and nodded.

"You see how easily your daughter's instincts tell her what is correct?" Gianini said as Alicia automatically put both hands on the steering wheel. Gianini took them in his for a moment. "Now, my child. While I crank the engine from the front, you must depress this throttle."

He placed her hand on the linkage next to the steering wheel.

"*Sì*, Padrone. I pray I won't fail."

"You won't fail, my dear child. I guarantee it." He gave her hand a long squeeze.

Alicia's heart pounded. Just seeing an automobile like this was a thrill. An opportunity to sit in it was a reward beyond her wildest dreams. Wait until Rafael heard. He would probably even know the car, she thought, holding tightly to the linkage. He had probably sat in this same position while working on it.

"Thank you, Padrone," she said, sinking back in the comfortable seat with its soft new leather.

Gianini moved to the front of the auto and with three quick cranks, the engine chugged to life. Quickly, he walked back and slipped in to the seat next to Alicia who was still waiting for instructions with an iron grip on the throttle.

"*Bene . . . Bene!*" he said, patting her on the knee several times. "You see how easy it was?"

"*Grazie, signore,*" she said, unaware that she'd done nothing.

She started to slide out. But Gianini kept his hand firmly on her knee.

"You can see much better from here," he advised.

"*Scusi,* Padrone. I don't understand."

"As a reward for your help and for being so charming to an old man, I've decided to reward you with a short ride. If, of course, your mother has no objections."

Maria felt a heaviness in the pit of her stomach as she nodded approval. She was afraid to offend this man who held the future of so many people in his hands.

"*Va bene!*" He smiled as he eased the car into gear and

20

pulled away from the curb. "Don't bother waiting for her. I will see to it that she gets home safely."

Alicia laughed and gasped and screamed with excitement as Gianini sped through the narrow cobblestone streets, his horn blaring, tires squealing.

"I'm glad it excites you as much as it does me," Gianini called over the sound of the engine as he circled back through the main plaza and around the fountains. "Touring in the automobile has become one of my greatest passions."

On the outskirts of town, they passed a procession of homeward-bound families sitting crowded together in the backs of donkey-drawn drays. Gianini watched as Alicia sat as tall in her seat as she could to make sure they recognized her.

As they passed another dray pulled by a struggling donkey, one of the black-shawled women looked up. The woman's dark eyes flashed at Alicia for an instant before she suddenly looked away.

Alicia stared back with pride and arrogance. Then it dawned on her. The woman had not looked away in envy. But in embarrassment. For Alicia.

Suddenly her pride was displaced by the reality of what all the old hags would be saying about her. She'd heard their cutting condemnations many times before about young girls seen alone with the Padrone . . . or with any man for that matter. Mortification flooded through her along with a terrible foreboding.

Slowly she inched away from the middle of the seat where the Padrone had his leg pressed against hers. Then she began to feel more relaxed. He didn't seem to have even noticed. Perhaps she had been wrong. After all, he was the Padrone. What would he want with someone like herself?

She was just starting to feel embarrassed at her foolishness when he looked at her and patted the empty space that had grown between them.

"What's wrong?"

"Nothing, Padrone. It's only that I thought . . . well . . . that you would need the room. You know . . . to steer better."

21

Gianini patted the pleated seat again and pointed to the empty space with his jeweled index finger.

"I am an expert driver, my dear. I have more than enough room to steer comfortably. And it will help warm this aging man's heart if you would sit here next to me."

He smiled. But Alicia recognized it as a command. Slowly, reluctantly, she moved back to the center and sat so that her leg pressed next to his.

The countryside beyond this city was a patchwork of rolling, green hills broken by long lines of hand-quarried stone walls that separated row after row of vineyards that stretched toward the horizon.

Slowing to a speed that kept them just ahead of the roostertail of dust kicked up by the tires, Gianini said, "I meant to compliment you earlier when we were leaving the cathedral, Alicia."

She had been staring off at the horizon lost in apprehension. Now she turned her head and looked at him, not having heard what he'd said.

"Your dress. It's a very beautiful dress." He reached over and traced her flowing hairline down to the nape of her neck. She tried to speak, but her throat was dry.

Her mother constantly warned her about the young men who worked alongside her in the fields. But it was her mother who had let her take this ride. She was confused. She didn't know what to do.

With casual indifference, Gianini reached over and pulled the hem of her dress up past her knees, exposing her thighs to the warmth of the sun.

"Please, *signore*." Tears welled into her eyes.

It was as if he didn't hear. And Alicia was paralyzed with confusion as he moved his hand along the inside of her bare thigh. The faint sensation she'd felt watching the skinny man secretly rub the woman's breast the previous week suddenly flowed back into the pit of her stomach.

She knew it was wrong. But the way his hand was moving up and down the inside of her leg was so pleasurable, it seemed to contradict all her mother's warnings about the terrible pain she'd suffer if she ever dared let a man touch her.

In a storm of dust, Gianini swerved into a narrow, rutted lane that led deep into one of the vineyards. The spike-

22

trained grapevines were higher than a man's head and the luscious green leaves that hid the ruby grapes were so thick it was like being in a forest.

Gianini switched off the magneto. The engine died and the glistening oak-spoke wheels slid to a stop. With the exception of the gentle breeze that rippled the tops of the leaves, the vineyard was as quiet as the cathedral during confession.

Quickly he slid across the seat to where Alicia was now rigidly pressed against the door. His face had turned a deep red. Alicia could see that his shirt was soaked with perspiration and he seemed barely able to catch his breath.

"*Dio . . . Dio . . . Dio!*" he whispered, moving his hand softly over her firm breast.

"No! *La prego!* No, Padrone." She screamed as panic finally overtook her. She thrashed and tried to twist away so she could leap out of the car.

Gianini grabbed her by the back of her dress. Her treasured white dress was torn almost in half as he pulled her back into the seat.

"Listen . . ." he spat. "Listen, you stupid little bitch. I'm not going to do anything that will do you any harm. I'm only going to bring you pleasure."

"No . . . In God's name, Padrone. Please . . . please. My mother!" She was almost hysterical now.

"*Stupida!*" She saw only the blur as his hand slashed across her mouth. "Now! You sit there. And you do nothing unless you want your mother on the streets by nightfall. Don't forget . . . your cottage stands on my land. Do you understand?"

The numbness in her upper lip was replaced with a burning pain as she tasted the blood from the cut inside her mouth. Alicia squeezed her eyes shut and clasped her hands over her ears trying to keep the nightmare from creeping into her brain.

"Do you understand?" Gianini tore her hands away from her ears and screamed at her.

"*Sì. Sì*, Padrone," she whispered. She tried not to think of what he was doing to her. She tried to concentrate on the sound of the breeze and the rustle of the leaves on the vines. She stared at the distant clouds floating across the sky and her eyes started to get a distant glassy look.

23

Gianini glanced up at her face and his anger suddenly drained. He smiled in relief as he saw a look of pleasure crossing her face.

Alicia suddenly felt a rush of relief explode deep within her as spasms racked her body.

Gianini felt the sudden wet warmth creeping into her soft cotton pants.

"*Dio!*" Her scream echoed through the quiet vineyard. She'd never imagined any feeling like this could exist. "*Dio!*" She whimpered as her hips thrust back and forth against his hand. The more his hand met her pants, the stronger and more frequent the wonderful sensation.

Suddenly she felt Gianini's hand start to tremble. Looking at him through half-closed eyes, she saw his whole body was shaking.

Dio! she thought, terrified. *Is he dying? Isn't it bad enough what people will whisper? But now . . . I might have killed him as well.*

She wasn't sure if she felt relief or anger when the Padrone's eyes flickered open and his breathing returned almost to normal.

He wasn't dead. But the problem of the gossiping hags still loomed over her head. They would never understand that there wasn't anything she could have done to prevent what happened.

The Padrone started the car, got back in the driver's seat, and drove back toward town in silence.

"*Cara mia!*" he whispered as erotic images filled his mind. He would keep this woman child in his villa. A still virgin toy that he would take in a moment of supreme ecstasy.

Alicia's brother, Pietro, was dozing in the shade of a giant, almost symmetrically square boulder overlooking the picturesque valley. It was an ideal place from which to watch over the more than three hundred sheep grazing across the slopes below.

Everyone believed Pietro had the ideal temperament for a shepherd. But when he'd first taken charge of this flock, the isolation and loneliness had almost driven him to the edge of insanity. And even now his moods were unpredictable. It had been his brother's job when the war had started, and Pietro had been the one marked for conscription. But Rafael had argued that Pietro was the head of the household, responsible for their mother and sister and was needed at home. And so, Rafael had gone to war in his place.

He had prayed for his brother during those days, guilty that his brother was risking his life in his place. But that was Rafael's nature. He'd helped to support their family since their father died when he was eight years old. When Rafael returned, they had decided there was no future for him in Montepulciano. There was barely enough work to support one . . . much less two brothers. So with Pietro's blessings, Rafael had set out on his own. Pietro was delighted with his brother's success in Milan. But he was torn—Rafael's departure doomed him to this life of loneliness.

But Rafael would be home for his holiday. And they would sit and talk half the night, drinking heavy red wine and smoking acrid-tasting cigarettes as Rafael told of the north, Milan, its women, and the Bugatti Motor Car Works.

To Pietro, automobiles were a mystery. He'd rarely seen an automobile before. Actually he'd only seen two trucks in his entire life. They were noisy, obnoxious things. But his brother was proving to be a magician with them and his future was bright.

Now a series of gunshots echoing up the valley brought Pietro back from his daydreaming and to his feet. He knew what the shots were even before he was fully awake.

Poachers!

Grabbing his ancient shotgun from the rock next to him, he sprinted up the path toward the crest of the ridge where several strays were fleeing back toward the main flock.

As he topped the ridge, he lowered the shotgun in disgust. He could see two men strolling casually toward an almost full-grown, black-faced ewe. The ewe stood shivering in the grass next to the trail, her shoulder shattered by one of the shotgun blasts. Near her two more half-grown lambs lay in dying spasms.

"Angela . . . Davilo . . ." Pietro called, following

with a shrill whistle. At the sound of his command, two sheep dogs, one a long-haired, rust-colored female, the other a massive, ugly mongrel male, came racing toward him.

"*Ciao,* Pietro. *Come stai?*" Two sweaty young men waved lazily at Pietro as he made his way down the rocky slope toward them.

Pietro cursed under his breath. They weren't poachers. They were worse. They were nephews of the Padrone.

Pietro pushed angrily past them and knelt next to the two half-grown lambs. They were dead. As his dogs raced up, Pietro motioned and they dropped silently in the grass at his side.

"We were target shooting." The taller man, Alvino Gianini, explained. He was wearing a leather vest and a felt hat that were both too small for him: hand-me-down's from the Padrone's son. "Unfortunately, these poor animals bolted in front of us."

Pietro didn't bother to reply. He walked to the ewe with the shattered shoulder, took out his knife, and quickly slit the animal's throat. She died instantly in an eruption of blood.

Pietro looked at both men with contempt.

"I hope we haven't caused you any problems," Ricco, the shorter, stocky man said. He smelled of sweet, flowery toilet water. "We merely wanted to do something other than sit around. Unlike those who are paid for sitting around."

Pietro didn't acknowledge the insult as he dragged the ewe out of the dust of the trail and onto the grass. He had never liked either man. But he liked Ricco least of all.

"Indeed an unfortunate beast," Alvino said referring to the ewe.

"*Sì,* Alvino. An unfortunate tragedy," Ricco echoed.

"But it has happened. And as it can't be undone, it would be a shame for such fine animals to go to waste. Don't you think, Pietro?"

"They won't go to waste," Pietro said. "They are still the property of the Padrone."

"Ah! The loyal shepherd," said Alvino. "But how would the Padrone ever miss a few small animals from a flock as large as this one?"

26

"It's enough that I'll miss them," Pietro said.

"They could have died from disease . . . or an injury." Ricco shrugged innocently.

"If they died from disease, then you wouldn't want to eat the meat. But since they died accidentally—as you both freely admit—then half of each animal belongs to me. The Padrone generously granted me that right. Maybe you could talk your uncle out of his half," Pietro said sarcastically.

The two men stared silently at Pietro for several moments. Even though they were related to the Padrone, shooting the animals had not been without risks for them.

"I have hungry mouths at home waiting for something to put in their bellies," Ricco said almost pathetically.

Pietro refused to respond. He knew that neither of these men, nor their families, had ever experienced hunger. They had killed the animals for sport. They often tested the Padrone's patience.

"It seems you share half of everything with the Padrone," Alvino said.

Pietro looked at Ricco, who was snickering at the remark. He didn't know what Alvino meant, but he wasn't going to be baited into a fight he couldn't gain anything from.

"To share a lamb with hungry friends hardly seems too big a favor to ask, Pietro," Alvino said.

"When I see hungry friends, they won't have to ask. If you want a share of these poor animals, again I say . . . ask your uncle. And at the same time, why don't you explain how they happened to die?"

"You don't think we will?" Alvino asked.

"No. I don't think you will."

"For the right to share half a dead animal, your family must truly owe the Padrone much," Ricco said.

"*Sì* . . . my family owes the Padrone much. As do your families."

"Do your mother and sister owe him much as well?" Ricco sneered sarcastically.

Alvino grabbed Ricco's arm as a warning not to push the volatile-tempered shepherd too far. It was true they'd wasted their food allowance from the Padrone on cards and a woman, but they should have tried another flock to take a couple of lambs from. He'd warned Ricco.

"Go fart up your sleeve, Ricco," Pietro said lifting one of the dead animals and starting back up toward the crest of the hill.

"Maybe the Padrone gives you half because of your mother. But she's old . . . and useless. So maybe it's because of your sister." Ricco's voice trailed off as Pietro whirled, his eyes ablaze.

"What did you say?" Pietro screamed as the anger exploded inside his head. In one angry motion, he dropped the ewe to the ground and leveled his shotgun at Ricco.

The explosion from Pietro's shotgun brought a scream of terror from both men. In disbelief at still being alive, Ricco cautiously opened his eyes and watched in horror as Pietro cocked the remaining chamber and leveled it at him once again.

At that last moment Pietro had moved the barrel just enough so the noise of the shell went off next to Ricco's ear. The ringing pain was excruciating.

"You insult my family . . . risk death for the carcass of a dead lamb? You are truly stupid!" Pietro said from his barely controlled rage.

Alvino grabbed Ricco by the arm and steered him down toward the valley floor.

As the two panic-stricken men slid and stumbled down the slope, Pietro pulled the trigger again. Alvino could hear the buckshot shrieking past his head. Before the sound of the blast had disappeared, Pietro had the shotgun reloaded and recocked. The sheer joy of seeing their terror almost made him fire again. But ammunition was expensive. He'd wasted enough on them already.

CHAPTER TWO

The dust along the path was so thick that Maria Orsini felt as though she were walking in fine sand as she made her way toward the valley where Pietro was tending the flock.

She was wringing with sweat and the rope that bound the canvas bundle she was carrying kept cutting off the circulation in her arm, making her hand numb.

Reaching a narrow strip of shade, she stopped for a moment to catch her breath and to wipe at her face where sweat mingled with tears of fear and frustration.

She eased the heavy bundle down. It was filled with cheese, wine, bread, rice, sausage, garlic, and seasonings she was bringing to Pietro, supplies for the next month.

The pungent smell from the musky, dry cheese mixed with the aroma from the garlic, filling the still air around her. Wiping her face again with her thick shawl, she silently cursed her husband's death. Giorgio would have known what to do. But he was gone and she had no one to turn to except Pietro.

Maria usually saw Pietro only once or twice a year, when the flock was driven down from the high pastures for shearing and the slaughter of spring lambs. Bringing supplies to him was usually Alicia's chore. But Alicia had been missing for more than a week.

Frantic with worry, Maria had searched every part of the city. She had asked the street merchants, fishmongers, vegetable farmers, and shoppers who lined the morning marketplace. But either they knew nothing or shook their heads before turning away and leaving her alone.

She'd even gone to the Padrone's. He had promised to see to it that Alicia got home safely. Though she knew he wouldn't have driven her daughter himself, he might remember which of those who worked for him did. But standing outside his villa, she became afraid. The residence was formidable. And he might be angered or insulted by her questions. Besides, she'd convinced herself, he probably didn't even remember them.

At the end of the first week, Maria's heart had jumped with relief. In a distant throng of shoppers, wandering down a canopied aisle in the sprawling open air market, she had caught sight of Alicia's white Communion dress.

"Alicia! Alicia!" Tearfully she forced her way through the shoppers, grabbed the startled girl, and smothered her in an embrace.

But a terrified girl had torn herself out of Maria's grasp.

"You're not Alicia!" Maria whimpered in disbelief.

"No, *signora*," the girl said backing cautiously away.

"Where is my Alicia?" Maria screamed. "What have you done to my daughter?"

"I don't know your daughter, *signora*." The girl started crying.

"Then where did you get her dress?"

"This dress was given to me by my mother," the girl said, looking around the gathering crowd for help.

"Take me to her," Maria demanded.

With Maria clutching the girl's arm in a grip the devil himself couldn't loosen, the petrified girl led her down the narrow cobblestone alley to a small room where she lived with her mother, father, and seven brothers and sisters.

"*Signora*," the girl's mother said as Maria and her daughter burst into the neat room.

"The dress! Where did you get my daughter's dress?" Maria raged.

The woman took her daughter in her arms and tried to soothe away her fright.

"I am Mira Correlli. I work in the villa of Pasquale Gianini," she explained, stroking her sobbing daughter's hair. "The *signore* himself gave the dress to me for one of my children. As you can see, it was torn. I mended it and . . ."

"The Padrone?"

"*Sì*," Mira Correlli answered. "It belonged to the young girl who now lives upstairs with the *signore*."

"Who is the girl? What does she look like?" Maria

asked, clutching her stomach as a shiver went through her body.

"I don't know, *signora*. I work in the kitchen. We are not allowed in that part of the villa. But others say she is very young. And the Padrone treats her like his most prized treasure."

"The Padrone!" Maria said weakly. "Why would he want my Alicia? She's only a child . . . and a peasant . . ."

Once it would have been an honor for the daughter of a peasant family to be asked to share the Padrone's house. His bed. But these were modern times. She knew her sons would consider it an insult to their family's honor.

She knew she had to reach Pietro before the gossip filtered up to his isolated valley. If she didn't, he would respond in a way that might destroy their family, their name, and their future.

"*Ciao*, Mama!" Pietro yelled as he saw his mother struggling up the hillside toward his flock. Dust and rocks cascaded down the narrow trail as Pietro ran expertly down the steepest part to meet her.

Throwing his mother's bundle over his shoulder, he kissed her and led her across a meadow to a small stand of trees in the hollow of the hill. In the middle of the trees, Pietro had constructed a small rock dam to check the flow from the stream as it spilled down toward the distant valley.

"What a fantastic surprise." He smiled, genuinely delighted to see his mother. "I was afraid I wouldn't have anyone to talk to except Alicia for the next couple of months. And you know how it is to talk to Alicia."

Maria nodded and half smiled as she sat down on a rock in the cool shade and swirled her swollen feet in the soothing waters.

"She's truly growing up, but still, when it comes to conversation, she's a child." He grinned. "I get more interesting conversation from my dogs."

Pietro looked up at his mother and knew something was wrong.

"Hey . . . Mama!" he said, splashing her with water as he slipped down onto the rock next to her. "What is it?"

She looked away, shaking her head. The cool of the shade . . . the gentle breeze . . . her smiling son. Dear God in heaven, she thought, as tears came rolling down her cheeks. Why can't everything be like this all the time? What sins have I committed?

"Rafael?" Pietro asked.

"No . . . no," she answered wiping her eyes. "Rafael is fine. A letter from him came almost two weeks ago. The priest read it to me and Alicia. He said to tell you he was leaving Milano on his way home for holiday soon."

"Then what is it, Mama?"

Maria shook her head and pulled her shawl across her face to hide the tears which were streaming down her face.

When Pietro pulled it back down, she pounded her hands against his chest and, in near hysteria, stumbled blindly toward the trail that led out of the little valley.

Pietro raced across the slippery dam after her.

"Mama!" he said, catching up to her. "What is it? Alicia? Mama, is it Alicia? Is that why you came instead of her?"

Maria grabbed him in a painful, near suffocating embrace. She was shaking with spasms of grief Pietro hadn't seen since his father's death more than ten years earlier.

"Yes," she said through the sobs. "It's Alicia."

"What has happened?" he asked, truly expecting to hear his sister was dead.

"She's gone."

"Gone?" He didn't understand. "What do you mean, gone? Gone where?"

"It's not important where. Just that she's gone. And I don't know if she'll ever come back." She wiped her face with her shawl and returned to the ancient olive trees where the bundle of supplies had been dropped.

She unknotted the rope and rummaged around inside until she found a hard bread wrapped in an old newspaper. She tore a length off and started filling the crusty bread with something for her son to eat.

"Mama . . . *ti prego*." Pietro grabbed her hands, stopping her. "Where is Alicia?"

"She is with the Padrone. Living with him in his villa," she said as calmly as she could.

Pietro felt as though someone had hit him with a club. Blood pounded in his temples. That was what Alvino and Ricco had meant with their insults.

"How did it happen, Mama?"

"I don't know. I mean I'm not sure. We were at church . . . the Padrone asked us to sit in his box . . ." Almost like a person in a delirium, Maria related the last Sunday she had seen Alicia. "I went to the Padrone's villa after *Signora* Correlli told me, but he refused to see me. His servant told me the Padrone was furious that I would even think she was there. That he'd put her out in front of the cathedral after taking her for a short ride as a reward for her help in starting his automobile."

Maria started crying again.

Pietro watched silently, filled with as much pain as his mother.

"What could I do, *figlio mio?* You know of the terrible things they say of the Padrone . . . I mean, others have lost their daughters to the Padrone . . ." She was rambling. "But no one can interfere in the Padrone's life . . . no one," she said looking at him directly.

"What did Alicia say about this?" Pietro asked.

"I haven't seen her. He will allow no one to see her."

"I will see her," he said standing.

"No!" His mother pulled him back down. "You cannot. You must not. It would cause great embarrassment to the Padrone. We wouldn't dare do that to him."

"What do you mean, I cannot? She is my sister!"

"Pietro. Listen to me. I beg of you."

"No, Mama." He shook his head angrily. "No man can insult another like this."

"*Sì* . . . believe me. This one man can."

"No. Not even the Padrone has that right."

"There's nothing we can do."

"There is the *polizia!*"

"The *polizia!* How can you even think of anything so stupid! He owns the police like he owns all the land. And all the money. And all these sheep . . . And now . . . Alicia."

Maria took Pietro in her arms again and held him, remembering how he used to feel as a baby. "There's nothing anyone can do," she said looking into his raging eyes. "That's why I came. I had to be the one to tell you that. You must understand that. Many people protect the Padrone from foolish boys like you. If you anger or embarrass him, it could also hurt your sister. And if, God forbid, you go to the *polizia*, you will simply disappear. And they will claim they know nothing about you."

"Then I will make sure enough people know about me and my sister that the Padrone and the *polizia* can't deny me." He started down the trail toward the path that led toward Montepulciano.

Alvino grabbed Ricco by the back of his coat and dragged him into an alleyway.

"What the hell you think you're doing?" Ricco twisted out of his grasp.

"Saving your ass! Pietro Orsini's coming up the street with murder on his face. I don't think you want to stop and chat with him."

Alvino pulled his felt hat off and wiped the sweat from his forehead with a dirty handkerchief.

"Shit!" Ricco said. There was only one reason for Pietro to be in town. And that was to report to the Padrone what they'd done to three of his sheep. "You said he wouldn't dare do anything." His ears still rang from the shotgun blast that came close to rupturing his eardrum.

"He's a fool!" Alvino said disgustedly.

"So what are we going to do? It was your idea . . . bastard! And I'll be damned if I'm going to take the blame."

Cautiously they walked back toward the street and watched as Pietro passed and made his way toward the Padrone's villa.

Sprawled on a treelined corner that bordered the city's busiest avenue, Gianini's mansion sat like a fort behind a high, whitewashed stone wall. Built nearly three centuries earlier by an aristocrat for a mistress sent into exile after she poisoned his wife, it was one of the most famous landmarks in the province.

As the two men watched anxiously, Pietro walked across the street and with his hands on his hips studied the formidable-looking villa. After a few minutes, he started

34

stalking up and down the sidewalk like a caged animal. His actions didn't make any sense to them.

Stopping in front of the villa, they saw Pietro suddenly reach down and pluck something out of the gutter. In a savage blur of motion, he hurled it as hard as he could across the flower-filled courtyard toward the house.

"Padrone! His angry voice reverberated back down the street to Alvino and Ricco like a thunderclap. "Pasquale Gianini!"

"Dio!" Alvino said.

When there was no response to Pietro's yell, he reached back down and picked up another rock. This time he managed to hurl it a dozen yards beyond the wall.

"Has he gone insane?" Ricco asked in astonishment.

"Let's hope so," Alvino said. "But before he comes to his senses, we better tell Carlo."

Even though he was their first cousin, Alvino and Ricco couldn't count Carlo Gianini, the Padrone's only son, as a friend. But with the information they'd be bringing him now, they could endear themselves to him and be owed a favor in case they needed one later.

Besides, they knew what his reaction would be. He thrived on physical confrontation and would come riding to his father's rescue like charging cavalry.

Since he was rich, powerful, brutal, and unafraid, they also knew where to look for him: in any one of a half-dozen bedrooms of the city's most beautiful wives.

The last rock thrown by Pietro had shattered one of the leaded windows over the entryway and ricocheted down a tiled hallway.

Enraged, Gianini rushed to the hall as the frightened housekeeper, a tiny, gypsylike woman tried to sweep up the shattered glass.

"Che cosa è?" he demanded, furious.

The old woman had spent most of her life working for the Padrone's family. "Some crazy boy," She said. "Shouting for you to come out and face him. I think he is *pazzo* . . . crazy."

"Who is he?" Gianini demanded. "Do you know him?"

"No, *signore* . . . a peasant, I think."

She turned back to her sweeping as Gianini climbed the

turretlike stairs that led to a small alcove overlooking the street. Cautiously looking out the window, he saw a young man in peasant clothes pacing back and forth in front of his gate like a caged animal.

He didn't recognize him. He might have seen him before. Possibly even often. But he seldom really looked at the faces of those who worked for him.

Confident the boy wasn't armed, Gianini unlatched the French doors and stepped out onto the terrace that overhung the garden. "*Stupido!*" he yelled. "What in God's name do you think you're doing?"

At first Pietro couldn't locate the source of the voice. Finally he saw the Padrone's face peering down half-hidden by the thick growth of vines surrounding the veranda.

"My sister!" He screamed shaking his fists at Gianini. "I've come for my sister, you molester of children."

"You stupid ass. You have the wrong house. There's no sister of yours here!"

"*Bugiardo!*" Pietro yelled, spitting toward the villa.

Gianini's face flushed with anger.

"You dare call me a liar? I am Pasquale Gianini. And, I warn you, you are going to cause your family great heartache if you don't shut your big mouth and move on. As a man of honor, I tell you, your sister is not in this house . . . Now leave me in peace."

"Honor? A man of honor, did you say?" Pietro jeered. "Who has ever known a molester of children to be a man of honor."

Gianini's face was burning. No one had ever dared talk to him in such a way. Normally, if any such threat of embarrassment arose, a quiet word or a nod of his head would bring a man to end the confrontation. But the boy was attracting curious onlookers. To do anything would be to admit the girl was here. He felt his eye start to tick in a nervous spasm.

The only way to handle this impudence is to ignore it, he thought, as he retreated back into the house and brushed past the housekeeper.

"I don't know why I bother wasting my time arguing on the balcony like an uneducated peasant."

"*Sì, signore.*" She nodded.

In the cool of his bedchamber, Gianini spent the next quarter hour trying to calm Alicia's fear and his own embarrassment. Usually people had enough intelligence to ignore his little passions. They would pass. And afterward, the families of the girls involved had always been generously rewarded.

He looked at Alicia as she lay in tears on the edge of the Roman-style chaise. God! What an enticing creature she was. She was unlike any of the others. With her, he felt like a master sculptor creating a magnificent work of art with the help of a model willing to follow his every direction. His every whim.

He had never experienced such abandon. Such freedom. Such a willingness to learn. Such a desire to please him. He couldn't let her go now.

"Let me talk to Pietro. I can make him understand . . . make him go away. Please!" she pleaded.

"No!" He ran his hand down her sheer chemise. She was naked beneath it and the touch of her soft, silky skin seemed to draw all the anger out of his body.

At first Alicia had been painfully embarrassed by the scanty clothes he had her wear. But they were elegant. And expensive. And they made her feel rich, like the big-breasted woman from the cathedral. The Padrone had whispered endless promises about the things he was going to buy for her. Gowns, jewelry, dresses, furniture for her mother . . . jobs for her brothers. Maybe even an automobile and a house of their own. Every night he filled her head with fantasies and dreams of things that she had never dared to hope for.

So, every night she let him dress and undress her. And stroke her. And play with her and excite her. And make her reach that wonderful moment when her whole body throbbed with pleasure.

"Che cosa è?" he asked as she lay her head on his knees and sobbed softly.

"I'm afraid," she said as one of Pietro's catcalls echoed through the villa from the distant street.

"Afraid?" He cradled her so his fingers could caress her breast through the iridescent black silk. "There's nothing for you to be afraid of. No one can harm you here."

37

"I'm afraid for Pietro," she said.

"Shh!" he whispered, marveling at how the faint trace of rose-petal cologne always seemed to excite him. He saw her nipples harden through the sheer material. "I would never threaten the life of anyone of your family." He stroked and squeezed her small breasts through the silky material. "I promise, on my soul, your brother is safe. His life is my gift to you."

"*Grazie,* Padrone!" Alicia said in relief as she put her hand on the inside of his thigh and stroked him in the way he'd shown her was most pleasing to him. "*Grazie . . . grazie.*"

But the jeering calls from the street continued and not even Alicia's supple ministrations could shut them out.

Finally Gianini stormed back to the veranda. Pushing the door open, he saw that the boy had attracted a large crowd of spectators now. When several pedestrians were forced to cross the street in order to avoid the mob, Gianini knew the time had come to end the confrontation.

"Enough, you stupid jackass!" Gianini yelled.

Pietro grinned with his success at forcing the Padrone to face him once again.

"I have told you, your sister is not in this house. I don't even know any girls as young as your sister."

"Liar!" Pietro interrupted. "How could you know how young my sister is if you didn't know her."

Gianini's face flushed at having been caught in such a stupid lie by such a simple boy.

"I warn you for the last time. Leave me and my home in peace. Or be prepared to suffer the consequences."

"*Sì,* Padrone. I will gladly leave. If you will just prove to me that my sister is not here."

"I don't have to prove anything to a stupid peasant like you." Gianini shouted back indignantly. "You have been warned. I will not warn you again."

"*Signore?*" The housekeeper called up from the hall. "Shall I send for the *polizia*?"

"The *polizia*?" It was Pietro who responded. "*Sì . . . sì, signora*. Send for the *polizia*. Tell them a molester of children is hiding in this house. And to come and take him away so the rest of the children in this town will be safe on the streets again."

"*Sì*. Send for the prefect of police," Gianini called to her so Pietro, as well as the gathering crowd, could hear. "Tell him to take care of this sheep dung. I have been patient. I have tried to keep a young man out of trouble and have been rewarded with abuse. Warn the prefect that I do not want to see this pile of manure on my street again."

Pietro remembered his mother's warning. The prefect of police was a man who owed his soul to the Padrone. He could easily see that Pietro suffered an accident.

"*Arrivederci*, Padrone!" Pietro picked up another rock from the gutter. "I will be back! Tomorrow, the day after that, and the day after that if need be. Until you set my sister free."

The crowd gasped as he hurled the rock at the Padrone. It glanced off Gianini's head, gouging a chunk out of his ear.

"*Fino a domain*," Pietro said, as he turned and melted into the crowd.

"*Sì . . . sì! Arrivederci*, you stupid bastard!" Gianini stormed through the house toward the kitchen, blood streaming from his lacerated ear. The pain was excruciating.

A moment after Pietro disappeared, a dust-covered, gray Fiat flew around the corner in a shower of smoke and gravel and spun to a stop. Alvino and Ricco dropped off the running board as Carlo Gianini banged the door open and bolted out.

He glared at the knots of people assembled across from his father's villa. Under his glare, they started evaporating.

"Well!" he screamed angrily at an ashen Alvino and Ricco. "Which one is he? Where is this goddamn idiot?"

Alvino looked over the disappearing crowd. "He's not here."

"Someone must have warned him you were coming," Ricco said, but Carlo was already storming across the street and through the gate toward the villa's front door.

"*Padre!*" he yelled angrily, banging doors open as he searched for his father.

Storming into his father's bedroom, he surprised an embarrassed young girl frantically trying to drape something around her half-naked body.

With no show of embarrassment of his own, Carlo let his eyes rake her tawny body. Even in his anger, she was exciting. "My father?" he demanded.

"In the kitchen, I think," the girl stammered.

In the sweltering kitchen, Mira Correlli buried her hands in the near boiling water in the galvanized sink and furiously scrubbed a heavy copper cauldron, hoping to mask her fear. Fear that some way the Padrone would learn that it was she who had told Alicia's crazy mother of her daughter's whereabouts.

"What the hell happened?" Carlo demanded as he stormed past the cook and her three scullery maids huddled near the stairway.

"It was nothing, Carlo." His father shook his head as the ancient housekeeper dipped a cloth from one of the stone cisterns and pressed it to the side of his bloodied ear.

"It is nothing, *signore*," she said to Carlo after inspecting the wound.

"It probably looks worse than it is," Gianini said.

Carlo took the towel from the housekeeper's hand and bent down to look at his father's ear.

"The size of the wound doesn't matter," Carlo said angrily. "Someone has attacked my father. And spilled his blood . . ."

"Thank you, Carlo, for your concern. But it's nothing to do with you. I will handle it myself," he said remembering his promise to Alicia.

"Nothing to do with me? You've been held up to ridicule by some filth in front of anyone who happened to be passing in the street. To men of little or no consequence. Men who did nothing but stand and watch. As your son, I am offended and suffer equally." He paced angrily.

"I told you, I will handle it myself, Carlo. And in my own way."

Carlo whirled and looked at him puzzled. He had learned from his father to place honor above all else.

"It's the girl, isn't it?" Carlo asked.

"*Aii!*" Gianini yelled at his old housekeeper as she added disinfectant to the open wound.

"You allow our honor to suffer because of some trollop hidden away in your bedroom?" he said, flushing with anger.

"You will talk civilly to me, Carlo," Gianini warned. "And about the girl as well."

"Maybe you should boot her out into the street. Let her brother have her back. Prove she isn't enough of a woman to share your bed. Let him take her back to the squalor they seem to thrive in."

"No. This child . . . this young woman . . . is different."

"Different or not, her brother has insulted the name of our family. I demand my right to . . ."

"No!" Gianini said angrily, tiring of his son's attempt to intimidate even him. "I have sworn an oath guaranteeing his life."

Carlo glared at his father in disbelief. "I refuse to let a man go unpunished who has brought such shame to you. He must be made to pay."

Gianini suddenly felt too exhausted to continue. Carlo was a mystery to him. Some of the time he lived like a common sailor drinking and brawling. Other times he was manipulating any one of a dozen of their family businesses, pushing him to grow, expand, take risks. Gianini wondered if he would ever be satisfied.

"Very well. Send Dominic to me," Gianini said to Mira Correlli as the housekeeper poured some more of the pungent-smelling liquid from the chocolate-colored bottle.

"I don't need Dominic to help me in this," Carlo said.

"He isn't to help you. He is to insure that you, my son, honor the promise I've given. I said for someone to get Dominic," he said angrily as the housekeeper added the cloth to his ear once again.

"*Sì, signore.*" Mira Correlli wiped her red hands on the full-length apron and rushed up the stairs that led to the rear courtyard.

A few moments later, Mira hurried back in, followed by the weather-aged Dominic. Stopping a respectful distance from the Padrone and his son, the gardener stood silently, his hat held in a massive hand.

"You heard the boy on the street earlier?" Gianini asked.

"*Sì,* Padrone."

"You think he should be punished?" Carlo interrupted.

"*Sì, signore,*" the man answered, emotionless.

41

"Then you are to go with my son and see that he is." Gianini sighed.

"Sì, Padrone," the man said as a smile crossed his face. He had been sent on this twofold mission before. Make sure the Padrone's son wasn't harmed. And make sure he didn't go too far.

"I don't want him killed," Gianini warned Dominic. "If he dies, I'll have your balls fertilizing my roses the hour after I learn of it."

The Padrone watched as Dominic turned to Carlo. As far as the Padrone could tell, Dominic was the only other man on the face of the earth Carlo respected enough to fear.

"I want the shepherd to feel great pain," Carlo said to Dominic. "Most of all I want to make sure this kind of insult to my father . . . and my family . . . can never happen again."

"Sì, Signore." Dominic nodded. He wasn't worried by the Padrone's threat. He knew how to deal with trouble-makers. And after he had dealt with them, they lived in the terror that the Padrone would unleash him on them again.

"Make damn sure the dogs aren't harmed either," Gianini said as Dominic followed Carlo toward the door. "They're more valuable than the bastard shepherd."

As his son and the gardener disappeared out the door, Gianini surveyed the nervous activity in his kitchen. Everyone knew the shepherd who had insulted their Padrone was to be given a lesson. But they scurried and buzzed around and between the counters and pantries like mindless bees.

Gianini smiled. He liked that kind of intimidation.

Outside the villa, waiting next to Carlo's car, Alvino and Ricco saw Dominic following Carlo like a faithful watch-dog and knew something was going to happen to Pietro.

They were both delighted. The bastard needed to be taught a lesson and they'd be more than willing to lend a hand.

After a few minutes of arguing with Carlo, they convinced him they'd also been insulted—and on more than one occasion. Dominic was reluctant, but he voiced no objection. So hanging onto their hats, they jumped on the running board as Carlo roared off into the late afternoon.

* * *

Pietro sat in front of his campfire staring at the checkerboard of red coals playing hide and seek with occasional wisps of smoke. A sound from the darkness startled him. Quickly, he pushed himself up from the smooth boulder he'd been propped against, set down his half-empty tin cup, and moved out of the light.

His eyes swept the slopes below, but all seemed normal. The flock was quiet and his dogs still lay close to the fire, their eyes half closed, enjoying the warmth.

The events of the day had left him tense and edgy, and he was still tormented by thoughts of Alicia and the Padrone. He'd faced the tiger on his own hunting ground and survived. But Pietro knew it was far from over. And with every sound, he expected to see the Padrone leading a charge of fanatics up the hill to his camp to extract vengeance.

No matter, he thought, picking up the ancient shotgun and cradling it in the crook of his arm. If they came, he'd be ready. In the end, he'd lose. But they'd pay dearly for it.

When there was no further sound, he moved back toward the fire. He spread the blanket roll and kicked it open. It unrolled toward the fire, stopping just short of the coals, close enough to keep his feet warm.

Taking his boots off, he stuck his feet inside the blanket and leaned back against the huge boulder. He reached into a crevice in the rock and pulled out the small cloth bag that held his supply of tobacco. He rolled a barely symmetrical cigarette, lit it, and sighed loudly as he looked up into the black, star-filled night.

Usually by this time of night he was already asleep. But the tension and anxiety weighed too heavily and though he was physically exhausted, his mind wouldn't allow him the luxury of sleep.

Pietro finally threw the half-smoked cigarette into the coals. It was stupid—childish—to be afraid of shadows and noises in the dark, he thought, disgusted with himself. He looked around his small camp and listened to the low sounds of the sheep. If anyone dared try to approach his camp, they'd warn him as fast as his dogs. And the noise would give him time.

He lay back, determined to rest, and finally the needed sleep fogged his consciousness.

The moon was gone and the coals of the fire had retreated behind white ashes when a noise brought his eyes open. Lying still, he looked over to the dogs and saw them peering into the darkness, silent but alert.

In one swift movement, Pietro rolled out of the blanket, grabbed the shotgun, and knelt in the darkness beside the boulder. Wiping his eyes, he checked the huddled mass of sheep that had moved closer up the slope to the fire. They were quiet, undisturbed by whatever had awakened him. He felt one of the dogs by his side and reached down and scratched the big male behind the ears. He saw a flash of motion as the female bounded away from the camp toward the sheep. In an instant the big male was after her and together they raced silently into the night.

Pietro waited and listened. The lack of sound told him they were probably rounding up strays and driving them back to the flock. Like all sheep dogs, they worked without sound unless a predator was attacking the flock.

Pietro circled down the slope toward the sheep. They parted as he made his way to their midst. A moment later he could hear the padded sound from his dogs as they raced back up the slope. He whistled and they trotted through the sheep to him.

Back in camp, he picked up a couple of pieces of firewood and threw them into the hidden coals. Ashes, sparks, and smoke erupted skyward as flames started attacking the dry wood. As the wood flickered into life, Pietro leaned over and picked up his blanket to shake the dirt and grass off before he lay down again.

As he shook the blanket, he was suddenly aware of a faint whistling sound. He spun toward the sound just in time to see a jagged piece of his firewood as it collided with the side of his head. His head erupted into a galaxy of shooting stars and volcanoes. He desperately fought to keep from falling into a bottomless void of blackness, but he had lost control over his muscles. Just before he hit the ground, a large, heavy man grabbed his arms from behind and yanked him back to a standing position. The momentum felt like the old crack-the-whip game he'd played as a child. The next thing he knew, he was falling again. Only this time, face first the other way. He tried to hold his arms out to break his fall, but the heavy man yanked him back to his feet and pinned his arms behind him. Not that it mattered. His arms felt as uncontrollable and as lifeless as his legs.

It was like a nightmare. A nightmare he was a part of, yet at the same time something he was watching from outside his body.

The savage blow to his head had blissfully numbed most of his senses. It seemed to him that the things the dark figures surrounding him were doing to his body should be excruciatingly painful. But they weren't.

From the nightmare on the inside of his body, he could hear the muffled impact, and feel their blows, as fists, clubs, and feet thudded into his chest, face, legs, and groin.

The stale, sweet-smelling toilet water permeated his senses. *Ricco!* His mind screamed from the ragged edge of his haze. "*Bastardo!* I will kill you for this!" he tried to yell. But a blow to his throat had paralyzed his vocal cords.

Through the slits of his rapidly swelling eyes, he saw the female sheep dog's yellowing fangs tear a jagged chunk of flesh out of one of the men's thighs.

The man screamed as the blood stained his torn pants.

Alvino, Pietro thought, recognizing the man's voice. Now he knew why the Padrone was so tolerant to these two worthless bastards.

Once again the rust-colored dog snapped and her fangs sank into flesh. The terrified Alvino brought a club down on her head with a sickening thud.

The female's instincts anticipated Alvino's move and she almost dodged the blow, but her age made her a fraction of a second too slow, and the blow almost crushed her small skull before blinding her in one eye.

Enraged, Pietro broke away from the big man's grip and had Alvino's skinny throat in his grasp. But only for a split second. Quickly, the big man grabbed his long hair and almost snapped his neck as he yanked him back into his bearlike hold.

While the female tried to struggle to her feet, her companion, the huge mongrel, raced in and out between the attackers, lunging, slashing, ripping.

On the edge of the melee, almost like a disinterested

spectator, Carlo watched his cousins' pathetic attempts to teach the shepherd a brutal lesson. Without Dominic holding Pietro, he doubted if they could have done anything, even after almost crushing his skull.

Carlo wanted to wade in and show them how to make an example of this man who'd insulted them. But he'd given his father his oath not to kill him. Dominic had given the Padrone his oath not to let Carlo kill the shepherd. But no one had said anything about turning these two idiots loose on the peasant. It had seemed like such a good plan. But they were so inept. He was afraid that if the dogs kept attacking, they'd spook and run.

He picked up Pietro's shotgun and raised it to his shoulder.

A roaring explosion from the shotgun caught the big mongrel full in the side. He fell in a heap across the dying coals of his master's campfire.

The smell of burning fur was the last thing Pietro was aware of before his body was swept into unconsciousness.

The sun was high by the time Pietro regained consciousness. The protective shock that had kept him from pain during the beating had gone. Now his body screamed in agony at every breath.

The horizon looked red through his one unclosed eye as blood seeped down from one of his many wounds.

He tried to sit up, but shattered ribs sent a bolt of pain shooting through his chest and took his breath away. It was as if someone had a giant rope drawn around his chest and was still tightening down on it.

Finally, using gravity and the slope of the hill, he rolled into a sitting position.

The effort sent an explosion roaring through the side of his head. It sounded like an angry surf he'd heard once when his father had taken the family to pick melons in a field near the sea. Everything seemed to be spinning, like the time he'd drunk too much wine at the harvest celebration. He remembered how his mother brought an old cooking pot and set it next to his pallet in case he got sick in the night.

"Angela . . . Davilo . . ." He called to his dogs so he could signal them to drive the sheep back down the slope

46

to the water. When he didn't hear them racing toward him, he opened his eyes.

The nightmare flooded back.

He turned as quickly as the pain in his chest would let him, and his eyes came to rest on the big male still sprawled across the cold ashes of the long dead campfire.

Spasms of grief and pain racked Pietro's body. He looked away and heard something scraping over the ground toward him. Angela, his once beautiful female shepherd, was half dragging her broken body toward him. Despite her pain, she was still ready to do his bidding. Her entire head was caked with blood. The bone above her eye glistened exposed like a grinning skull. Shivering from the shock and pain, she settled next to her master's leg.

Pietro reached across and stroked around the rupture pushing out from her abdomen where she had been kicked by a heavy boot.

Her tail slowly wagged at his touch.

Pietro felt his body start to shake. The sun was warm but he was chilled to the bone. He slowly reached across Angela, caught the edge of his grass-covered blanket, and dragged it across them both.

If he could just get the blanket over his shoulders, he'd be all right. Then he'd be able to rest. After that, he'd start back to town and show the Padrone it was going to take more than a beating to stop him.

He slumped back against the earth. The pain rocketed through his body, making him retch with nausea.

He pulled his hand over his eyes to shade them from the painful glare of the sun. For a few moments he stared, entranced by the shape of his hand, fingers . . . the joints . . . the pattern of hair gently woven over the faint blue lines of the veins on the back of his hand. The only thing that was different was the color of his skin.

Usually it was sunburned . . . olive colored. Now it seemed mushy . . . pasty white.

Slowly he clinched his hand into a fist.

"Good! It still works. That's all I need!" He started to smile. But his busted, torn lips had already dried and the movement tore the wounds open again, bringing tears back to his eyes.

"Goddamn!" he screamed in pain as the chills sent his remaining teeth chattering.

He struggled back up to a sitting position still clutching the blanket. The hot beating sun seemed to bring some relief from his chills, but his eyes ached. They ached almost as much from trying to stay open as they did from the pain from his beating.

He looked around his pitiful, ransacked camp. Everything was smashed and broken. Dried salamis, the goat cheese, his bread, his other set of clothes, and all the things his mother had brought up just yesterday. Yesterday? It seemed like a hundred years ago.

He couldn't keep his eyes open any longer. The chills were gone. And the sun seemed to have soaked away some of the pain. At last his body was beginning to feel pleasantly numb.

Carefully, he lay back against the soft, cradling earth feeling the warmth from his dog next to him. As he closed his eyes, he felt a fluttering deep in his chest.

And his heart stopped beating.

CHAPTER THREE

The blazing sun caused glistening drops of sweat to shower down like holy water from Rafael Orsini's forehead as he shoveled the rocky soil back into Pietro's grave near the stand of trees by the stream that ran through the valley.

Dry-eyed, his mother stood next to him, staring down at her dead son.

Rafael had rolled Pietro's body into the blanket before lowering him into the freshly dug grave. He had also placed the broken bodies of the two sheepdogs on either side of his brother. Even in death they looked as though they were dozing, merely waiting to respond to a command from the sleeping master they adored, Rafael thought. He remembered the many nights when they both had huddled next to the dogs for warmth.

It was Rafael who had found Pietro lying in his blanket on the side of the hill.

Home for the holiday, Rafael had dropped his tiny suitcase at his mother's. He knew she and Alicia would be working until after sundown, so he decided to walk out and surprise his brother first.

Walking up the trail that snaked into the valley, he could see a distant figure lying on the side of the far hill.

"Hey . . . Pietro Orsini!" he called. "Is that you still sleeping in the sun? Hey! It's almost midday!"

There was no response from the figure, but the dog next to him lifted her head. From this distance, it looked to Rafael as though the dog had been brightly painted for some celebration.

Struggling down the slope as if her feet were overtaking her front, the dog positioned herself between the form in the blanket and the approaching Rafael. She growled a warning.

Rafael approached and knelt in the trail. He whispered her name. The growling stopped and her hackles lowered.

"Angela . . . *Povero cane! Poveretta*, Angela!" he cooed.

She recognized his voice.

Slowly, Rafael inched his way to her and carefully stroked her ears behind the painful wound in her head.

As the dog struggled to walk back up the slope behind him, Rafael, his heart pounding with dread, slowly pulled back the blanket.

Tears filled Rafael's eyes as the blanket fell away. The tears etched glistening lines down his sunburned face as he stared at his brother's swollen, discolored face, battered almost beyond recognition.

As the earth showered down on her son, the blanket that covered Pietro, woven by Maria as a girl, seemed to absorb all the noise. She was thankful for this small relief. The thing she remembered most about her husband's funeral was the lonely sound of the dirt pelting down on his wood coffin. Slowly the hole filled with dirt until it formed a mound above the level of the meadow grass. Letting the shovel fall, Rafael squatted down and stared silently at the mound.

A noise brought him back to reality. He and his mother found themselves surrounded by the crush of grazing sheep. Untended, they wandered from their grazing.

As Rafael stood up, the silent sheep suddenly seemed to burst into almost synchronized bleating.

"Even the flock misses their master," Maria said as they started across the meadow.

"No. They don't miss their master. They miss the shepherd their master has slaughtered," Rafael said as the sheep bolted away from a sight and smell now unfamiliar.

"There is no one to tend them now," she said, looking back at the flock that was starting to fragment into little white puffs against the green grass, now that there were no dogs to keep them bunched together.

"There will be no need for anyone to tend them now, Mama," Rafael replied.

Fear started to creep over Maria as she stared at her son for a moment. He was taller than most and his curly, thick, black hair reminded her of that of a warrior hero from one of the old stories her father used to tell her when she was a child.

She threw her arms around her son and locked him in an embrace that almost squeezed his breath away. He returned her embrace and for several long minutes, they cried in each other's arms.

Finally, his tears dried. He stepped back so he could look directly into his mother's eyes.

"It is time, Mama. The Padrone will be waiting."

"*Sì*," she nodded, knowing it was useless to argue. He'd always been the strong-headed one, the one they looked to.

"*Ciao*, Mama," he said, quickly embracing her again before sending her out of the valley.

She suddenly turned back. "Rafael . . . please!"

"Shh . . . shh . . . shh . . ." he whispered, and with his arm around her shoulder, walked with her for a while.

"I tried to tell Pietro . . . to warn him. He wouldn't listen. Please, Rafael. What can you do that won't end up the same way . . . with you dead?"

"Mama. It will be better if you know nothing."

Maria moaned and sank to her knees in the middle of the dusty path.

He knelt down next to her.

As the shadows lengthened, Pasquale Gianini strolled down the treelined street toward where he had parked his Bugatti.

As he walked, he primped his mustache and bushy gray sideburns. He was in an angry mood. He had spent the entire afternoon playing *bocci* and he'd had to use more intimidation than skill to triumph over an old man.

He was also furious with Carlo, Dominic, and his two idiot nephews. He could understand why they might have gone a little too far with the shepherd. Men lose control when their blood is pumping from the excitement of a battle.

But they'd killed the dogs, and that irritated him. Too many irritating things seemed to be happening all at once, and he wanted to put a stop to them, once and for all.

Maybe it's the stars, he thought. He'd have his housekeeper read his cards in the morning. Maybe she could explain why he seemed to be suffering so many personal irritations all at once.

After Mass, and after taking an espresso on the veranda of the Hotel Montepulciano, he'd driven around town flirting with all the young girls and smiling at their tight-lipped fathers before parking in the shade of these stately trees and walking the two blocks to the *bocci* park.

He didn't care for the walk. But the shade from the trees had kept the interior of his car cool.

He reached in now, turned on the ignition, and adjusted the choke and throttle. Walking around to the front bumper, he cranked the engine. After three or four spins, the car chugged unevenly to life. The engine seemed to skip every three or four beats.

Damn thing! he thought, angry at still another irritation. The Bugatti shuddered badly, coughed, backfired, and finally died.

Gianini fiddled with the ignition and throttle linkage. He stepped out of the car and tried several more times to start it. But each time, it shuddered badly and died.

A tall young man strolled down the sidewalk engrossed in his Sunday missal. Approaching, he stopped a few feet away and watched Gianini's vain attempts for a few minutes.

"*Signore.*" The young man smiled warmly as he put his missal in his suit pocket. "Possibly I can be of service."

Gianini jiggled several wires before looking up and scrutinizing the young man. He was well dressed. Not expensive clothes, but not like the ragtag locals either.

"How could you possibly help?" he asked. "This machine is one of a kind. A Bugatti. It's merely being temperamental. Like a young lady. Besides . . . it doesn't need prayers," he nodded toward the missal bulging out of the man's coat.

"*Sì . . . sì,*" the young man replied. "But it's possible I worked on your automobile originally."

"What do you mean?"

"I have the honor to work at the Bugatti factory near Milan," the young man said as he took off his coat and bent over the raised hood.

Gianini's eyebrows raised. It was a good omen. At last maybe things were returning to normal.

Gianini watched as the young man's hands seemed to fly over the wiring, around the generator, the plugs, tracing the course of his problem.

"What brings you to Montepulciano?" Gianini asked.

"I'm on holiday. I'm on my way to Bari, which is my home. I took a room at the Hotel Montepulciano. It's rather fine. Though I must admit, more expensive than I'd hoped for."

Gianini nodded. The young man could evidently afford the hotel. But he was being wise with his money. He would prosper as he matured.

"That should do it," the young man said confidently. He walked around to the front and spun the crank. Once again the car sputtered, coughed before seizing up.

"Stupido!" Gianini said impatiently. "I thought you were an expert."

"I assure you, *signore*, I am."

"Then I warn you. This is a very valuable automobile, as you know. And I will hold you responsible, especially now that you have tinkered with it, if it is not repaired within the hour, *signore*."

The young man dropped his eyes in acknowledgment.

"Ahh!" he said, from beneath the cowling. "I think I see what the trouble is now, *signore*. If you please . . . would you lend assistance?"

Gianini shook his head. He had no intention of dirtying his hands to help this young man.

"Signore, please. I merely need you to hold one of the wires while I crank. To see if there is any spark coming through the wire. Once I locate the wire that doesn't have a spark, we will have isolated the trouble."

Reluctantly, Gianini grabbed the wire out of the young man's hand.

The young man spun the crank and Gianini heard *tick . . . tick . . . tick . . .* as the spark rattled out its staccato.

This definitely wasn't the wire causing the trouble. The young man unplugged another wire. Gianini held it and the young man spun the crank again. This time there was no sound.

"This is the wire, *signore*," he said, taking it from Gianini. "You see . . . it has no spark."

Gianini shrugged as the boy reconnected one end of the wire to something deep within the engine compartment.

"Now, *signore*. If you will hold it again, while I test it? I think I have your problem solved."

Gianini raised his eyebrows to let the man know he was becoming impatient.

As the young man cranked the engine, the current coursed through the reconnected wire, roared through Gianini's body and out the soles of his shiny patent leather shoes and through a previously unnoticed puddle of water.

The surging current flung him against the car in semi-consciousness.

"*Dio! Dio mio! Signore,* I am terribly sorry," the young man said as he struggled to help Gianini into his car. "Have no fear, *Signor* Gianini," the young man assured him. "I will see you safely home."

Gianini slumped back in the seat, his eyes closed, as the car rumbled off into the growing darkness.

Gianini was lying across the cold, pleated leather in the back seat of his car. His eyes fluttered as he tried to force himself into consciousness. He was shivering from the cold, and his muscles ached with cramps. He tried to move, only to discover his hands and feet were bound.

He tried to struggle up to a sitting position to orient himself. Then realized he was naked.

The damned automobile repairman must be a bandit . . . a thief, he thought. But he'd gone to a lot of trouble for nothing. Gianini never carried any cash. He never needed any. Everyone knew who he was. If he felt like it, he paid. If not, he didn't. And no one ever dared complain. This fool had gone to a lot of trouble for nothing. He grunted as he struggled against the ropes. Craning his head around, he saw that he was only several hundred feet from his villa. He wanted to yell for help but he was gagged with a heavy piece of coarse material.

The thought of having to spend the night in the back of his car, half freezing to death until someone wandered by and found him, enfuriated him. But he found some consolation at being so close to the safety of his villa.

A heavy wooden door in the wall that surrounded his grounds suddenly opened and he saw two figures emerge.

As they approached the car, he recognized the tall one as the thief.

The second figure came into view, and his heart skipped a beat. Draped in one of his expensive mohair topcoats was Alicia. The young man opened the door and helped her into the front seat.

She was strangely quiet, and Gianini could tell she'd been crying. He tried to turn away to hide his nakedness. But all he succeeded in doing was attracting the attention of the young man. No doubt he'd hold the two of them hostage until one of Gianini's agents paid a large sum for their release.

"Don't let your nakedness embarrass you, Padrone," the man said after starting the engine which now purred softly. "Soon you won't have anything to hide."

Gianini's heart pounded as the man stepped into the driver's seat and reached back to tear the gag away from his mouth.

"Alicia, what did he mean? Please . . ." Gianini said. "Who is this man? What does he want?"

She looked over her shoulder at him, and he could see the hatred in her eyes.

"What is it? What has happened?" he asked her.

"You promised on your soul that my brother wouldn't be harmed," she said, tears flooding into her eyes.

"He wasn't. At least not badly. Besides, you misunderstood," he informed her like a spiteful child. "I only promised he wouldn't die. Not that he wouldn't be hurt. He had to be punished. His insults were intolerable."

"He's dead!" Alicia said quietly. "And your soul is forfeit."

"Impossible! It's not true!" Gianini's teeth chattered as they roared through the deserted streets.

"Then the boy I buried must have been my brother's twin," the young driver said.

The Bugatti bounced over a heavily rutted road and slid to a stop in front of a delapidated hovel. Rafael opened the car door and Alicia, clutching the heavy coat around her naked body, slid out with Rafael behind her. The door opened and Maria Orsini rushed out and took her daughter in her arms.

But when she saw who was in the back seat, the short stocky woman tried to reach for the car door. "Pig! Murdering filth!"

Rafael held her back.

"Mama," he whispered, "you must be kind to this poor condemned soul."

"I hope his death takes as long . . . and is as painful as the one Pietro suffered," she said.

"It will be," Rafael said to Gianini's growing horror. "I promise."

He embraced his mother and Alicia one last time. Maria reached out and for a long moment, their hands grasped each other.

"Where will you go, Rafael?" Alicia asked, tears rolling down her cheeks.

"It's better if neither of you knows that," he said. "But as there's a God in heaven, we'll be together again . . . as a family."

He unwound himself from their embrace.

"It's time."

Gianini's teeth were chattering from the cold and from his fear.

"Where . . . where . . . are you . . . you . . . you . . . taking me?" he pleaded to the black image sitting in the driver's seat in front of him.

Rafael turned and stared into the Padrone's eyes without answering.

Gianini's heart sank when he saw the look on Alicia's brother's face. He had expected hatred. That he'd seen many times before. Hatred was something the rich and powerful lived with daily. It was something they taught their children to deal with or ignore. He could tempt hatred. Reason with it. Confuse and distract it. But this was a look of absolute calm. What frightened Gianini most was the total absence of emotion.

Rafael turned back toward the front. The headlights lit a bumpy, rutted road that seemed to lead toward a black abyss. The longer they drove, the more bumpy, the more primitive it became.

Gianini winced as the car scraped over heavy rocks that kicked up and thumped and banged along the undercarriage. Alicia's brother was heading into hilly country where no car had ever been before.

As the Bugatti creaked and groaned over one violent bump after another, it threw Gianini high enough in the seat so he could see Rafael dodging white boulders along the dusty trail.

The car headed down a steep hill toward a black hole of a valley. The thumping from the rocks stopped, to be replaced with a staccato *flap, flap, flap*, as they drove into a grass filled meadow off the rocky trail.

Rafael put on the brakes and turned off the ignition. For a few moments they both stared silently up into the black, star-filled night.

Rafael finally crawled out of the driver's seat and opened the back door. Gianini tried to pull away, but his body was numb from the cold and barely responded.

Rafael grabbed Gianini by the ankles and dragged him out of the car like a side of beef. Gianini's backside scraped painfully across the door frame and his head banged against the running board as he fell heavily onto the dew-filled grass.

The stars seemed to explode in his head, blending momentarily with those in the sky. He prayed to lose consciousness, so he could escape the coming nightmare. But Rafael slapped his face several times until he was sure he was awake. Satisfied that he was, Rafael pulled him around to the front of the car and slammed him hard against the grill.

Gianini's scream pierced the night as the heat from the shiny brass radiator branded his fleshy white back. Through the tears that flooded into his eyes, Gianini saw the huddled forms of a large flock of sheep sleeping in the distant meadow. Strange, he thought. Even my scream didn't startle them. Then he saw that many of their woolly coats were stained a dark, glistening color.

"*Dio!*" Gianini whispered when he realized why the mass of three hundred bodies was still. The whole flock was dead. Their throats had been slashed.

"*Sì* . . . " Rafael said, bending and untying the Padrone's feet. "They were without a shepherd. So I had to destroy them. It took almost two days."

"Cristo!" Gianini's whisper was barely audible.

"*Sì*, Padrone," Rafael said quietly as he grabbed Gianini by his well-trimmed hair and dragged him toward the dead animals.

Gianini stumbled and tripped as burrs and small sharp rocks stabbed into the bottoms of his pedicured feet, but Rafael's grip kept him from falling until they reached a grassy knoll near the center of the dead flock.

"The grave of your shepherd, Padrone," Rafael said as he pushed Gianini down next to the mound of newly turned earth. "Unblessed, unconsecrated. A poor boy with a gentle soul. He died without last rites. Worst of all, he died alone . . . and in great pain."

There was another gaping grave next to the new mound of earth.

"And the other grave?"

"It's for you."

"You are going to kill me?"

"When I dug it, that was my plan," Rafael admitted as he went to a canvas sack by the grave and began rummaging around in it.

"Then please," Gianini said trying to impress Rafael with his bravery, "have the decency to make my death as quick as possible."

Rafael strolled almost casually back to him. In his hand he carried a pair of sheep shears. They were made from a single piece of heavy metal bent into a figure eight.

"That was when I was digging the grave. I changed my mind since then. Now, Padrone, I mean to keep you alive. As long as I can. And in as great a pain as I can."

Gianini shuddered and his knees finally buckled. He sank to the ground in total panic as Rafael started honing the blades of the shears on a black, oily sharpening stone.

"It was with these very shears that I destroyed the lives of your flock for you," Rafael explained without looking up. "I'm afraid it made them dull."

"Please . . ." Gianini blubbered. "Please . . . listen! You must stop this terrible game. We're both intelligent men . . ."

"We're what?" Rafael asked as he put his thumb on the blade to test its sharpness. "You're not a man. You're

58

lower than an animal. And I'm going to take away your ability to create another animal like you. I'm going to guarantee that you can't spawn more filth . . ."

"Please . . . Please I can make you a rich man. Your family as well. If you just won't hurt me . . . please!"

"Please!" Rafael mimicked him. "What could you pay?"

"Anything!" Gianini said, suddenly filled with hope.

"A trade then. I will make you a trade," Rafael offered.

"*Sì . . . sì!* A trade. Anything."

"The life of my brother and the innocence of my sister. In return I will give you back the life of this flock of sheep . . . and your life as well."

"I cannot change what has already been done," Gianini cried, his heart sinking. The young man had been playing with him.

"*Sì . . .* that is true," Rafael said sadly. "Not even the great Padrone of Montepulciano can do that. What a pity."

Rafael rolled Gianini over and grabbed the knotted rope that held his hands behind his back. Lifting violently on the heavy rope, he forced Gianini painfully to his feet. Bending him over, Rafael brought the Padrone's arms up as high behind his back as his shoulders would allow.

He spun Gianini around and half dragged, half steered him back to the front of the car. Pulling the Padrone's arms up till he was on his tiptoes and screaming in pain, Rafael slipped the old man's hands over the hood ornament. It left Gianini's arms pinioned behind him so he couldn't move or drop off his toes without excruciating pain shooting through his shoulders.

Spotlighted by the headlights, Rafael slowly moved toward Gianini's naked body with the sheep shears. The shears seemed to sparkle in the light as Rafael held them in front of Gianini's eyes and slowly pressed the blades together.

Gianini's breath stopped and his eyes widened in terror as Rafael lowered them toward his manhood. Gianini's screams echoed off the nearby hills and roared across the stark landscape.

When Rafael stepped back, the front of his white shirt was splattered with blood.

* * *

59

The early morning, low-floating white clouds were stained blood red from the rising sun as dawn broke over the sleeping city and Gianini slowly regained consciousness. Through an ice cold, babbling haze, he saw blurred figures rushing back and forth, gathering a few meters from him. No doubt they are here to pay respect to their Padrone, he thought.

He started to motion for them not to bother him so early in the morning, but his arm wouldn't move. He looked over his shoulder and out along his arm. To his disbelief, he saw it was tied to the distant arm of a marble statue. His head turned slowly to the other arm; it was tied to the marble shaft of a horse's tail. He had been spread-eagled between the two statues in the city's main fountain. Fragmented pieces of the previous night flashed through his brain like an electrical short circuit.

A black automobile raced up the wide boulevard toward the fountain and shrieked to a halt. The prefect of police bolted out of the car, followed by an ashen-faced Carlo. Carlo waded into the blood-tinted waters of the fountain and covered his father with a blanket thrown him by the prefect.

His face distorted with hate and rage, Carlo sliced through the stiff fibers of the thick rope that held his brutally disfigured father between the cold, grinning statues.

If it took a lifetime, Carlo promised in whispered sobs, he'd find some way to erase this horror.

His father was unhearing though. His mind had sunk into the depths of insanity.

BOOK
TWO

CHAPTER FOUR

New York City!

The name itself seemed almost magical.

Rafael stood on the corner and drank in the sights. Even though it was still early morning, the streets were already alive with people, and buzzing with the excitement of a new day: the black automobiles, the lumbering double-decker buses, the dusty overheated trucks, clanging street-cars, shiny checkered taxis, and pushcart peddlers.

Almost two months had passed since he'd fled from Montepulciano in the Padrone's blood-splattered Bugatti. It had taken him almost a month to wind his way over the rutted, dusty roads that connected Montepulciano to the province of Lazio and its capital, Rome. He could have made it in half the time, but he had cautiously left a dozen false trails to confuse anybody following him.

In Rome, getting rid of the Bugatti was easy. He found a sleazy shoe merchant anxious to take advantage of a young man on his way to visit his sick father. With the money from the sale of the car, he bought steerage-class passage on a ship bound for the United States. During the voyage, he spent most of the time wrapped in a damp, mildew-smelling blanket shivering his way across the stormy Atlantic.

Some of the Italians he met during the voyage were on their way to places named Chicago and Wisconsin. One of the young men, a carpenter from Palermo, was headed for a place in one of America's southern provinces called Leedle Wrok.

But mostly their destination was New York.

They were on their way to join families who had gone ahead years earlier to build new lives. Some, like Rafael, had gone to escape the law. Or a vendetta. But the main

63

lure, the bait that took them to the United States was that there they could do something that was all but impossible in the old countries: they could buy and own land.

The rumble of the New York streetcars seemed to shake the very concrete Rafael was standing on as they shuddered and jerked and clanged up and down the building-lined streets.

Walking through a small cloud of steam escaping from an iron grate covering the sidewalk, Rafael stepped up to a storefront counter that opened onto the sidewalk. A young girl, no more than ten years old, wearing a soiled apron that was too long for her, hurried to wait on him. The dark circles under her eyes and her red, cracked hands told him that although it was barely past seven o'clock, she'd already put in a long, hard day.

Rafael scanned the blackboard menu that hung on the wall behind the counter, looking for something familiar. But the day's offering had been written in chalk over words erased a hundred times, so it was unreadable.

When he didn't order, the girl turned away to serve a man in worn work clothes. Rafael watched as she refilled the man's cup with coffee from the spigot of a steaming urn. The man spoke and she took a thermos from his lunch pail, a shiny dented metal pail that looked like a miniature milk can, and filled it from the spigot.

She quickly cut two sandwiches in half with a butcher knife that seemed to dwarf her tiny hands rolled them in a piece of newspaper and put them in the pail along with his thermos.

The coffee's aroma made Rafael's stomach rumble with early morning hunger.

"*Signorina*," he said as the girl rushed past the window to deliver another order from the back room.

"Yeah? Watta ya have?" she said wiping her nose on her apron.

"*Caffe.*" He pointed to the urn hoping she could understand him.

She nodded and poured a steaming crock cup full.

"Ya want cream?" she asked wiping a spill.

Rafael smiled, not understanding what she'd said.

"Ya want cream or dontcha?" she demanded. Her husky

voice hardly seemed to match her tiny, almost delicate body. "Cream?"

"Ah, sì! Crema," he said nodding as he dumped heaping spoonfuls of sugar into the steaming black liquid.

He lay a twenty-lire note on the countertop and turned back to enjoy the jostle and color of the crowded street.

"Hey, bub," the little girl said, pushing his money back across the counter. "We don't take no funny money in dis joint."

Rafael turned to her. He smiled and shrugged.

"Da money," she pointed at the twenty lire. "Dis ain't 'merican money. You owe me for coffee and I ain't takin no funny money for it."

"Scusi, Signorina," Rafael apologized. "Non capisco."

"She says you owe her American money for the coffee," the man in worn work clothes said to Rafael in Italian.

"Ah . . . a paisano?" Rafael asked.

"Sì." The man sipped his black coffee. "I'm Italian."

"Tell me, how much do I owe. Surely twenty lire is more than enough for a cup of coffee."

"You owe her a nickel. A nickel is five American cents. Twenty lire is more than enough. But her father, the cook, would beat her if she took your 'funny money' . . . that's any money that isn't American."

"Ah . . . sì." Rafael felt embarrassed. All his money was still in lire. The landlady where he'd taken his tiny room hadn't questioned it. And the attendant at the public bath had taken it when he soaked the two weeks of ocean voyage off his body.

The man rattled something to the girl that sounded to Rafael like a steady stream of unrecognizable noises, then dug into the bottom of his grimy pocket and picked a small, thick coin out from a collection of lint and sulphur-tipped wood matches.

The girl nodded, took the coin, and dropped it in the cash drawer before returning to her other customers.

"Thank you very much," Rafael said realizing the man had paid for his coffee. "Please take this in return," he said trying to force the twenty lire into the man's hand as he picked up his lunch pail and came out the door.

"No. Thanks." The man smiled. "Save it. You can exchange your money at that bank on the corner." He nodded toward the enormous gray building.

"My name is Rafael Orsini," Rafael said holding out his hand. "Thank you."

"Hello, Rafael Orsini. I'm Tomaso Fierello. You have a job yet?"

"No. Not yet." Rafael followed the man as he wove expertly through the morning rush. "But I am an automobile mechanic, so it seems I shouldn't have a difficult time finding one." His hand swept toward the traffic-jammed street.

"*Sì*, but you do not speak English," the man said, taking a toothpick out of his flannel shirt and sticking it between his teeth.

"True. But a mechanic is a mechanic. All engines speak the same language."

"Yes. But unless you speak English, no one's going to hire you." The handle of his lunch pail seemed to squeak above the noise of the street as he shifted it from one hand to the other. "Outside of Little Italy that is. And if they do, they will try to cheat you. To steal from you."

"I'm not worried. Others have tried before," Rafael warned.

"*Sì*," the man said smiling. "Many of us are here because of those same reasons. But in this country, we can't deal with those who cheat us like we did in the old country. They have many laws here. And many police," he warned as they passed a blue-coated policeman. "Besides, tell me. Where would you run from here?"

"*Sì*. From this country there would be no place else to run."

They walked on for several minutes in silence.

"So where do you work, Tomaso?"

"I work on a street gang as a laborer. I help dig up the streets. Then I help fill them in again. Sometimes we even repair something in the ditch we dug. But it's mainly a political thing for the bosses."

"I see."

"There's always an extra shovel if you want to work. And have a strong back."

"No, thanks. I didn't come to American to dig ditches."

"Oh! Excuse me!" Tomaso said sarcastically. "I on the other hand, unlike you, came halfway round the world

66

from digging ditches in Napoli, to dig in the gold-paved streets of New York."

"I'm sorry," Rafael apologized. "You're right."

"Of course I'm right." A wide grin flashed across Tomaso's face. "And between now and the time you hear from Henry Ford, I suggest you stick with me."

"Who?"

"Forget it."

"I do need the work, though."

"Good. And if you keep your ears open, it will help you learn the language. So you can become a big, rich mechanic," Tomaso said.

"Okay, Tony," the foreman said as the smoke curled up around his nose from the cigarette that dangled from the side of his mouth. The smoke seemed to hang under the brim of his greasy, brown fedora as he handed Rafael the small envelope with his pay in it.

Rafael nodded.

He hated being called Tony. But the Irish foreman delighted in calling every Italian in his crew that. The only way they could tell who he was yelling at was by the description he added. There was Fat Tony, Old Tony, Greasy Tony. But Rafael was just plain Tony.

He folded the tiny brown envelope and stuck it under his handkerchief in the bottom of his front pocket.

"Grazie, molto grazie, padrone mio!" he said, mocking the Irishman with his thick accent as he wiped the sweat from his face on the back of his shirt sleeve.

A couple of the other Tony's snickered under their breath.

"Don't give me none of that Dago crap, you wop bastard," the man warned, his face flushed.

"Watta you talka bout?" Rafael smiled innocently in his pidgin English.

"You know goddamn well 'watta I talka bout,'" the foreman said, his face a few inches from Rafael's. This greaser was asking for it. He'd fire the son of a bitch, but he was the hardest worker he'd ever seen. Maybe he'd just have some fun and rough him up a bit. It was a shame he couldn't break his head, but the wop did most of the work in his gang.

Rafael raised his hands in submission.

"Ima promise boss. I no giffa you no Dago crap."

"Damn well better not. 'Specially if you wanna keep working," the foreman said as the ash dropped off the end of his cigarette onto his coat. The Irishman hacked, clearing his throat and spit on the sidewalk next to Rafael. "Okay. Tomorrow morning. Six o'clock on the dot. Corner of Seventy-third and West End."

The men waited anxiously for him to tell them how many men he would be needing.

Everybody . . ." he said, smiling maliciously at Rafael. "Even you, Tony."

"Thanks, bossman," Rafael said, bowing like a gentleman. Though he was sweating heavily, he was starting to feel the cold as the icy wind whipped through the deserted street. He winked at Tomaso as he slipped on the coat from his only suit. It was almost winter, but he hadn't bought an overcoat. He came to work in his suit coat, folded it, and put it in a protected place, then worked the whole blustery day in his shirt sleeves.

He was sending as much money as he could to a priest in Montepulciano for his mother and Alicia. The rest he was spending on English lessons.

Tomaso told him it was stupid. Especially when ultimately he would learn English for free.

But Rafael was impatient. There was too much in life to do and he was determined to do it at his pace, not the slow, unhurried pace of the other immigrants around him. They were satisfied to toil so their children could prosper.

Rafael Orsini wanted prosperity for his mother and sister and himself. Now. The future generation could take care of itself. The sooner he learned the language, the sooner his chances for success. And the sooner they'd be reunited.

"What are you doing, Tomaso?" Rafael asked a few weeks later as the two men hurried down the crowded avenue toward little Italy on the lower East Side.

"Reading," Tomaso said glancing up from the magazine to make sure his pathway down the sidewalk was clear. "About California."

"What's a California?"

"California is not a what, Rafael. It's a place. A state on the Pacific Coast."

"It's still in America?"

"Of course."

"They need ditchdiggers out there?"

"I don't know. Why do you ask?"

"Was wondering why you were reading about California."

"Because, my dear friend, it's the place for me. They grow things out there. Oranges. Grapes. Lettuce. Strawberries. That's what I want, Rafael. That's why I came. For land. My land. To grow my own things on."

"Maybe when you're a big, rich farmer, I'll come and fix your tractors for you," Rafael joked.

"Are you kidding? You think I'd let some dumb wop touch my tractor? You're crazy." He smiled at his feeble imitation of the foreman.

Later that night, Rafael lay on the rickety bed in his tiny room and stared up at the decaying plaster. His work shirt, washed by hand in the bathroom at the end of the hall, hung on a nail near the radiator. He'd already finished his cold supper, a sandwich left over from the lunch prepared by the little girl who wouldn't take his "funny money" his first week here.

He had only one change of clothes that he'd brought with him from Italy, and a shaving brush, a straight razor, some salt, and a brush for his teeth.

His stomach had food in it. He was clean and warm. And he had a growing cache of money hidden in an envelope taped under an empty drawer in the bureau. When he'd saved enough, he would open a garage to repair automobiles, send for his mother and sister—and maybe think about finding a wife.

His body ached with exhaustion, but he couldn't allow himself the luxury of falling asleep. He had a forty-five-minute English lesson and he had to pay for it even if he missed it.

He swung out of bed and raised the yellow shade.

He checked the ornate clock hanging on the corner of the building in the next block. Time to go. He put on his extra shirt, his suit coat, wrapped a towel around his neck as a scarf and started down the four flights of stairs to the street.

It was a brisk thirty-minute walk in the near-freezing night. Rafael took the steps that led to his English teacher's ornate door two at a time.

Almost as soon as Rafael pulled the doorbell, Sophia Secchio opened the door, smiling at him.

Sophia was his English tutor. She lived with her father and mother in what the Italian community considered an opulent apartment. Unmarried and overweight, with few hopes of finding a husband, she taught newly arrived immigrants, hoping to rouse some desperate bachelor's interest.

Her face was broad and treble-chinned. Her gold-lined mouth grinned out at him from between the swelling V of two of the most enormous breasts Rafael had ever seen.

"*Buona sera,*" Rafael said, returning her smile.

This was only his third lesson. But she was already infatuated with him.

"Good evening, Mr. Orsini," she replied in English to remind him of her rule. They would speak only in English during the lesson.

"Ah . . . *sì, sì!* Sorry. Good evenin', Miss Secchio. May I into your house come?"

"Of course," she said, realizing she'd been blocking the way, and holding the door open. "Won't you please take a seat in the parlor and we will begin," she said slowly and without inflection so he would be able to understand the individual English words.

Rafael followed her into the brightly lit parlor and nodded to her father, a short, balding man whose face was buried behind a newspaper. He walked across the room and took the hand offered by Sophia's mother.

"Good evening, *signora.*" One or both of Sophia's parents were always present with their daughter during her lessons with an unmarried man.

"*Buona sera,*" Rafael said to the father as he sat down on the straight-backed chair that had been placed across from Sophia's place on the overstuffed love seat. Nearby the warm hearth of the coal fuel stove bathed the parlor in luxurious heat.

"Good evening, Mr. . . . ah . . . Orsini," her father

said very deliberately without looking up, to remind him again of his daughter's rules.

A salami-maker by trade, Secchio had used his wife's money to open a factory that had flourished so well that he'd become the New York Italian community's leading dry salami manufacturer.

Signore Seechio scrutinized the handsome young man seated across the deep carpet from him. Orsini seemed to be creating more of an emotional turmoil in his daughter than any of her past pupils had.

He's too handsome to be trusted, he thought. But then he had never really liked any of the young men who passed through his daughter's life.

The boy was Italian, of course. And strong. And he could read. More than Secchio had been able to do when he came to this country. And there were his eyes. They had a quality about them that said the boy had seen much, including pain, and had survived.

Sophia was in her element when she was teaching. Then she held the upper hand. She had something they wanted . . . needed. And she could give it.

Her father was pleased that she was so dominant during the lessons. So forceful. So precise. Maybe this personality will help her find a husband, he thought. He sighed loudly to himself, drawing their attention.

"Pardon me." he said as he got up and went toward the kitchen for his nightly cup of espresso. As he passed behind his wife's chair, he glanced down at her.

Her once pretty face seemed tiny and out of place as it sat above a fortune in satiny material that hid a body almost twice his weight.

As the lesson progressed, Sophia placed the primer she'd made by hand for Rafael on her lap and leaned back. Through the shiny material of her dress, Rafael could see the outline where her stockings were rolled so they wouldn't sag around her ankles. Most of the women of the day wore stockings to hide the hair on their legs. In Sophia's case. the hair was so heavy under the stockings that a pattern of dark swirls was visible.

After the lesson, Sophia came back from seeing Rafael off and sat silently between her parents.

"A very nice young man," her mother finally said. "And so handsome."

Sophia blushed. "Mama, please!"

"What do you mean, 'Mama, please'? I've seen the way you've been acting. Now tell me. Is there something you want to tell your mama?"

"Like what, Mama?"

"Like is there something happening between you and this nice young man?"

"Mama, please." Sophia said looking away. "Rafa . . . Mr. Orsini is very nice. But he's also very young."

"And you're so old?" her mother asked, putting down her needlework and waddling to the love seat. "I'll tell you a little secret," she whispered as she sank down next to Sophia. "I myself am three years older than your father."

"How does this young man earn his livelihood?" her father interrupted to change the subject. Many times during his life, he'd been accused of marrying an older woman for her money.

"At the present, he's just a laborer, Papa. That is, until he learns to speak English. But he's very smart . . . and . . ."

"You mean a ditchdigger," Secchio said, contempt lacing his voice. It was degrading for anyone to have to dig ditches. Especially an Italian. They should find more honorable work. But his daughter was nearly past marriageable age. And growing older and fatter each day. Just like her mother, he thought, looking at the two women sitting side by side.

"Maybe you could help change that," Mrs. Secchio said.

"Change what?"

"If the young man's as smart as Sophia says he is, maybe you could help him."

"How?" he asked, not really wanting to hear the reply.

"You've complained a hundred times about never being able to find anyone with brains to work for you. Idiots! That's all you claim you can ever find."

"So?"

"So, hire the young man. You said if you could ever find a man with a brain as well as a strong back, he'd be worth his weight in gold."

72

"I'm sure Mr. Orsini would be a hard worker, Papa."

The thought that her father might provide a job that would make Rafael accessible to her socially made Sophia's blood pound.

In bed later that night, wrapped beneath a thick, down comforter, the thought of their being together excited her so much she had to stroke herself before she could fall asleep.

"My daughter tells me you have a reputation as a hard worker."

"Your daughter is very kind, *signore*."

"So tell me, Orsini. Why did you come to America?" Signore Secchio asked in Italian as he placed the tiny demitasse of syrupy black liquid under the spout of the espresso machine. He cracked the tiny brass valve, and steam hissed and bubbled through the black liquid.

Rafael wondered why the old man had invited him into the kitchen, but he was impressed by it. The room was big enough to be a restaurant's kitchen. He had never seen such abundance; entire baskets of onions, potatoes, and vegetables sat on a sideboard under garlands of garlic drying between long chubs of salami. The air was thick with oregano and spices, the pungent, heady smells of home.

"I would think I came for the same reasons as yourself, *signore*. A new life . . . a new country," Rafael said.

Secchio looked up and studied him. "I might have need for a hardworking young man in my factory. If he's a man who can follow instructions."

Rafael looked at the man without any outward display of interest.

"I couldn't offer this person much as far as a salary was concerned. But he would have an opportunity for a bright future. And it wouldn't be in the bottom of a ditch."

"What type of work would this person be doing?" Rafael asked as he sipped his espresso through a cube of rock sugar.

"Everything. In my factory, everyone does everything. Men and women alike. They grind and blend meat. Chop garlic . . . spices. Stuff casings . . . pack . . . lift . . .

deliver . . . ship. We make the finest Toscana salami in America. I think it's the finest in the world. But I'm a modest man." He smiled.

Rafael acknowledged his humor, then continued to stare down into his espresso.

"If you're interested," Secchio finally said, "as I said, it would be a great opportunity to get out of the sewer business. Of course the pay couldn't be much. Not while you'd be learning. No more than you're already earning probably. But you'll be learning a trade."

"I already have a trade, *signore*. I'm an automobile mechanic."

"*Sì*. I know. Sophia told me. But there are hundreds of mechanics in New York. And your experience was in manufacturing. Automobile manufacturing in America is in Detroit. A terrible place. But in all America, there are but a few salami-makers."

On the other side of the door that led down the back stairway from the upstairs bedrooms, Sophia waited in the dark, her heart pounding. Why hadn't her father been more forceful? Made the job more attractive, more glamorous? She leaned forward to try to hear better, and the stair creaked loudly under her.

Rafael saw Secchio glance up at the noise . . . then quickly away. He chuckled to himself at Secchio's embarrassment.

"I don't know, *signore*." He sighed. "I have invested much time becoming a mechanic. All my plans for the future are based on that trade."

Secchio's anger flared. He was afraid it was his wife listening on the back stairway. She would scream bloody murder if he didn't push the boy into accepting the job. He was sure the boy had heard her shuffling around. Even a fool could figure out why she was there. And any fool would hem and haw until he got more money. God! He hated being in this kind of situation!

"All right. Maybe I can pay a little more than what you're making now. But what I'm offering is a good opportunity for a man fresh from the old country. And don't forget. Winter is coming. Pretty soon those lovely sewers

74

you seem to enjoy working in will be filled with snow. And you'll be without work."

"It sounds like an opportunity I can't afford to miss," Rafael finally said, knowing the man was right. The snow-clogged streets were short weeks away and his desperately small income would disappear. And when his income disappeared, so did his mother's and Alicia's. "When does this job begin?"

"What's wrong with tomorrow?" Secchio said.

"I've already promised to work tomorrow. It would create a hardship for the other workers if I failed to report. How about the day after?"

"Fine. That will be fine." Secchio was pleased Rafael was honoring his commitment. A show of character in someone so young was a pleasure to discover.

The sidewalks looked as though they'd been dusted with a layer of flour as the light snow filtered down between the gray, stone-faced buildings.

"Goddammit!" the Irish foreman muttered. "This shit keeps up, we'll really have to bust ass tomorrow." He cursed himself. He'd arrogantly promised his pissant of a brother-in-law that they'd be able to finish the job on schedule.

He jerked around toward the dark trench that ran ribbonlike past the pile of cobblestones wedged out of the street by the crew at the crack of dawn. They were whistling, cheering, and calling. He hurried toward the trench to see what was causing the work stoppage.

"Well, I'll be damned," he said as he saw Rafael squatting next to the trench talking and joking with his old friends. "Hey! Goddammit! You want to keep this crew from working, then you either take their place or pay their wages."

"Oh, I no wanna do either one," Rafael said, standing.

"Didn't think ya would." The Irishman leered. "Sorta missed not having your cute little ass around here causing trouble, Tony. You sure ya don't wanna come back?"

"No, thanks. Itsa nice and warm there. Plenty new salami."

"Sorry to hear that, Tony. Thought for sure by now,

they'd a caught onta you. Kicked your ass back out in the street." He leered at Rafael through the lazy trail of smoke that drifted up from his cigarette.

"Rafael . . . Mr. Orsini!" a voice echoed in the cold air.

They both turned and saw the figure of Sophia lumbering toward them.

"Hello, Miss Secchio," Rafael said as she rushed up mildly out of breath.

"I'm sorry I missed you at Papa's. I stopped by earlier but you were already gone."

"Sì . . . it was my day for deliveries," he said uneasy as the Irish foreman snickered.

"Yes, I know now. Papa told me. He says he's very pleased with your work. Well . . . I know you're probably very busy. But I was wondering . . . I mean, I have a cancellation this evening. So if you would like an extra lesson . . ."

"Thank you, Miss Secchio. Yes. That would be very nice."

"Well, then, I'll see you at seven."

"Well, I'll be dipped in shit!" The foreman roared with laughter, flashing cigarette-stained teeth after Sophia walked away. "You mean to tell me that fat little doxie's done gone and hooked your ass?"

Rafael's face flushed. Sophia was a lady. And in his father's house, it was a sacrilege to talk about a lady with less than respect.

"It is her papa I work for. Not her," he said seething.

"Shit! You poor dumb wop bastard! She's the most famous little twat on this side of town. Her old daddy's probably hired a hundred cocksmen like you," he lied. "He's been trying for years to get her laid so's he can get her off'n his hands 'fore she eats him into the poorhouse."

"Not a good idea for to talk about her like that." Rafael's voice was barely above a whisper.

The Irishman wailed with laughter. He had finally gotten the smart-assed wop's goat.

Rafael never saw the punch coming.

One minute the Irishman was laughing with his hands at his side. The next second, Rafael was on his knees, his nose clogged with blood.

He thrashed around in the snow, trying to get back on his feet.

"Stay down, Tony," the man sneered, still laughing. "I don't want to hurt you."

"Bastard!" Rafael spat, getting to his knees. He barely managed to dodge the Irishman's boot. As it whistled past his head, Rafael grappled it and hung on. The snow had made the sidewalk slippery and the Irishman's other foot slipped out from under him. His stomach hit the cobblestones with a sickening thud. As he rolled over, Rafael swung viciously. The blow landed full on the Irishman's ear, knocking his hat into the gutter. The man lunged at Rafael, wrapped him in a crushing bear hug, and used Rafael's closeness to butt him with his forehead.

Rafael managed to twist free, but as soon as there was space between the two men, the Irishman's arm shot up toward Rafael's chin like a runaway piston.

Rafael felt stars explode in his skull. He shook his head trying to clear the cobwebs. He was sprawled painfully on his face only a few inches above the snow-covered cobblestones. He watched almost hypnotized for what seemed like an eternity as a pool of blood from his nose coagulated on top of the snow.

"Now . . . goddammit! Stay down, you wop son of a bitch! Stay down, or I swear, I'll kill you. I'll break every bone in your goddamn face!" The Irishman wheezed, gasping for breath, and held his side trying to squeeze away the fire in a lower rib that Rafael had cracked with one of his punches.

Rafael pushed himself back onto his haunches, gasping for breath.

The Irishman was willing to stop. He knew the laborers in his crew had had their wind taken out of them. They'd been cheering for the Dago to whip his ass. But their hero had just got his ass kicked.

He started to smirk at the circle of tight-lipped men when a blur shot toward him. From his squatting position, Rafael's fist landed in the pit of the Irishman's stomach. Rafael could hear the air escaping from the man's throat in a loud hiss as his knees buckled. Yet the stubborn foreman still tried to grab for Rafael.

The Irishman's agony was short-lived as one final blow

caught him between the eyes. Almost in slow motion, he rolled over the pile of dirt and cobblestones and into the black trench.

"Pretty good fight." Tomaso smiled to Rafael who was still gasping for breath.

"*Prego*," Rafael said, trying to stem the flow of blood from his nose.

They walked to the edge of the trench and stared down at the still figure of the Irishman.

"Dead?" Rafael asked, his mind filled with the dread of being a criminal in this new country.

"Christ no!" Tomaso answered. "But he's going to have one hell of a headache for a couple of days."

One of the others, known as Old Tony, slipped down into the trench and pulled their pay envelopes out of the Irishman's back pocket.

Tomaso gave him a hand back up the slippery side of the trench, and each man grabbed his envelope before melting into the night.

"What are you going to do now?" Rafael asked Tomaso as they headed away.

"What do you mean?"

"Well, I heard some pretty loud cheering. And it wasn't for the foreman. Not going to be too hard for him to figure out who it was coming from. Seeing as how you're my best friend and the one who got me on his crew in the first place."

Tomaso nodded. Rafael was right. The Irishman would remember and be looking for someone to take his fury out on. Tomaso knew he couldn't stand up to the man the way Rafael had. "Who knows? Maybe I'll head on out to California. Now's probably as good a time as any."

Rafael put his arm around his friend. "Listen. You took care of me when we first met. Right?"

"*Sì.*"

"Well, it's time I did the same for you. We're friends, so we stick together."

"You mean become a sausage-maker?"

"*Sì* . . . why not?"

CHAPTER FIVE

The Secchio salami factory was a stubby two-story, West Side brick building overlooking the Hudson River and the shoreline of New Jersey.

Once a week, through the grate of the elevator that opened up through the sidewalk onto the street, more than two tons of meat was hauled down to the butcher in the preparation room.

By the end of the week, Rafael, Tomaso, six other men, and four women had diced, ground, measured, and stuffed the meat into four-foot linen casings. The meat—one third of it lean bull meat, the rest, fatty pork, laced with pepper, garlic, spices, and wine—was then hung in neat rows on steel hooks in the Green Room.

Five days later, when a hard white mold started to form over the casing, they would move the meat to the curing room, where a month and a half later it would emerge as brick-hard, marble-colored, pungent-smelling salami. Then, cut into foot-long chubs, Secchio's sweet-tasting Toscana salami, identical to that used two thousand years earlier to feed Roman armies, would be crated and carted back out the elevator and loaded on the back of Secchio's wood panel delivery truck.

Rafael was sweating as he looked up from the thick handle that turned the worm gear of the meat grinder. Coming up the ramp into the cool room where he and the other workers ground, diced, and mixed the ingredients were Signore Secchio and Sophia.

"Good morning, Mr. Orsini," she said cheerfully as she picked her way carefully through the sawdust on the concrete floor.

"*Signorina* Secchio. *Come stai?*" Rafael smiled, putting

down his huge butcher knife and wiping his bloody hands on his stained white apron.

"Good morning, Mr. Orsini," she said, again in her teacher's tone. "It's nearly lunchtime. And as I was in the neighborhood, I thought maybe I'd have lunch with Papa. If you'd care to join us, it would be an opportunity to practice your English."

Rafael was aware that the other workers were busying themselves to keep from grinning at him. This was not the first time Sophia had just happened to be in the neighborhood. And everyone who worked in the factory was aware that she had Rafael in her sights.

"*Sì*. Pardon me, yes." He was embarrassed, but she was an excellent tutor. And the lesson was well worth the embarrassment as far as he was concerned. "I that would like very much."

"Come upstairs when you're washed up," *Signor* Secchio advised, taking Sophia by the elbow and guiding her toward the stairs. He knew if he didn't take her along, she'd stay, hovering around Rafael like a moth circling a bright light. He preferred that she maintain some vestige of ladylike pride.

After they were gone, Rafael looked around at his coworkers. Across the long butcher's block from him, Rafael could see Tomaso shaking with suppressed laughter.

He ducked as Rafael's wadded apron came whistling across the block and smacked him in the face.

"You better watch your ass!" Tomaso said, his laughter open now as the catcalls and whistles from the other workers echoed off the stone walls.

Secchio's office was small, cramped, and always too warm. In the summer he refused to open the windows, and in the winter he kept a brazier going for heat. Temperature and humidity were the two most critical things in salami-making, and he wanted his office kept at an even temperature. That way, when he made his twice daily inspections of the different green and curing rooms, he could tell instinctively by the feel whether more or less heat was needed, or more or less sawdust was needed to control the humidity.

Sophia had taken off her fur-lined cape and gloves, but

still wore her hat. Rafael wondered how she managed to keep the little pillbox of a hat perched on the broad top of her head.

When he came in, she started laying out an embroidered tablecloth. From a basket, she took a length of hard Italian bread, several pound-size chunks of cheese, and a deep crock dish filled with rich red lasagna. A second bowl contained a pungent delicacy of chopped olives, muscles, and squid marinated in an oil vinaigrette. A roast chicken filled with an eggplant stuffing completed the main course.

That Sophia had managed to carry the heavy basket, let alone prepare all the dishes during the short morning was an indication of her determination.

"Please sit down, Mr. Orsini." She pointed to a chair at the small table next to her father's desk.

Rafael nodded as he squeezed past her and her father.

As Sophia ladled out huge portions from the dishes onto Rafael's plate, her father poured glasses of Burgundy from an emerald-green bottle. Rafael felt very honored. Prohibition was in full bloom. So Rafael understood that either Sophia's father had private stock from before Prohibition, or made his own wine, or knew a bootlegger. It was amazing he was willing to share the precious liquid with Rafael.

"Evviva!" Rafael said, raising his glass after Secchio handed it to him.

"Cheers," Sophia said correcting him.

"Evviva!" her father interrupted as their glasses touched. A toast was a private thing and didn't have to be given in English.

The flavor of the wine seemed to burst in Rafael's mouth like a bouquet of flowers. He hadn't tasted a good hearty glass of wine since leaving Italy. Every drop of this wine seemed to be filled with a musky flavor similar to that born in the agonized soil of his homeland. He looked up from the bottom of his glass and saw them both watching him.

"Sorry," he apologized for ignoring them. "The *vino Italiano* is much good. Makes me remind of home."

"This is California wine. Not Italian," Secchio said.

"This is the California what is on the Pacific?" Rafael asked in amazement.

81

"Actually the grapes are grown in California. I make the wine myself," Secchio said. "Every year at this time, trains arrive from the west with the grape harvest. For fifteen years I've been buying grapes from the same family in California. Every year I make wine from their grapes. And every year the wine is always sweet, red as blood, and as robust as the wild wind."

"I think is not okay for to make," Rafael said.

"Not exactly. Beer is illegal. Bourbon, scotch, all whiskies. Brandy. And wine also. Unless it's medicinal, sacramental . . . or made at home. Each family is allowed to make so much a year for home use."

"But they can't sell it," Sophia added.

"Shows we Italians have some pretty strong politicians on our side." Secchio winked as he poured each another glassful.

Rafael nodded as the robust flavor of the Burgundy lingered in his mouth. He'd have to talk to Tomaso some more about this California.

"You excuse me, please. I'm 'fraid time come for back to work."

Sophia was disappointed. The wine and the heat in the small office had made her giggly and coquettish. Hidden from her father's view under the small table, her leg kept pressing against Rafael's. At first it had seemed accidental. But when her hand wandered to his knee, Rafael pushed his chair back and stood up.

"Raf . . . Mr. Orsini," she said as she stood and followed him to the door. "I have another extra hour this evening if you haven't anything planned. We could work in another lesson."

Secchio cleared his throat, and they both looked at him. Rafael was thankful her father had come to his rescue.

"Your mother and I have plans for this evening."

"Oh, really," Sophia said disappointed.

"Yes," he beamed proudly. "The man I buy some of our meat from gave me two tickets to the new showing of D. W. Griffith's *Intolerance* over at the Liberty Theater. I promised to take your mother to dinner first. So, you see, there would be no one at home."

Sophia suddenly brightened. "Well, maybe Mr. Orsini could meet us for dinner. I would love to go to dinner with you and Mama. I haven't been out for weeks. And Mr. Orsini could join us. It would be an excellent time to use his English in a totally different environment."

"Please, *signorina*," Rafael protested. "Plan have already been done. I no think . . ."

"Shh . . . shh . . . shh!" she shushed him. "Papa would love to have you join us. Wouldn't you, Papa?"

Secchio was trapped. He shifted uncomfortably in his squeaking swivel chair. It might be worth a big dinner check to soothe Sophia by allowing her to invite Orsini to dinner. At least they wouldn't be unchaperoned.

"But how would you get home?"

"Mr. Orsini can see me home after dinner. Can't you, Mr. Orsini?"

"Alone?" Secchio asked, slightly indignant.

"Papa . . ." Sophia blushed. "Mr. Orsini is a student of mine. Besides it will hardly be a scandalous time. And if it'll make you feel better, you can give us money for a taxi."

To Sophia's delight, her father nodded consent.

"Then, we'll see you at seven. At Valente's. At Forty-eighth and Broadway."

"*Grazie, signorina.*" Rafael headed down the corridor toward the aging room where he knew Tomaso would be wiping mold spores onto the new casing from the older chubs and waiting to hear the details of their lunch.

The restaurant, a sea of white linen-topped tables, was crowded and the smoke and din seemed to fill the building.

Rafael searched the crowd for a sign of the Secchios. Finally at one of the rear tables, he spotted the giant proportions of the two women.

Sophia was wearing a dress of tiered, transparent material, a gauzy silk layered over a bright patterned lining. From the top of her expensively decorated floppy hat to the bottom of her patent leather shoes, everything seemed a little out of place.

Rafael felt totally out of his element in the fashionable restaurant. Everyone seemed well-dressed and affluent. The women wore silk, ostrich feathers, handsomely tailored velvets, or carried oversized fur muffs.

The men were dressed in thick, dark woolen suits and looked out at the world from behind the smoke of expensive, hand-rolled Havana cigars.

As Rafael made his way toward the Secchios' table, he had to dodge several bow-tied waiters carrying huge, heavy laden trays to the party-sized tables.

Rafael had never seen such abundance, such opulence—racks of lamb, sizzling steaks, melon-sized bowls overflowing with mashed potatoes, steaming green vegetables.

America was truly enchanted, he thought, comparing it to the meals in the province he'd left behind.

"Mr. Orsini," *Signora* Secchio said in her melodic singsong voice. "Please sit down. Sophia told me you'd be coming. I'm so pleased."

"Thank you. Good evening, *Signora* Secchio. *Signorina*. I'm pleased for to sit with you." He took the empty chair between the two women. They seemed to have been bathed in an overpowering mixture of pungent perfumes.

"We were just talking about *Intolerance*. Have you heard about it? Aren't you just dying to see it?" *Signora* Secchio said as the hovering waiter filled Rafael's water glass and handed him a menu.

"I not think I know what is 'Entollerence,'" Rafael apologized.

"It's a film," Sophia said coming to his rescue. "A three-hour extravaganza by D. W. Griffith. He's a film director and, they say, a genius."

Rafael nodded. He'd seen the marquees and signs over the dingy little nickelodians whose posters and glossy pictures promised an hour or more of entertainment. He'd even bought a ticket and poked his head inside one once. But the men all had black lips and looked overly feminine. And the grainy, jerky pictures hadn't captured his imagination. They seemed like a waste of a good man's time. So when he started getting a headache, he'd left.

"I hope you'll forgive us. But we've been terribly rude and already ordered our dinners, Mr. Orsini," *Signora* Secchio said. "That way, if the service is slow, we won't be late for the film."

"*Sì* . . . yes. Of course." Rafael opened the menu.

Signora Secchio reached over and took the menu out of

his hands, like a mother impatient with a young son who couldn't make up his mind. "We also took the liberty of ordering for you. I hope you like steak."

"*Sì* . . . yes. Thank you." Rafael was delighted. More that she'd ordered for him than for the steak. He recognized very few things on the menu, and the prices were more than he would care to spend.

"All the newspapers say *Intolerance* is the greatest achievement the film world will ever produce."

Rafael raised his eyebrows to show how impressed he was.

"And can you imagine, Griffith used over fifteen thousand people in it . . . and it's over three hours long." Sophia had a gleam in her eyes at the prospect of three heavenly hours alone with Rafael.

"Fifteen thousand peoples?" Rafael was amazed. That was more than the entire population of the province of Puglia.

"Yes. And it cost over two million dollars to make. And there hasn't been an empty seat in the Liberty Theater since it opened." *Signora* Secchio patted her husband's cheek with her gloved hand in acknowledgment of her pride that her husband had been given tickets by a grateful supplier.

"Two millions of dollars for a moving picture." The way Americans spent money took Rafael's breath away. "For two millions of dollars, I could buy all the *provincia* where I born!"

The Secchios smiled at his naivete as the waiter returned with the heaping tray that held their orders.

The Emperor's steak that *Signora* Secchio had ordered for Rafael was easily enough for two people, maybe three. It was four inches thick.

Rafael stared at it in disbelief.

"Something wrong with your steak?" *Signora* Secchio asked.

"Oh no! It is beautiful." He smiled without taking his eyes off the cut of meat. In truth, he'd never had a steak before in his life. And to start with one this size was overwhelming.

* * *

As the waiter cleared away the heavy dishes, Secchio lit a thick, stubby cigar. Stiffling a belch, he took a gold watch out of his vest pocket. "We're late," he warned his wife who was finishing off an ice-cream laden dessert.

"Oh dear." Grudgingly, she put down her fork and pushed her plate away.

"Mr. Orsini! You will please see my daughter home. Straight home!" he warned.

"*Sì* . . . yes. Of course." Rafael said standing and helping *Signora* Secchio as she struggled into her capelike coat.

Seeing them getting ready to leave, the waiter hurried over. Secchio took him by the shoulder and placed a small wad of bills in his palm.

"This will cover everything," he said to the waiter. "I think my daughter should have . . . would like another cup of coffee. Then please see that they have a taxi," he said nodding to an ever smiling Sophia. "And nothing to drink," he warned the waiter who nodded understanding.

"Are you sure you'll be all right?" he asked Sophia.

Before leaving home she had drunk a few glasses of wine mixed with a shot of brandy to soothe her jitters. The excitement and the heat from the crowded restaurant had brought her to the verge of outright drunkenness.

But the risk of losing her night with Rafael was enough to keep her in control.

"Papa, please!" she said, dismissing his concern. "You and Mama had better hurry or you'll be late." She gave her mother a knowing look. Her mother took her father by the arm and steered him toward the door.

"Have a good time," Sophia said as she took Rafael's sleeve and pulled him back down in his chair.

"How 'bout a little after-dinner brandy?" she whispered in his ear as she tried to slide her chair closer.

"I do not think that a too good idea. Besides, I not know where find speakeasy for to buy. And no forget, your papa say . . ."

"Well, I think it's a marvelous idea," she giggled, ignoring his efforts to bring the meal to an end. "And we don't have to go to any dingy speakeasy."

She leaned over to whisper in his ear. "For a price, the waiter here will provide . . . how do you say . . . a little libation which helps aid the digestion." She patted the material stretched across her middle. It seemed close to its limits. "Waiter!"

"Yes, ma'am."

"My friend and I seem to be suffering ever so from a little after-dinner distress. Do you think it might be possible to get something that might offer some relief?"

"I'm not sure I understand, ma'am "

"Two of your finest brandies," Sophia beamed, slipping the man a large bill.

"Yes, ma'am. Two of our best coming up." A few moments later he brought them two coffee mugs half filled with triple shots of their cheapest rotgut. If the old bastard who'd left earlier wanted someone to watch out for his daughter's virtue, next time maybe he'd remember to tip better.

An hour later, Rafael was panting and sweating after half carrying, half dragging Sophia out of the taxi and up the steps to her front door.

He hoped he could get her inside and upstairs before her parents got back from that motion picture thing and blamed him for the condition she was in. The lock clicked open and he pushed the door open with his foot while he tried to hold Sophia against the doorframe, so she wouldn't slump to the ground.

"Oh . . . my . . . my . . . my!" she slurred cheerfully as Rafael pulled one of her arms over his shoulder, put his arm around her waist, and dragged her inside, kicking the door shut behind them with his foot.

A stairway led to the second floor where the bedrooms were. They made the first three steps with almost no problems. But suddenly Sophia's legs buckled, and she slumped face down on the carpet runner.

Panting heavily, Rafael rolled her over on her back and grabbed her quickly under the arms so she couldn't slide back down the staircase. Holding her from behind, with his hands locked under her massive breasts, he dragged her toward the landing at the top of the stairs.

Feeling his strong hands under her breasts, Sophia's

blood raced. Could he be so excited that he'd take her right here on the stairs? The thought made her quiver.

With a final burst of strength, Rafael heaved Sophia to her wobbly feet atop the landing. But the sudden motion sent her stomach churning.

"Oh God!" She tried to fight away from his hold and stagger down the hallway toward her room. But the minute she succeeded, she sprawled in a heap.

"Oh, God! Help me, Rafael! Please!" she moaned.

"Are you all right?" He was panting, trying to catch his breath.

"No!"

"Then what's wrong for you?" he said as his anger rose.

"O, God! Help me. I'm going to be sick."

Not wanting her to get sick on the expensive carpet, Rafael called on another reserve of strength. He lifted her bodily off the floor and into his arms.

"Which room is yours?" he asked staggering under her weight as he moved down the hallway toward the doors.

"That one!" She feebly tried to point.

Kicking open the door, he staggered across the room and dropped her on top of the thick comforter that covered the bed under the frilly canopy.

"Oh, God!" he heard her moan again.

In almost hypnotic fascination, he watched as she staggered to her feet and lumbered across the room toward another open door. She banged into it and fell into the small bathroom on the other side.

Rafael wasn't quick enough to help her to her feet. It was too late anyway.

Like a grotesque statue crowning the top of a fountain, she spewed forth the total intake from her evening's revelry: wine, steak, dessert, vegetables, brandy. Rafael turned his head away, but the sound of splattering against the tile floor sent his own stomach churning.

Sophia struggled back to her feet, wiped her face on a robe that hung on the door, and lunged across her room toward the safety offered by her bed. She didn't quite make it. She sank down on the carpet next to her cedar hope chest at the end of her bed.

"Please help me," she whispered as she tried to undo the stubborn buttons of her dress.

Rafael watched in fascination as she slowly pulled the dress off her shoulders. But before she could pull it completely off, it became tangled around her wrists. She struggled to free her hands from the sleeves. But she hadn't unbuttoned her cuffs, and her hands were hopelessly tangled inside.

Not knowing what to do, Rafael took her arms and yanked at the sleeves until the buttons popped off. He slipped the sleeves over her hands until they were finally free.

"Help me into bed," she pleaded. "Papa can't find me like this."

"My shoes . . . please . . ." she asked from behind closed eyes, enjoying the feel of his arms as they helped her into the soft bed.

Rafael straightened her legs and yanked off her shoes. He walked around to the other side of the bed and pulled back the comforter. Reaching across the bed, he rolled Sophia over to where the covers were pulled back.

Sophia giggled with delight.

Rafael shook his head and covered her with the comforter. He'd never seen anyone so drunk before in his life. His father had come home drunk a couple of times. But his mother had taken off his clothes and put him into bed with half this much trouble.

"Would you get me a wet towel?" she asked as she heard him start toward the door. "Please. I'm getting a terrible headache. Just a wet towel and I'll be all right . . . I promise."

Rafael nodded. In her bathroom, he grabbed a thick towel that lay on the side of the claw-footed bathtub. He turned on the cold water and soaked the towel in it while trying to focus away from the repulsive remainder of her dinner curdling on the floor.

A few moments later, Sophia opened her eyes and smiled as he placed the cloth over her forehead. Slowly she reached up and took one of his hands. She brought it under the covers and placed it on her breast.

She'd gotten completely undressed while he'd been in the bathroom. His face flushed as she moved his hand slowly over her nipples which seemed to be growing with his touch.

Slowly . . . carefully . . . she moved his hand across her stomach and down onto the top of her thigh.

Rafael started to speak but she shushed him.

She drew his hand halfway to her knees before releasing it. He started to move it away, but she squeezed her knees together and held it in place.

Her legs suddenly started moving, bicyclelike, back and forth until she'd worked his hand up to the dark patch of hair between her legs. It was as velvety and soft as the hair on a newborn babe.

Slowly she spread her legs open and his hand rested full on her soft, warm mound. She reached up and took his other hand. Slowly, she rubbed it over her breast before bringing it up to her mouth.

His hand pressed against her soft, warm mound was suddenly hot and creamy.

God! He'd never felt anything so exciting. Cautiously he started exploring, probing the slit hidden beneath the velvety hair.

God! He'd never felt himself so hard before. The throbbing in his groin was at a height he'd never imagined.

Suddenly, Sophia started bucking and groaning and biting her lower lip. Rafael couldn't stand it any longer. As her spasm started to quicken, he unbuttoned his trousers.

He let them fall to the floor and stepped out of them, taking a moment to pick them up and lay them carefully over the back of the chair so they wouldn't wrinkle. Unbuttoning his knee-length boxer shorts and letting them fall to the floor, he slipped into the warm bed beside her.

Sophia's eyes were glazed from the wine and brandy, but she realized what was happening. Smiling at him, she put her arms around him and dragged him on top of her. Her breath smelled like stale wine as she crushed her lips against his. Rafael didn't care. He strained to force himself into her.

"*Dio! Dio! Dio!*" He was shocked to hear his yell echoing through the still house.

For a moment, she had him locked between her massive legs as he pounded uncontrollably up and down, up and down.

His climax was starting to erupt from the deepest part of his stomach when he felt her legs go slack. He couldn't hold it any longer. He couldn't have even if he'd wanted to. As the first spasm of his orgasm erupted into her, one of her legs fell off the bed. Frantically, Rafael looked at her. Sweat was pouring down his chest onto her undulating breasts. He was afraid that she might be trying to leave . . . to flee . . . his almost violent sex. But she wasn't.

Sophia had passed out.

Still panting from the explosive orgasm, he was staring down at Sophia's slack mouth, when he heard an automobile braking to a stop in front of the Secchio apartment.

"*Cristo!* They're home!" Panic swept over him, turning the sweat of passion into clammy terror.

It took a moment to gain control over his panic.

Quickly he swung out of bed and threw the comforter over the snoring Sophia. He pulled on his pants, walked across and closed her bathroom door so that if her mother came in to check, she wouldn't see or smell her mess. He turned off her bedroom lamp and slipped down the back stairs into the dark, cold kitchen.

Holding the swinging door into the parlor open a crack, he saw the Secchios come into the entryway. As the taxi whined off in the street below, *Signora* Secchio picked up her skirt and waddled laboriously up the stairs toward her daughter's room.

Rafael's heart pounded in terror as *Signor* Secchio turned into the parlor and walked toward the kitchen door he was holding ajar. Rafael's mind blazed in panic. *He always makes himself a cup of espresso before bed.* He cursed himself for not remembering.

Rafael's knees almost buckled from relief when Secchio stopped at the table next to the love seat and pulled the chain that turned off the night light they'd left on for themselves.

Secchio walked back and rattled the front door to make sure it was locked, then followed his wife up the stairs.

Gingerly, Rafael slipped out of the kitchen, across the parlor, and unlocked the door. Stepping out into the cold night air, with a burst of energy that came from surviving a disaster, he rushed off down the street into the dark night's embrace.

* * *

Rafael's deep rejuvenating sleep was shattered by an explosion of sounds as someone pounded on his flimsy door. In a fog, he glanced at the dollar pocket watch lying on the table next to his mattress. Barely six A.M.! What the hell was going on?

"Bastardo!" He heard the muffled voice of *Signore* Secchio screaming at him from the hall.

Rafael's face burned as the previous night flooded back to him. The old man knew! He had talked to Sophia!

It took Rafael barely more than a minute to slip on his clothes, grab the envelope with his savings from its taped hiding place under the empty drawer, wrap his extra set of clothes in a towel, and slip through the window and down the fire escape.

His head was pounding from the wine and brandy from the night before. And his mouth tasted as though someone had relieved himself in it. In the quiet of the morning, he could still hear Secchio cursing and pounding on his door as he disappeared around the corner of the building.

Trotting across town through the early morning shoppers, he raced up six flights of rickety stairs and knocked on Tomaso's sagging door. Rafael could hear him coughing and mumbling complaints as he shuffled across the room toward the door. He opened it a slit and peered out into the dimly lit hallway.

"Son of a bitch! You just coming in . . . or going out?" Tomaso smiled through bleary eyes that said he'd also had a hard night.

"I'm in trouble. I need your help."

"Come in." Tomaso swung the door open.

Rafael had been to Tomaso's before, but he still couldn't believe the chaos. The room was cluttered, disorganized, and as unkempt as Tomaso: a pile of filthy work clothes in the corner, a two-burner hot plate buried by dishes on a dirty sink, a stained mattress nearly hidden under a knotted mass of tattered blankets, and next to the mattress, two crates of newly opened grapes. On the sink next to the hot plate was a galvanized bucket in which Tomaso had started to crush some of the fruit for wine.

"You look like you been running from the police."

"No," Rafael said as he slumped down onto a box next to the sink. "Worse!"

"Worse? *Che cosa è?*" Tomaso put a dirty, stained coffeepot on the hot plate and started to boil coffee that was at least three days old.

"Sounds like big Sophie's after his sweet little ass," yawned a voice from under the blankets heaped atop the mattress.

A head poked out. It was Nell McFarland, a flashing-eyed redhead from the salami factory.

Swinging her legs over the edge of the mattress, Nell pulled one of the blankets from the knotted mess and draped it around her naked body. Shivering in the morning cold, she crossed gingerly to the stove and started to wipe out two cups and a chipped glass.

Rafael was speechless, as much from his surprise of finding her here as from her apparent lack of modesty. The way she held the blanket around her pink, freckled body barely hid anything.

Nell was witty, bright, and the only non-Italian at Secchio's. Everyone felt the old man had hired her because of her long, silky legs, the exact opposite of his wife's short, fleshy pillars. Brought up in a half-Irish, half-Italian neighborhood, Nell spoke Italian as easily as English, and had taken to Rafael in a big-sister fashion. He liked her as well, but had no idea she and Tomaso were friends, much less lovers.

"Go ahead. Don't let me interrupt," Nell said, taking the glass and pouring it almost full of the barely warm, oily black liquid. Then she darted across the room, sprawled on the mattress, and pulled the covers over her before lighting a cigarette.

"Okay. What the hell's going on?" Tomaso asked, truly concerned.

"The Secchios," Rafael said, like a man repeating a prison sentence to Devil's Island.

"My God!" Nell said, buried in the warmth of the blankets. "It really is Sophia then, isn't it?"

Rafael looked at them both for a long moment before nodding his head.

"God, I'm sorry," she said. "I was just trying to be funny when you came in."

"Come on over here where it's warm," Tomaso said, patting the mattress. "I think we better talk about this."

Rafael walked across the room and slumped onto the mattress as Nell scooted over to make room. Exhausted and embarrassed, he explained in detail what had happened the previous night.

"It's not exactly your fault, you know?" Nell said trying to relieve him from some of his guilt.

"Doesn't matter. I ran. I ran when I should have stayed and faced her father . . . and done the right thing."

"Oh dear! Oh dear me! I see . . ." Nell said dropping her cigarette into the dregs in the bottom of the glass.

"You see what?" Tomaso asked irritated that he might have missed something.

"It was his first time," she said, running a motherly hand through Rafael's black uncombed hair.

Rafael nodded.

"My God!" Tomaso whispered. "You really did come from out of the dark ages, didn't you? Didn't they teach you men anything in Montepulciano?"

Rafael stared at him. "I don't know what happened. I thought I was strong. I should have stopped before it happened. But . . ."

"Don't you understand? Poor baby, no one could stop at a time like that. Sophia knew that. There's an old-fashioned word for what she was doing. It's called seduction."

"Nell's right, Rafael," Tomaso said. "Everybody knows she's had her eyes on you. It would have been like trying to stop the tide."

"More like a tidal wave," Nell giggled.

"It doesn't matter. I've known all along what's been on her mind. In a way, it was me who seduced her. Maybe not seduced. But at least I used her. I figured I could use the extra lessons . . . save some money. Now . . . I have to do the honorable thing."

"Honorable thing?" Nell shook her head in disbelief. "God! Why didn't I run into you first? Rafael, there's nothing dishonorable about what you did. Won't you understand? For Christ's sakes!" She was screaming now. "You were a damned victim!"

"If it was anybody else, you might be right." Rafael shrugged. "But there's something you don't understand.

Something you don't know that makes this different. I have to do the honorable thing. Because I made a man pay a terrible price for the same thing. The same thing in which he didn't do the honorable thing with my sister."

Nell and Tomaso nodded. This was the first time Rafael had revealed anything about his past.

"Chances are no one will ever find out," Nell said after a few moments of silence. "For sure Sophia's not going to say anything. She wouldn't dare. Besides, from what you said, I doubt if she'll remember anything this morning . . . other than throwing up."

"Her papa already knows," Rafael said as he related how the old man was pounding on his door with murder in his voice at the crack of dawn. "I shouldn't have run," he repeated. "I've never run from anything in my life before. But when I woke up . . . heard the pounding on my door . . . Well, my brain wasn't working too good. And the next thing I know, I'm sitting here between you . . ."

Before he'd finished his sentence, the sounds of a commotion from the room directly beneath Tomaso's drifted up to them.

"It's Secchio!" Nell whispered.

"What are you talking about?" Tomaso asked.

"Listen! That voice yelling . . . downstairs."

"Impossible!"

"Goddammit, it is, I tell you. I'd know that squeal anywhere. He's yelled at me enough times after I left him slobbering in one of the aging rooms." Nell flung herself off the mattress and grabbed her clothes from the piles scattered around the floor. "Come on, dammit! Move." She grabbed Rafael and jerked him and Tomaso off the mattress.

"What's he doing here?" Tomaso said in a panic.

"It don't exactly take a genius to figure that one out. Rafael got you the job. Everyone knows you two are friends." She was struggling with the row of tiny buttons that joined the front of her blouse together.

"I'm not going to run," Rafael said quietly.

Without answering, Nell found Tomaso's grimy pants and threw them to him.

"Okay. So you're not going to run. But it's not going to do any good to talk at a time like this," Nell said as she stepped into her silk panties. "It'll make it a lot easier after everyone's had time to cool down. Know what I mean?"

"No."

"Jesus H. Christ! Look. You take this lame brain, Tomaso, and hide in the john down the hall, I'll stay here . . . all nice and innocent like. When the old son of a bitch comes pounding, I'll keep him here till you get a chance to hightail it out of there. I'll talk to him . . . see what's on his mind. Then in a couple of hours, we'll meet and set things up."

Nell grabbed Rafael and shoved him into the hallway. Throwing Tomaso his shirt, she pushed him after Rafael whispering for them to get down the hallway to the bathroom at the end of the corridor.

She barely got the door closed when she heard Secchio's footsteps pounding up the stairs. As an afterthought, she tore off her blouse and quickly wrapped one of the sheets around her, before innocently opening the door.

Secchio's angry face, red and sweaty from the climb, turned an even darker shade of red as his mouth fell open. Standing in front of him with a sheet wrapped around an apparently naked body was the apparition he'd been lusting after for almost a year.

"What are you doing here?" He was astonished to find her in this pigpen.

"The pipes broke at my place," she explained innocently. "Mr. Fierello was kind enough to offer me the use of his . . ." She saw him trying to peer in past her. "Oh . . . he's not here. I think he stayed at the 'Y.'"

Huddling in the bathroom, Rafael and Tomaso heard the voice that had been angry and threatening downstairs suddenly become throaty and charming. When the door into Tomaso's apartment closed, the two men slipped down the stairs to the street.

Almost at a full run, Tomaso pulled Rafael through the morning shoppers and onto a clanging trolley. They slumped down on the hard, wood bench and sat mute trying to look inconspicuous. Silently they rode the grinding, clanging trolley around its whole route. An hour later they looked out the window anxiously as they approached Tomaso's building again. Nell was sitting on the stoop eat-

96

ing a red hot dog from a pushcart. They quickly hopped off.

"Want some breakfast?" she asked, offering the steaming hot dog to them. "It's on the old man."

They both shook their heads as they waited for her to tell them what had happened. But Nell took her time, savoring each bite.

"Well . . ." she said wiping her mouth on the thin tissue the hot dog came in. "Sorry to break it to you like this."

Both men moved closer.

"But I'm afraid you're going to have to learn to live without Sophia." She grinned.

"What?" Rafael said as he couldn't keep a grin from breaking across his face.

"No kidding?" Tomaso said, pounding his friend on the back.

"You sure?" Rafael asked seriously.

"God, yes!" She laughed. "Don't worry. When I opened the door and Secchio saw me standing there in nothing but me, I probably could have had him sign over his life insurance. But, dear Rafael, I'm not sure I would have taken him to bed even for you," she said squeezing Rafael's arm.

"If it wasn't Sophia and Rafael, what the hell was he doing coming to my door and pounding like some lunatic?" Tomaso asked suddenly indignant.

"It didn't have anything to do with Sophia." She hitched her arm through theirs and they stared down the middle of the sidewalk as the sun broke through the gray and started warming the crisp air.

"Then what was it?" Tomaso asked impatiently.

"Every Saturday, and he's been doing it for years, he goes to the factory to one of the aging rooms to mark the chubs that are ready to be shipped. It seems one whole room, the one near the elevator, had about four thousand chubs that exploded. Like sausages in a frying pan. Rotted instead of curing. He was almost crazy from the anger. Rafael lived closest to the factory. I guess that's why he picked on him. When Rafael wasn't there, he blamed the next closest . . . you, Tomaso. If I hadn't been there, he'd have blamed whoever lived next closest."

"Wonder what the hell happened?" Tomaso said. "Do you think someone did it on purpose?"

"Naw! Most of the time when it happens, it's caused by cheap garlic . . . which the old man has been known to use on more than one occasion. There's something in it. A blight or something that kills the mold on the salami."

"Most of the time?" Rafael asked. "Garlic causes it most of the time?"

"Yeah. But in this case, I told him you did it."

"What?" Both men's heads shot around.

"Yeah. I told him everybody knows you're a dastardly fellow after his daughter so you can get his money."

Rafael's puzzled look turned to a grin.

"You don't want little Sophia to be able to talk him into forgiving you now, do you? I mean, she just might remember what happened up in her little room. And in her innocent way . . . blackmail you a little." She grinned triumphantly.

Rafael swung Nell around and into his arms. With her feet off the ground he hugged her and twirled her for almost half a block. "You're a wise woman, Nell McFarland," he said setting her down as startled pedestrians passed.

"You really would have stayed and faced the music though, wouldn't you, Rafael?"

He nodded.

"Damn! I still wish I'd found you first." She laughed.

"You better make yourself scarce for a while," Tomaso suggested. "The old man will probably get drunk this weekend to forget his troubles. But he still might go to the police or something soon as his head clears."

Rafael nodded.

My place's over at ninety-eighth and Amsterdam." Nell grinned as she took Rafael's hand and squeezed. "You could stay with me."

"Hey! What about me?" Tomaso protested.

"You already have a place," she answered linking her arms through theirs once again and leading them down the street. "Tomaso's right though, Rafael. What with the old man . . . Sophia and all, it might not be a bad idea to take it on the lam for a while."

"What's that mean?" he asked.

"Take it on the lam . . . a trip . . . get out of town. Till things cool down," Nell said. "Course if you want to know what I think, I think you ought to get out of New York period. For keeps. Ain't nothing here for someone like you."

"Thanks, Nell. But even if I wanted to, I don't have the money."

"Are you kidding?" Tomaso said. "Everybody knows you got a wad stashed away."

"*Sì*. But that's to bring my mother and sister to America."

"So . . . grab a freight, then," Nell said. "Head south to Florida. California maybe. Someplace warm."

"California is Tomaso's dream." Rafael said.

"Yeah. It's Tomaso's dream," she answered, "and it's not a bad dream either. But as far as Tomaso's concerned, it'll always just be a dream. Right, Tomaso?"

Tomaso shrugged and walked in silence for a while.

"Come on," he said suddenly heading for another streetcar.

"Hey . . ." Nell protested as he jerked her along with him. "Where the hell's the fire?"

"You'll see. It's a surprise." He motioned for Rafael to hurry.

Almost an hour later, after crossing the river into New Jersey, they got off the little streetcar in front of a block-long warehouse that opened onto a central freight yard.

Like an army of ants, people were swarming in, around and even over the boxcars parked on the sidings next to the warehouse. It was worse than downtown New York City during the height of the evening rush hour.

As the three of them crunched along on the gravel between the faded wooden boxcars, Rafael saw whole families haggling with vendors standing in the open boxcar doors. The further into the throng of people they walked, the fiercer the haggling.

Rafael smiled to himself. The haggling, the din of noise, and the crush of people made him feel comfortable, because everyone was bartering, shouting, laughing in Italian.

And what they were bidding so fiercely for were boxes full of grapes.

"They're from California," Tomaso said. "Like the ones you saw at my room." Some were ruby red, some golden colored, some whitish green, some almost berry black. But they were all hard and fresh having been picked only the week before and shipped in iced carloads to the Italian community in New York.

Rafael stopped next to a steel drum in which a fire blazed warmly. He watched as one of the selling agents, wearing a derby over the scarf knotted around his head to keep his ears warm, used a pair of pliers to unlock one of the boxcar doors. The man worked the metal fastener back and forth quickly until the heat built up and the fastener snapped. Unlatching the door, he rolled it open to expose its contents.

The aroma within the boxcar seemed to pour out over the spectators like scented water. Rafael had never smelled anything so sweet and alive. It was like a field of fruit blossoms.

The man in the boxcar took one of the crates from the top of a stack, pried open the top, and held up a bunch of heavy maroon grapes that looked as though they were ready to burst. Almost instantly, a cacophony of shouts and yelled bids were hurled at him.

A nod of the head by a man in the boxcar door sealed the deal with the successful bidder. No contracts, just a nod of the head and a handshake.

"It's not such a bad dream, eh, my friend?" Tomaso said.

Each family was buying the quantity they needed for next year's supply of wine. A supply of wine that the U.S. government allowed them to make despite Prohibition.

Delighted at having made a purchase at what he thought was a bargain price, a wizened old man offered Rafael a bunch from an open crate.

"Thank you, *Signore*," Rafael said, putting one of the grapes into his mouth. The grape burst as he crushed it in his mouth, full of liquid and flavor. It tasted like manna from heaven. "Your wine will be special this year," Rafael complimented the man.

The old man was delighted. "Thank you," he said. "The longer into the season you wait, the bigger and sweeter the grapes. Some people are so impatient, they buy early . . . from the first trainloads. But I have found, after almost thirty years, it's best to wait almost to the end of the season."

"You mean this is not a special day?" Rafael asked, not sure he'd understood what he heard.

"Special? Special, how?"

"With so many people, I thought maybe this must be one of the only trainloads of grapes."

The old man banged the case of grapes shut. "This goes on every day for almost three months."

Rafael shook his head in amazement. The place called California that could send trainload after trainload of grapes for months at a time must indeed be smiled on by God . . . an Eden.

Tomaso was right. This was a dream worth chasing.

"Is it a long way to California?" Rafael asked his two friends.

"Yeah. Almost to the other side of the world. My place is a whole lot closer." Nell grinned up at him.

"That's a place I have to see," he said almost from a trance.

Nell nodded, knowing he didn't mean her apartment.

By the end of the hour, Rafael had walked deep into the freight yard leaving Tomaso, Nell, the haggling families, the sales agents, and the din of noise behind. Nearly crushing Nell in his embrace and squeezing Tomaso's neck until his face turned red, Rafael promised to start Tomaso's dream for him and to find a place for them all to be together again.

But when he disappeared around the bend in the tracks, Nell knew they'd seen the last of him.

It took Rafael awhile to determine which of the freight cars were inbound and which outbound. Finally he located one of the main westbound lines. Within another hour, he was huddled out of the wind on a flatcar stacked with crates of machinery bound for St. Louis.

Despite the cold, as the train clattered across the steel latticework that spanned a nameless river, his eyes started to ache from exhaustion. As he drifted into sleep, his mind raced with colorful dreams of what lay ahead.

California!

Deep fertile valleys, warm running rivers, lush greenery, and sweet grapes. As he finally drifted off, his mind was transported to his mother's hovel. His heart ached, realizing the torment she and Alicia would be suffering without him.

"Soon, Mama. Soon!" he cried as her warm. smiling image magically appeared. "You and Alicia will be here with me. Safe. Warm. And with plenty to eat. I promise."

CHAPTER SIX

Mira Correlli glanced around and hoped she wouldn't be recognized as she climbed the tile stairway toward the third floor of the squalid building at the end of a narrow, garbage-littered street.

She stopped on the landing and leaned against the iron rococo railing to catch her breath. From behind one of the closed doors, she heard a woman yelling. The door opened and slammed shut as an embarrassed little man hurried into the gray light from the skylight, the only light these dingy musty hallway had known for years.

Mira Correlli hid behind her shawl and acted out a bad cough as the man hurried past, fixing his hat and trying to straighten out his sweat-stained clothes.

She closed her eyes, but his odor lingered. Evidently a field worker, he was probably in town for his only day off in months. And this was the only place in town where a man from the fields, for a price, could find the luxury of a woman with a warm, willing body.

Mira Correlli shuddered with pain for the lost souls trapped behind these doors. As a woman, she understood what they were going through merely to survive in a country where there were barely enough jobs for the men.

She made her way down the hallway that hung over the courtyard, finally locating the room she was looking for.

She raised a trembling hand and knocked lightly.

There was no response.

She knocked again, a little harder.

"In a minute!" The sullen young voice on the other side of the door yelled.

Mira Correlli waited. Finally after a few anxious minutes, she knocked again, hoping the girl on the other side of the door would read the anxiety, and urgency in her signal.

"All right! All right!"

Mira Correlli heard the girl's high heels echoing across the tile floor as she stormed across the tiny cubicle toward the door.

The sagging, creaking door was flung angrily open, and Mira stood eye to eye with Alicia Orsini.

Tears burst into both women's eyes as Alicia dropped her arm to let the door swing open so Mira could come in.

"I'm sorry," Alicia apologized to the woman from the Padrone's kitchen. "I was afraid it was another . . ."

They both stood for a moment without speaking. An overheated fan hanging from the ceiling protested loudly. In the early morning chill it shouldn't have been on at all. But in her desperate times alone, it gave Alicia some motion to follow.

Alicia crossed the room and sank back against a tattered satin couch. Mira followed and stood uncomfortable and embarrassed in this girl's alien world. As she looked down at Alicia's pathetic figure, she felt more than guilt at the girl's situation. She had news she dared not give the girl. There were letters at the central post office for Alicia and her mother, addressed to them in care of their priest. Letters that undoubtedly contained money as they were from her brother, Rafael, in the United States.

But Carlo Gianini had invited the aging postmaster for coffee one morning and assured him that his future would be less than bright if any letters that arrived for Alicia or her mother weren't conveniently misplaced.

While clearing the table where they were talking, Mira had overheard. She knew it would be too easy to trace the source of the information. And if she risked it, and if Carlo Gianini found out what she'd done, he would do to her what he had done to the Orsinis. She and her family would be like refugees in their own country with no one daring to extend a helping hand.

She was taking a terrible risk even by being here now, and they both realized it. She looked at Alicia for a moment. Alicia's mouth had become hard; it was no longer the smiling, happy thing she remembered. Her body was more mature, more alluring as her young breasts showed invitingly through the gauzy material that barely covered her nudity.

The dress was held together in front by a single sash which made it easy to get out of. Or, if the man preferred, she didn't have to get out of it. She merely had to spread the front of it to reveal her legs, her youth.

After Rafael had left, the hovel which had been their home had been torn down. As she and her mother watched, Carlo Gianini, with the help of a crew of laborers recruited from their neighbors, dismantled it mud brick by thick mud brick. Sitting alongside her mother on her mother's brass bed, with their meager belongings stacked around them, Alicia prayed for something from heaven to strike Carlo dead.

After that day, unable to find anyone willing to take the chance of giving them work, her mother had sold one small treasured possession after another for enough to feed them on. The only shelter they had been able to find was in the open air stalls of the town's marketplace. Windblown and ever damp, their lives were a nightmare until one day when she alone, Alicia was invited to the house of a heavily rouged old woman who offered her tea and the prospects of earning a few lire.

Alicia had been excited. She searched for her mother who had taken to wandering the streets hoping to find a coin or something of value. Not able to find Maria, and not wanting to miss the appointment with the old woman, Alicia brushed her hair in the splintered mirror in the public toilet in back of the marketplace and rushed off.

Less than an hour later, tears of rage streamed down her face as she watched the fat, gaudily dressed woman casually shrug off Alicia's indignation. The room was small, made even smaller by the oversized, overstuffed furniture and the walls filled with crosses and paintings of Madonnas and saints.

"You must know, dear girl, there is no other way for you to earn money in this province. If you are to survive, this is the only occupation open to you. No one in Montepulciano can even offer you or your poor sainted Mother help. Now . . . I have discussed your situation with the young Padrone, Carlo Gianini . . ."

"What? You discussed this with another person . . ." Alicia cried in disbelief.

"Sì, of course. After all, you are not a virgin. You were experienced . . . with his father."

"But I wasn't a . . . a . . ."

"A prostitute?" The woman added the word Alicia couldn't get out of her throat. "Of course you were, my child. How were you different? You provided the gentleman certain pleasure, certain fantasies, gratification. And in return the gentleman rewarded you."

"But that was different." Alicia's voice was filled with revulsion.

"That's questionable, to say the least. No matter . . ." The woman returned to the original proposal. "Carlo Gianini has no objections to you living under my roof. Be thankful that he has decided to be generous to you and your mother. And above all . . . think of your mother. Her health."

"I would rather die . . ." Alicia said angrily rushing toward the door.

But two weeks later, a gaunt, hollow-eyed girl with hair matted and soaked from the rain that hadn't stopped since they last talked knocked on the old woman's door.

"Come in . . . come in." The gaudily made up woman smiled like a glowing patroness.

"Only if my mother never learns . . . Never!" Alicia said, shivering as the heat of the small room started seeping into her soggy clothes.

"Of course," the woman said putting her arm around Alicia's shoulder and drawing her toward the fire.

"And a room. I need a room for her. Someplace warm and dry."

"Of course . . . of course." The woman smiled, knowing that buried within this drowned rat of a girl lay a delightful treasure through which she would profit greatly.

That had been almost a year ago.

Mira Correlli shook her head at the thought of the change that she'd seen in Alicia during that period of time.

"I'm here because of . . . of your mother," Mira said finally.

Alicia looked at her anxiously. "You need more money?"

Signora Correlli had been the only one willing to take the chance of helping Alicia or her mother. She had become the go between, the one who met Alicia at some out of the way place and took her money, the pitiful few lire the old woman allowed her, and relayed it to Alicia's mother.

Maria had been told Alicia was in another town working in someone's household and that her address had to remain a secret lest the Padrone interfere.

Alicia dreaded the answer. More money meant she would have to double her efforts that night.

Mira shook her head. "No. No extra money is needed."

"What then?"

"I'm afraid your mother has found out."

"*Dio!*" Alicia cried as tears flooded her eyes. "But how?"

Mira shrugged. "Who can say? Sooner or later, it was bound to happen. A careless word here. A vindictive old hag . . ."

Alicia turned and started to take a dress out of the mirrored wardrobe that stood next to her bed.

"I will go to her."

"She is not . . ." Mira hesitated. "They have had to take her."

"Who's taken her? Where have they taken her?" she asked, not understanding.

"They had to take her to the hospital."

"Oh, my God! Is she dead? She didn't . . ."

"No." Mira said as she took Alicia's face to her breast. "It was the other hospital . . . the asylum."

"The madhouse? Oh *Dio* . . . *Dio* . . ." Alicia sobbed.

"*Sì . . . sì,*" Mira whispered, rocking her gently back and forth like a baby. She stroked the hair that had once been soft and downy. Now it was curled and primped into greasy little waves. "Her mind just couldn't take any more pain."

"When did she . . . when did they take her?" Alicia said as her resolve started to return.

"This morning. She was at the main fountain where . . . well . . . she had a knife. She would have mutilated herself if they hadn't stopped her. I would have come sooner but . . ."

"*Sì*. I understand." Alicia embraced her, knowing the risks the woman had taken just by coming.

"I'm sorry, my child."

"There's nothing for you to be sorry for, *signora*," Alicia said, resignation in her voice. "We had to eat. Or starve. No one would help. We had to live . . . until my brother returns for us."

The thought of her brother brought a stab of loneliness to her numb body. Every day she prayed to hear from him. That he was well. That he was thinking of them. That they would be together soon. But each day . . . there was nothing. She was terrified something had happened to him. Maybe the Padrone's men had caught up to him and murdered him. *Oh God, Rafael, please be all right,* she thought trying to fight the panic welling up from the thought that if he was dead, they might as well be also.

"I have to go to my mother," Alicia said as she stepped to the bed to change.

"*Sì*, of course." Mira nodded as she turned to leave.

"*Signora* Correlli," Alicia said as Mira went through the door.

"*Sì?*"

"I may never be able to thank you for all you have done. But God in heaven knows. He will truly reward you."

"*Dio!*" Alicia said under her breath. Her mother, Maria, was in the corner, pressed against the stone wall amid a hundred hysterical, tortured souls.

"Mama! Mama . . . please!" She called through the din. But there was no trace of recognition on her face. Only the echoing "Mama . . . Mama . . ." from several haggard-looking crones who mindlessly mimicked any sound.

Alicia turned and fled up the stone stairway that led through the iron gate back to the street.

"*Buon giorno! Buon giorno!*" an overly cheerful voice behind her said as she sagged against the cold granite wall of the asylum. "What a pity to see a beautiful young whore in such pain."

Alicia saw the boyishly handsome Carlo Gianini grinning down at her from his father's Bugatti.

"Do you like my car? Oh, I forgot, you've seen it before. Isn't it wonderful that Dominic happened to find it in Rome. After a little talk, the man who had it decided he should like it returned to its owner. By the way, I understand your mother has suddenly taken ill. What a pity!"

His voice dripped with mock sympathy as he opened the door and lazily swung out of the car and walked toward her.

"It was you, wasn't it, Carlo Gianini?"

"It was me . . . what?"

"It was you who told my mother about me."

"I don't recall. I've never tried to keep it a secret. Have you? I mean if I violated some confidence, I'm sure you'll understand."

"Someday . . . when Rafael returns, you will suffer as you've made us suffer, Carlo Gianini." She pointed her finger at him. "I promise."

"I hope he returns soon." Carlo smiled. "We did try to find him though, my dear. Even the little man who had the misfortune of having my car could shed no light on his whereabouts. Clever . . . your brother. He seems to have vanished without a trace. I was afraid for a while it might run in the family. But now, with your mother here . . ." His smile darkened. "I'm sure you won't be in such a hurry to leave our charming city."

"When my brother comes back, I promise you, your father's pain will seem like a thing of joy compared to what he will do to you."

At the mention of his father, Carlo's face contorted.

"Your promise has about as much worth as the dead sperm men spill between your legs. Poor Papa," he spat, "if only he'd known how cheaply he could have had your affections. A few lire, at most."

Alicia laughed defiantly. She felt a powerful sense of accomplishment at creating such anger in Carlo.

"He paid the full price for those affections. And now he stands naked on his veranda for all the world to see, screaming profanities at passersby like some madman. No . . . Carlo. You don't hate my brother for what he did. You hate him because now your father is such an embarrassment to your name. The madman who, servants say, flaunts his disfigurement like a badge of honor whenever he's left unattended . . ."

"Enough!" Carlo screamed. "Don't forget, my not so enchanting little whore, that you and your mother are alone. Your brother has run like a frightened dog. Out of compassion, I have allowed you to survive. So, if I were you, I would be as nice as I could to your benefactor . . . the only one who can . . . and has helped you. Do you understand?"

He reached over and slipped his hand under her shawl and pressed against her breast. His heart suddenly pounded. Since he had first set eyes on her, half naked in his father's bedroom, she had excited him. He looked into Alicia's eyes as he felt himself becoming hard.

"If I want to survive . . . and for my mother to survive . . . you might help me?" she asked with all the smiling innocence of a child.

"Yes . . . of course." His face flushed with anticipation.

Her innocent smile exploded into hatred as he felt her saliva splattering his face. Carlo took his hand away from her breast and took out an expensive handkerchief trimmed with the intricate lace that bore the Gianini family crest.

Carefully, he wiped the spittle from his face and dropped the handkerchief into the gutter. Without another word, he turned to the Bugatti, started the engine, and drove angrily into the evening.

Alicia stood in defiant silence watching the car disappear. Suddenly she started shaking. Tears streamed down her face and she couldn't control her sobs. "Rafael!" she called in pain and in terror. "Help us! Please . . . help us!"

CHAPTER SEVEN

The old Ford vibrated and the fenders rattled as Rafael steered around the rutted gully. The roadbed had washed away in the unusually heavy rains and the repair crews still hadn't repaired the damage. Rafael glanced at the gasoline gauge that had stopped flickering a few miles earlier. He needed gas. He had for the past hour. He'd run out once already and had used the last few gallons in the five-gallon lard can he kept on the running board.

He checked the winding road ahead as it disappeared in the elbow of two distant rolling hills. It didn't look too promising. No stations. No roadside cafes. No sign of any farm buildings.

There was a grade crossing at the bottom of the small hill he was coasting down. As Rafael nursed the car to a slow stop, he saw out of the corner of his eye the billowing contrail of a locomotive thundering toward the deserted crossing. He turned off the engine to preserve the last of his precious gas. Out of habit, he adjusted the spark, got out, and sat on the bumper waiting for the rumbling train to pass so he could crank the engine back to life.

As he sat there in the wind and dust kicked up by the fast freight, the ground around the grade crossing rumbled as if torn by an earthquake. The train hurricaned past the fragile old Ford that he'd reconstructed out of several wrecks. The caboose finally passed in a red blur and the storm of wind died and left him in silence.

Rafael reached down, spun the crank, and quickly got in and nursed the engine to life. Carefully, he eased the tender tires across the steel rails. On the other side, he pushed the clutch and gears through their sequence, set the manual throttle, and slouched back to watch the passing countryside.

It reminded him of the rolling farmlands of northern Italy. Though it was far into the summer, the rains had kept everything an emerald-green color. A nice part, Rafael thought, as he made a quick mental evaluation as to whether or not this was a spot he'd consider staying in. Was this the place to toil, work, settle down, and bring his mother and sister to . . . and marry and raise a family?

Nice! Even better than okay, he thought. But it didn't have what he was looking for. He really couldn't describe what he was looking for. He only knew that when he saw it, he'd know it.

It had been over a year since he had boarded the freight train in New York. Faithfully during that time, Rafael had worked from dawn to dark, seven days a week if he could, to earn enough money to send to his mother and Alicia.

There were weeks when he wasn't able to count on three meals a day. He could have. But that would have meant not having anything to add to his savings—savings that were growing toward the amount he knew would buy their passage to America. To miss a few meals really didn't matter to him. It just meant he'd be able to get in an extra hour of work during the day.

The farmers he worked for loved that quality in him. They'd rather pay him for the extra hour than have to feed a man of that size. And in just a few months this past summer, the work and the sun had tanned and matured his face and molded his body rock hard.

Many was the farmer, or shop foreman, who had tried to persuade him to stay. Put down his roots wherever they were. But in the end, he'd felt the need to move on in his more or less westward migration. His was the path of a drunken bumblebee, governed as it was by the roads that might run north or south before meandering back west.

Rafael's reputation as a prize laborer had become almost legendary. If a farmer needed an outhouse dug or a smokehouse built or livestock slaughtered and butchered, or if a rural machine shop or blacksmith needed a strong back, there was Rafael, a master at working with metals and at getting the mysterious "infernal combustion" engines back to life.

People started looking forward to his passing. They'd

even save up jobs hoping the giant Italian with the wide warm smile would pass again. He never did, of course, which also added to his legend. The car he was driving, which doubled as his home, was the result of three weeks of that labor.

Outside of Omaha, he'd sweated and broken knuckles and assembled two big harvesting machines for a small local distributor. In the back of the main shop, the skeletons of a half-dozen flatbed trucks, an old ice truck, and several boxy four-door convertibles had been dragged to a corner of the storage yard and forgotten, consigned to scrap and destined to rust.

"What you going to do with those old clunkers out back?" Rafael asked as he stopped by the owner's cubicle to pick up his pay at the end of the first week.

"Don't know for sure. Haven't made up my mind yet. Couple of 'em are still pretty valuable." The man shrugged. Actually he wished someone would haul them to the dump for him. He'd even have paid to have it done. But his horsetrader's instincts clanged a warning. He smelled a trade . . . a deal. "Whatta you think could be done with 'em?" the old man asked, as he and Rafael walked through the barnlike doors of the shop and around back to where the rusting hulks sat. "I have to admit, couple of 'em are pretty well done for. But a couple of them ain't so bad, despite what they look like. Sorta like jewels under them tattered exteriors."

Rafael didn't answer. Suddenly the old man sounded as though he was talking about a herd of prized horses, or his firstborn son. Everywhere cars teetered precariously on top of each other. It reminded Rafael of the carnage left over after some horrendous wreck.

"Looks like a lotta junk to me." Rafael shrugged. He knew the old man's reputation as a trader. And he wasn't about to give him any ammunition. "I was thinking maybe I could haul a couple into town and sell them. Whatever I get, I split with you—half and half."

He knew he could build a car or truck by scavenging parts from several of the wrecks sitting there in a heap. Afterward he could sell what was left for junk. And he'd willingly split that with the old man.

The old man looked at the mounds of lifeless mechanical bodies. He knew Rafael was a magician when it came to engines. But no one could get one of those running. And there wouldn't be more than twenty, maybe twenty-five dollars' worth of scrap there.

"Tell you what," the old man finally said. "Rather than split fifty-fifty. You give me . . . oh . . . say seventy-five dollars and you can have the whole shooting match. That way you don't have to worry about splitting. And if you're good, really good, you can probably make more than my share of what it cost you."

"Seventy-five dollars!" Rafael grimaced. He kept looking at the pile of hulks like a poker player not daring to give away his hand. He already knew he could get at least two of the trucks running. The only thing he couldn't salvage were the tires. But he wouldn't worry about them until after he got one running. "Looks like maybe ten . . . no more than fifteen dollars' worth of scrap," Rafael finally countered.

The old man nodded. "That would be a good price for you. If it was nothing but junk. But there's some pretty expensive pieces of machinery sitting out here, ya know? A man'd be a fool to take fifteen dollars for something worth a whole lot more."

The old man reached in his back pocket and pulled out a pint bottle of moonshine. He uncorked it and took an eye-watering swig before handing it to Rafael as a signal that the bargaining was underway in earnest.

Rafael gasped as the drink took his breath away. America's raw, harsh liquor was something he'd never be able to get used to.

"What's the matter, boy?" The old man grinned at him. "Can't take a little drink?"

"It just went down the wrong pipe," Rafael said, coughing and wiping the tears on the back of his greasy sleeve.

"Shit, boy! You only got one pipe! You just can't take it."

"And I suppose you can?" Rafael taunted him.

The old man took the pint out of Rafael's hand, tilted it back, and drained it, then sank down on the tailgate of the old ice truck.

An hour later, dead drunk, the old man made a deal with Rafael for fifteen dollars, cash, for the whole shooting match. When Rafael peeled fifteen one-dollar bills out of an old crumpled manila envelope, the old man knew, through his drunken stupor, that he'd been had.

It took Rafael three days to overhaul the engine of the ice truck, remount it on a drive shaft cannibalized from one of the battered convertibles, and sell it to a farmer as a combination haybaler, mill, and water well pump, replacing the farmer's ancient windmill. A few days later, from the remaining derelicts, Rafael reconstructed one of the convertibles. Not long after that, he was on the road again, ever westward toward the magical place called California where the rich lands flourishing with unending harvests waited.

Now, as he started down a hill, the engine sputtered and finally died. He shook his head in disgust. He was finally out of gas. He didn't mind the walk for gas. It just irritated him to have to waste the time.

He pulled the gearshift to neutral and the car picked up speed as he coasted toward the bottom of the long hill. In the distance, in a heavily rutted turnout at the side of the road, he saw a small caravan of vehicles pulled over to the side of the road. With any luck, they'd have a few extra gallons of gas he could buy.

As he coasted toward the turnout, he could see that three of the cars in the caravan were in almost as bad shape as his. Two of them were old four-door sedans that had their back halves cut off and replaced with flatbeds on which were loaded household furnishings, pots, pans, suitcases, and cardboard boxes.

Another of the autos was an ancient four-door convertible, so covered with dust and mud it was hard to tell what model or make it was, or what the original color might have been. Like Rafael's, it was a mongrel made up of parts and pieces fitted together.

The people surrounding the cars were migrants who lived and worked out of their cars and trucks. As he coasted off the road, he could see four men huddled around the raised hood of one of the flatbeds.

Two women were unpacking a big wooden crate strapped to the back of the other flatbed. It contained their roadside kitchen. While one of them busied herself with setting it up, another woman directed a little band of children in gathering firewood.

The men looked up from the hood as Rafael's tires thumped across the rutted dirt and coasted to a stop. Rafael set the hand brake and got out through the hole where the door had once been.

The men watched him silently for a moment. They were all dark-haired and dark-eyed, deeply tanned from the endless days working under the sun in the open fields. One of the men set down a ball peen hammer on the fender, wiped his hands on a rag, and came toward Rafael.

The two men surveyed each other.

"She sure runs quiet!" the man finally said. His face warmed with a growing smile.

Rafael nodded and returned the smile. The man was shorter than he by a head, but no less muscular.

"I have found," Rafael said, "that the less gas the engine has, the quieter she runs."

"Not good to spoil an engine with too much gas. Makes them fat and useless." The man's smile seemed like a permanent part of his face. Rafael liked him immediately.

"That's why I quit giving her some a couple of miles back." Rafael nodded toward his car.

"I think I must have given mine too much. Sure seems to have spoiled her. Now she says she don't want to run." The Mexican nodded in disgust toward the truck.

Rafael surveyed the bastardized old car for a few moments. "Maybe she needs someone else to talk to her. If I could convince her to run, maybe she would share a little of her gas with mine . . . who at the moment is starving."

"My friend, if you can get this stubborn pain in the butt of a car to run, she will share with you." The man's hand shot toward Rafael. "I am Guillermo Rivera."

Rafael took his hand and shook it. "Rafael Orsini." Their hands clasped in mutual crushing grips.

The lantern wedged between the firewall and the engine block cast a yellow light over the oily engine as Rafael finally tightened down the last bolt before leaning on the fender to survey his work.

Across from him were Rivera and three other men.

Enrique Quintera, a young Mexican with a scraggly beard, turned and nodded his approval at his brother, Ramon. Were it not for an ugly scar that had claimed his right eye and covered most of the right side of his face Ramon would have been handsome. He delighted in making up bizarre stories about how he got the scar. Actually it was from an accident, a fall from a picking ladder: he'd landed on a stack of wooden crates, face first.

The car rocked and creaked in protest as the fourth man, Benito Obregon, leaned on the fender. He was a bull of a man, silent and unsmiling.

"Es bueno?" he asked. *"Es bueno?"*

"With a little luck," Rafael said as he checked his work. He wiped his hands on a towel, took the lantern out of the engine compartment, and lowered his side of the hood.

"I think that's it," he said, as he turned and sat down on the running board. Rivera came around the car and sat down next to him. Benito, Enrique, and Ramon followed and stooped down in front of them. Benito deftly rolled a cigarette from dark-brown tobacco in a red tin can and handed it to Rafael.

"Don't you want to see if she runs?" Ramon asked as he craned his head around so he could focus with his one good eye.

"The *señor* has said it is fixed." Benito sat back in the dirt and crossed his legs.

"No. He's right," Rafael said. "We should give her a little test. But after I work on one of these old ladies, I like to wait awhile first."

They waited for him to explain.

"When you feed someone something new, you should give him a chance to taste it before you ask him if he likes it. Like a new pair of shoes, you must let your toes feel the leather before you start running in them. It also gives me a chance to sit here and think. And make sure I fed her what she needed to be fed."

He glanced around their tiny campsite. Under a roof of diamond-bright stars, their roaring campfire had long ago died to red coals. Sitting on top of the coals was a trunk-sized iron box that served as their stove.

Though dinner had been done cooking for hours, and the children were cranky from not eating, as long as Rafael worked, no one had eaten. They were waiting until he finished.

"I think you got the bad part of our deal," Rivera apologized. It had taken Rafael more than three hours and a couple of cracked knuckles to repair their old engine.

"A man is only as good as his word. We had a bargain," Rafael said, exhaling the pungent smoke.

Rivera nodded appreciatively and held out his hand to pull Rafael to his feet. "Come, share our meal and our fire."

"Thank you." The offer had sealed their friendship. "I am honored."

"Maya!" Rivera called as they walked toward the warmth of the fire. *"Estamos listos para comer."*

"Sí. Bueno." A young woman answered. Her exotic, dark beauty was almost breathtaking.

"Rafael Orsini," Rivera said, proudly introducing her, "this is my wife, Maya."

Before Rafael could open his mouth, Maya and the other women descended on him. Maya pointed to an upholstered chair sitting in the dirt near the warmth of the fire. It was evidently the only chair among their possessions.

"Please, *señor*. To sit here." Maya said, patting the hand-sewn cushion.

A small woman with denim trousers hidden under layers of work shirts handed him a delicate china plate with a chip in the floral pattern that ringed it.

Rafael noticed that the others ate from tin plates. This one piece of china was a treasure saved for special occasions and special guests.

A skinny child, with one eye that crossed slightly, struggled under the weight of the biggest iron skillet Rafael had ever seen. She reminded him of the overworked little girl in New York who'd refused to take his "funny money." He wondered for a moment what had become of Tomaso, Nell, and Sophia.

118

The little girl placed the skillet on a crate that served as a table. The smell of the brown pasty-looking substance wafted over to Rafael, and his stomach churned with anticipation.

A raven-haired woman whose pregnancy bulged out from her men's overalls took a broad wooden spoon and heaped his plate half full of the wonderful-smelling frijoles.

"Please," he protested, "that's too much. Please . . . no more."

The woman looked at Maya. Maya smiled and shook her head ignoring his protests and filled the other half of his plate with stew from a pot that had been simmering over the coals.

The woman doing the cooking was Benito's wife, Muriella, a stocky Indian woman with a broad toothy smile. She patted out circles of mealy-looking dough in the palm of her hand. In one quick movement, she dropped the thin pancakes on the sizzling metal and quickly jerked off the ones that were already done, dropping them into a piece of cotton cloth before they could burn her fingers. She nudged a little boy barely old enough to walk and nodded toward Rafael.

The child ran toward Rafael holding out the cloth filled with the freshly made tortillas.

Rafael had never tasted anything so delicate yet so hearty. The beans were gone and more added in their place before he made a dent in his plate.

He looked at the tortillas in the dish towel in his lap and didn't know what to do with them. The little boy took great delight in showing him how to fill them with beans and use them as a scooper to push things onto his fork.

"*Fantástico!*" Rafael moaned between mouthfuls as he heaped the white meat from the stew into his mouth. "I never tasted chicken so good."

"*Qué dice?*" Maya asked

"He says is the best chicken ever he eats," Benito interpreted for Rafael.

"Chicken?"

"*Sí. Pollo.*"

"*Pero no es pollo.*"

"Not chicken, *señor*," Benito said.

"Not chicken?"

"Rabbit," Benito said tearing a mouthful off the legbone.

"Rabbit?"

"You don't like?" he asked as a smile finally crossed his usually solemn face.

"I love it. It reminds me of home. In my province, gentlemen on holiday hunt rabbits. They bring their families and after their hunt, they have a picnic . . . eat and drink ⌐ . ."

"In this country it's not the gentlemen who eat rabbit. But the farmers . . . the peons," said Rivera as Maya started toward them with another laden pot.

"No . . . please. No more!" Rafael begged.

"You no like?" Maya pouted coyly.

"Show him mercy, Maya. *Por favor*. At least until we know for sure if our truck will run again." Ramon laughed.

"It will run, Ramon," Rivera said, standing and walking toward the back of the truck. "If our friend says it is fixed, it is fixed."

Rivera opened the wooden supply box tied to the tailgate and took out a large half-gallon bottle covered with wicker.

"Vasos, mujer," Rivera barked at Maya.

She looked at him and the faint trace of a smile crossed her face. *"Sí,* my husband." she quickly wiped out two small mason jars with a cotton towel and brought them to him. She kept her eyes lowered lest they meet Rivera's and make them both laugh.

Unlike most Mexican men, Rivera treated his wife as an equal. She shared everything in her husband's life—love, fears, responsibilities, decisions, angers, and plans.

It couldn't have been any other way.

He'd fallen in love with her the first time he set eyes on her. She'd taken his breath away. He'd seen her dropping flower blossoms in front of a huge crucifix carried by their village priest during a religious holiday. He'd been headed in the opposite direction toward Manzanillo with a band of friends for an afternoon of drinking, smoking, and gambling at the weekly cockfight where one of his birds was to fight. Despite the excitement of the fight, he hadn't been able to stop thinking of her and for days afterward wasn't able to sleep.

All the following week he searched the giant open-air

market for a glimpse of her. To the surprise of the priest he even attended Mass every morning, but he never saw her.

The last place he thought of was the river—or, rather, the series of pools that dotted the side of the river. These pools were where the village women did their laundry. Standing on the trail, he spotted her coming toward the river, loaded down with her family's laundry.

As he wandered down to the water, a buzz swept through the women. To find a man at the river was more than unusual. The older women cackled and whispered back and forth among themselves as he casually made his way toward Maya.

She looked up from the sun-warmed water in the pool and knew the others were watching. Flustered by the unexpected attention, she dropped a shirt in the swirling water. It rapidly disappeared downstream. But Rivera hopped across several rocks and reached down into the rushing water and retrieved the worn shirt amid a chorus of giggles.

Maya blushed as he held the sopping garment over his head like a trophy. He started to retrace his route back toward the bank, but he lost his balance and fell seat first into the river. As he came back to the surface, the old women were howling with laughter. Maya was standing on the bank over him with her hands on her hips.

"*Gracias, niño!*" she said as she took the shirt while he dragged himself out of the water.

His already flame-red face deepened. She had referred to him as a boy.

Another week passed before Maya's father came into the kitchen where she was helping her mother with the evening meal.

"Someone has asked to see you," he said.

Standing awkwardly at the door was a grinning Rivera, a handful of flowers in one hand and a bucket of water in the other. "Hello," he said, setting the bucket down and abruptly thrusting the flowers toward her. On his way over, he'd thought of so many things to say, but now that she stood before him, he couldn't remember a one.

"Hello, *niño*," she said quietly, her face aglow. "Did you save the water from your clothes?" She nodded toward the bucket.

"No," he answered, suddenly feeling even more foolish and wishing he could summon the courage to turn and flee.

They stood there in embarrassed silence for a few moments.

"Then what is the water for?" Maya finally asked.

"Oh!" He said. His throat felt as if someone was strangling him. "I thought maybe . . . well . . . if you wanted . . . you could go with me to water my birds."

"I would like that," she smiled. It was a great tribute. Fighting birds were a man's most treasured possession.

"Gracias, mujer!" He had called her "woman."

Around Manzanillo, the small port city near their village, cockfighting was the local passion. Every peon, farmer, widow, and shopkeeper had a half-dozen fighting birds caged or penned next to their huts.

That year, though, no bird could threaten that bird known as Bloody Red, owned by the amiable, lovesick teen-ager, Guillermo Rivera. The red-and-orange rooster would destroy anything thrown in the ring with him.

One day, when Bloody Red's reputation was at its peak, Rivera was challenged by Rico, an arrogant young man from Mexico City. The purse and the betting odds were too much for Rivera. So he went to all his neighbors and together they formed a syndicate to back him and Bloody Red.

As the day of the fight approached, Rivera and Maya touched, whispered, giggled, and made fairy-tale plans for their future with the wealth from Bloody Red's victory. And finally, for the first time, they made love.

Later that week, under a thatch roof in the hot moonless night, the spectators watched the macabre spectacle as the two birds fought. On one side of the ring, Rico strutted for a group of well-dressed ladies and linen-suited gentlemen who'd journeyed from Mexico City to join him in the promised victory celebration.

Each time Rico's trainer and Rivera would leap into the ring to separate the birds at the end of the alloted time, Rico would chide, insult, and taunt Rivera about his cowardly bird. Rico was a master at psychology. The taunts and insults were the bait he used to raise the bets and change the odds. Without fail, they worked every time.

As the fight went on, the tension grew. Sweat ran. No one could sit or remain silent around the ring lit by flickering candles, coal oil lamps, and the occasional flare from a cigar being lit by a flaring match. Even Rico's suit started showing signs of the tension.

The cocks inflicted terrible wounds on each other. But neither would back off the attack or yield ground. Their yellow, phosphorescent eyes blazed with ferocious hatred. Finally, Rico's bird, Black Death, went down and couldn't move. The next instant, Bloody Red's deadly beak crushed his skull.

As Rivera held his filthy, blood-covered bird over his head in exultant triumph, hundreds of hands pounded him on the back. But a few minutes later, in the quiet and dark stall behind the arena, Rivera knew from the sticky, metallic smell of the blood that still pumped out of the bird's wounds, that his wonderful Bloody Red was doomed. He tucked the bird gently under his shirt to keep him warm, but suddenly Bloody Red went limp and was dead.

An hour later, the drunk Rico locked himself in his hotel room and reneged on his bets.

The next morning, as the peasant women of the village gathered to wash their laundry against the rocks where Rivera and Maya first met, they found Rico's body floating in one of the quiet pools, his skull crushed.

Before the man's body was discovered, Rivera had disappeared.

Maya waited for him. Her family and friends tried to tell her he was gone for good. But she knew he'd return or send for her. Then, one moonless night, she was struggling up the winding pathway along the riverbank where they'd first made love, when a hand shot out of the darkness and covered her mouth. She was jerked off her feet and into the briarlike underbrush.

"Dios!" She tried to scream.

"Hola, mujer," a voice whispered.

"Rivera!" she screamed as the hand left her mouth. She pounded him on the chest with both hands as much in a rage for being scared half to death as for her uncontainable joy that he'd come back for her.

* * *

Rafael watched as Rivera filled each mason jar with a clear liquid. Rummaging around in a burlap sack, Rivera took out a handful of lemons from the last grove they'd worked and sliced each one in half. Next he handed Rafael the jar and a shaker of salt.

Not knowing what to do first, Rafael took a tiny sip from the jar. It definitely wasn't wine. It burned so much he couldn't tell what it tasted like or even if it had a taste.

"No . . . no . . . no!" Rivera said, grabbing the salt shaker out of his hand. "This is the only thing that can help your stomach after a meal like that."

"But for to work," Benito smiled, knowing what Rivera was up to, "es necesario for to drink like so."

As Rafael watched in fascination, Benito poured a lick of salt on the back of his hand. He took the jar and lemon from Rivera, and to Rafael's disbelief, drained half of the deadly liquid in one gulp. Smiling at Rafael, he licked the salt and squeezed the lemon juice into his mouth.

"Ah!" He breathed a sigh of relief as he patted his barrel of a stomach. "Now I feel much better." He handed the salt to Rafael.

Rafael took the shaker and stared at the jar for a moment. *What the hell,* he thought. *If they can do it, so can I.* Before he could change his mind, he finished draining the jar, licked the salt, and squeezed the lemon into his mouth.

Almost instantly he realized he'd made a terrible mistake. The first thing he noticed was that his forehead had broken out in sweat. The next thing he knew he was unable to catch his breath.

"Holy Mother of God!" He gasped as his breath returned.

"Es bueno, yes?" Ramon's one good eye beamed.

"I'll say," Rafael wiped his forehead, "Sort of like kerosene."

He handed the glass jar back to Rivera, who instead of taking it, tipped the big wicker jug up and refilled it, expertly stopping just short of the brim.

"It starts to taste better after the first one," Rivera promised.

Rafael nodded as the men raised their glasses toward him in a toast. He took a deep breath and downed his second glass.

"Better, *sí?*" Benito smiled wiping his mouth with the back of his hand.

Rafael shrugged. His vision was blurring.

"If you don't know," Benito said taking the jug from Rivera and refilling the glasses, "then you no have *suficiente* tequila for to drink yet."

From Rafael's growing haze, another jar full seemed to appear magically.

A half hour later Rivera stumbled over to the truck's tailgate and broke open another wicker bottle. The Italian was a better drinker than they'd given him credit for. It had started out as a game. Now it was becoming a matter of national pride.

"I think," Rafael finally managed to say, "instead of gas . . . if I could have a gallon or so . . . of this tequila stuff, my car'd run forever. 'F not, she'd sure die happy."

"*Es mucho* too strong for you old car." Benito giggled from his growing stupor.

"That reminds me . . ." Rafael struggled to as steady a standing position as he could and looked toward the car he'd worked on earlier. "Funny," he scowled at his disorientation, "a little while ago, that car seemed a lot closer."

With the four drunken Mexicans following, Rafael managed to stagger to the front of Rivera's car. Hanging onto the spare tire tied to the running board, Rafael worked his way on rubbery knees around to the front and grabbed at the rusty crank. But inserting it into the engine block was about as difficult as passing a camel through the eye of a needle. He felt a hand prying his away from the crank. Looking up through a haze that seemed like a thick fog, he saw Maya take the crank, put it through the slot, and give it a spin. The engine caught instantly.

"Thank you, my friend," Rivera said to Rafael from where he had a death grip to keep him from falling. His knees were rigidly locked and he didn't dare let go.

They all stood there as the engine chugged on.

"Someone oughtta shut . . . the . . . ah . . . engine off," Rafael said. He held onto Rivera to keep from falling.

"True. You are a wise man, my friend." Rivera nodded,

looking around at the others whose heads bobbed up and down in unison.

The last thing Rafael realized as he was passing out, was that he'd already forgotten what they were bobbing their heads up and down in agreement with.

Rafael's eyes fluttered open and he found himself looking up into a bright blue sky filled with snowy white clouds.

He was in agony.

He didn't know if the noise he heard was the sound of his engine or of his head pounding. The only thing he knew for sure was that he was slouched in the passenger's side of his car. And his car was either moving down a treelined road, or an earth-shattering tornado was blowing everything past where he lay in his car. The thought of either was equally painful.

He managed to crane his head around. Sitting in the driver's seat, propped up on a soda crate, and driving with her feet barely touching the pedals, was Maya.

He sat up, but that was a mistake. The top of his head felt as though someone had smacked it with the flat side of an ax handle.

"*Buenos días, Señor* Orsini," Maya said with a singsong cheerfulness.

Rafael tried to reply, to make a sound. But his throat felt as though he had just spent a week on the desert. And his mouth tasted as though he'd been eating rabbit fur. Out of the corner of his eye, he caught a glimpse of a body sprawled across his backseat. It was Rivera.

"Where are we?" he finally managed to say.

"Oh . . . I think maybe twenty, thirty kilometers from Sacramento. We go to pick crops *norte* from there. Every years we pick for the same peoples. We have to be there *mañana*. We no could leave you alone and sick. My husband says we take you with us. Others are little sick also. But they are with us just little bit behind."

Rafael glanced over his shoulder and saw the caravan following. The other men had been loaded in various stages, half in and half out of the cars, and their wives fought to keep the various vehicles on the road.

Rafael would have laughed at the comic sight. But the

thought of the pain that laughing would cause stopped him.

"Looks like they're having trouble keeping the cars on the road. When we stop, I'll check and see if I can do something that will make them easier to steer."

"Oh, it is easy for to steer. It is just that we never before have to steer."

Rafael groaned, half with fear, half with the pain from breaking into laughter.

"You ever pick in field?" Maya asked holding her hair behind her head with one hand while steering with the other.

"Many times." Rafael nodded. Which was a mistake. From now on, he told himself, he would just grunt an acknowledgment.

"Is pretty hard work. But if you like, is possible for you to work with us. I think Rivera mean for that when he tries to get you drunk on tequila."

Even if he'd wanted to protest, he was too weak. But Rafael didn't want to. He liked this little band of migrants. Rivera's clan was like a family of friends he'd known all his life. It felt right being among them.

All that summer of 1925, they crisscrossed northern California, Oregon, and touched southern Washington before heading back toward central California.

In most of the migrant crews Rafael had worked with, the men and women went about the backbreaking work in silence. The only sounds were the scraping of a corduroy sleeve against a branch, the dull thuds as short-handled hoes chopped endless rows clogged with weeds, the exhausted grunts as tubs and boxes and sacks were filled, and the heavy breathing as they hurried to drop them in bins or stack them at the end of completed rows.

But in Rivera's crew, it was like a party. A picnic. Not the work, but the easy exchange between them. They'd yell back and forth and insult and laugh and tease and sing. And whenever he could find Maya alone, Rivera would whisper a suggestive, almost obscene love message to her as they passed down the rows.

Rafael grew to love this band of friends. Rivera had become a brother. And they relied on each other.

One hot day the following summer, they were working a berry farm in southern California before heading north. It wasn't a very big farm. And they'd seen it from the road on their way south. The farmer had hired them providing they could finish in a day as his crop was on the verge of spoiling. They were lined up in the rows looking lke a ragtag line of rebels ready for a charge at some imaginary enemy.

Rivera passed Maya working the other direction. Their backs screamed in protest, but they were nearing the end of the day and the job was going to be finished on time.

"Hey . . . *señora*. How would you like to take the rest of the day off? I know a man who can arrange it," he whispered. "All you have to do is be nice to him . . . whatta you say?"

"And what would I do with all that extra time?" she asked, removing the bandana which seemed to dwarf her delicate neck. She slipped off her straw hat and wiped her brow with the back of her sleeve.

Replacing her hat, she stooped back down to her work and her fingers disappeared back into the leafy plant.

"We could . . . you know . . . mess around."

She shook her head. "No. We already did that. And I'm paying for it."

She worked her way away from him almost a half a row before he hurried up to her.

"What do you mean? How are you paying for it?"

"I'm going to have your child, that's what I mean by it."

Suddenly he let out a whoop that made the heads of everyone in the patch look up.

As they watched, he galloped, leaped, and shouted. Finally he picked her up and swung her around, ecstatic with joy.

"What's that all about?" Rafael asked, stooping next to Muriella.

"*Maya está con niño.*" She beamed back her broad grin. "She just tell Guillermo."

"Hey!" Benito yelled from across the hot field. "You telling us it's time to quit?"

"No! I'm telling you Maya's pregnant," Rivera yelled back beaming.

"You just finding that out?" Benito yelled back unimpressed.

"What do you mean, just finding out?" Rivera said as he finally let Maya's feet touch the ground again.

"You must be the last one. Everyone else has known for at least a month," Benito teased.

"*Vasos, mujer!*" Rivera hollered after dinner that night as Ramon tinkered with a guitar he was trying to learn how to play.

"*Sí, esposo,*" Maya said as she produced the mason jars.

"My wife," Rivera said raising his jar and looking at Maya. He reached out with his other arm and pulled her to him. "The one who makes my heart sing. The one who warms my feet at night. And the one who will soon be the mother of my family."

They threw back their drinks and Rafael's mouth recoiled from the memory of the first time he'd tasted tequila.

"*Uno mas,*" Rivera demanded. Quickly Maya refilled their glasses.

Rafael was about to protest. He wasn't ever going to get into another drinking bout like the last one. But Rivera's toast brought the glass to his mouth.

"To my friend Rafael's family. May they join us soon."

"Thank you." Rafael said. "With luck, maybe in a few months I'll be able to send for them."

Everyone cheered.

"You will go from us then?" Maya asked sadly.

Rafael threw the lemon he was sucking on into the fire. The smoke from the rind wafted the fragrance to him as he looked around their warm faces. "I hope not. I hope we will be together for a long time. But if there is some reason we can't, we'll always be friends. And in my heart, we'll always be together."

Later that night, as Maya and Rivera lay on their summer quilts under one of the trucks, they watched Rafael still sitting by the coals staring into the dying ashes.

"He has helped us in so many ways, and has so often worked more than his share, maybe we can help," she said.

"How?"

"I don't know."

They watched him quietly for a few minutes.

"Maybe we can help him send for his mother and sister." Rivera suggested.

"He wouldn't take money," Maya warned. "Not if he knew."

"Then we won't tell him."

"There's barely enough now." Maya giggled. "What we could save, he might not notice."

"But we'll try."

"He'd try for us," she said, squeezing him. "And it will help make things sooner for him.

Rivera squeezed her back tightly, unable to get enough of her warmth, her smell. He couldn't believe he could be so happy, that life could be so perfect.

During the following weeks, he managed it so that at any time during work, he could look up and watch her as she toiled alongside the other women. Sometimes he'd become so enthralled, he'd find himself holding his breath. The farther along in her pregnancy, the rosier her complexion seemed to become. She seemed to possess a whole new vibrancy as the new life flourished within her body.

CHAPTER EIGHT

The glow from the candles lit the tiny alcove off the main cathedral hall, as Alicia Orsini dropped the last coin in the metal poor box. She took out another waxed taper and finished lighting all the remaining candles in the wrought-iron rack.

She glanced over to the plain, wooden coffin that sat in front of the altar. Looking around, she made the sign of the cross and rose to leave. A priest picked up his missal and walked down the aisle toward Alicia, who paused next to the cheap wood box that served as her mother's coffin.

The two stood there for a few moments, alone.

No one else had come. But that was unimportant. Alicia didn't know if anyone else knew her mother had died. But no one would really care that she'd died a hard death anyway. From starvation, exposure, and finally, pneumonia. Mostly, though, she died from the shock of the pain-filled nightmares suffered in those rare moments when she returned to the brink of sanity and found herself in the squalor and din of the asylum.

Alicia doubted if anyone would have dared come anyway. She handed the priest a little packet of lire and shook his hand.

"*Grazie, Padre*," she said as she turned and walked away. Her high heels rang against the marble floor as she made her way out of the tiny alcove where her mother lay and down the aisle toward the double doors.

As she disappeared into the gray rainy morning, the priest turned and knelt before the statue of the Virgin Mary behind the rack of flickering candles. He crossed himself and buried his head in his hands praying for forgiveness.

131

He was caught in a soul-wrenching vise. In the sanctity of the confessional, the postmaster had confessed a knowledge of letters that awaited Alicia and her mother. But because of the Padrone's son, he was forced to withhold them even though they were addressed to the women in care of the priest.

The priest was helpless. It was information gained in the confessional; he couldn't reveal any of it to anyone without condemning his soul to hell for eternity. Yet the pain of knowing a woman had died without learning that her son was still alive was a terrible burden for him. His thoughts drifted to Alicia. He clenched his hands together until they pained him as he prayed for forgiveness and guidance.

At the Padrone's villa, there was a knock on the door. It opened and Dominic entered the book-lined study.

"Well?" Carlo Gianini asked as the man stood there still dripping from the rain.

"*Niente.* There is nothing to tell, *signore*," Dominic said. "The girl left the cathedral and returned to her room where four men—clients—were waiting for her to entertain them."

Carlo moved closer to the crackling fire. "She stopped nowhere? Talked to no one? Mailed nothing?"

"No, *signore*. Since I talked to the Correlli woman who used to work in your kitchen, she has confided in no one. And no one other than the men who frequent her services has talked to her."

Carlo nodded. It was a pity the old woman had died. He would have preferred her alive. But not out of compassion. A crackling laugh echoed down the corridor from a room upstairs where his father spent his days ranting mindlessly.

"We must watch her more carefully now that her mother is gone," Carlo mused, almost to himself.

"*Sì, signore.*"

"Someday Rafael Orsini will try to contact her other than by his letters. We must make sure Alicia stays here until that happens. Then we will know where he has settled and is making his life."

"*Sì, signore.*"

"Then we'll finish this business, once and for all."

"*Sì, signore.*"

"Padrone." Carlo corrected him.

"*Sì*, Padrone." Dominic backed out, closed the door and headed up the stairs to tend his old master.

Long after Dominic was gone, Carlo stared into the fire. His mind was consumed by thoughts of Alicia Orsini. The times were growing when he could think of nothing else. He quickly bent down and kicked one of the logs farther into the flames.

CHAPTER NINE

"Where are we?" Rafael asked, jerking up with a start. He had dozed off. He looked at the countryside as Rivera steered down a narrow winding road.

"We just passed through Healdsberg. It's seventy, maybe eighty, miles north of San Francisco," Rivera answered.

"Where are we headed?" Rafael yawned.

"Through this little valley toward Napa. But first we have to stop at a farm about twenty miles east. Just before we cross those little mountains over there into Napa valley." He pointed toward a tiny range of craggy mountains that formed a crown surrounding the rolling green valley they were driving through.

Rafael stretched and tried to shake away some of the exhaustion. Late the previous afternoon they'd finished working a field near the little central California town of Gilroy, south of San Francisco, where they were harvesting onions. Rafael'd had to work another six hours on two of their cars before they could get on the road again.

Looking down toward the valley floor, Rafael could see the fields laid out like a patchwork quilt. Trees overhung the road like tunnels. An occasional open space framed fertile fields guarded by weathered barns.

They passed over a bridge crowned by hand-hewn stones. For the next few miles, the river and the road wound along together like strands of rope.

It was breathtaking. Rafael had never seen anything so beautiful. Oak trees blended with evergreen; purple and gold leaves mingled with the dark emerald needles of the stately sequoias. He sat forward on the edge of his seat.

"You like, *sí*?" Rivera asked noticing his interest.

"It's one of the loveliest places I've ever seen."

Maya leaned forward toward Rivera as he steered down

the snaking road that wound through the central part of this northern California county. She gently stroked the shaggy hair on the back of Rivera's neck.

The gentleness of her touch brought a smile to his face. They drove into the heart of the valley.

"It never stops making me breathless," Maya said.

Rafael nodded. "What's it called?"

"Just the east part of Sonoma County, I guess," Rivera said. He slowed and turned off onto a rutted drive that led toward a white two-story frame house in the distance.

The house sat nestled in a grove of shade trees. Though nearly a quarter of a century old, it looked new. The paint was hard and white; and the windows shone as though they'd just been washed.

When Rivera slowed to a stop, Rafael could see a tall, weathered older man standing in the doorway outlined by the screen door.

As the others braked to a halt behind Rivera, the man came out onto the veranda.

"So, you finally made it, Rivera," the man said gruffly.

"*Sí, señor.*" Rivera hopped out and walked up the flagstones framed with grass. The two men shook hands.

"You're late. I figured you weren't coming."

"This is the same day we get here the last two years, *señor*," Rivera said, still smiling. It was a game he always played with the older man. He always smiled; Ferrara never did. As a matter of fact, Rivera had never seen any sign of emotion pass across Ferrara's tan, leathery face.

"Yeah, but I was ready to start picking two days ago."

Rivera took off his straw hat and wiped his forehead. "*Sí,* I understand. This nice heat makes for early picking."

"Thought maybe I was going to have to hire me up a new bunch of Mexicans. But Angelica talked me into waiting."

"My thanks to your daughter when you next see her, *señor.*"

"How is your daughter, *Señor* Ferrara?" Maya called from the back seat.

"Fine, Mrs. Rivera. Just fine. Matter of fact, when she heard your old clunkers turning into the drive, she made a beeline for the kitchen. Figured you'd need to cool off, so she's making something for you."

"She is indeed a girl worthy of her name," Rivera said standing in the refreshing shade of the eucalyptus trees Ferrara had planted as seedlings years before.

"You get yourself a drink of whatever it is she's fixing up," the old man said. "Then I want to see the backsides of those baggy pants shining up at me in the sunlight."

"You will, *señor*. I promise," Rivera said. Of all the men they worked for, this one had always been the most fair. He wasn't friendly. He wasn't sociable and many in this valley didn't like him. But they all agreed, he was fair and honorable.

Rafael looked up as a tall young woman in her early twenties pushed open the screen door, struggling to balance a tray laden with glasses and pitchers. As she walked off the porch and down the flagstones, Rafael's mouth watered. She was carrying fresh lemonade in pitchers filled with mounds of snowy white ice.

Few farmers were extravagant enough to buy ice this time of year. And this farm was isolated enough that it was indeed a luxury she was sharing. It was then Rafael noticed the single strand of wire that ran from the road to the roof of the house. This old man had electricity, which explained the ice. He probably had one of those new ice-making boxes in his kitchen that kept food cold and prevented spoiling.

"She's a very nice lady, *sí?*" Maya whispered. She had noticed that Rafael hadn't taken his eyes off the old man's daughter.

Angelica Ferrara wasn't an especially pretty young woman. But there was a magnetism about her. Her coal black hair was pulled back and knotted in a bun. Her olive skin had a natural glow as though it had just been scrubbed. And her smile, gleaming and white, rivaled Maya's.

"*Señorita!* Thank you . . . thank you . . . *mil gracias.* I think you have saved the lives of all my families with your generosity." Rivera bowed.

Angelica curtsied and handed him the heavy tray.

"Don't go trying to turn on your charm with her, Rivera," the old man said. "You're just looking not to have to get to work until tomorrow. I know you and your kind. And I'm warning you . . . it ain't going to work."

Rivera grinned and started to protest, but the old man cut him off.

"I need you and your bunch out there now. I got bushel baskets already stacked at the head of every row."

"*Sí, señor.*"

Ferrara turned and headed for the barn.

Rivera put down the tray on the hood of his car, and the others piled out as he poured each a glass full of the frosty liquid.

"*Como está*, Maya?" Angelica asked as she walked to the side of the car and hugged Maya.

"*Bien . . . gracias.*" Maya returned her embrace. Although they saw each other for only a few weeks each year, they considered themselves friends.

"I am . . . how you say . . . *con* . . . with baby," Maya whispered.

"That's wonderful, Maya," Angelica squealed. She had tears in her eyes as she grabbed Maya.

"*Es fantástico, sí?*" Rivera beamed. "Soon we'll have many sons to help their poor old father!"

"How soon? I mean, when are you due?" Angelica asked.

Maya stepped back to show off her condition. "I think three months more."

"I'm really happy for you," Angelica said. As she looked past Maya, she found herself less than a foot from where Rafael was still sitting in the backseat.

"Oh . . . *señorita.* This is our friend, Rafael Orsini. Rafael this is *Señorita* Ferrara. Rafael is from *Italia.* Like your papa."

"Miss Ferrara." Rafael stepped out of the car and extended his hand.

"Mr. Orsini," she answered, taking his hand. She was suddenly self-conscious. She'd never met a worker bold enough to shake hands before. She blushed as she walked back to where her father was standing, deep in conversation with Rivera about the plans for the harvest.

Rafael watched her go, noticing how tall she was, how strong her body was under her long cotton dress.

He watched as she crossed her arms and leaned slightly against her father as he talked. The old man put his arm around her without noticing and kept talking.

Later that afternoon, Maya passed Rafael working in the opposite direction. They were harvesting a vegetable field that ran almost to the back door of the Ferrara's house. Ferrara's farm was basically a truck farm. The vegetables he grew were trucked twice a day to a barge in Petaluma where a broker would buy them and ship them across the bay to San Francisco.

"Pretty girl, *sí*?" Maya said standing up and massaging the small of her back. She had been feeling pain lately. And strange discomforts which she blamed on her pregnancy.

"Who?" Rafael asked innocently.

The metal shaft squeaked as Angelica pumped the handle up and down. The water that flowed into the pot was cool and clear. She added it to the vegetables simmering on the wood cookstove, as she heard her father's footsteps coming up the back steps.

He entered, drenched with sweat. He went to the sink to wash as she finished setting the table for the noon meal.

"You angry, Papa?" she asked after sitting down. He hadn't said a word since he came in.

He didn't answer as he dished out heaping portions of the half-dozen vegetables she'd prepared. He buttered a thick slice of freshly baked bread as she placed the ham on the table. "It's just been one of those days," he said finally. "The thieves at the landing take half a day trying to talk me out of a fair price for our vegetables—all the time screaming that everything's too ripe and half rotten."

He poured a glass of cold milk from the white pitcher. "Sure it is!" he said, banging the pitcher down. "It's been sitting on the damn dock in the sun for half a day while we argue price."

"You never had to leave it on the dock before . . ."

"The truck broke down. By the time I got to the dock, the first barge'd already sailed down."

"What's the matter with the truck?"

He shrugged, buttered his third piece of bread, and took another helping from the green beans flavored with bacon.

"Maya told me one of their men has been keeping their trucks and cars on the road. He's supposed to be able to fix almost anything. Maybe you could have him. . . ."

"No." Ferrara shook his head until the white hair rippled.

"But, Papa, I know he'd help if you asked Rivera."

"I said no. I know which one you mean. And I ain't askin' Rivera to ask him. I don't like the man to begin with."

"Are you sure you know which one I mean? Maya told me he was the hardest worker in their whole crew."

"Don't matter none to me. I don't know why . . . I just don't like the man." But he knew exactly why he didn't like the tall Italian. He reminded him of the young man who had worked on his farm almost twenty years earlier. The young man who had run away with his wife.

He got up from the table and went out to the truck. He opened one side of the hood. Halfway up, he had to drop it. The dark paint had absorbed the burning rays of the midday sun. He got a horse blanket from the work shed and draped it over the fender so he could lean against it without being burned.

After tinkering with the engine for over an hour, Ferrara wiped the sweat off his face, rolled down his sleeves, and gave up. He'd have to ask the Italian for help: the vegetables couldn't wait, and right now, he couldn't afford his pride.

Rafael lifted the galvanized pail that sat at the head of the row. He tilted it back until the water ran into his parched mouth. Even warm from the hot sun, the water tasted silky and delicious. A motion attracted his attention as he set the pail back down so it was partially shaded by the vines. He peered over the row of beans and saw Angelica Ferrara walking down one of the dusty ruts that formed the road leading toward where their crew was working.

He started working down the row so he would come out near her. His hands almost flew as he stripped the vines into his pail. His timing was perfect. She passed just as he ended the row.

"Good afternoon, Miss Ferrara." He smiled, half hidden by the stringy vines.

The sound of his voice startled her. She smiled and nodded a silent reply and passed by. She walked another dozen yards before she thought it would be safe to look back to catch another glance at him as he worked.

She did.

He was still staring at her.

They both looked hurriedly away and she walked faster until she spotted Maya.

"*Hola*, Maya."

"Angelica . . . *como está?*"

"Fine. And you?" Angelica stopped opposite the row Maya was working.

"A little tired. But okay."

Actually Maya was more than tired. She was deeply worried. For the past several months, she'd grown familiar with the feel of her child's every movement. Even his moods, she thought. But for the past week, she'd felt nothing. Nothing but the constant pressure of his weight pressing down on her abdomen. Then this morning, for the first time, a sharp pain had sent her to her knees.

From the next row, where Rafael was working near her, he had seen her doubled over and rushed to her.

"You all right?" he asked as he started to pick her up and carry her toward some shade.

She pushed him away. "What are you doing, Rafael? It's only the baby kicking." She forced a smile to relieve his concern. "He's telling me he's going to be here soon."

Rafael nodded as he studied Maya's face. He didn't know anything about women and babies. But he saw from her pinched face that she was still hiding some pain.

"*Es verdad*, Rafael. I promise." She pulled herself erect.

Rafael wiped the thin line of perspiration from her upper lip. Maya smiled and squeezed his hands from behind closed eyes.

Later, during the noon break, when she went behind the windbreak of eucalyptus trees, she discovered a liquid had stained her legs and pants. It wasn't blood. She was used to spotting. This was a brownish, almost clear fluid. And it frightened her.

Something was wrong and she didn't know what to do. If she told her husband, it would frighten him. She knew he'd insist that she see a doctor. But she'd never been to one before and the thought of exposing herself to a stranger filled her with dread. Besides, there was no money. So Maya tried to convince herself that the pain was normal for a woman as pregnant as she was. It wasn't so bad, she thought. But if it kept up, she would ask Benito's wife, Muriella. She'd had many children and would know.

Maya looked up to find Angelica studying her.

"You sure you're all right?" Angelica stooped down next to her pale friend.

"*Si* . . ." Maya smiled. "Rivera's son has growing pains."

Rafael was watching the two women from across several rows, trying to figure a way to work in their direction, when a vine snapped behind him.

"Better watch your ass," a voice whispered.

Rafael turned quickly and realized the sound was Rivera working down the opposite row toward him.

"You get into pretty big trouble sneaking looks at another man's wife. Especially my woman."

"How about if I look at her friend, then?"

"Go ahead," Rivera said. "Just stand around and look at the pretty girls. You think those beans are gonna jump into the bucket? You want to look? I'll pay you for looking. You want to pick beans? I'll pay you for picking beans!"

Rivera grinned as Rafael attacked the row. It ended perpendicular to a row of grapes that flowed down the slope from above.

"What about the grapes?" Rafael asked. The lime green canes and the lush green leaves reminded him of the trainloads of grapes that had come into the freight yard in New York almost three years before.

It was as though the leafy plants were beckoning to him. He felt a cluster and popped a grape into his mouth. It was still a little sour.

"What do you mean, what about the grapes?" Rivera answered.

"Who's going to pick them?"

"Us probably."

"Little too early, isn't it?" He was delighted at the prospect of work that would keep him at the Ferraras'.

"*Si*. It's too early. But first we'll cross the mountain and work on into Napa County picking vegetables. It's the next place that way from here." He indicated east. "Then we'll circle back into this valley again. By then the grapes should be ready."

"You always pick Ferrara's grapes?"

"Only sometimes. The old man's plenty tough. Besides, it depends if he is able to use them or not. The last few years of this Prohibition thing has been a problem for him and the others around here who grow grapes."

The sound of a wagon plodding toward them made them both glance up. They saw Ferrara sitting on a bale of hay as he turned the horse down the break toward them.

"Now for sure you better watch your ass. Old man Ferrara see you looking at his daughter, *muy malo*. Very very bad!" He whistled softly.

"I'll be careful," Rafael whispered as Ferrara reined in the old mare.

"Can I talk to you?"

"*Sí, señor.*" Rivera put down his pail.

"Not you, Rivera. The Italian."

"You in trouble already, Rafael?" Rivera whispered so only the two of them could hear.

"Not that I know of," Rafael said heading down the row toward the waiting man.

"What did he want?" Rivera asked after the old man drove off.

"I don't really know for sure," Rafael said. He had gone back to work alongside the shorter Mexican. "Something about . . . a shotgun and his daughter . . . and a baby . . ."

Rivera jerked up, staring at Rafael.

Rafael burst into laughter.

"He wanted to know if I'd take a look at his truck. Seems like it isn't running and he can't get it to shift when it is."

"Ah . . . *sí*. That is why he didn't pick up a whole day's work. Usually he picked up almost before we have it in the baskets." They worked on down the row. "You think you able to fix it?"

"I better be."

"Why?"

"I promised him we'd use our trucks to deliver everything we picked today and load it onto his truck when we quit tonight. That way he can leave before sunup tomorrow."

Ferrara watched as Rafael started up the engine and eased it into gear. Slowly he drove around the barn before parking the truck in the shade under the trees in front of the winery.

Ferrara was pleased. Orsini had fixed his truck. Now he wouldn't lose a day getting to market. But it was the first time in years he could remember owing another man a debt of gratitude.

Rafael refused the money he offered. "No, *signore*. My payment is that you provide us with work."

Ferrara looked at the Italian, unsure whether to allow himself the luxury of believing him. He hadn't trusted another man since his wife ran off with his hired hand. Even knowing she was dead hadn't been enough to wipe the bitterness out of him. Though he'd heard it was pneumonia, he knew better. It was God's punishment.

"Come with me then," he barked. Rafael followed as the old man walked toward the heavy oak door to his small stone winery across from the house and barn. The stones of the winery seemed hand shaped, one overlapping the other, like the work of some ancient mason. It reminded Rafael of a sculptured castle.

As he waited for Ferrara to find the brass chain for the bare bulb that hung in the center of the room, he remembered the first time he'd been in a winery. He'd been five or six years old. He'd gone with his father to help with the crusher. Now, years later and in a land a half a world away, here was the same refreshing coolness behind thick stone walls and the fruity smell that permeated everything.

There was nothing in the world like it.

"If you won't take money for your work, then you must share some of my wine." Ferrara insisted.

"That is different, *signore*. I consider that an honor."

Ferrara went to a heavy oak barrel in an arched alcove and took two stemmed glasses from the work bench next to it. With a wood mallet he carefully tapped open the wood spigot and filled the glasses with the clear Burgundy liquid. Ferrara put the glass to his nose and inhaled its bouquet. He smiled, satisfied.

"I'm impressed, *signore*. That you are allowed to have so much wine in times such as these."

"Most of it's wine I had before this damned Prohibition. The rest is what I'm allowed to make each year as head of the family." He handed Rafael one of the glasses.

"To your health and prosperity." Rafael lifted his glass. He downed half the glass. It was marvelous, like the homemade wine he'd had during lunch in New York with Sophia and her father. Its flavor seemed to burst in his mouth.

"Thank you, Orsini." The old man had watched disappointed as Rafael almost swilled the wine. He hoped Rafael was watching as he took another sip, closed his eyes, and swirled the wine around the inside of his mouth before swallowing.

When he opened his eyes, he caught Rafael imitating him.

"Better, *sì?*" Ferrara asked.

"Yes. Much," Rafael agreed. "It's a very hearty wine. It tastes the way the fruit tastes the day it comes off the vine."

"Thank you. Wine is the mirror of the soul of the country in which it is born."

"God then has smiled on the soul of your land. It is sweet. And it tastes like it's been born on land that has never known pain."

"I can assure you, Orsini, this land has known pain."

Rafael nodded silently.

"Where are you from in Italy?" Ferrara asked.

"Montepulciano. It's on the east coast . . . in the middle of . . ."

"*Sì.* I know where it is. I was there once."

"Really?" Rafael was delighted.

"I was still a boy . . . passing through on my way to America. I am from Bari, which is south of Montepulciano. My father was a fisherman. Now there was a man who knew what it meant to work."

Rafael nodded as the old man held the bottle toward his glass.

"He left the harbor every morning before dawn. He rarely returned until well after sundown. And only then to give my mother the catch so she could sell it the next day."

"Why did you leave Italy, *Signore* Ferrara?"

"He died . . . my father. So the boat went to my older brother. It was only fair. He had a new wife and a child on the way . . . plus my mother and me to feed."

"It seems strange that a man from the sea should end up so far from it." Rafael smiled.

"I sailed for a while." Ferrara shrugged. "The last ship was a three-masted ketch. Steel hulled. Sailed from Vancouver up north down to San Francisco. Damn thing nearly sank and killed us all . . . hurricane in the middle of winter. So I took that as fair warning. Took my share from that trip and bought that piece of land over there, the hill the grapes are planted on. Next few years I bought the rest of this." He suddenly became silent. He hadn't meant to talk so much. He felt embarrassed about opening up to this young man he barely knew. "Anyway . . . Montepulciano is a beautiful city. I can remember the fountains . . ."

"You are a fine winemaker, *signore*," Rafael said as his last memories of those fountains flashed through his mind.

"I'm afraid this isn't a country to be a winemaker in."

Rafael looked around at the stone cellar. Except for the single tier of barrels, the place was like an empty warehouse.

Ferrara walked toward a distant door and Rafael followed.

As he swung it open, Rafael could see four enormous redwood fermenting bats.

"Empty!" Ferrara said bitterly. "By now they should be scrubbed, ready for the harvest. But . . ." He shrugged his helplessness.

"Prohibition?"

"Yes. When I first built this winery, I had planted almost a hundred acres of new vines. Already had seventy-five acres on the hill in back of the field where you worked today. Since Prohibition, six, maybe seven years, I've hardly had a chance to make use of it."

Rafael shook his head in sympathy. "It still smells like you just crushed," he said, enjoying the fermented fruity aroma that still permeated the building.

"Oh . . . each year I get my permit to make some homemade wine."

"What happens to the rest?"

"Nothing." Ferrara looked down at the Burgundy-colored liquid in his glass. He swirled it around, then stuck it under his nose to catch its bouquet. "I haul it back to the vineyard and pour it into the ground. Which isn't exactly profitable. If someone doesn't help us soon, most farmers I know'll be pulling out vines and planting something else."

"When I was leaving New York, I saw a crowd of people fighting to buy fresh grapes from California. Grapes they also used to make their wine. Italians . . . Germans . . . Swedes. They were begging to buy grapes."

"Sure." Ferrara acknowledged. "It's a seller's market there. But it's too expensive for me. And the mighty railroads only want whole trainloads, or else they won't guarantee delivery."

"It seems a crime to have a law that creates such waste."

"But it is the law nevertheless. And breaking an unjust law does not make it any more just." Ferrara said. Then, unexpectedly he set down his glass, put a gallon jug under the spigot, and tapped it open. "Share this with Rivera and his tribe."

"*Mille grazie!*" Rafael said, delighted. "They will enjoy it."

He answer was gruff. "At least it'll be a change from that rotgut tequila."

"*Sì, signore.*" Rafael smiled as Ferrara turned off the spigot and handed him the uncorked bottle. They had turned to leave when Angelica called from the doorway.

"Papa? Dinner's ready. I saw the light and thought maybe you forgot and left it on." In fact, she'd seen the two men entering the winery from the kitchen and had been curious. Her father wasn't known for his hospitality. He had never invited anyone else into his private domain before.

"No, I didn't," Ferrara moved toward the door. But Angelica was already halfway across the room.

"Good evening, Miss Ferrara." Rafael smiled.

"Good evening, Mr. Orsini."

"Mr. Orsini was kind enough to repair our truck, so I was sharing some wine with him in return."

"It's all done then . . . the truck, I mean?" she asked. Rafael nodded.

"Then you're just in time. Maybe . . . perhaps Mr. Orsini would like to join us for supper?"

Ferrara felt himself bristling. He didn't like to share his table with anybody, much less those who worked for him.

"I'm sure Rivera's ladies already have supper waiting for Mr. Orsini," he said.

"They eat at sundown." She smiled innocently. "By now everything's cold. The least we can do is offer the hospitality of our table."

Rafael knew that out of politeness he should decline her offer. But he didn't want to.

"Don't you agree, Papa?" Angelica said.

"Yes," he finally grumbled.

Rafael and Ferrara sat in cold silence as Angelica bustled around, setting the heavy old oak table with steaming bowls from the stove.

"Where are you from, Mr. Orsini? I mean, which part of Italy?" she asked.

"Montepulciano." He watched her as she moved around the room. What an exciting creature she was.

"I don't think I know where that is. Do you, Papa?"

"Yes," Ferrara said without offering more.

"It's on the eastern coast . . . a beautiful stretch of coast," Rafael explained.

"Were you ever there, Papa?" she asked as she brought a large pan of hot bisquits from the oven.

"Yes," he answered coldly. "But I don't remember too much about it."

Rafael suddenly stood.

Ferrara looked up, hoping the young man had finally understood that he wasn't welcome at their table.

"Here. Let me help," Rafael said as he moved quickly to pull Angelica's chair out for her.

"Thank you," she said blushing.

Ferrara felt disgusted. Angelica was perfectly capable of setting the pan down and pulling her own chair out.

"Did you like it, Papa?"

"Huh? What?"

"The town Mr. Orsini's from."

"Not particularly."

She nodded, embarrassed, and for a few moments they

passed the bowls back and forth. Rafael took small helpings, hoping to impress her with his manners.

"You don't seem to have much of an appetite, Orsini," Ferrara said. "What's the matter? Don't you like my daughter's cooking?"

"On the contrary, *signore*. It's the best food I've ever tasted. I just don't want to abuse your hospitality." He smiled at Angelica.

"How long have you been here. In America that is?" Angelica asked.

"A little more than three years."

The dinner ended as it began, with Angelica asking questions, Rafael answering them, and Ferrara sitting silent as a stone. She got him to tell about his train ride from New York, his favorite food, and his most unusual job.

"Knocking the horns off steers, then painting them with tar so they could be shipped," he answered.

She grimaced. She smiled. She laughed. She gushed enthusiastically. Finally, Ferrara could take it no longer. He picked up his half-empty plate, set it in the sink, and stormed out the screen door to smoke his pipe in the solitude of the shed next to his barn.

"Papa hates girls who gush and talk on mindlessly. He especially hates it if I'm the girl doing it."

Rafael smiled as he sipped his coffee.

"If I want to get rid of him for a while, it works every time."

Rafael looked at her in amazement.

"Come on," she said starting to clear the table. "I'll wash—you dry. That way Papa can see you helping through the window. He hates wiping dishes even more than I do, so he'll leave us alone."

For the next hour they both did everything they could to drag out the simple chore of dishwashing.

"You are very close to your mother," Angelica said after he told her of his plans to bring Maria and Alicia to America.

"*Sì*. Yes, of course. Isn't everybody?"

She stood there and wiped her dripping hands on her apron. "I never knew mine. She died when I was a baby."

"I'm sorry. It must be sad not to know a mother."

"Let's not talk about sad things," she said, smiling to change the mood.

"The saddest thing that I can think of right now is that I see your father coming across the yard."

She suddenly looked down.

"I . . . maybe . . . was thinking . . ." he began, stopping as he heard Ferrara's footsteps on the porch. "Maybe in a few days, when we're caught up on the work . . . we could, I don't know . . . maybe . . . go on a picnic or something?"

Ferrara was in the door scowling at them before she could answer.

"It's late," he said. "You'll have to excuse us, Mr. Orsini."

"Of course." Rafael folded the dish towel and started for the door.

"Thanks for helping with the dishes." Angelica smiled.

"And for the truck," Ferrara added. He stood in the middle of the room, a signal that their evening together was at an end.

Rafael hesitated as he went out the door, wishing he could reach out and touch her, and wishing they had more time.

"Do you like fried chicken and potato salad?" he heard her whisper as she closed the door behind him.

The smile burst across his face as he nodded. She had accepted his invitation to a picnic. He would spend half a sleepless night planning and dreaming about just the right spot.

"Nice man, Papa," Angelica said after his footsteps disappeared off the porch.

"Just another migrant," Ferrara said. "Here today and gone tomorrow."

The next week, Ferrara could be seen hovering at the head of whatever field they happened to be working. He'd fuss at them, load and unload crates in the back of his truck, and spend hours with them on jobs he seldom bothered with before.

And he saw to it that not once did Rafael catch sight of Angelica.

149

Pressed into service on jobs that suddenly couldn't wait, Angelica spent the better part of every day in the old coupe traveling up and down the county from farm to farm, to Healdsberg, to as far south as Santa Rosa. She rounded up seed, wire, lumber, leather for harness repairs, coal oil, parts for threshers and implements that had long sat unattended.

Suddenly there was a great rush to fix, mend and repair, and paint. Rarely arriving home before sundown, she barely had time to fix her father's supper and clean the kitchen before falling into bed with a list of things that urgently needed to be done "first thing" the next day.

But Angelica knew what her father was up to.

"You've been a real godsend this week, Angelica. I don't know what I'd a done without you," he said as he finished breakfast and headed for the door.

"It has been a little rough," she answered, her hands buried in dishwater.

"Well . . . Rivera's gang should be finishing up today. After that, things'll slow down. Get back to normal."

"In that case, as long as we're both headed toward town today, why don't we celebrate? You can buy me lunch."

"Got yourself a deal." Now he didn't have to worry about an excuse to keep her gone all day.

Rafael was in a black mood. He'd given up hope of seeing Angelica before they left. He was sitting precariously on the tailgate, his feet hanging barely above the pavement, as Benito steered the truck toward a shady grove of eucalyptus where Muriella, Maya, and the other women were preparing the noon meal.

He shook his head in disgust at the sight of Ferrara's truck. As Benito pulled between the cookfire and the table filled with the waiting food, Rafael couldn't believe his eyes. Leaning against the table talking to Maya was Angelica.

She smiled and waved as he hopped off the tailgate.

"Hey!" she called as he stood there openmouthed. "I thought you were going to stand me up."

"I . . . ah . . . no."

"Then we better get a move on. Your boss tells me you only got a half hour."

"Better not be late either. Or I'll take it out of your pay," a sweat-stained Rivera threatened as he walked over and hugged Maya.

Maya closed her eyes and leaned against her husband. The low, penetrating pain was almost constant now. Though she smiled and talked, she rarely remembered what she'd said or to whom she'd been talking, she was in such a daze. She'd seen Muriella looking at her a few times, but she smiled and ignored her silent inquiry.

Beside her father's truck, across the grove from where Rivera and the others ate, Angelica opened a wicker basket. She took out a heaping plate of crisp golden-fried chicken, mashed potatoes, fresh bisquits, a mason jar of gravy, and a pitcher of iced tea.

"Sorry. No potato salad," she said.

"You're really incredible," he answered, unable to take his eyes off her. She started to become embarrassed. "I'm sorry," he said realizing he'd been staring.

"Don't be . . . please. Actually I love it. And I'm terribly flattered." She handed him a heaping plate.

"This isn't exactly what I had in mind." He waved his arm toward Rivera and the others.

"What do you mean?" she asked indignantly.

"Oh . . . I don't mean the food. It's wonderful."

"You haven't even tried it yet!"

"If you cooked it, it has to be. What I meant was when I thought of a picnic with you, I thought we'd have it . . . well, you know . . . in a quiet place without a crowd. Maybe next to a stream."

She grinned. "You mean alone?"

He shrugged, then nodded.

"Guess I better hurry," he said, digging in. "If Rivera doesn't dock my pay, I expect your papa will come riding in any minute."

"Not today," she said, barely touching her food.

"Oh, he'll be here!" Rafael promised. "He hasn't missed a day since we had dinner together."

"I know. But not today." She handed him a bright polka-dotted napkin. He held onto her hand for a moment as he took it from her.

"Why not?" he asked.

"Something's wrong with my car. I had to leave it at the

151

garage in town." She acted the wide-eyed innocent. "He went to check on it for me. I got tired of waiting and took his truck and came on home."

"What's wrong with it?" Rafael asked, delighted with her ingenuity.

"Nothing really. A loose wire or something."

"Then we can expect to see him roaring down the road any minute."

Angelica smiled and held up her car keys. "Not without these."

"You are marvelous." He laughed from deep within.

"Thank you." She said, reaching over and touching the lines on his cheeks formed by his smile.

CHAPTER TEN

Alicia shivered as the chilling scream echoed down toward the entryway where she waited.

"The Padrone says to come upstairs," the old woman said.

Pulling her shawl around her shoulders, Alicia followed her up the stairs and away from the sound of the old Padrone raging in the far wing of the villa.

The old woman opened the door into Carlo's room and stepped back.

"In here, *signorina*." She turned and shuffled back down the stairs.

Alicia walked in and looked around the room. Across the bedroom chamber, past the canopied bed in a book-lined alcove, Carlo was sitting, talking to a delicate-looking young man whose glasses seemed dwarfed by his balding pate. The room was little changed from the first time the old Padrone had brought her here. The man with Carlo smiled a quick greeting, but Carlo talked on without acknowledging her.

"You asked to see me?" she interrupted, returning his rudeness.

Carlo stared at her coldly before returning to his conversation with the stranger.

Alicia turned to leave. She had no intention of being insulted by this man.

"You will stand there and wait until I have finished my business and am ready to talk to you. Do you understand?" he said his eyes blazing.

The man with Carlo shifted uneasily.

"May I introduce Alicia Orsini," Carlo said, his voice filled with contempt. "Alicia is the . . . girl . . . woman . . . creature . . . responsible for my father's

. . . condition. Tell me, Maxmillian, do you think she was worth the price?"

The man took out a handkerchief and wiped his forehead nervously. He was Maxmillian Buntz, a Swiss solicitor from Lugano. He and Carlo were taking Pasquale Gianini to a sanitorium in Switzerland where he would be cared for and cease to be a continuing embarrassment.

Like Carlo, Maxmillian was from a wealthy family. The two had met when Carlo was in Lugano to negotiate a merger with a larger company from Zurich to distribute the wine that bore his family's and Montepulciano's name.

Maxmillian had thought that Carlo was a brash, immature, spoiled aristocrat who'd unfortunately gotten his hands on the family fortune. But he had watched Carlo use the Swiss company's low opinion of him to his advantage. It was a masterful job that led ultimately to Carlo's taking over the larger company. Maxmillian wasn't as ruthless as Carlo, nor was his reputation ever going to grow so meteorically. But the two men had one thing in common. They both lacked a conscience.

"I have no intentions of standing around so you'll have someone to insult, Carlo," Alicia said, turning toward the door.

"You will, if you want a letter from America."

She stopped and whirled back toward the two men. Carlo was leering at her and she couldn't tell if he was lying or telling the truth.

God, she thought. Word from Rafael! Could it be? Her heart suddenly ached with the hope. She saw Carlo tap the polished wood tabletop. Her eyes darted to his fingers. On top of the table she saw an envelope encrusted with a cluster of foreign-looking stamps and several official-looking seals.

Completely forgetting the men, she rushed to the table. But Carlo quickly picked the envelope up and buried it in his coat pocket.

"Give it to me, Carlo!" she demanded as her anger almost took her voice away.

"Soon . . . soon, my dear." As she watched, he took the envelope back out of his pocket and peeked into it. Raising his eyebrows as if greatly impressed, he whistled softly and took out a small folded wad of money and waved it tauntingly in front of Alicia's face.

She grabbed for it but he was too quick.

"Bastardo! Damn you to hell, Carlo Gianini. Give me my letter!" she screamed as tears filled her eyes.

"First you must earn the right to have it," he said looking up from the envelope.

"Earn it?" she shouted. "Don't play games with me, Carlo. Just tell me what you want."

"Are you clean?" He smiled casually as he lit a cigarette and exhaled the smoke in her direction.

"What?" She choked. She couldn't believe what he'd asked.

"I said, are you clean? You see, my friend Max is accompanying me as I take Father to a clinic. It is a long trip. It was a long trip here from Lugano. I can tell Max is in need of some entertaining . . . some diversion. So I naturally thought of you."

"You pig! You are beneath contempt!" She would have spit but her rage had dried her mouth.

"Pity . . ." Carlo smiled and shrugged to Max. "I am sorry, Max. I know you're not use to this kind of scene. But our Italian women have spirit, *sì?*"

Max nodded silently.

Taking a match from a dish, Carlo struck it and held it under the letter. It seemed to take forever, but finally the edge of the envelope blackened and started to burn a soft yellow.

Alicia's heart ached with pain and rage. It was as if the hungry little flame was searing her soul.

"No!" She screamed and sank down. She grabbed Carlo by the pants leg and pleaded. "Please, no. Please! Don't burn it!"

"Well, that's better." He quickly doused the flames in a cup of cold coffee left on the table. "Does that mean you've changed your mind?"

"Sì." She sobbed without looking up. She wiped her nose. "Just tell me what you want of me."

The next hour was a nightmare for Alicia as Max ravaged her. He'd never known such a young woman . . . such firmness of thigh and magnificent breasts. In his chair across the room, Carlo watched her degradation. He made Alicia answer every fantasy Max or he could imagine.

Slumped against the end of the bed on the floor, the naked and nearly hysterical Alicia stared at Carlo. Max, hastily bathed and dressed, entered and Carlo led him out of the room.

"*Ciao!*" Carlo said as they left. "You know, you should truly be in the cinema."

"The letter!" she screamed.

"Calm yourself. I will leave it downstairs with the maid. In case it's not good news, I don't want a naked hysterical whore chasing me through the streets. She will give it to you after we have Father on the train."

Back in the bathtub in her room, she sat shuddering with spasms of hate and betrayal. For hours she tried to get the dirty feeling off her body. Even the peasant men smelly after months in the fields hadn't made her feel so filthy.

She knew someday . . . somehow she would kill Carlo Gianini.

There had been no letter from Rafael. There was a letter. And it was from America. And it had money in it. But it wasn't from Rafael. It was a worthless piece of business correspondence Carlo had used. But, of course, Carlo had never said it was from Rafael.

CHAPTER ELEVEN

"Twenty days, Rivera," Ferrara said as the crew sweated to finish loading their trucks before heading east toward their next jobs in Napa County. "If you all aren't back by then, I'm hiring another crew."

"Don't worry," Rivera assured him with his toothy smile. "We will be here."

Twenty days! Three weeks! Rafael thought, as the old trucks and cars strained and clattered and slowly lumbered out onto the road, leaving Ferrara and Angelica standing behind staring after them.

He rarely thought in terms of time. But now! Three weeks without seeing Angelica seemed like an eternity.

They went down the gravel road that led up into the little ring of mountains that overlooked the Ferrara farm. After winding through the wooded mountain, the road would drop down again near the little town of Calistoga. They'd work there for a week, then head on east to St. Helena, Oakville, and Yountville before circling back through the town of Sonoma, then to Ferrara's.

Three weeks! By then, old man Ferrara might have Angelica packed off someplace where he wouldn't be able to see her again.

Thinking of Angelica, as the miles drifted behind, he barely realized that the rest of the convoy had disappeared ahead of him until he rounded a curve and the road dropped toward a grove of pine. The other cars and trucks had already parked in the shade and they were all waiting for him.

"We bet you got lost . . . and had to go back and ask Angelica Ferrara for directions," Rivera teased.

Rafael smiled blankly. Maya recognized the blank stare. Her dear Rafael was showing his first symptoms of love.

During the next two weeks, they worked four different jobs for four different farmers. Each job had taken them further east. And each job seemed to go so slowly that Rafael was convinced time was standing still.

At dinner after the fourth job, Rivera drove up from scouring the farms to set up the next day's work.

"*Hola, amigo.*" Benito said as Rivera came up to the camp stove and poured a cup of coffee. "You look like you're in a foul mood. What's the matter? No work tomorrow?"

"There's work. But I'm not sure we want to take it," he said quietly as the others gathered. "I saw one of the Pacheco brothers on the road from Oakville. He wants us for three weeks," he announced.

"We promised Ferrara we'd be back in less than two," Rafael said.

"Old Ferrara knows if we're not back, he finds someone else," Ramon said. "*No es importante.*"

"But do we want to work for the Pachecos?" Maya asked her husband.

No one answered.

"Who are the Pachecos?" Rafael asked.

"Very rich, very big farmers," Benito said.

"*Es seguro.* They have the first *centavo* they ever made," Ramon interjected.

"They own that big farm on the road between Calistoga and St. Helena," Rivera explained to Rafael.

Rafael remembered the big plantation-sized house that sat near the highway.

"They pick . . . pick . . . pick . . . yell . . . yell . . . yell . . . !" Maya said. She carefully eased down on the running board as a wave of nausea swept over her.

"Sounds like we don't need their work," Rafael said.

"But they pay the best in the whole valley," Benito said.

"They have to," Muriella snorted.

"It's too much money for us to say no," Benito said.

Ramon, Enrique, and finally Rivera nodded glumly.

"I'll tell them we'll be there at sunrise," Rivera said, walking back to his truck and heading off into the growing darkness.

As the sound of the truck faded in the distance, Maya

struggled to her feet and walked to Rafael's side. "I'm sorry," she said taking his hand.

"Benito's right. Three weeks' work is too much to refuse." He squeezed her hand in return and walked back to his car where he would try to force himself to a restless sleep.

They had been right. The Pachecos made the money hardly seem worthwhile. They constantly hovered around Rivera's crew, complaining, criticizing, everything, everyone. The speed at which they worked; quitting too soon even though it was dark; starting late, even though it was before sunrise. The plants they damaged during harvest, even though within days they'd be plowed under. Nothing escaped them.

One of the brothers, Paolo, was skinny. The other, Nicchio, was fat. And they worked as a team. The fat one, Nicchio, was basically the farmer. The skinny one, Paolo, was the banker.

Not unexpectedly, at the end of their first week, their pay was short. At Rafael's insistence, they watched and listened as he discussed collecting the difference with the brothers.

"You must think we're pretty stupid," Paolo Pacheco said arrogantly. "The tubs were half filled with culls . . . dirt . . . anything you could pick up off the ground. We don't pay for picking garbage off the ground. We only pay for what's fresh."

Rafael walked slowly toward the man and placed his huge hand on the back of the man's neck. Paolo felt his eye start ticking in nervousness.

"You are mistaken," Rafael said. "No doubt it is an honest mistake. But you should know this . . . and remember it. We have never cheated anyone. And no one has ever cheated us."

"Well . . ." Paolo Pacheco said quickly taking out his wallet. "Maybe I was misinformed."

"That's possible," Rafael said, taking the money extended by the man's trembling fingers and counting it one bill at a time.

Paolo was furious. His brother Nicchio had been wrong about them not daring to complain. "Don't forget, though," he said, trying to regain some authority as he heard Benito chuckling behind him. "Any damage, any shortages, and we deduct them from your last week's wages."

Rafael smiled politely. "Of course."

That night as they sat around the coals of the cookfire, Rivera and Maya walked over and sat down next to Rafael.

"Thank you," Rivera said.

"It was my pleasure," Rafael smiled. "The little one's like a dog. Yap . . . yap . . . yap. And even if he bites, his teeth are very short."

"I need to ask you to do us another favor," Rivera said.

"Of course."

"*Señor* Ferrara is always kind to us. I'm sorry we won't be able to pick his grapes I've been thinking . . . Maya and me, that is. We should send a man to tell him. That way, for sure, he'll have time to get some other pickers."

They smiled at each other for a moment before Rivera stood up. "Try not to get yourself lost, *sí?*"

Rivera's grin almost covered his face.

"But we both know I can't go."

Rivera's grin faded.

"We've got to get the Pachecos finished." Rivera started to protest but he knew Rafael was right. After the scene Rafael had made, if he disappeared all of a sudden, the Pachecos would be impossible. "I love both of you for thinking of it." Rafael smiled. "But the time will pass. Things will work out if they're meant to."

Rivera grabbed Rafael's hand, squeezing it in his powerful grip. "I hope for you they do, *mi hermano.*"

Rafael smiled as he watched Rivera walk away, his arm around Maya. A family. How he wanted a family, his family. With him now. After hundreds of sacrifices, he was close to having enough in his manila envelope to bring his mother and Alicia to America.

The moon had gone down and the cookfire coals had turned to ashes. Maya carefully pushed herself from beneath the truck. Another pain had awakened her and she felt as though she was burning up from the heat.

She stumbled over to the back of the truck and took out a rag and dipped it into the cistern of water.

She had wrung it out and wrapped it around her neck when a figure slipping out of the darkness almost brought a cry to her throat.

"Muriella!" she whispered in relief.

"Sí." The Indian woman whispered back. "I couldn't sleep."

Maya smiled, but Muriella couldn't see it in the darkness.

"And you?"

"Me neither."

"Pains again?"

Maya nodded, praying the pain would psss.

"You should tell him, Maya," Muriella warned. "The work will get done without you. I told you. I could take your place and you can do the cooking for me. It's easier . . ."

"You're having a baby, too. Don't act the fool. Yours is due before mine."

"But it is not my first, Maya."

"Listen! It's good for me to work. It will help make my baby strong. Rivera will be proud, sí? A strong son and a strong wife."

Muriella exhaled her exasperation and tiptoed back toward her blankets. She had promised Maya not to say anything. But she had the feeling that she'd done the wrong thing.

Lately, Maya's complexion had paled. Her mouth seemed pinched and rarely showed the smile the old Maya was rarely without. And her proud bearing seemed to have slipped. She seemed to tire at the slightest exertion.

Through the darkness, the troubled Muriella tried to drop back to sleep. But every time she opened her eyes, they fell on Maya's shadow. She sat on the edge of the tailgate of the truck, occasionally dipping the cloth in the cistern before wiping it over her burning body.

Angelica sat at the table listening to the sounds of the new day—the distant chirping of protesting birds, the occasional crack from the tin roof over the barn as the sun heated it.

What she didn't hear was the sound of Rivera's clattering caravan. But she knew they weren't coming. By now they would already be here. Her father's deadline had been yesterday.

Frying chicken sizzled on her stove. She smiled, remembering Rafael's grin when she'd asked him if he liked chicken. With a pang, she realized how much she'd looked forward to seeing him again.

At the sound of an approaching engine, her heart leaped. But it was her father on his way back from town with the men he'd hired to pick his grapes. With arms folded, she waited at the doorway while he parked. She listened as he gave orders to the two dusty, windblown boys who hopped down from the back of the truck.

"Hello, Papa," she said as the boys headed toward the empty lugs in the vineyard.

He nodded without answering.

"Found some help, I see."

"That's a matter of opinion. They were the only two in town that weren't working. And they didn't seem too keen on the idea. I figure they'll work till they get a couple of dollars, then light out."

"I thought for sure they'd be back by now," Angelica said.

Nodding, her father turned toward the vineyard and left her standing alone.

From where he stood in the field, Rafael watched as Rivera and the rest tried to look busy. They'd finished the harvest almost three days earlier, but the Pachecos had contracted for three weeks and they were working out the week. From the small field near the riverbank, Rafael could hear Benito yelling at the four-horse team he was driving to harrow the field. He was sitting on top of the steel sulky seat with his bandana covering most of his face to keep from suffocating in the heavy dust kicked up by the steel wheels and the team of huge draft horses.

Rafael looked at the sun. It was only an hour after midday. It was their last day. He'd collect their pay after dinner and in the morning they'd be on their way west at first light. He knew they wouldn't be able to work the Ferrara vineyard, but no one was going to be able to stop him from stopping and saying hello to Angelica.

The big horses strained against their traces, making the reins slippery in Benito's sweaty hands as he neared the end of the field. He kept the team moving faster than they were used to going. He wanted to be done with this field and with the Pachecos. But mostly he wanted to get the hell away from here so Rafael would return to normal and they'd stop feeling so damn guilty about making him miss seeing his sweetheart.

He clucked to the lead horse, pulled on the reins, and in unison, like a roman chariot, they swung in a tight circle and headed back toward the opposite end of the field marked by the Pachecos' new windmill and water tower. At the end of the circle the outside horse kept pushing in and Benito had to crack the whip near his ear to get him to straighten up.

He was a spirited animal. Even after pulling alongside a team a whole day, he quivered with strength and pent-up energy. Three more like him and I'd have to tie myself to the seat, Benito thought, as the animals broke into a canter.

He tried to duck a huge fleck of lather one of the horses had shaken off. But it hit him on the forehead. He shifted the reins to one hand to undo the knot in his bandana and wipe it off with the other. He should have halted the team. But he was making too good a time. He knew everybody was waiting for him, just marking time until he finished.

He had got the bandana retied and nearly readjusted so the dust wouldn't blind him when he looked up and realized it was nearly too late to turn. He cursed himself. He could stop. But if he did, he'd have to unhitch the team, handle the harrows by hand until they were turned in a different direction, then rehitch the team before starting again.

He pulled hard on the reins and yelled at the lead horse. She responded almost immediately. But the outside horse lagged, making the whole team late in its turn.

Angry at the big animal, Benito gave him a couple of hard wacks on the flanks and the horse kicked and tried to rear. Benito wacked him again. This time the horse tried to break and run.

For a moment the other horses strained to follow.

The trailing harrows were too wide for the turn. One of them collided with one of the stanchions that formed the legs of the Pachecos' new windmill.

Benito heard the clang of metal against metal, and, glancing over his shoulder, knew what had happened. In horror he watched as, almost in slow motion, the galvanized leg of the windmill separated at the bottom where the harrow had struck. After teetering for several heart-stopping seconds, the whole thirty-foot tower came tumbling down.

With hands trembling and heart pounding, Benito finally got the spooked team stopped.

Benito was the picture of dejection and humiliation as he sat on the running board of the car listening to the Pachecos rant, rage, curse, and insult the whole crew.

"Do you know how much that's going to cost to replace?" Nicchio yelled as spittle flew out of his mouth.

"It was new. Double-geared, self-oiling, and everything," Paolo shouted nearly as loud.

"Three hundred and fifty dollars . . . that was the windmill alone. Not to mention the gearbox, what it cost us to bring it out here . . . a crew to set it up . . ." Nicchio was wining.

Rafael walked into the light of their kerosene lamps after inspecting the windmill.

"Thought maybe you'd run off, Orsini," Paolo said sarcastically. "You get a good look at the Mexican disaster?"

"I tell you," Nicchio said to his brother in disgust, "far as I can see these Mexes are good for two things: making babies and wrecking other people's property!"

In a blur of motion, Rafael had the fat Pacheco by the throat and almost off the ground. "I tell you this only this one time. And never again. Never insult my friends again. Or I'll squash you like a sow bug under a rock. Your property was damaged. It was an accident. We'll repair the damage. Because these Mexes, as you call them, are honorable men. And not because of your stupid insults . . . or threats."

"But it took a whole crew of men to put it up," Paolo

informed him cautiously. "How in the world are you going to do it with your . . . friends?"

"If we can't do it, you've got me. I'll stay till the cost of putting it back up is worked off."

"That's half a year's wages, at least," Paolo warned.

"You sure we can fix it?" Benito asked after the brothers had gone.

"I'm pretty sure. The shafts are bent. But the gears weren't damaged. Just pulled out of their housing. I'll need some help, though."

"I'm your man," Benito nodded.

"We can all help," Rivera insisted.

"No. I don't need anybody else. You'd just get in the way. I only need Benito. Mostly I need his car. And mine . . . to get the tower standing again. After that, with a little luck, it'll only take a few hours to straighten the shafts and get the gearbox back together."

"Just the two of you are going to lift that big iron tower?" Rivera asked in disbelief.

"No. We're going to use the drive shafts of the cars . . . make a hoist. We'll let the engines do the hard work."

"I'm staying too!" Rivera insisted. "You're crazy if you think you can do it alone."

"That's okay with me." Rafael shrugged. "You're more than welcome to stay and sit in the shade on your butts all day. But it's a waste of time. While Benito and I finish this, you can be on the road looking for work. That is, if you dumb Mexes think you can find any."

"How about I stay and Benito goes? He knows the routes . . . where the work is."

"No!" Benito said adamantly. "I did the damage. I stay."

Benito stared at his old friend who finally shrugged. "I am the boss," Rivera grinned. "The boss should be able to stay if he wants."

"I am the wife of the boss," Maya interrupted. "I will stay in his place."

Everybody looked at her.

"What do you mean you'll stay? This doesn't have anything to do with you." Rivera said.

"It has a lot to do with me. They will need someone to cook for them at midday. And like Rafael says, someone should be out looking for more work for us. Unless you'd rather sit around here like it was the Navidad. And as the boss can't stay while the work is completed, the boss's wife will take his place."

"But how will you find us?" he asked as if he'd discovered the flaw in the plan.

"Leave word at the Ferraras' where you will be," Maya said, smiling at Rafael.

"Bien," Rivera finally said, reluctantly.

As the first gray started to appear in the sky, Rafael, Maya, and Benito watched as the caravan pulled away and drove down the dusty road that led to the highway.

Maya felt a wave of loneliness sweep through her—the same feeling she'd known when Rivera had fled north after Rico was killed after the cockfight.

As Rivera's car turned onto the highway and disappeared, she went to the back of Benito's truck and started putting away the dishes Muriella had already washed before leaving.

Maya felt a burning, cramplike pain in the bottom of her abdomen as Benito and Rafael hopped into the other car.

"We're going on to get everything rigged up. Meet us next to the river when you're finished, okay?" Rafael asked as he pulled up and stopped next to her.

He watched as she looked up and smiled. The pale light of the dawn seemed to mask her face in drab gray, Rafael thought. As they drove away, she let loose of the tailgate she'd been clinging to and sank down next to the back tire. Her breath came in short pants from the growing pain. She knew it was still too early for her baby. But she also knew that whatever was wrong might make him come early.

At least if he does come, I'll have some peace and quiet, she thought. I won't have to worry about Rivera being scared half to death. She smiled at the vision of her husband rushing around frantically. She closed her eyes as the pain subsided and for a few moments allowed her some relief.

An hour later, she followed Rafael's directions and positioned the car so the windmill was between her and Rafael's car. She switched off the engine and sank back in the seat in pain.

Bouncing over the rough, uneven field had taken its toll on her.

"Hey! Just because your husband's gone, don't think you can sit on your bottom the rest of the day," Rafael said as he passed and set a thick plank across the front bumper. He started to attach the plank to the bumper for the added support he'd need once they started lifting the tower.

"Why? You need a woman to lift that old windmill for you?" She sat up, trying to find a position that was comfortable in the seat. Half the springs seemed to be poking her through the threadbare upholstery.

"I might. If this doesn't work," he admitted.

"Well, just remember. I'm the boss's wife. And I don't do any of the hard work."

Rafael laughed as he slipped under the front of the car and tightened the bolts that held the plank to the bumper.

Maya felt her eyes growing heavy as the sun started to warm up. It felt wonderful. She'd never known the luxury of sleeping late and she felt guilty. She should help, she thought, as her eyes fluttered shut. Even the motion of the car rocking back and forth as Rafael worked under it didn't disturb her as she drifted into an exhausted, dream-filled sleep.

Her eyes suddenly snapped open when a pain exploded through her abdomen. Her arm was asleep from leaning on it against the door. And she had to look around for a moment before she remembered where she was.

At the edge of the field she could see the Pachecos watching the progress at a safe distance from Rafael. She didn't realize she'd been asleep that long. She hadn't even heard them drive up.

Looking around, she saw the other car already rigged. Rafael was near the top of one of the old trees near the river. He'd already secured a pulley to the tree trunk and was pulling a length of cable through it.

Benito walked toward her dragging the other end of the cable. As she struggled to get the door open, she felt a wetness flowing between her legs. She sat back, her heart pounding with dread.

Rafael hopped down from the lower branch of the tree and trotted after Benito. "Hello, Princess!" Rafael grinned as he and Benito pulled the cable tight and wrapped it around the plank and front bumper. "You finally awake?"

"Not unless it's noon." She tried to smile.

Rafael dropped the wrench in his toolbox. He and Benito stood and surveyed their work. Like some prehistoric skeleton, the windmill tower lay on its side in the dirt attached to the two cars on opposite sides by the cables.

"How's this supposed to work?" Benito asked. He had merely been following Rafael's instructions. But now that they were getting ready to start their engines, he was getting a little nervous.

"When I back my car up, I'll be like a crane." Rafael pointed to one of the cables that snaked from the windmill through the pulley and back to his car. "I'll be lifting the top of the windmill till it's sitting on two of its legs."

"Con suerte!" Maya teased in a weak voice.

"Yes, with luck. That's for sure," Rafael said. "Anyway, about half way up, I'll signal to you. You start backing and the weight'll shift to your cable . . . and she should pull right up."

"Ah! *Sí . . . sí!*" Benito said as he started to understand. "The tower will be like a shark on the end of a hook waiting for gringos to take its picture."

Rafael nodded. "I'll come back forward to keep tension on my cable. And again . . . with a little luck," he winked at Maya, I'll keep it from falling back over your way. That makes sense, huh Maya?"

Maya shook her head. She was sure now that she didn't understand. It just seemed to her like a giant tug-of-war with the tower in the middle, the prize.

"I think it'll be safer for the boss's wife if she waits over by the windbreak," Rafael said.

Maya nodded and looked at the shade under the trees of the windbreak. It seemed a million miles from where they stood. She struggled out of the car, wrapped a blanket around herself, and slowly walked toward the distant trees.

"Ready?" Rafael asked.

"Sí, listo."

Rafael hurried to his car. He cranked the engine to life and hopped in. Putting the car in reverse, he slowly eased out the clutch, backing until the cable grew taut.

He revved his engine to its peak and let out the clutch a little more. He could hear the pulley in the tree creaking and complaining as the greased cable started rolling through it.

Now if the tree just doesn't fall, he thought as he backed slowly away from the tower. As he backed, his tires started slipping. The dust kicked up under his car, almost hiding him in a reddish-brown cloud.

If the field had been wet, or newly irrigated, they'd never have been able to try it. Their cars would have dug themselves into the wet ground. But the hot sun had baked out the field the last few weeks. All he had to worry about was not suffocating in the storm of dust.

Benito watched gleefully as, like a drunk being lifted to his feet, the uppermost part of the tower started rising skyward. Quickly Benito backed in the opposite direction to keep a strain on his part of the cable as Rafael had ordered.

At the peak of Rafael's lift, Benito heard a thundering crack. The top of the tree, which anchored the pulley, sheared off. It felt to Benito as though he'd backed into a brick wall as the sudden weight of the tower shifted to his cable and dragged his backing car to a shuddering halt.

He felt his locked wheels dragging forward. The top of the windmill dropped slowly back toward the ground. Frantically, he gunned his engine to a roaring pitch and let out the clutch. In a whirlwind of dust, shuddering and bucking, the truck slowly inched away, raising the tower back toward the sky.

One of his rear tires blew out with a loud explosion. He could smell the burning rubber, but the tire stayed on the hub. Even as the tire started shredding, he kept the shuddering car backing inch by inch in a straight line. Slowly the windmill lifted.

Benito half stood in his seat to see how high the tower was. It was almost to the position where it would fall into place. But Rafael's car was tangled in the snarled cable and treetop. He couldn't keep the tension on the other cable to prevent it from falling in the other direction. It was totally up to him, Benito realized, his heart pounding with excitement and fear.

Benito waited for the dust to clear. He could hear the cable groaning and stretching under the strain and knew it might snap if he didn't hurry. He wasn't afraid. He knew he could jump clear if the tower fell his way. But if it fell, they'd never get it off the ground again. There were no trees close enough on this side of the field to hook their pulley to. And Rafael would lose a half year of his labor.

As the dust settled, Benito saw Rafael running toward Maya who lay collapsed in the middle of the field. Benito's heart felt like a locomotive had run through it. Had the cable hit her? Had the tree?

"Dios! Dios! Dios!" his mind screamed as he jammed the car back in gear. He felt the weight shift from the front of his car as the tower fell toward him It felt like an eternity as he watched. Then joy and relief swept through him. The tower had dropped onto all four legs with hardly a sway and settled into the dusty soil. It was perfect.

"Maya!" Rafael yelled as he knelt beside her. Like Benito, he thought she might have been hit by the whipping cable or pieces from the splintered tree.

He lifted the blanket and saw that her face was contorted in terrible pain.

"Maya," he said and shook her gently trying to break through the pain.

"Rafael . . ." she cried. *"Es el niño.* Something is no good. Help me . . . please."

He reached under her to pick her up and carry her back to the car. But she couldn't stand the movement. Her scream echoed across the quiet field.

"Dios, Rafael! *Por favor,* help me . . . *Dios!"*

Frantically he looked around, surveying the possibilities. Benito was racing toward them but both rear tires on his car had blown. The front end of his own car was half torn off.

The Pachecos!

They stood like two frozen statues, their delight at getting their tower standing again short-lived.

Rafael sprinted past the terrified Benito toward where the Pachecos leaned against their car. They watched as though paralyzed as he charged toward them like an enraged bull. Finally without a word to each other, they clambered into their car, started it, and without a backward glance, roared away.

"Goddamn you! Come back, you goddamn bastards! Come back!" Rafael screamed.

He scooped up a baseball-sized dirt clod and hurled it at the speeding coupe as it raced away in a swirl of dust.

Benito was kneeling, white-faced, next to Maya. She was moaning and in pain. Blood was coming from her lower lip where she'd bitten partway through it. Her glazed eyes were open, pleading.

"It's time for Maya's *niño*," Benito croaked in terror. He'd been present when all his children were born. But he'd never seen Muriella suffer like this.

The next hour was a nightmare for the two men.

While Benito got water from the river and swabbed Maya's face and tried to keep her shaded, Rafael transferred the tires from his wrecked car onto Benito's.

The sounds of Maya's stifled screams made it seem as though his efforts were mired by quicksand. Nothing went right. The hubs on Benito's tires were so hot, it was almost impossible to break them loose from the studs. And when he finally did, after a herculean strain, they were too hot to handle.

Finally, sweat pouring off both men, they lifted her toward the car and lay her on a bed of blankets in the backseat.

The stiff springs of the old car magnified the bumpy field and the joggling as Rafael drove across the field toward the road. Maya's jaw ached from biting the blanket to try to keep from screaming. But in the end, she couldn't stop herself. After an eternity, Rafael eased the car onto the asphalt and roared down the road toward the Pachecos'. He knew they had a telephone. He'd call a doctor from there and find out where to take her or what to do.

The terrified faces of the brothers peered out the window as Rafael turned into their driveway. Before the car stopped, Benito was out and running toward their porch.

"*Señores!* Please. We need your help!" he yelled as he pounded on the front door. He pounded again and again, but they wouldn't answer.

Benito sensed, more than felt, the motion next to him as Rafael hurtled past. The door, frame, molding and plaster splintered from his charge.

Nicchio Pacheco was just coming into the foyer with a shotgun in his fat hands when the door exploded off its hinges. He screamed in panic, dropped the gun, and fell to the floor blubbering.

"Where's your telephone?" Rafael screamed, pulling him to his feet.

"Please don't hurt me . . . It was my brother's fault . . ."

Rafael's hand slashed across the man's fleshy cheeks and mouth. "Where's your telephone?" he screamed in a rage. But the man was too hysterical to answer.

Paolo Pacheco suddenly appeared in the doorway down the hall holding a small chrome revolver in shaking hands. Despite the gun, Rafael went down the hallway toward him. Pacheco waved the gun, closed his eyes, and pulled the trigger. The sound of the explosion was deafening in the narrow hallway.

Benito opened his eyes after the explosion in time to see Rafael rip the gun out of the man's hand. He crossed himself when he saw the shot had missed completely and ripped through the door next to where he stood.

"Goddamn you! Where's your telephone?" Rafael lifted the man completely off his feet and flung him against the wall.

"In the kitchen . . . on the wall next to the back door!"

"Yes . . . may I help you?" The nasally disinterested voice came onto the line as Rafael frantically spun the crank.

"It's an emergency . . . I need a doctor."

"Yes sir," the voice came to attention. "What kind of emergency, sir?"

"My friend's having her baby. And it's not her time . . ."

"Sir," the operator interrupted. "Who's her doctor? I'll put you through to him."

"She doesn't have a doctor. We've been working over here at the Pachecos' place and . . ."

"Oh dear!" the operator said, genuinely concerned. "There're only three doctors in the valley. Dr. Crowley's in San Francisco. Dr. Fleming just went over to the Murphy farm—he turned his tractor over and half cut off his leg. That leaves Dr. Aidman. He doesn't usually treat migrants. But . . . well . . . let me try his office. Hold on, sir."

172

Rafael wiped his face on his shirttail as he waited for the operator to come back on the line.

"Sir . . . Dr. Aidman's sorry. But he has an office full of patients who already have appointments."

"Ma'am . . . please!" Rafael pleaded. "She's in terrible pain. And it's a couple of months before her time."

"Well sir, just a moment." The operator sighed. "Let me try to talk to him again."

After what seemed another eternity, the operator came back on the line. "Sir . . . Dr. Aidman says there isn't too much he could do anyway . . ."

"Operator . . . let me talk to the man . . ."

"He already hung up. Said he was too busy. But he said not to worry. Nature'd take its course. If you'll leave your name with me, and where the lady'll be, he'll try to swing by later tonight or first thing tomorrow."

"Ma'am . . ." Rafael felt his rage starting to fill every part of his body. "Something is wrong. Terribly wrong. Believe me . . . please. She can't wait. Just tell me where this doctor is and I'll take her to him."

"I'll tell you, sir. But I want you to know he doesn't handle deliveries there. That's something he always does at home. I can tell you that for sure. I got four . . ."

"Ma'am!" Rafael yelled into the mouthpiece. "Please! Just tell me where he is and tell him we're on our way."

"He's on the main street, sir, between the post office and the grange hall. You can't miss him."

"Get the door open while I get Maya out. See if maybe they don't have a stretcher or something," Rafael barked to Benito as he skidded to a halt in front of the doctor's pale green office building.

"Rafael!" Benito called in panic after leaping out and racing up the steps. "The door! It's locked."

Rafael lay Maya back on the seat. His heart pounded with fear. There was a large stain of blood where she'd been lying.

Her skin felt cold and clammy and her breathing was so shallow, Rafael could barely feel it. This was the first time she hadn't screamed from the pain when he moved her. Her eyes were half open and glazed. He couldn't tell if she was conscious or unconscious.

173

He raced up to the door. Benito was right. It was locked. He cupped his hands to the window and peered through the glass. A gray-haired nurse sitting in front of a fan shook her head and waved them away. "I'm sorry," she said through the door. "The doctor's having lunch."

"Please, ma'am! We have an emergency. The operator called for us and . . ."

"I'm sorry. Maybe you could try over at the county hospital. It's over in Santa Rosa. It's only about an hour . . ."

"It's too far. I'm not sure she can make it that far. Please!" he pleaded.

"I'm sorry. But . . . well. You see, Dr. Aidman doesn't really handle your kind of people."

"Our kind of what?" Rafael asked in disbelief. The rage within him made his whole body numb.

Angelica watched as the dusty, black sheriff's sedan pulled off the road and came toward their house. She'd been waiting anxiously all day for Rafael, Maya, and Benito to show up since Rivera and his band chugged down the road just after sunup. He'd apologized for not being able to pick their grapes. And he'd explained that the others were going to stop by later in the day to find out where their crew was working.

"Miss Ferrara?" The sheriff took off his battered hat and fanned himself. He was wearing his badge on the lapel of a rumpled suit.

"Yes." She tried to smile. Something was wrong. It couldn't be her father. He was working on the other side of the field from her.

"Do you know a Mr. Rafael Orsini?"

"Yes," she said quietly, feeling a dread.

"And a Mrs. Maya Rivera?"

"Something's happened, hasn't it?"

"I'm afraid so." The sheriff nodded.

"An accident?"

"Not exactly, ma'am. It seems Mrs. Rivera was having some kind of pain and well . . . she had her child afore it was due."

Angelica waited, trying to control her trembling as the man continued.

"Seems she was suffering this terrible kind of pain and this Orsini fellow went berserk. Busted into some doctor's place over to Napa. They say he sorta got outta hand. Broke up the place something awful."

"Where's Mr. Orsini now?" she asked.

"Over to the jail in Oakville. They had to take him over there cuz that's where the judge was this week."

"The baby?" Angelica asked.

"Nip and tuck." The man half smiled. "But the little fella oughta be okay."

"And Maya . . . Mrs. Rivera?"

The man looked down at his feet and shook his head. Angelica felt her skin start to tingle.

"I'm afraid she died, ma'am."

"Oh, dear God!" Angelica felt pain throughout her whole body.

"Yes, ma'am. It's a terrible thing. But it happens every now and then. Terrible thing for you womenfolks."

Angelica didn't hear the words that came out of the man's mouth. She sank down on the steps and sobbed into the dishcloth she still clutched in her hands.

"Ma'am, I'm sorry to be bothering you at a time like this. But the judge needs someone to vouch for this Orsini fellow. He can make bail. But the judge wants to make sure he stays around to pay for the damage . . . or else he'll have to go to jail."

"Of course. I'll get over there as quick as I can."

"Thank you, ma'am." He was relieved. He hated telling people about the death of loved ones. It was the worst part of his job.

Angelica sat staring at the distant clouds that looked like puffs of cotton. She heard a sound that filled her with dread. As she looked toward the road, she could see Rivera's dilapidated car and truck turning into the drive, chugging toward her.

From where she sat on the porch, she could see Rivera searching the yard for a sign that his wife and friends had arrived.

"Hello, *señorita*." He smiled over the clattering engine as he braked the overloaded truck to a stop.

Angelica couldn't force a sound through her throat. She remembered how she used to love watching Rivera and Maya laugh and fight and play their almost childlike games of chase until they both fell exhausted into each other's arms. She couldn't imagine one without the other.

Rivera studied her when she didn't answer. He saw that her eyes were red and her face puffy from crying.

"Hey . . . *qué pasa,* my little *señorita?*" he said sympathetically.

She looked at his sunbaked face through a blur of tears.

"It's Maya," she said softly.

Rivera stood there without speaking or moving as she choked out what the sheriff had passed on to her. He had the frantic look of a child lost in a huge crowd, numbed with the possibility of being abandoned.

Slowly he shook his head. "No, *Señorita. Es imposible.* No . . . no . . . no! Not my Maya. It is a mistake . . ."

Tears flooded into his eyes. Angelica saw Muriella sink to her knees, her huge girth shuddering from the sobs. Ramon and Enrique and their wives were silent. Dumbfounded. Their emotions frozen by the horror.

"No . . . no . . . *no es posible.* Not Maya," Rivera kept chanting over and over in disbelief. "Please, *señorita,*" he pleaded like a child violently torn from his mother's arms. "*Digame . . .* it's not true."

She could only stand there and nod. She could force no sound through her throat.

"No!" he cried as the pain of realization sizzled through his nervous system. He began pounding his chest with his fists, faster and faster. Losing all control, he smashed his body against the truck as if to destroy himself.

"What in the name of God is going on?" Giuseppe Ferrara demanded, as he rushed down the path toward them from the field.

"Maya," he heard his daughter answer. He never heard her finish her sentence. He didn't have to. Her voice told him Rivera's wife was dead.

Although it was not yet midmorning, it was already stifling. Angelica sat on the varnished wood bench and waited while the bailiff and clerk complained about the heat.

She and Muriella were waiting for the sheriff to bring Rafael and Benito before the judge for their preliminary hearing. Her father had taken Rivera to the mission to make the arrangements for Maya's burial.

The noise made by the people in the courtroom annoyed and irritated Angelica. It was unfair for anyone to be happy or flippant when others were suffering from so terrible a loss. She felt Muriella suddenly tense. The door behind the bailiff's desk had opened. Two uniformed deputies brought in a line of men. They were all chained together on a common line: the men scheduled for hearings or sentencings.

In the middle of the chain were Rafael and Benito. Muriella could see that her husband's eyes were red from crying. She starting sobbing when their eyes met. Angelica stared at Rafael. She'd never seen him look like that before. His jaw was set, his eyes radiated a wild, deadly coldness.

"All rise!" the bailiff barked. Everyone stood as the judge came in.

The men were unchained and ordered to sit on the bench in front of the railing that separated the courtroom from the spectators.

As Benito started to sit, Muriella couldn't restrain herself and flung herself sobbing against her husband's shoulder. The bailiff started to separate them, but the judge stopped him. "Don't appear to me that they're doing anybody any harm," he said as he perused the paperwork already arranged on his bench by the clerk.

As they sat down, Rafael turned so he could look at Angelica. He put his hand on the railing and she covered it with hers.

"Rafael Orsini!" the bailiff finally called his case.

"Mr. Orsini," the judge said from his bench. "It seems you caused considerable damage to the property of Dr. Aidman, including Dr. Aidman himself."

"Yes, sir." Rafael was prepared for the worst.

"How do you plead?"

"I did what it says I did, sir."

The judge continued to study the report. He shook his head and looked at Rafael. "Though the circumstances ap-

177

pear to be unusual, there can be no allowances for taking the law into a person's own hands."

Rafael nodded.

"However, this court is not without sympathy for what you were trying to do. Because of that, if you can show some ability to compensate the doctor for his damages, I'd be willing to suspend sentence on the assault charge."

Rafael thought of the money remaining in his envelope. He'd already thrown half of it in the doctor's face when the man had sneered that he didn't trade his work for chickens or eggs. The surprised doctor had taken the money and had him carry Maya into his examination room. But by then it was too late.

"Mr. Orsini? Do you have the money to pay restitution to Dr. Aidman? Do you have any money at all?"

He knew if he didn't pay, he'd go to jail. Probably for a year, maybe longer. "Yes, sir," he said reluctantly. At least if he stayed out of jail, he could start earning money for his mother and Alicia all over again.

"How much?"

"After paying that butcher for murdering my . . ."

"Mr. Orsini," the judge interrupted before he was forced to add contempt to his charges. "You're stretching this court's patience. Do you understand?"

"Please, Rafael," he heard Angelica whisper from behind him.

He knew the judge was trying to be fair. He nodded. "Yes, sir."

"Good. Now, do you have any money?"

"Yes, sir. Two hundred and sixteen dollars."

"I know that money represents a great many hours of labor. But I'm afraid it doesn't cover the cost that the doctor has estimated."

"Your honor? Can someone else pay the difference for Mr. Orsini?" Angelica asked.

"Yes, of course, Miss." The judge looked up at the young woman who stood in the first row. She came forward taking a small wad of bills out of her purse.

Maya was buried under a young tree in the mission's little walled cemetery overlooking the winding road that

178

first brought them into the valley she and Rivera loved so much.

Rafael sat in the grass next to Rivera as they both kept a vigil on the hillside overlooking her grave. They sat in silence for more than an hour before Rivera finally looked at his friend. "You must not blame yourself. You did more than anyone else could."

"I still can't believe it. I just can't believe she's gone," Rafael said. He closed his eyes and used sheer willpower to keep the tears from flowing.

"Who can understand the way of God?" Rivera answered, sadly. He looked away from Maya's grave and up into the crystal blue sky, still unable to relate the tiny patch of earth to the place where his wife now lay. "I'm sorry you had to spend your money."

Rafael looked at him in genuine disbelief. The man who'd lost the most treasured thing in his life was trying to console him.

"The money didn't mean anything."

"That's not true. It was for your mama and sister . . . to come here to be with you."

"Money is easy to make."

"*Sí. Verdad.* But I know it was many years of your work. Someday I'll pay it back to you."

Rafael put his arms around Rivera and embraced him. "No," he said. And Rivera knew he'd never take it even if he could earn it. "Benito shouldn't have said anything."

"His pain was too great not to tell everything about what happened. He feels it is his fault too."

"It was the doctor's fault," Rafael said bitterly.

"He didn't make her die, Rafael," Rivera said sadly.

"He may not have made her die, but he let her die."

"No, my friend," Rivera said. "There is no one to blame. If we must blame him for her dying, then we must thank him for saving my son."

Rafael looked across the hill toward the car where the others waited. Wrapped in a soft white blanket, Rivera's tiny, fragile son lay nestled in the warmth of Muriella's giant soft bosom.

Less than a week old, the scrawny, wailing boy seemed too tiny to survive the harsh world that awaited.

"Well, *hermano mio*. It is time." Rivera pushed himself to his knees. "My son, Roberto, will need much food and care and love. Especially food."

Rafael nodded. Rivera had wanted to name the boy after him. But Rafael knew he and Maya had long planned on naming him after both their fathers in Mexico. So he had insisted Rivera stick to that name.

"I've been thinking," Rafael said, still sitting in the grass. "I should probably stay somewhere around here for a while. At least until I can repay the money Angelica put up for me."

Rivera nodded. "I understand. But I will miss you. Everybody will, more than we can say."

"Me, too." Rafael rose quickly and took his friend's hand. "Maybe someday . . ."

"*Sí*, someday . . . ." Rivera said.

Rafael could see the tears in his friend's eyes as he made his way to the caravan and shepherded everyone into the cars.

BOOK
THREE

CHAPTER TWELVE

Ferrara wrapped the chain around the trunk of the spike-trained grapevine and dragged it back to the oak pole attached to the harness behind his lathered horse. He connected the chain to the hook fitting and whistled to the animal. As the links of the chain pulled taut, the gnarled, five-foot-high spike pulled out of the wet soil like a giant gray carrot.

He'd almost finished stripping two rows of the spikes when he saw Rafael's battered car on the road below him. He dragged the heavy spike to a pile already drying in the midday sun and waited as Rafael parked and walked up the hill toward him.

"How are you, *signore*?"

"What can I do for you, Orsini?" the old man answered coldly.

"Two things. I was on my way to your house. I have the balance of the money I owe Angelica."

It had been more than a year since Maya's death. Rafael had stayed near the Ferrara's farm in Sonoma County taking the most grueling jobs so he could repay her as quickly as possible.

"I'll take it to her. Save you the trip up to the house," Ferrara said.

"Thank you." Rafael smiled, wishing he'd kept his mouth shut so he could have seen Angelica. "Also, *signore*, I have some tires and coal oil for sale. I thought you might need some in case the weather turns."

When the weather turned cold, the farmers burned old tires to create a heavy sooty smoke that hung close to the ground and offered some protection to their crops against the frost.

"You're wasting your time," Ferrara said. "Weather's bound to hold to summer."

Rafael nodded. The old man was probably right. It had been an easy spring. More rain than normal, but other than that, the weather had remained gentle.

"You hauled your tires out here for nothing," Ferrara said pointing to the pile of gnarled spikes that had started showing the first signs of new life just before being uprooted. Had they not been jerked out, their leaves would have shaded heavy clusters of grapes within months. "Pulling out all my muscat. No sense spending time or effort on them. Probably couldn't find a buyer for the grapes anyway."

Rafael surveyed the field the old man had been clearing. The holes left by the spikes made it look as though it had been bombarded by artillery.

"A pity, *signore*. They have known much love and care."

"That was before Prohibition." Ferrara gazed down the newly exposed mounds of earth. When he'd set the vines out almost twenty years earlier, they had been shorter than his forearm. "Unless you can figure a use for a whole lot of grapes, most of us don't have much choice."

"I'm always thinking, *signore*. I might just do that."

"Ain't a man in this valley that hasn't racked his brain trying to figure out something. Everybody knows there ain't nothing to do with them except try to outwait this Prohibition thing."

"Maybe that's the problem."

"What?"

"If everybody knows nothing can be done with them, maybe they stopped looking for a solution."

A sound attracted their attention. Angelica was clucking to an old horse as it pulled the steel wheeled farm wagon toward them. The old man scowled, but Rafael could barely keep his delight from showing.

"Rafael! How are you?" The old horse stopped automatically as Angelica slacked off the reins. "It's been so long. I thought maybe you skipped town. How about a hand down?" she asked, wrapping the reins around the back of the seat.

Rafael grinned and started to help her down but Ferrara beat him to it.

"Join us for lunch?" she asked Rafael, picking up the basket filled with food she was bringing to her father.

He started to shake his head, but she insisted.

"There's plenty. I always bring more than we can ever eat."

As the men sat in the shade cast by the pile of weathered spikes, she spread out the lunch buffet style on the tailgate of the old wagon.

Halfway through the meal, Rafael was refilling his glass with iced tea when it struck him that they'd experienced this particular scene once before in their lives. Then he remembered that first night they'd had dinner together. Now, as then, Angelica and he were doing all the talking, laughing, storytelling. Old man Ferrara was the same now as he had been that night: ramrod straight, stern, cold, and silent.

"What's wrong?" Angelica asked as her father stared toward what were now empty rows where his lush vines once grew.

"Hate pulling the muscats. But they're just not worth the money to harvest. Soon as I can get them out, I'll drop in a quick money crop. Course that's just till Orsini here comes up with his big idea that's going to solve all the grape grower's problems."

Angelica looked at Rafael waiting for him to respond. But he was silent, red-faced.

"Course he doesn't have it yet," Ferrara laughed.

Angelica had to slap the reins to keep the old horse moving as she drove Rafael down the hill toward where his car, loaded with old worn-out tires, was parked.

"You shouldn't let it bother you," she said.

"What?"

"The way Papa acts."

"It's hard not to. It might be easier if I knew what I'd done to him."

"It's not you. He'd just getting old . . . crotchety. I've been noticing it lately."

"That's not it."

185

"I guess he just feels you're a threat."

"What could I possibly threaten him with?"

"Me," she said quietly.

They rode for a few yards in silence before he finally looked over at her.

"I think of you often," he admitted.

She felt the heat on her face as it turned red. Her heart raced. This was the first time Rafael had actually come right out and admitted his feelings toward her. She turned back and looked at him. Now it was his turn to become embarrassed.

"It's a crime to have so much and not be able to use it. Especially when so many others have so little." He was trying to change the subject. "I wish I could figure something to do with the grapes your father's taking out."

"There're plenty of things to do with grapes to make money."

"Then why is your father putting himself through such pain pulling the things he loves out of the ground?"

"Because he's stubborn."

"That much I know . . . from firsthand experience. But aside from that?"

"The only way Papa knows to use grapes is for wine. He planted them for that. Besides, he's in the middle. He's bigger than a small grower. Smaller than the big ones."

"What's that got to do with it?"

"Plenty. The big ones, like Italian Swiss up in Asti, have all the clout with the railroads and politicians to get the shipping and Treasury stamps they need to make really huge batches. They make the big batches and call it 'sacramental wine.' They can ship 'sacramental wine' all over the world."

"I thought your father told me he got one of those stamps every year."

"Sure. There're always a few left over for the little guy to make some for pharmacies, small churches. But they don't let him make enough under those licenses to cover his whole harvest."

"So then what can he do with the rest?"

She looked at him. "Rafael. What are grapes?"

"Fruit?" he answered, sheepishly.

"And what is a fruit?" she asked, taking his hand like a child being taught a lesson.

"Something you eat?"

"Very good. You get a gold star."

"When?" he asked, leaning against her.

"Not now," she said glancing around to see if her father was still watching them. He wasn't. He was hard at work pulling out vines.

"So what are we going to do with all these grapes that we got left over after we make our little batch of wine?" He grinned.

"We? Well, since I'm being recruited, let's see. There're lots of things *we* can do with the grapes. Raisins, jelly, even make concentrate to sell to soda pop companies."

"Then why doesn't your papa do that. Instead of pulling those damn beautiful vines out of the ground to make room for something like cabbage?"

"Rafael. He's a farmer. Not a packer or a canner. Not a businessman either. It would take all his time. And then he wouldn't know where to sell the stuff. The only thing he knows is what he's done for the past twenty-five years. I swear if they tore down the docks at Petaluma, we'd probably starve. He's too old and too stubborn to change. He and the rest of the farmers in this valley just grow things they hope someone will buy. The grapes have always been his dream. Something that gave him pleasure."

"It was more than just for pleasure. He built the winery."

"That was a dream that went back to the time when my mother was still with him. Back then he used to brag how someday he was going to be the best winemaker in all America and have vineyards stretching all the way to the horizon. But that was just a dream. It died with Mama."

"Sounds a little something like mine." Rafael smiled. "And it seems foolish as hell to kill the things that your dreams are made of. Even if you can't make money with them."

"Then why don't you do something about it?"

"What do you mean?"

"You've got a strong back. And it looks like a lot of time on your hands. Or else you wouldn't be hanging around with me in the middle of the afternoon. So why don't you stop dreaming and make it real. And another thing. Stop cursing around me. It's a bad habit you picked up somewhere."

"How?" he asked, ignoring her temper.

"I don't know. Try washing your mouth out with soap. That would probably be the easiest way."

"No. Not the cussing. How could I make my dream come true with his grapes?"

"You couldn't if they were his."

"Even a stupid Italian immigrant knows that."

"Then why don't you figure out that you could probably rent the damned vineyard. And I told you what you could do with the damned grapes."

"That's a very good idea."

"Of course it is."

"I mean about washing your mouth out with soap."

She blushed. "I think we almost had an argument," she said.

"No. I could never argue with you. I have a feeling I'd never win."

Rafael was silent as he thought about what she had said. He looked back over the vineyard and felt a rising excitement inside him. Was this where his dream lay?

"What are you thinking about?" she asked.

"Just trying to figure out how to rent a vineyard with no money."

"You're really going to try it?" She grinned.

"Yes. Something tells me I have to do it."

"I wouldn't wait too long then." She nodded toward her father. "There might not be any vines left."

He nodded glumly.

"I could talk to Papa. I'm sure if I asked him . . ."

"No!" he said with absolute finality. "A man's dream is something he must pursue alone. It can't be given to him by someone else. You've already done too much for me already. First, the money . . . now, inspiration. An idea. Now it's up to me. I have to work out how to get the rest. And I will, I promise you. And without you having to ask your father for it for me."

"That's not fair. I want you to have your dream. But I want to help you with it."

He pulled her to him, holding her close and not caring

whether or not her father was watching. God! She made his heart sing and hurt and laugh, all at the same time. "You can help. But you have to let me do it. Before, it was just a dream. Now, I think it's more than that. And the only person I would want to share it with is you."

Her whole body was tingling. She pulled back and looked into his eyes. She'd never felt so filled with joy . . . love. Slowly she leaned toward him and for the first time, her lips touched his.

They pulled apart and looked at one another.

"Well, I better get going," he said awkwardly.

She smiled and nodded.

"Do you think your father would really rent his vineyard to me?"

"Are you kidding? Not only will he rent it, but I can guarantee, you'll become a very popular fellow with him."

"That'll be a switch. And how about with you?"

"You already are."

The next morning, Ferrara came out onto the porch, the screen door banging shut behind him. Dew was glistening off the hood of his truck, birds sang, and the fields were covered with a brilliant green carpet of new growth.

He had lifted his steaming cup of coffee to his lips to blow across it when a figure sitting on the bottom step turned. "Good morning, *Signore* Ferrara!" Rafael said cheerfully. "Isn't it a beautiful morning?"

Ferrara half nodded, hooking one of his hands through his suspenders. "What can I do for you, Orsini?"

"I have a proposition to make. One that might give you a way to make a little money from your grapes."

Ferrara waited, an impatient look on his face, for the young man to make his revelation.

"I want to rent your vineyards," Rafael said enthusiastically as though a great crossroad had been achieved.

"What?"

"*Sì*. I want to rent them. All of them if possible. I'll tend them. Harvest, crush, and take all the risks. You fix a price and I'll agree to it."

"If it's something you're so all fired hot about, why is it that I'm the one that has to set the price?"

"Because you are an honorable man. And I would trust you to set an honest value on it."

"Just hold on a minute. You come out here at the crack of dawn to catch me at a weak moment, is that it?"

"No, *signore*. Not at all. I'm just anxious for you to hear my proposition."

"Then let me hear it. But the way things are supposed to be done. One step at a time."

"Of course, *signore*." Rafael repeated his proposal pertaining to the vineyards Ferrara was going to pull out or not harvest.

"How much can you pay?" Ferrara asked sarcastically. "As far as I can tell, it can't be much."

"I would trust you to set the value for me."

"Okay. Half the price I received for the last full harvest, and it's yours," Ferrara said, suddenly serious about the idea.

"Agreed," Rafael said, offering his hand to seal their deal.

"Not so fast. How are you going to pay it?"

"How about a deposit now, the balance after the harvest?"

"Nothing doing. You want the risk, the chance to make a profit, you have to pay for it. And in advance. Not afterward. It may be a bust for you, and I'll be stuck for all the costs you rang up . . . not to mention having to harvest."

"Would you consider a deposit now and the balance after the harvest, if I gave you an equal share of the profits?"

"That's great. Assuming there are any profits. But what if there aren't any?"

"If there are none, I promise to work for you all next year at no cost to you," Rafael said quietly.

"I'd still have to feed and house you."

"*Signore!*" Rafael tried to control his exasperation and keep his voice calm, "I'll willingly pay you what you want and in the manner you want. I just want to keep as much cash on hand as I can to use in the field and on the crop. Better for it to be in the field than in your bank, no?"

Ferrara studied the young man for a long time.

"Give me half the rent in advance," he finally agreed.

"Balance due thirty days after your harvest . . . or you're mine for a year."

"The profits?" Rafael asked.

"If there are any, you took the risks so they're yours. The rent'll be money—profit—enough for me." Ferrara stormed off the porch and roared off toward the fields in his truck.

The screen door banged and Angelica stood on the porch in the spot occupied by her father a moment before. "Congratulations," she beamed as she sat down on the step next to him.

"Thanks."

"Hey! I'd think a new vineyard operator would be a little happier. Why so glum?"

"The vineyard operator had better come up with some money in a day or two. Or else he's going to be your father's laughing stock for a long time."

"I have an idea."

"I already told you . . . no."

"Not that one. Another one."

He looked at her and shook his head. He leaned over and once again he marveled at the gloriously soft feeling as their lips touched ever so lightly.

"Okay," he said as he continued to nibble at her cheek. "Let's hear it."

"Okay," she giggled, pulling away. "I've been giving it a lot of thought and I think I know who you should go to for the money."

He couldn't believe the name that came out of her mouth.

"The Pacheco brothers," she said again to emphasize she meant it.

"Are you all right? I mean you haven't been out in the sun already this morning?" he asked.

"Rafael. I know what happened. And I also know the Pachecos. I've known them all my life. For what it's worth, despite the way they treat their help, my father trusts them. Once when my father was in trouble and needed money, they gave it to him. They didn't even ask for an I.O.U. or anything. They just rushed over and helped a neighbor in trouble. And they've done it more than once. A lot of people owe them everything."

"You know them one way. I know them another."

"Rafael. A terrible thing happened. And they panicked. Stop and think for a minute. If someone came running at you screaming and yelling with blood in his eye and you didn't know why, what would you do? Knowing you, you'd probably stay and face him. But they're just ordinary men. Rafael, they just panicked."

Rafael spent most of the day thinking of what Angelica had said. He had a little money. But not enough to give her father a full half-year's deposit. And he knew that no matter what, he would not take hers again.

Finally, he turned his car around and headed toward the mountains that led into Napa County.

As he passed Angelica's, he honked. He saw her come out onto the porch and wave as he sped by. He didn't dare stop for fear he'd not want to leave.

It was the first time he'd traveled east from the Ferraras' toward Napa since Maya's death. The mountains were alive with new life. Spring was bursting forth everywhere. Oak trees were turning green with new leaves, wild flowers and wild poppies gave the hillsides a brilliant patchwork of color as he dropped down on the opposite side of the mountain and passed through the sleepy town of Calistoga.

Fifteen minutes later, he felt a lump in his throat as he passed the field where the windmill stood. He pulled over to the side of the road and stopped. The windmill squeaked softly as it turned. Rafael shivered as he listened. Around the curve in the distance, he could make out the white, plantationlike house belonging to the Pachecos.

He finally started his car and drove slowly toward the dusty lane that led toward the house. Then he honked a couple of times to let them know that he wasn't coming unannounced.

Paolo Pacheco came around the house and stopped, his face turning red. "*Signore* Orsini," he said nervously. He was wearing overalls over his suitpants. He rolled down the sleeves of his white shirt. He'd been tending his flower garden, a passion that occupied almost all his free time. He watched Rafael cautiously.

"How are you, *Signore* Pacheco?" Rafael asked, still sitting behind the wheel.

"Fine." The skinny man nodded. He breathed a little more easily when he saw Rafael smile. "What brings you to our neck of the woods?"

"Several things."

Paolo looked apprehensive again as Rafael moved to get out of his car.

"I come in peace," Rafael said to relieve him. "Whatever has happened in the past has to remain in the past."

For the next half hour, Paolo showed off his garden to Rafael. Rafael was genuinely impressed with the man's talent. His brilliantly colored flowers and already blooming hybrid roses were exquisite and showed his dedication. The time spent among the flowers seemed to soothe both men and help wash away the memory of that terrible day.

"I would like to rent Crystal Rock," Rafael finally said when they were sitting under a shade tree sipping a new pitcher of lemonade.

Pacheco looked at him in surprise. The old two-story rock building was their family winery located across the mountains near the Ferrara farm. It hadn't been used since their father's death almost ten years earlier, even before Prohibition.

"I'm sure we could work something out. But what could you possibly want with it?"

Rafael explained to him his proposal to Ferrara and that their agreement didn't include use of Ferrara's winery. He hoped that since the Pacheco winery was not in use, it would be cheaper to rent.

"It's yours, then." Pacheco smiled.

"That brings me to the second thing I'd like to discuss with you."

Pacheco raised his hands in submission after Rafael presented his proposal which included not only the rental of the winery, but a loan as well.

"Whatever you need, if it's within reason . . . for you, just ask. We've never forgiven ourselves for what happened. I'm not sure we ever will."

The next few months were the happiest Rafael had ever known. He was tending land. Not his land, true. But, for the first time in his life, the fruits of his labor would be his.

Every day from dawn to dark, he worked the vineyard.

With three crudely built waterwheels he made from lumber salvaged from a blown-down barn, he routed water from the pipe laid from the Pachecos' Crystal Rock winery to his vineyard at the Ferraras'. He sculpted the water's route through the dirt so it spiraled down, snakelike, from the highest plateau of the vineyard to the lowest rows.

He weeded, pruned, fertilized, and pampered the vines. In return, they responded like growing children. The broad leaves turned emerald green. The flowers turned to massive, purple clusters of heavy fruit.

From the early days, when the grapes were small and as hard as rocks, he anxiously pinched off clusters at random and popped them into his mouth.

At first, they were hard and bitter. But as the days fluttered through the early summer, they filled out, softened a bit, and turned sour. He smiled at the sourness. They had entered their adolescence.

Everyone who used the road past the vineyard became familiar with the sight of Rafael working somewhere in the field on his vines.

He sang.

He talked to the vines.

He smiled.

He pleaded.

He sweated.

He worried, lest the vines he'd pampered and grown to love might give a disappointing crop. But they were like his own children and regardless of how they turned out, he knew he would still love them.

Angelica had become almost as familiar a sight as Rafael in the vineyard. As soon as she finished her housework and cooking, she'd stop by and work alongside him for hours at a time.

At first her father was angry. He felt Rafael was taking advantage of her infatuation with him to get an extra hand for nothing.

"You weren't brought up to work in the field," he said at dinner one night.

"You work in the fields."

"Yes. But they're my fields. I have to or we don't eat."

"Won't they be mine someday?"

He couldn't argue with that. His whole life had been

dedicated to building a monument to her through this farm.

Every stone wall. Every honeysuckle plant. Every tree had been planted with her in mind. And now was the first time she had shown real interest in the land he loved so much.

On his way to irrigate or plow or drive into town, he found himself stopping by the vineyard more and more often.

"Want to make sure Orsini isn't killing our vines," he barked his sullen excuse.

But over the weeks, he found ways to offer advice that he knew would help. It was always presented gruffly, almost as an afterthought. But both Rafael and Angelica realized he wanted to roll up his sleeves and dive in with them. He just couldn't let himself.

As much as he wanted the vineyard to prove its worth so the Italian would have no excuses in case their deal didn't work out, Ferrara could barely stand to watch Rafael with Angelica. A demon inside him hounded him with a vision of himself, old and lonely, while his daughter, the woman he'd dedicated his life to, was off in the arms of this man whom he considered unworthy. He felt like two people. The one who loved her new involvement with the earth, her sweat-stained clothes covered with dust, her newborn knowledge about the vines, her delight and joy when she brought him a cluster of nearly ripe fruit. And the pain-filled, hurt, and lonely old man.

CHAPTER THIRTEEN

An exhausted Alicia opened the door and stepped down the stone steps into the small restaurant. It was late and most of the customers were already gone. It was also the only time ladies in Alicia's profession dared be on the streets.

She sat down at a table in a tiny alcove and ordered a pastry and coffee from the proprietor who nodded and shuffled off to fill her order. He knew Alicia and what she was, but he was sympathetic toward her. He had a granddaughter who had made her First Communion with Alicia. His restaurant was one of the few havens open to Alicia in Montepulciano.

Alicia added heaping spoonsful of sugar to the inky black Moroccan coffee he had brought her. As she sipped the sweet, almost boiling liquid, she heard the scrape of chairs as patrons in another part of the restaurant rose to leave.

Suddenly the footsteps stopped.

Standing behind her were Ricco and Alvino Gianini, both swaying from the effects of too much wine after a night on the town. She could smell Ricco's sickening toilet water as he leaned toward her.

"Pardon me, *signorina*," he slurred, placing his hand on her shoulder.

She jerked her shoulder away and glared at him.

"Well . . . well . . . well!" He smiled. "Look what crawled in from the gutter."

He looked around at the few remaining patrons and pointed at Alicia. "Isn't it disgusting that decent people have to be exposed to something like this . . . a common streetwalker allowed to sit among us?"

The embarrassed patrons turned away from him.

In another small alcove, a big man set down his after-dinner brandy, took out a pack of crumpled, strong cigarettes and settled back in his chair to watch the two cousins.

"Waiter!" Alvino Gianini called indignantly through the nearly deserted restaurant.

"*Sì signore*," the old proprietor said coming out of the kitchen.

"My name is Alvino Gianini. Are you familiar with that name, old man?"

"*Sì, signore*." The old man nodded. War and age had made him immune to intimidation.

"Well, *signore*, my cousin Ricco Gianini and I are insulted that you would serve someone as disgusting as the woman there." He pointed to Alicia who was sipping her coffee pretending to ignore them.

"I afraid I don't understand. As far as I can see there is nothing for you to be insulted about, *signori*."

"My name is Gianini. And if a Gianini is insulted, it could be the end of your business. Now do you understand?"

"How can the presence of a mere girl insult you two gentlemen? I'm at a loss to understand why you are disturbing her as well as my other customers."

"Don't play games with me, old man," Alvino warned, stepping toward him.

Dominic would have remained out of this confrontation had not the two men flaunted the Gianini name so flagrantly. Alicia Orsini meant nothing to him. But he was the protector of the Gianini name and he could not tolerate its abuse any longer. In a movement alien to one so large, he appeared out of the blackness of his alcove and spun Alvino around. He took the man by the shoulder and steered him toward Ricco.

"Perhaps the *signori* were mistaken," he apologized to the old proprietor. "I'm sure they meant no disrespect."

"Just a damned minute." Alvino jerked away from the powerful grasp. "How dare you take liberties with a Gianini. If there's any apologizing to be done, it's by this man. He should keep trash like Alicia Orsini out of the view of respectable people."

"Respectable people do not cause an embarrassment to

their family's name," Dominic said softly as his smile faded.

"Don't assume for a moment that you speak for all the Gianini," Ricco said, poking his index finger into Dominic's chest.

Faster than the eye could follow, Dominic's hand closed around Ricco's throat. "I speak for the Padrone, Carlo Gianini. Do you understand?"

Taking both men by the shoulder, he guided them toward the steps that led up to the door.

Carlo glared at his two cousins who slouched in the chairs in front of him.

"It's bad enough to have to tolerate being related to fools like you, but it's worse to think that you have no respect for your family's name. The next time you flaunt it in public, I will instruct Dominic to handle your situation without bothering me."

"But Carlo," Alvino pleaded, "we thought you would want the girl humiliated. After all it was she who . . ."

"You goddamn fools," he raged, moving toward them menacingly. "What exists between Alicia Orsini and myself is strictly between us. Do you understand? The girl is mine. As is her brother. They have nothing to do with you. I have to suffer with the knowledge that it was you two idiots who were responsible for her other brother's death."

"But you were . . ."

The force of Carlo's slap knocked Ricco completely out of his chair.

"You need to be taught a lesson," Carlo hissed. "Tomorrow morning, before I have my breakfast, you are to offer Alicia Orsini your apologies. You are to offer her flowers and perfume and assure her you were drunk and the asses people think you to be. You are then to extend her an invitation to join you and your families on the veranda of the Hotel Montepulciano."

Both men gasped. To be seen with a whore was bad enough. But in public, at the city's finest restaurant and with their wives? That was unthinkable.

"Do not disappoint me," Carlo warned. "Tomorrow, when I drive by on my way to the train to Rome, which leaves at one, I want to be able to wave and smile and make sure everybody is having a good time. Do you understand?"

"*Sì*, Carlo," Ricco answered, wondering how he was going to explain this to his wife.

"The next time you touch her, I'll chop off your hand. The next time you insult her, I'll cut out your tongue. Do you understand?" He loomed over his terrified cousin.

"You don't like them either, do you, Dominic?" Carlo asked the man who stood quietly in the shadows after Ricco and Alvino hurriedly departed.

"I have no feelings about liking or not liking them, Padrone."

"An opinion then?"

"Every man should have a value, a reason for living. I have trouble finding reasons for them. But they are your blood. And that and your name are entrusted to me, Padrone *mio*."

"My family's champion, eh, Dominic?"

"*Sì*, Padrone."

"And what about the girl?"

"I feel neither hate nor pity for her," Dominic shrugged.

Carlo nodded at the man's logic. He had been thinking of her often of late. Her face. Her smile. Her defiance. Her willingness to sacrifice herself for the prospect of a letter from her brother. "My hate . . . and passions are reserved for her brother," he said.

"*Sì*, Padrone."

"There is much to do before my departure tomorrow. But before those buffoons make an appearance at her doorstep, bring the girl to me."

"What do you want, Carlo?" Alicia said, exhaustion etched on her face.

"Only to offer my apologies for the disgraceful way my cousins acted toward you."

"You had Dominic drag me across half a city in the dead of night for that?"

"*Sì*."

"I don't believe you."

"I'm sorry about that, Alicia." He watched her for a few moments. She had grown more beautiful than ever, despite the spirit-shattering work and unending hours. He'd been back in Montepulciano for several months and had seen her dozens of times. But always at a distance And always without her knowing it. This was the first time they'd been face to face.

"No more games, Carlo. I'm past any pain that you can threaten me with."

"No more games." He nodded.

"I wish I could believe you."

"We are merely two of fate's sad victims." He shrugged.

"It's much more comfortable being a victim in your palace than on the street with me."

"I cannot change our positions. Nor can I alter the events that brought us both to this time . . . this place. If it were in my power, I would. But . . ."

"It's in your power to let me go . . . to stop hating my brother."

"No. Your brother was the creator and author of this all."

"No!" she interrupted angry. "Don't place the blame on my brother. It was your father. Make no mistake about that."

"All right." He was suddenly too tired to argue. "But don't deny that you enjoyed living with him. Under this roof. What it promised. The luxury and position that was beyond your most secret dreams. He gave you all those things."

"Sì. And I'm still paying."

"Do you think what I want from your brother is any different than he would want from me if our roles were reversed?"

Alicia shook her head, knowing what he said was true. "Then it's not over."

"I wish it was. But . . . no."

Long after she disappeared into the night, Carlo stared through the window into the darkness thinking about the possibilities that might have existed between them had not fate dealt with them both so cruelly.

A deep sadistic chuckle rumbled through his chest at the thought of his frantic cousins attempting to persuade Alicia to accompany them for a conciliatory lunch with their families.

No matter the consequences, he knew she'd refuse.

CHAPTER FOURTEEN

Rafael and Rivera embraced.

"Hermano mio!" Rivera said, lifting the taller man off the ground with joy.

"Rivera!" Rafael whooped in joy at the unexpected pleasure of seeing his old family sitting at the side of the road. They were at the bottom of the hill from his vineyard. He waved to Benito and Muriella who was carrying the infant daughter they had named after Maya.

"What do you think of this big fellow?" Rivera laughed, the proud father, as he swooped his newly walking son out of his truck and deposited him piggyback on his shoulders.

The closer Rafael came, the more the baby's lower lip stuck out as he tried to hide behind his daddy's thick curly hair.

"Thank God he took after his mother and not his father," Rafael teased, taking the pouting little boy's pudgy hand and trying to get him to smile. Rafael was amazed at how much he'd grown and filled out. When they had left the valley, the child had been so tiny and scrawny Rafael had worried about whether he'd survive. Now his button nose had almost disappeared between two fat brown cheeks. And it looked as though he was about to burst out of the clothes that Muriella had made for him.

Roberto spotted Muriella and started crying for her to take him.

"He's spoiled rotten," Rivera said.

"Well . . . he may not look like his father, but he takes after him." Rafael laughed.

"Looks like old Ferrara got a pretty nice crop this year." Rivera beamed. "Been taking pretty good care of the vineyard for him, I see."

Rafael felt good. Not just at seeing his old friend, but

because the pain seemed to have faded a little. The sparkle was back in Rivera's eyes. Once again they could joke and insult each other.

"It's not the old man's crop," Rafael said.

"What happened? He sell the farm?"

"No. It's my crop."

Rivera's eyes widened. "You rob a bank like that Dillinger fellow?"

"Nope. But if I don't make some money, I may have to. I rented everything from him, stopped him just before he was going to tear everything out."

Rafael saw Rivera suck in air, knowing the risk Rafael had taken. Table grapes were chancy at best. But wine grapes!

"*Chihuahua!*" He whistled. "Well. You'll need a crew to pick pretty soon, *sí?*"

Rafael shrugged. "Maybe."

"Whatta you mean, maybe?"

"Your crew available?"

"Maybe!" It was Rivera's turn.

"Well . . . if you are, the pay's bad. Working conditions are worse. And the boss is harder than the Pachecos," he warned.

"Pretty tough cookie, huh?"

"You better believe it."

"Sounds like it's too good to pass up," Benito said as he came up and flung his arms around Rafael.

"Don't see how we can miss out on such a good deal," Rivera added.

It was just before sundown when Angelica drove by on her way home from town. Her joy at seeing the dust-covered ragtag caravan at the side of the road almost made her lose control of the unwieldly little coupe. She barely missed careening into the drainage ditch.

To her embarrassment everyone cheered heartily from the hillside above her where they'd gone to inspect Rafael's vines. Rafael ran down the slope and brought her up to where the others waited.

From the side of the hill, the sunset that night looked as though it had been painted just for them.

"A sign from God!" Rivera said breaking the quiet.

"I hope so," Rafael replied as he and Angelica sat quietly mesmerized by its magnificence.

"How do you plan to pick?" Benito asked.

Rafael surveyed the rows around them. The leaves were speckled and dying, showing the change of color that signaled that the season was ending and the fruit ripe for picking.

"By variety. There are four different ones. The whites are ready now. The muscat and mission grapes, maybe next week. The week after that, the zinfandel. There are not many of them, so it should only take a day, maybe two, at most."

"*Vasos por favor, mujer,*" Rivera called to Muriella, who'd become matriarch to the crew.

The familiar cry brought a twinge to Rafael. And when she brought the glasses, he half expected to look up and see Maya handing the tequila to him.

"May God bless these weeks for you," Rivera said, lifting his glass.

Rafael's mouth tingled at the thought of the smooth, burning liquid. He swallowed a hearty slug and passed his glass back to Muriella.

"You not have time for drink with poor peones?" Benito said with as much sarcasm as he could muster.

"Oh . . . now he's big *rico* . . ." Enrique hopped in, with an ever-ready insult.

"Not tonight, *amigos*." Rafael shook his head. "I have to be able to keep my eyes on all of you tomorrow."

"You're not going for help us?" Enrique asked.

"Help you? Are you joking? I'm the boss man. Bosses aren't supposed to work." He smiled at them. "Enjoy yourselves. This might be the last time for a long time . . . I'll see you bright and early tomorrow," he warned.

He held out a hand to Angelica and together they walked down the hill. When they were standing next to Angelica's car, they looked back up the hill at their friends sitting in the vineyard bathed in growing shadows.

"I want you to know, I could never have done it without you," he said, putting his arm around her shoulders.

"Nonsense! I just got in the way. At least more often than not."

"True! But that helped too!" He thought of the many

times he'd delighted in catching her in his arms as they tried to jockey past each other in one of the narrow rows.

She turned and locked her arms around his waist and they stood very close and very quiet for a while, lost in one another's warmth.

"It's true, though. If it wasn't for you, I wouldn't have had sense enough to think of renting from your father."

"I'm full of good ideas."

"You're the brains . . . I'm the muscle," he said, suddenly aware of how delicate she felt.

"Beauty and the beast," she answered. But her heart was pounding with her love for him.

"You better get home," he said as he lifted her onto the running board. "Before he comes looking for you."

"Or you!" she teased.

She looked down at him from the seat as she drove away and wondered if he knew how her body felt when she was close to him . . . how it seemed to crackle with desire when she was in his arms . . . those arms that lifted her so effortlessly, yet gently, off her feet.

Their day finally dawned.

Harvest time!

But this wasn't the bright, sunny day Rafael and Angelica had dreamed and talked of. This day dawned cold, rainy, and windy. It was as if suddenly summer was over and an early, dismal winter was on them.

It never got completely light. The gray clouds were outlined with black as the rain drizzled down onto the crew trying to pick in the vineyard.

Rafael looked out over the vineyard as he unloaded old tires and cans of coal oil every few rows. He pulled up his collar against the cold and wet as he surveyed Rivera's band in the distance, making their way through the mud-clogged rows to strip the vines of their fruit.

They moved slowly, affected by the weather, the mud and the cold, slipping and sliding up and down the slopes and standing in little streams of water that were coursing down toward the drainage ditch near the road. Steam erupted from their nostrils and mouths as they toiled to strip the vineyard for Rafael before a freeze followed the rain and destroyed the fruit.

It was damn cold, a grim-faced Rafael thought, as he steered further into the vineyard and dumped off another batch of tires. He would douse the old tires with the coal oil and light them. Without the warming thick smoke, he could lose the whole harvest.

Finishing with the load, he slithered to a halt at the bottom of the field as Ferrara's truck, headlights flickering, waited with the engine idling.

"Hello, Mr. Ferrara."

"Orsini. Thought I'd come down and check and see how this stuff was draining."

"We're not getting much fruit picked. But at least it's not washing out any of the vines." This wasn't the way Rafael had planned it, the script his dream was supposed to be following.

"Oh, it's not so bad. I've seen worse," Ferrara said. "You going to light them tires?"

Rafael nodded. "I haven't heard anything about the weather on the radio. But I'm not going to take any chances."

"Waste of time," Ferrara said. "It's not going to freeze. You'll save yourself a lot of time and won't gouge up the rows if you just pull Rivera's crew out till this blows through. Once it does, it's gonna turn hot again. Mark my word. I've seen it happen enough times the last thirty years."

Rafael felt someone standing next to him and turned. It was Angelica.

"Hi," she said, holding a raincoat over her head. "How's it going?"

"It isn't." He shrugged.

"I brought some hot coffee for everybody." She'd been riding in the back under the canvas tarp to keep several pots from spilling. She turned and started taking the big pots out of her father's truck and putting them in the back of Rafael's.

"Maybe I'll just light every other row then," Rafael said, not convinced Ferrara was right. "That way, if things start getting any worse, at least we'll have a head start on it."

"Suit yourself." Ferrara shrugged as he put the truck in gear. "You going back with me, Angelica?"

"No. You go ahead, Papa. I'm caught up at home. I think I'll stay and help Muriella."

He nodded grimly. "Once you get them tires lit, they won't stop till they're burned out. This rain passes, it'll turn hot again, I guarantee it. What with the water and the extra heat from them tires, it's gonna be miserable working out here," he warned.

Rafael nodded, but Ferrara could see he was determined.

"Borrow your truck?" Angelica asked Rafael as her father backed out.

"Might be easier to swim up." But he nodded.

"What do you think?" she asked, squinting as she looked up into the rain.

"I can't take any chances. Your father might be right. But I'm the one that loses if he's wrong. I'm going to fire them up just to be on the safe side."

Angelica nodded as he helped her into the cab. She half-smiled, trying not to appear worried, as she reached out and touched his face before chugging up the hill toward Rivera with the hot coffee.

A couple of hours later, the black smoke billowed up from the tires. Rafael watched from under the canvas tarp stretched between the trees at the bottom of the hill where Rivera's camp was. He could feel the heat pouring from Muriella's cookstove as she and Angelica put the finishing touches to the noon meal.

The fragrance from the freshly cooked food seemed to spill into the air before vanishing in the cold, windy mist.

"Ready, Rafael?" Muriella asked as she rushed past on her way to one of the cars with plates for her baby daughter and Roberto.

He nodded, put his finger to his mouth, and whistled.

"Want me to fix you a plate?" Angelica asked as, in the field, a couple of heads popped up over the rows of vines and waved.

"No, thanks. I'm not hungry."

Huddling under the canvas tarp, standing on wood planks to keep them out of the mud, Rivera's crew started peeling off some of the layers of clothes that they wore to shield them against the cold.

Despite the chill, they stripped off their high-topped shoes or boots because they were caked with pounds of mud. They set their footwear near Muriella's cookstove to dry out and then went after their food.

"I was getting a little worried about you," Rafael said, standing next to Rivera who was eating standing up.

"Why, *amigo*?" Rivera asked.

"Thought maybe you forgot you were supposed to come in out of the rain."

"If the bossman we worked for had a heart, we wouldn't have to be out in it at all." Rivera grinned.

"You're right," Rafael said. He knew Rivera would keep his crew out all night for him if need be. But in this weather there wasn't any sense in sending them out again. They weren't able to pick half what they could in good weather. Ferrara was right.

The only thing they could do was wait. But if the rain kept up too long, cold or not, the fruit would start rotting on the vine. Rafael shook his head and uttered a silent prayer.

The rain kept up the rest of the afternoon as Rafael and Angelica, looking like two drowned rats, slogged back and forth between the piles of tires, adding fuel oil to make sure the heavy shroud of protective smoke continued drifting over the vineyard.

It was late when Rafael looked over the vineyard before heading to his tiny room next to the aging room at the Crystal Rock winery. The glow from the piles of tires dotted the night. He was satisfied they'd burn until morning. He lay there in the dark listening to the rain as it beat against his roof. Finally, he drifted into an exhausted, uneasy sleep.

Another dawn finally came.

Rafael opened his eyes and listened. Thank God, the sound of rain was gone. He walked to the front and opened the door.

The sky was bright and sunny with almost no clouds left in the sky. The cold front was gone, it had passed through. Ferrara had been right!

It was the kind of day he and Angelica had dreamed of. He felt like yelling, like singing, like giggling as he steered through the puddles that dotted the road toward his fields.

He felt as though the weight of the world had been lifted.

It was a day of joy for Rafael. His and Angelica's work, their endless hours of labor would be rewarded with an abundant crop. That much was evident. But now came the race. The race against time. The leaves that remained on the vines were already turning brittle. Gone was their green softness of spring and summer. The moment the fruit was picked, it started to die. Before it rotted, they had to get it started toward whatever it was destined for.

A month earlier, he and Angelica had made plans for the fruit. A portion of it, the major portion, was to go to the Crystal Rock winery for crushing and fermenting. Through the Pachecos, Rafael had received a license to ferment five thousand gallons of sacramental wine destined for the church in Mexico. Another portion would be made into grape jelly, preserved in mason jars. He and Angelica had spent two days in San Francisco overwhelming grocery store owners with their sales pitch. It became a contest as to who did the best selling job. But it paid off. The grocers ordered and were promised delivery before Christmas.

The selling job was easy compared to the blistering heat-filled days ahead when Angelica would be tending the big iron stove they'd installed in the barn next to the Pachecos' winery. While Rafael finished the harvest, Angelica volunteered to boil the fruit down, strain it, and store it in the cool aging room until they got back to making the finished product after harvest.

They had also convinced the grocers to take boxes of fresh grapes which would be trucked down by Angelica's father to the landing at Petaluma for ferrying down the bay.

The balance of the crop would be made into raisins. If, that is, the weather held and stayed dry. The sun didn't cost anything, Rafael explained when he noticed doubts about the market for raisins. Angelica remained biased. She just didn't like raisins. But Rafael spent a week after work making flats to hold the stemless fruit. After the harvest, he'd tend them till they were dried.

"It doesn't matter if we sell them right away or not," he argued. "They won't spoil. And if things don't work out, at least I'll have a three- or four-year supply of food."

The wet morning turned sweltering by noon, but Rafael never stopped moving, running, working. He did the work of a half-dozen men. Running up and down rows, he emptied tubs, pots, and pans—all the containers they were using to pick with—into the wood bins on the wagon at the head of the rows.

As the fields started drying out, and the puddles started evaporating, the mugginess became almost unbearable. He toted pail after pail of drinking water to the long line of sweaty, suffering migrants working down the slopes toward the flatland.

At noon, Rafael ladled out lunch to the exhausted workers, and while they ate, drove the team of horses with his loaded wagon to the winery, returning to the vineyard with more empty bins stacked in the winery.

By dusk, he was sore in muscles he never knew existed. Every tendon screamed. He was filthy. He looked as though someone had hosed his clothes down and then caked them with mud.

Angelica untied the big knot that held his bandana around his head and started to unwind it.

"Ugh!" she said, uncoiling it.

Rafael cocked his head and stared at her.

The only part of her body visible was her face. Her hair, worn in a bun, was hidden under a layer of scarves on top of which perched a broadbrimmed straw hat. Her father's oversized overalls and work shirt made her look like an abandoned orphan. Rafael started to laugh when he saw her gloves. They had been new, white cotton gloves she'd bought especially for the occasion. Now, at the end of the first day, they looked as though they'd been dipped alternately in sticky grape juice and mud.

"You're pretty as a picture."

"A picture of what?"

Muriella laughed at them as she brought a heaping plate and set it on Rafael's knees.

For once, the noisy band was unusually quiet. They weren't out of things to say. But true to his promise, Rafael had worked their tails off.

"*Hola*, Rafael!" Benito moaned as he stuffed his mouth with a bean-filled tortilla dripping with butter.

Rafael looked up from his own exhaustion and waited to hear what the man was going to ask.

"You see the Pachecos soon, *sí*?" Benito asked.

Rafael nodded, too tired to do more than pick at his food.

"Ask them if they need help. After today, I'll never complain about them again."

Rafael smiled and bowed as the others cheered.

As he picked at his food, he watched Angelica wolf down her food and hurry to help Muriella. He smiled to himself. She'd worked alongside him all day. Now, this woman, clad in a sea of muck-covered denim, still had strength enough to help another.

Slowly, achingly, he got up and stretched, trying to get the blood flowing and to ease the exhaustion that was crushing down over him.

"See you all in the morning," he said, heading out of the firelight toward the mud-splattered team of horses. "And I do mean bright and early," he warned.

He was barely in the seat when he saw a shadow hurrying toward him. It was Angelica. He held up the horses and reached down to pull her up. Her muscles screamed a protest as she crawled up next to him.

"Where do you think you're going?" he asked.

"With you."

The picking was over for the day. But his day was not over yet. If he was going to keep ahead, he had to crush the grapes they'd already picked before he could call it a day.

"Aren't you even going to try to talk me out of it?" she asked.

"Would it do any good?"

"No, but it'd make me feel better." She locked her arm through his and slumped against him in exhaustion.

He clucked to the tired team and reluctantly they moved out of the field toward the road. He was almost halfway there when he felt a lurch in the wagon. He glanced around to see what he'd run over and saw Rivera helping Muriella into the back.

"You damn gringo!" Benito muttered. He was huffing and puffing. "Better slow those *caballos* if you don't want to kill these poor old Mexicans."

Rafael felt tears coming to his eyes. Fanned out across the field behind him, every one of Rivera's crew was hurrying to catch up and hop onto the wagon.

As the wagon creaked and protested toward the winery, Rafael saw the double barn doors of the aging room standing open. Inside, coal oil lamps cast light that flooded out into the workyard and gave the winery a rich, warm glow.

Rafael reined the horses to a halt. Aching, the crew climbed down.

"Chihuahua!" Enrique whispered as he followed Rafael into the light of the winery. He'd never been inside a winery before, and the coolness, the fruity smell swept over his exhausted body like an elixir. "Must be how it smells in heaven."

They looked around the big, stone-walled aging room for some sign of life, but it was deserted.

Two floors up they could hear the shrill squeak of the basket press as someone turned the handle that moved the gear down onto the fruit until it was crushed. Then it stopped for a few moments while more fruit was added to the hopper. Again the squeaking sound.

The thick plank stairs that rose along the side of the wall seemed miles high as they all shuffled up toward the crusher.

Standing at the crank handle, covered with sweat and splattered from head to foot with juice that spurted from the sides of the press like a leaky hose, stood Giuseppe Ferrara.

"Hello, Papa." Angelica smiled, feeling a deep love for her father.

"Evening all," he said gruffly. He hardly looked up. He cranked the handle which turned the huge gear under which the fruit lay waiting to be crushed and reached for another tub of fruit. Before he could dump it over the wood-slat sides of the press, Rafael was at his side, lifting with him.

"I figured you'd probably be still trying to put them tires out and wouldn't be able to make it tonight," Ferrara said. "And long as Angelica . . . well . . . I mean, I didn't have anything else to do anyway."

"Sì, signore. Grazie!" Rafael smiled. He watched as the

clear juice from the almost black berries trickled into the pan beneath the press before draining into the line like a frothy mountain stream.

"Don't thank me. Thank my daughter." Ferrara turned back to the crank.

By the third day, Rivera and his crew had reached an orchestrated routine in which Rafael was more of a bother than a help.

"You can help better in the winery . . . or with *Señorita* Angelica," Rivera convinced Rafael. "Take Benito and this load to the winery. Stay there. Benito'll drive the wagon back from now on."

"Trust us." Benito complained. "We have done this work before. Remember?"

Rafael knew they were right.

After unloading the wagon and sending the beefy Benito back to the vineyard, he climbed down the side of the hill to the open storage shed attached to the winery where Angelica was tending the boiling cauldrons of sweet-smelling mess.

As he came around the corner, he saw her fanning herself in the shade at the end of the shed, trying to catch a breath of air.

"More . . . more!" she pleaded as he picked up an end from a cardboard box and helped fan her. Her overalls and work shirt were drenched.

"Please, Angelica," he said, suddenly worried by her paleness. "Sit down for a while. Cool off!"

"Are you kidding? I'm already behind schedule. Look at all those boxes stacked up over there."

"Angelica, please. Sit down. At least until the sweat stops pouring off you. You could get sunstroke . . . even die . . ."

"Women don't sweat!" she said indignantly as she sat down on one of the crates. "They glow!"

"Well, you're glowing so much you're leaving a puddle."

She laughed. "When the heat starts to get to me, I go stand under the hose."

He followed her glance. An old black garden hose was snaked through the rafters at the end of the shed, its brass nozzle dripping in a fine spray.

A hissing sound erupted from the stove.

"Come on," she said, jumping to her feet. "Give me a hand." She rushed to the cauldron. "What are you doing around here this time of day, anyway? Hiding so you won't have to work?"

"Naw!" he complained glumly like a little rejected boy. "They kicked me out of the field. Said I was just getting in the way."

He picked up an old shirt cut in half for rags, grabbed the wire handle, and helped her lift the pot off the burner.

"Well, don't think that I'm going to let you hang around down here and get in *my* way!"

As they walked together, carrying the cauldron, he could see the smooth, rounded white skin revealed by her half-buttoned shirt. His heart pounded and his groin ached.

He laughed and shook his head as the sound of a backfiring truck sputtered up the road toward them.

"What's so funny?" she grunted as they strained to carry the pot toward the cooling table.

"Nothing . . ." He held the handle while she tilted the end up and poured the batterlike liquid into a shallow tray.

"Probably sunstroke. I understand it makes you hysterical," she teased.

"Just seems to me like your father always comes just in the nick of time."

She looked up and felt her face flushing.

"He's a master at timing," she muttered. "It'll drive you crazy sometimes."

"He might not . . . but . . ."

"But what?"

"But you might."

"Hello, Angelica." Ferrara started tossing off a load of firewood that had been cut in short lengths and split so it would fit easily into her stove. "Thought you might be running out. So I brought you some I had extra."

Rafael started to jump onto the truck to help, but Ferrara stopped him.

"No sense'n us both doing this. Won't take me ten minutes."

Rafael nodded. He knew Ferrara was right. "Then let me pay for the wood."

"Nope. But as long as you're going to stand around for

ten minutes, you could take a look under the hood. See if you can't get all those cylinders to firing."

"Sounds fair." Rafael smiled.

"Course it is," Ferrara said gruffly. "Wouldn't offer it if it weren't."

A half hour later Rafael had the truck purring again. Ferrara was just finishing stacking the last of the wood next to the stove. As soon as he did, he rushed to help Angelica take one of the cauldrons off another burner and carry it to the cooling table. He shook his head and snickered. The concoction looked like lava as it oozed into the tray.

"What are you laughing at?" Angelica asked, while setting the cauldron back on the stove and refilling it from a bucket before it had a chance to cool.

"Just wondering what you're brewing up." He poked at a couple of the trays where the concoction had cooled and hardened. "Looks to me like them rubber mats."

"Never thought of that." She poked at one of the trays with her fingers. Its dark purple surface truly felt like a piece of rubber.

"Maybe you could make tires out of it."

"Funny! Very funny, Papa," Angelica said.

Ferrara was roaring with laughter now.

"What's so funny?" It was Rafael's turn to ask. Angelica, taking his hand and poking his fingers into the pan, explained, and he joined their laughter. It felt good, warm. He'd never known the old man to smile, much less laugh. Even if it was at his expense.

"Wouldn't make a bad mattress either," Rafael added.

" 'Cept on a hot night," Ferrara warned. "You start sweating and I guarantee you'll wake up in a pool of juice."

By now they all were in tears from laughter.

" 'Fore this sets up, you could add straw," Ferrara continued. "Once they harden you could use them instead of adobe."

"If we molded them like bottles," Angelica said, "we could sell them as bottles of wine. Let the people go crazy trying to figure out how to get them open."

"Not a bad idea," Rafael said. "Think of the money we could save not having to buy real bottles."

"Not to mention corks," Ferrara added.

"They have hard-rock candy. Why not hard-rock wine?" Angelica asked.

Everyone was finally laughed out. And Rafael saw the change come back over Ferrara. He was distant once again. A little more so now that he'd allowed a chink to show through his armor.

"Maybe we could make some money with it this way," Angelica said. She had begun to have another of her ideas. "Chop it into squares . . . like fudge. Let the people add water and presto! A fresh grape drink."

"Wouldn't be worth your while," her father advised. "Barely make it worth that with your jelly."

"Wouldn't have to spend any money on jars . . . sugar . . . or anything else," Rafael said rising to her idea.

"You can get one of those fizzy drinks now for a penny," Ferrara said, taking out his pipe and lighting it. "Besides, you go adding water back to it and who knows what it'd taste like."

"Weak grape juice . . . and unsweetened at that," Angelica nodded, starting to agree with him.

"In Italy, when I was a shepherd, my mother made something like what we're talking about out of grapes the Padrone allowed us to pick after the harvest. It stayed hard . . . unless you left it in the sun. She used to save it and bring a block of it out to where I was. Every now and then I'd cut off a piece and mix it with water."

"How'd it taste?" Angelica asked.

"Not bad." Rafael shrugged.

"Those fizzy drinks are made out of chemicals that taste like grapes. They don't taste bad either. And they sell for a lot less money than you could sell yours for," Ferrara said.

"Maybe we can sell it to people just like it is. They can add water and turn it back into grape juice . . . then into wine." Angelica started feeling enthusiastic about her idea again.

Ferrara and Rafael both smiled.

"When you boiled it, you killed the yeast," her father said. "It's the yeast in it that makes it ferment . . . makes it wine."

"I can sure vouch for that," Rafael said. "Once I was moving a flock of sheep to a high pasture and I forgot to

216

bring the bottle I had just filled with the stuff. A few weeks later, when I came back, I remembered where I'd left the bottle. It was hot, like now. And on the trail I kept dreaming of that bottle. I thought it had probably turned to wine by then. For miles I thought of how it was going to taste after I cooled it in the stream for an hour or two."

"So what happened?" Angelica asked impateintly.

"I sat for almost two hours on the side of the stream watching that bottle get cooler and cooler." Rafael saw Ferrara puffing on his pipe, already knowing what had happened. "My mouth was watering as I took it out and pulled the cork."

"And?" she pleaded.

"It was probably sourer'n vinegar." Her father laughed. Rafael nodded. "It was terrible."

"No yeast . . . no wine," the old man shook his head grinning.

"What if we put a little packet of yeast in with each block?" She asked. "Wouldn't it ferment then?"

"Probably," Ferrara agreed. "But there are two problems. Number one . . . what's it going to taste like? Number two . . . it's illegal."

"What could be illegal about selling our grape rubber and a package of yeast," she asked. "It's not wine. It wouldn't have to be wine. Unless the people wanted it to be."

Rafael stood in absolute awe of her. Her mind never stopped working.

"And making wine is not illegal, *signore,*" he added thoughtfully. "If you have a permit, you're allowed to make enough for your family."

"When they can buy grapes, why would they buy your grape rubber?" Ferrara asked.

Rafael thought about it for a while. Then he looked up. "Not everybody knows how to make wine. And they can only buy grapes one time a year. The way this rubber's cooked down, it won't spoil. So if we could get it to ferment, we could sell it all year round."

"Still sounds illegal to me," Ferrara insisted.

"But Papa. Rafael's right. It has to be perfectly legal. No one has to make wine out of it. It could be used like . . .

217

like lemonade." She beamed, but her father shook his head and scowled.

"Angelica. If it isn't specifically against the law, it for sure violates the spirit of the law."

Rafael looked at her and shook his head in exasperation. He didn't understand this old man's logic any more than that of the country. It was all right to make your own wine for your family. But you couldn't give it or sell it to anyone else. Even though those others could make it also and had the same rights.

"I think Angelica may have come up with something that the growers have been looking for all these years," he said.

"Even if you could do it, where you going to sell it?"

"Papa," Angelica said, "if there's anything that's a problem in this country, selling booze isn't."

"You mean bootlegging?"

"Of course not, Papa. But you know yourself that if you want a drink, all you have to do is go to the barbershop or drugstore. I'm just saying that this might be a way to make a few dollars from a crop that usually ends up rotting anyway. Can't hurt trying. Let's see what happens to our rubber stuff if we add back some yeast."

"Lotta smart people have tried to outsmart this Prohibition thing. They always failed. And most ended up in the clink. It needs Congress to give us a Constitutional Amendment. And that'll probably be coming down the road apiece."

"That could be years."

"Longer than that, more than likely. But you're heading for a pack of trouble, girl. I warn you . . ." He stopped. If he pursued it, they'd probably try it out of spite. "I got to be getting back to work." He turned abruptly and pulled himself into the cab of his truck.

"He's probably right," Rafael said to ease her discomfort at her father's sudden change in mood.

"Probably." She shrugged.

They watched as the truck disappeared into the heat waves shimmering up in the distance. They sat there looking at each other. One of Angelica's eyebrows raised impishly. "It wouldn't hurt just to try it out."

"Course not."

"I mean, we've got the grapes and it's only a little time wasted if it doesn't work."

"True."

"And it probably won't work anyway."

"Probably not," he agreed, not meaning it.

"Good!" she said with enthusiastic delight. "Then what are we waiting for?"

Rafael couldn't keep from laughing as she stormed determinedly toward the "grape rubber."

A week later, in the shadows in the back of the barn, Rafael and Angelica uncorked their experimental bottle of the grape-rubber brew. They knew it wouldn't be ready. But they had to find out if it was fermenting at all.

Rafael started to put it to his lips but Angelica stopped him.

"You're supposed to let it breathe for a little while."

"How long?" he asked.

"I think that's long enough." She giggled.

He put the long-necked bottle to his mouth and took a swig. He swirled it around his mouth imitating her father and finally swallowed.

She watched impatiently for a few moments waiting for his opinion. She started to reach for the bottle to try it for herself, but he held it away from her and took another, maddeningly slow sip.

She waited impatiently.

Suddenly he seemed to go into a convulsion . . . gagged, rolled his eyes up, and sank back unconscious.

"Rafael!" she screamed, grabbing his cheeks between her hands. "Damn you! Damn you!" she yelled when she felt him shaking with laughter.

"Scared you, huh?"

"Yes. I didn't know who I was going to get to try the next bottle if this one killed you."

They rolled along the floor, laughing. Finally, nestled in his arms, she said, "Well?"

"Well what?"

"What does it taste like?"

"So so." He squinted.

"So so, how? So so good? Or so so bad?"

"Didn't seem to take the white off my teeth. So I'd say

about halfway between the bottle that I had when I was a shepherd, and your Papa's."

"My God! Rafael, really?" She screamed in delight.

"I think it could use a little more aging though."

"What for? It already had a week." She buried her face in his chest, loving the hard feel of his muscles through his shirt. "Rafael . . . do you realize what this means? It really works!"

He nodded, delighted with her childlike excitement.

"I love you, Rafael," she said barely above a whisper.

He squeezed her until she thought he was going to crush her. "Thank you," he whispered.

"Thank you?"

"Yes . . . thank you. Because . . . I love you too." He reached down and gently kissed her.

It felt as though their lips barely touched. But she had never been more excited. Her heart pounded and she felt tears of joy in her eyes. He moved his head and kissed her gently on her neck . . . then her shoulder.

Gently, more gently than she would have ever imagined, he slipped his hand under her shirt and caressed her back. The thought never entered her mind to stop him. Carefully, he traced her back, brought his hand around to the front and pressed it gently over her breast.

Her nipple grew hard in his hand and sent his hand trembling. He picked her up and carried her into the cool shadows in the back of the barn.

CHAPTER FIFTEEN

"I need advice, *signore*," Rafael said.

"I'm not in the business of offering advice, sir. I'm in the business of interpreting the law." He was a small, nattily dressed man, nearly overwhelmed by his huge desk.

"Ah . . . *sì. Sì.*" Rafael smiled charmingly.

Warren Forsythe, ex-attorney general for the State of California, studied the young Italian sitting across from him. Forsythe hadn't wanted to see him. But the man had made five trips to his office in San Francisco from somewhere north of Santa Rosa. And two of his oldest clients, Paolo and Nicchio Pacheco, had called to ask if he could see him.

"I need for you to interpret something about my business."

The ex-attorney general listened, mesmerized as Rafael cajoled and charmed the man with his vision of how a variety of grapes, now ready for harvest and destined to rot on the vine, could offer a tremendous profit through a new product developed by the man and his partner. These profits were possible if the attorney general could lay out a course for them that would guide them around the possible legal pitfalls that might lie ahead.

Forsythe sat listening attentively as the young Italian led him through the presentation that he'd rehearsed with Angelica.

"And as to payment for your services, I hope you will consider participation in our organization . . . being at this very moment set up in the Sonoma and Napa valleys," Rafael concluded.

"I don't know who the hell . . . or what the hell you are," Forsythe said finally. "But I think I want to know some more about this project of yours. I haven't been flim-

221

flammed into working for nothing since Harvard." He extended his soft, manicured hand and they shook heartily.

A week later, Rafael was talking to Rivera as Angelica helped Muriella with the food on the camp stove. His harvest was over, but the crew, still working the area, remained camped next to his vineyard.

It had been an anxious week for Rafael and Angelica. They hadn't heard a word from Forsythe. They wanted to make a deal with some of the other farmers in the valley whose grapes still remained unharvested. But they didn't dare make any financial commitment until they heard from the lawyer.

They looked up as a new, shiny pearl-colored Oldsmobile slowed to pass the assembly of vehicles that was partially blocking the farm road.

The driver waved to the group and pulled into the weeds in front of one of Rivera's battered trucks. As they watched, a gray-haired man got out, put on his suit coat, adjusted his hat, and walked up the hill toward them. Rafael smiled and squeezed Angelica's hand in anticipation. It was Warren Forsythe.

Forsythe smiled and shook hands as he was introduced. Rivera's crew felt ill at ease because of the man's impressive appearance. But in only minutes, Forsythe had them relaxed, laughing, and feeling at ease.

"How'd you find your way here?" Rafael asked, pleased Forsythe had made the effort.

"Oh, dear fellow." He wiped the inside brim of his expensive hat. "Don't forget, I'm an old politician. Before I left that arena, if there was a warm body . . ." He paused. "Well, at least relatively warm . . . a body capable of voting, I could sniff it out. Additionally, I might add, I'm here for reasons better than those. I'm here because I believe . . . or have every reason to believe . . . you've hit on a product that has remarkable possibilities."

That evening, coatless and with shirt-sleeves rolled up, Forsythe sat on a box next to Rafael, as Rivera and his crew cleaned up after dinner.

"Fine meal, ma'am," he complimented the blushing Muriella. "As far as I can tell," he said, returning to Rafael, "I think I can guarantee you won't go to jail for it."

"See. Papa was wrong," Angelica said.

"The federal government may try to stop you. But the way I see it, they'd ultimately have to ban grapes totally. And I can't see that. Even in the New Testament, in the second chapter of John, Jesus changed water to wine. Right?"

"Right!" Rivera and Benito chorused. They'd have agreed with what Rafael wanted to do, legal or not.

"Besides . . . it's bound to help shore up some of the local economy. And, more important, provide some tax money for the local coffers."

"I don't know about those things." Rafael shrugged. "But if you say they're important . . ."

"Trust me. In the government's case, the product or issue is never important, or unimportant for that matter. It's only what they'll provide the community, state, and federal governments on the tax rolls."

Rafael looked at Rivera who shrugged as if Forsythe were talking Latin.

Forsythe smiled. "If Uncle Sam can make a buck, they won't mess with it," he said putting it in language they would understand.

"Why didn't you say so in the first place," Rivera said bringing out a bottle of tequila and a paper sack of limes. *"Vasos por favor, mujer!"* he called to Muriella.

It became almost a common sight the next week to see Rafael and Angelica passing each other on some out of the way crossroad as they raced the clock canvassing the valley looking for growers who still had grapes left for harvest. Often as not, when they saw each other, they wouldn't bother to pull over. They'd just stop in the middle of the road. Like children on a treasure hunt, they'd laugh, kiss, embrace, and compare lists.

They never beat around the bush with the growers. They came right to the point and told them they wanted to buy their grapes, would pay either top dollar or a share in the profits. They openly told each one what they planned to do with the grapes.

The growers liked the idea. And unlike Ferrara, they all felt it had a chance for success. Of course they could do the same thing on their own. But Rafael and Angelica were confident because Forsythe was already working on a market for their product.

Without exception, the farmers who accepted their offer took the money rather than the share. As much as they liked the scheme, they were cautious conservative men. They were happy with their unexpected little windfall of cash, courtesy of the line of credit arranged by Forsythe.

Angelica had been reluctant to allow Rafael to make theirs a partnership. She wanted nothing more than to be a loving supporter in his scheme. They were Rafael's grapes, she explained. But it was her idea, he countered. Without it, he'd be making raisins by now. She had finally agreed, saying she knew the real reason he wanted her as a partner: cheap labor.

A few of the growers who'd known Angelica since her birth took nothing. They said she and her partner could have whatever they could pick and haul off. It couldn't do anything but help the vines and make sure they produced another crop next year.

It was a wonderful moment for Rafael and Angelica when the grapes started arriving. From down the road to the Crystal Rock winery, a line of vehicles stretched, waiting to unload. Single- and double-horse teams pulled wagons loaded with grapes spilling over their rails; trucks pulled gondolas and trailers with sides boarded up to hold their load.

Even the thought of the grueling work and the terrible heat they faced didn't dampen their enthusiasm.

As the work began, Rafael insisted on doing the fire tending and the cooking in the six black-iron wood-eating monsters. It was Angelica's job to cut and weigh the "Angel's Butter," as Rafael insisted on calling it.

"Sure sounds better than 'Grape Rubber,'" he said before they wrapped it in cheesecloth and heavy butcher's paper for shipping.

Originally Rafael had intended to go on the road with their "butter" to peddle it from store to store, but Forsythe had stopped him.

"It would take months," he said. "By then Prohibition could be over."

"Then how do we sell it?" Rafael asked.

"Dear fellow. You leave the distribution to me. I've already been working on it. I have friends, relatives actually, who are already set up. They sell other products, true. But they're already in the business of sales and have salesmen on the road. Most important of all, they have customers! Customers just waiting for the goods."

"Well, you can believe we're going to have the goods," Angelica promised.

By the end of the second day, they were swamped. Everywhere they looked, there were grapes waiting to be boiled down into concentrate. Boxes, crates, baskets, even wagons were filled with them. Crushing the grapes and filling the vats wasn't a problem. But they had to get the "must," the newly crushed grape juice, from the vats into the cauldrons and boiling before it started fermenting. If it fermented, the Feds might come out, see what they were doing, and confiscate the whole mess.

As more and more loads arrived, Rafael felt like a man trying to hold back the tide with a bucket.

Shirtless and covered with soot from emptying the ashes of one of the stoves, Rafael turned as Rivera and Benito stopped in the glow outside the shed next to the winery.

"How's the big businessman?" Rivera grinned at his sweaty friend.

"Planning a vacation to the French Riviera and South America on one of them luxury liners." But Rafael couldn't afford the luxury of stopping to talk. All the stoves were belching smoke into the starlit night and he was rushing from one cauldron to the other to stir them so the grape mixture wouldn't stick and burn on the bottom.

"Where's your partner?"

"She had to drive the Evangelistas back home. They didn't need their wagon. So they said we didn't have to unload it till later."

Rivera and Benito each pulled up fruit boxes and leaned back on them against a wagon parked near the shed.

"Nice to see a man who's worked his way from the fields to the top and is now *numero uno*," Rivera grinned cockily to Benito.

"*Si.*" The big man nodded. "He gets to the top and it's 'Easy Street' from then on."

Rafael stopped for a moment and looked into the darkness at his two friends' grinning faces.

"You two busy?" he asked, wiping his chest and arms on his shirt that was hanging on a nail.

"No. Why?" Rivera shrugged. "You need some help?"

"No. But if you're not busy, I'd like to hire you just for the pleasure of firing you."

Benito and Rivera both laughed as they stood up and pitched in to help.

With their help, the work seemed to fly.

"Okay," Rafael said as they emptied the last cauldron just after midnight. "You're both hired. If you want jobs, that is."

"You were right," Benito said as he unbuttoned and pulled the shirt-sleeve out of his wringing wet shirt. "You always told me. Work hard enough and you'll get out of those dusty, hot fields someday."

"You sure you're going to be able to take all this easy life?" Rivera asked, fanning his face with his straw hat as the rivulets of sweat poured down his neck.

The next two weeks, Rivera split his crew up. Half of them kept harvesting the crops in neighboring farms. The other half worked with Rafael and Angelica. Hauling, crushing, boiling, emptying cauldrons, chopping the rounds of wood into kindling so it would fit in the cookstoves.

It was like the old days. They were all a family again. Complaining, insulting, moaning, laughing, sharing.

"I arranged for a warehouse earlier this week. Though God only knows why," Forsythe said one day after driving up from the bay. He tried to stay out of everybody's way as he escorted a wide-eyed young lady, at least twenty years his junior, through the hubbub of activity. "The orders are already coming in," he said as Rafael passed straining under a load of firewood. "As a matter of fact, we're getting them so fast I don't think we're going to have anything to store . . . except maybe our money."

Rafael was skeptical about the way Forsythe just assumed the money would come rolling in. Superstition, if nothing else, kept him from talking about profits.

But finally the end was in sight. Most of the wagons and

gondolas had been returned, the firewood chopped, and it was almost time for Rivera and his crew to be on the road again, chasing the crops that ever needed harvesting. The coals in the stoves were approaching ashes as Rafael and Rivera cleaned up after the long day's work.

"Won't be long now," Rivera said.

"I think we finally have it licked." Rafael nodded.

"That's good. I am happy for you, *hermano mio*."

"Thanks," Rafael said, slapping him on the back as they started for Rafael's car.

"If your partner from San Francisco is right, the money should be rolling in soon."

"Money never rolls in," Rafael scoffed. "I think there's a few wishful dreams mixed in with his reality," he said, as he steered down the hill.

"Well, if he's not dreaming and the money comes rolling in, what then?"

Rafael looked at him and smiled. "I send for my mother and sister."

"You'll be able to go back to Italy and pick them up in a big limousine. Benito and I will even drive it for you."

Hardly a day passed that Rafael didn't think of his mother and Alicia. He wondered how they were and worried about them. How much had his little sister grown in the nearly six years since he'd been gone? He ached for word from them. He often wished there was some way they could have answered his letters over the years. But until now, he'd never been in one place long enough. And there was the chance that the Padrone might find out where he was. So, until he was able to send for them, it was safer for all of them the way it was. Soon, though! he promised himself.

"I don't think I could go back for them," he said.

"*Por qué no?*"

"It might be a little too risky."

Rivera nodded. He understood the risk of returning to one's homeland.

"Not for me. But for my mother and sister." As they drove toward Rivera's camp, Rafael told his best friend the story of what had happened to his family.

Rivera sat there in silence after Rafael had finished.

"I'm sure you will see them soon." The whiteness of his teeth flashed in the darkness. "I can feel it in my old bones."

"I hope those old bones are right."

"They always are. But I'm afraid that it also means we won't have the honor of meeting them."

"Why not?"

"Because, *hermano mio,* tomorrow we must be on the road again."

"No. You can't leave."

"Why not? Can't you handle the rest without us?"

"Of course. But tomorrow, we're celebrating. The fair is opening down in Santa Rosa. And Angelica and I are treating. You . . . the whole crew . . . have to come."

"Sounds good. It's been a long time since we took time off. Maybe it'll do everybody some good. Stop some of the complaining."

"I doubt if anything would stop your crew from complaining."

They both laughed.

"Besides. You haven't got any choice," Rafael said.

"Why not?"

"Because I haven't paid you yet. And I'm not going to till after we've celebrated, had some fun, and maybe a few drinks! Dinner's on us. I hear they have some fantastic barbecue. They've been cooking whole steers in a pit for almost a week, they tell me."

Dressed up in a stiff starched shirt, studs, and straw skimmer, Rafael walked arm in arm with Angelica down the midway of the carnival section of the county fair.

He'd never seen such a sight in his life. It was a miniature magic city. Banners and colorful hand-painted signs showed men swallowing swords, ladies with giant snakes, tattooed women, fire-eaters, even a half-man–half-woman.

Everywhere barkers, hawkers, and shills tried to challenge, dare, and even coerce them inside a sideshow to see harem dancers from the Arabian desert who looked suspiciously American, or freak shows that cost an extra dime.

Passing under a brightly painted banner of a muscled man with a whip, they stopped in a crowd of people gazing at an iron-barred red cagewagon where a half-maned lion gnawed on the glistening white joint of a meat-covered bone. He looked a far cry from the roaring savage beast depicted on the canvas sign atop the cage.

The fields around the fairgrounds had filled with an assemblage of stake bed trucks, dust-covered sedans, two- and four-horse wagons and a sea of black Model-T Fords.

The harvest season was over in the valley. Crops had been shipped, gardens stripped, their contents stored in mason jars on a shelf in a pantry. The fields lay empty, ready to be plowed and planted with a winter crop.

The women were also done with their sewing and canning. Everywhere, everyone seemed to be filled with a holiday spirit.

As isolated as most of the farmers in the area were and as little as they saw of each other, there was a great camaraderie and competitive spirit among them. True, they had come to relax and play and have a good time. But they had also come to show off new kids, pies, cakes, and canned goods for judging. Most of all, the men came to show off their prized livestock. Bulls, sheep, hogs, and horses had been bathed and groomed.

Wide-eyed, knee-scraped children held onto older brothers or sisters in fear of being lost in the huge crowd as they gazed with longing looks at the amusement rides. There was a haunted house, a tub filled with little boats that went in a circle, a Tilt-a-whirl, a cyclone centipede, and the biggest and brightest ride, a Ferris wheel.

Everywhere booths were set up with glasses, vases, dishes, and crystal of all shapes and descriptions. Housewives lined up to pitch a penny into them to win something for their kitchen.

At the head of the midway, a huge red, glass-encased calliope boomed, tromboned, and rang music that added to the din. And everywhere, exasperated mothers yelled threats as they tried to peel cotton candy off Sunday clothes or to pull it out of matted hair.

Rafael had never been to a fair before. He was as wide-eyed and excited as most of the children. He and Angelica stopped near the line that was waiting to get into one of the twelve baskets of the Ferris wheel.

"Want to take a ride?" she asked.

"You bet."

"It's more romantic at night," she winked.

"I hadn't thought about that," he grinned. "I just wanted to see it up close to see how it worked."

He yelled in wounded glee as she pretended she was going to strangle him.

As their basket reached the top and started back down the other side of the arc, Rafael cheered like a kid on his first ride. He put both arms around Angelica and squeezed her, filled with a sudden, heart-bursting joy.

"Isn't it wonderful?" she laughed, hugging him back. The wheel stopped and the basket swung gently back and forth as the grease-covered operator gave everybody a brief stop at the top before releasing the brake.

"Angelica . . . Angelica!" A distant voice called from the basket above them as the little engine strained to turn the giant, red, white, and blue decorated wheel.

Craning around, she saw Sue Vinson, her best friend since first grade. Next to Sue sat a curly-haired young man with a smile that seemed to cut his head in two.

Rafael raised his arm to wave at Angelica's friend. The basket swung dangerously back and forth.

"Oh God, Rafael" Angelica shrieked. "Don't wave . . ."

"Hey . . . I bet we could get this thing to turn a complete flip." He shifted his weight and started the basket swinging dangerously.

"Don't you dare!"

"What?" He laughed. "I can't hear you."

"Rafael! I'm warning you!" she screamed grabbing him around the neck and hanging on for dear life, as he roared in delight at her terror.

"What's the matter?" he teased. "I thought you liked it."

"You're not going to if you don't stop."

"Why not?"

"Because I'm getting sick." Angelica laughed now as Rafael grabbed the metal strut and quickly stopped their swinging.

"This is Frenchy," Sue said as the two couples made their way down the sawdust-filled midway.

"Hello, Frenchy," Rafael smiled returning the man's hearty handshake.

"He's a trucker," Sue said. "Got his own truck and everything."

"Sounds like a good deal," Rafael said.

"I hear you got yourself a pretty good deal too," Frenchy said. "Congratulations!"

"Can't be sure yet. But we think so," Rafael nodded.

"Say, if you ever need anything hauled, I'm your man. I've got my own truck'n everything. Like Sue says, I'm an independent. I'll haul anything . . . anyplace . . . anytime. That's my motto."

"Thanks. I'll keep that in mind."

Even though the sun had set, the sky was still a beautiful pale blue and the moon shone brightly in the predark sky. Rafael and Angelica were sprawled, exhausted, in the grass in front of the white, gazebolike pavilion after spending the afternoon racing from one ride to another, from one booth to another, from one sideshow to another. As they watched, the uniformed high school band filed in, tuned up, and started playing a concert for the picnickers who were gorging themselves on fried chicken, potato salad, baked beans, and cake provided by the local church.

Rafael grinned and nudged Angelica as some of the farmers tried to make their rusty waltz steps match the tin pan alley and ragtime songs adapted for a band heavy with flutes and clarinets.

"How about you, Orsini?" Angelica asked, wiping the fried chicken off her fingers on her napkin.

"How about me what?"

"Dance . . . you know?" She twirled her fingers in a circle. "Surely they dance, even in Italy."

A pained look crossed his face. "They might. But I haven't been there in a long time so I can't say for sure."

"Come on," she said pulling him reluctantly to his feet.

He started to protest but she kept yanking. He led her into the center of the dancers where he hoped he'd be as inconspicuous as possible and took her in his arms. He fumbled and bumped and twirled Angelica as he tried to lead her in his charade of a dance. On a truck next to the road, he heard a generator roar to life and the string of lights throughout the midway and on the pavilion flickered on. A cheer rose from the crowd.

"Not bad," Rafael said as they swayed close together during a slow number.

"Wanta bet?" she asked, faking a limp.

Rafael tilted his head and roared with laughter. Angelica felt ecstatic. It was wonderful to see him having such a good time.

She hooked her arm through his and they walked back toward their blanket.

"I guess it's almost time to call it a night." He sighed reluctantly as several groups around them were gathering up sleeping kids and dogs and heading across the field toward where they were parked.

She nodded and started gathering their belongings.

"Got a busy month ahead of us," he said, "Not going to have any time to sit around and dance and eat."

"Do you have to remind me?" She picked up the blanket and handed him one end so they could shake it out.

"Got to finish the last of the grapes."

She nodded as she stuffed their napkins and chicken bones into a paper sack.

"Load the stoves on the truck and get them back . . ."

She grimaced at the thought of the hours they had spent in the shed working in the grueling heat from the iron monsters.

"Angel Butter to cut and weigh. Boxes to pack."

"Boy! You really know how to thrill a girl. I can hardly wait."

"Then . . . there's flowers to buy." He folded the blanket under his arm, took her by the elbow, and started through the remaining dancers.

"Flowers?" she said. "What do you need flowers for?"

"I don't think you can have a wedding without them."

"Wedding . . . flowers?" She stopped as she suddenly felt her heart pounding. "What are you trying to say, Rafael?"

"I was trying to say . . . I love you."

She tried to put her arms around him, but the blanket got in the way. It fell in the dirt and they both bent to pick it up.

"You're not doing this very well, you know?" she said softly as she brushed the blanket off and stuck it back under his arm.

"I know," he admitted, standing there like an embarrassed schoolboy. He finally continued. "I was wondering . . . well . . . if you wanted to get married?"

She shook her head and broke into laughter as he dropped the blanket again. "If we don't, who in the world is ever going to be able to take care of you? You're helpless without me. You know that."

He nodded as she brushed the blanket off again and stuck it back under his arm.

"If you want . . . I mean . . . maybe you need some time to think about it. Think it over. You know what I mean."

"I don't need any time. I already thought it over."

Rafael nodded, waiting for her answer.

"I was starting to think I was going to have to ruin my reputation and ask you," she said, leaping up in his arms and kissing him. They broke apart as several people sitting on a blanket near them started cheering and clapping.

"Do you mean it . . . I mean . . . are you sure?"

"Yes, Rafael. I'm more sure of that than anything in my life."

Rafael hitched the blanket securely under his arm, and pulled her to him. He was ecstatic. He had never realized anyone could be so happy; he never thought he would have a life that was going so perfectly.

They were halfway through the crowded midway before Rafael realized someone was calling his name. He searched the crowd before Angelica finally located Benito and Muriella and their children waving from a shooting gallery where Ramon, Enrique, and Rivera were lined up trying to win kewpie dolls for the kids.

"We're getting ready to leave. So why don't you come out to the truck with me so I can pay you. Before I run off with it," Rafael warned.

"Oh, *Señor* Rico," Ramon said squinting and resting the battered little rifle on his hip like a bandit. "We trust you. *Verdad*, Rivera?"

"You still better get it while you can," Angelica warned. "He's going to be needing a lot of money in the next few weeks."

"If he needs it, it's his," Benito croaked, thinking she was serious.

"You need more grapes, use our money. It's yours," Rivera added.

"He won't be needing it for grapes," Angelica said.

"Then for what you need it, *hermano*?" Benito asked.

"Oh . . . for flowers . . . and dishes . . . and pots and pans . . . and linens . . ." Angelica smiled proudly as she slipped her arm around his waist.

Muriella shrieked with joy and rushed to Rafael and threw her arms around them both.

Giuseppe Ferrara sat picking at the tablecloth.

"I think it would be wise for you to wait for a while. This will pass . . ." he said without looking up at his daughter who was sitting across from him.

"Wait for what to pass, Papa? I'm not a schoolgirl with a crush on a schoolboy. I'm in love. Deeply in love with this man. My whole body, my heart, and soul feel empty when he's not around. Can't you understand?" She reached across the table and took his hands in hers. "Please, Papa. Say yes."

He let his hands stay between hers, but he wouldn't answer.

"Papa. What's wrong?"

"I just think he's the wrong man for you. You deserve better. What can he offer you, Angelica? Believe me. Nothing! Someone better will come."

"Someone better? Papa, he's loved by his friends. He's honest . . . and you've even admitted that you've never seen a harder worker. As for what he can offer, he offers himself. That's enough."

"It should be more."

"It's enough."

"I won't argue with you about him, Angelica. It's just something inside me."

"You can't hate and distrust every man who smiles at me and looks like he looks . . . because of Mama!" she said.

Ferrara looked at her as though she'd hit him.

"What do you mean?" he said weakly.

"You know what I mean, Papa. You let hate ruin your life. Please. I'm begging you. Don't let it rub off on mine."

"I'm sorry. You know how I am. Once I form an opinion, I'm damned if I can change it."

"You're going to have to change it, Papa," she screamed at his stubbornness. "You probably lost Mama because of it. Don't force me to make a choice."

He looked at her, and a terrible loneliness filled him.

"Papa. I'm of age. I don't need you to say yes. But I want you to say yes. I want you there. I want you happy. We both do. And we both want you in our lives."

"Why?" he said as tears rolled down his cheeks.

"God only knows," she said putting her arms around him. "You're a grouchy, cranky old man. But we love you."

"I'll try, Angelica," he said embracing her for the first time that either could remember.

"Thank you, Papa." Relief flooded through her. Her father had finally faced the pain that had haunted them both all their lives.

"I can't promise, though."

She laughed and shook her head. "Just try, Papa . . . that's all."

CHAPTER SIXTEEN

Carlo Gianini sighed in contentment from the warmth that penetrated the room from his fireplace. It was good as always to be home in Montepulciano again. It was a place of security to him. The only place nowadays he could let down his guard and relax. He had originally started going north to Switzerland, France, Belgium, Austria every three to four months. But as his businesses flourished, the trips had become so frequent that Maxmillian had convinced him to move his headquarters to Zurich.

Now he visited Montepulciano only every three or four months. And the reason for that was Alicia. She dominated a part of his mind. And now he was threatened with the loss of that. He'd learned via a cable from Dominic that the postmaster was dying. Carlo knew that soon the little man would be obsessed with saving his soul by confessing and making amends and so would be beyond any threat a young Padrone could make. Alicia would discover the treasure that existed in the form of letters and money from her brother.

He shrugged. He would be losing control over her life. The domination over her very existence. But not for long.

For in the end, her discovery of that treasury of words and money would once again bind her to Carlo. For through those letters, Alicia would lead him to her brother. He should have allowed her to discover them sooner, he thought.

The stench from the little postmaster's cancer filled the room as the priest came into the garret that had served as the man's home for half his lifetime.

The priest covered his mouth and nose with a handkerchief, thankful he'd wrapped a small bead of incense in it.

He'd come to give the man the Last Rites. But he prayed to the Virgin to soothe his nausea.

The little cell of a room reminded the priest of the cell he'd occupied at the seminary. This room was bigger, but as spartanly furnished, with a single mattress with dirty stained ticking. The postmaster's eyes fluttered open and he stared at the brightly painted statue of the Virgin Mary which stood under his crucifix on the wall next to his mattress.

"Bless me, Father, for I have sinned . . ." the man's voice was a feeble whisper as with a trembling hand, he made the sign of the cross.

The priest nodded and clamped his eyes shut as he folded his hands under his nose in prayer and desperately inhaled from the handkerchief between his palms.

The priest thanked God that he could keep his eyes closed as the man rattled on, searching his soul, trying to confess every sin he'd committed so he could be absolved and enter the Kingdom of Heaven.

". . . and I have committed the most unpardonable of sins. Against the family of Orsini. Because of me, the mother died mad and the daughter . . ." Tears flooded the sunken eyes at the thought of Alicia. "A child once filled with life."

The priest nodded and was filled with anger as the man's confession droned on. He'd threatened him many times before during confession that if he truly wanted to obtain Jesus's forgiveness, he must go to Alicia with the letters from her brother in America. He had told the man he must beg forgiveness of the Virgin. Each time the man had promised fervently. But each time after leaving the confessional, he'd been visited by Dominic . . . and had failed.

This time, they both knew he was beyond Dominic's threat.

"Please, Father, give the letters to the girl . . . and beg her to pray for my soul."

Alicia sat nervously clicking her brightly painted fingernails as she sat across the desk from the priest. Even in his presence, she didn't bother to button the silky blouse that barely covered her breasts.

The priest's pain at what she'd become was almost uncontainable. He blamed his own personal weakness for not being able to persuade the little postmaster of the need for God's grace. If he could have convinced the man to have courage and to go to Alicia with her letters, she might have been spared her terrible life.

She stared at the letters in the worn cardboard box. Tears started streaming down her cheeks. She was consumed with rage at Carlo Gianini for what he'd done to her. But as the priest read her the letters, the words from her brother swept through her body and were as soothing as a cool breeze on a sun-drenched day. She was not abandoned. She was loved.

"The most recent letter is not from your brother, but from a woman whose name is Angelica Ferrara," the priest said as he unfolded the thin paper from the envelope.

Alicia studied the strong, bold handwriting that filled the pages as the priest read it for her.

"She and your brother are planning to wed. They live in a place called California . . . on the Pacific Coast of America."

The priest stopped for a moment as Alicia searched her string bag for a tissue to dry her tears.

"She wants to surprise Rafael and have you and your . . . your mother there at their wedding. She wants it to be a surprise, and a wedding gift for him. She's enclosed a draft that covers the two passages from Naples."

Alicia stared down at the draft from Angelica and the paper money neatly stacked under it from Rafael.

"At last, you will be able to leave this place."

"I've never needed money to leave." Alicia said, still staring at Angelica's letter. "The money I've . . . earned, I've kept. It's considerable. I just never dared leave for fear Rafael would return and find me gone."

The priest nodded as he folded the letter back into the envelope and pushed the boxful of letters and money across the table to her.

"No matter, my child. Your nightmare is over. The two of you . . . the three of you now, can be united."

"Father," Alicia said softly, "for the first time in a long time, I'm afraid."

"There's nothing for you to fear now. I promise you, your destination will remain a secret. It is safe with me."

238

"Thank you, Father. But it's not Carlo Gianini I fear. More than him, I fear myself . . . what I've become."

"Trust in God, my child. It's his will that your life is changing."

Alicia shook her head in confusion at the combination of pain, joy, relief, and hate that flooded her heart.

"I will say a mass for you," the priest said.

"Thank you, Father." She started to stand but sat back down. "I need a favor. For you to write a letter to this kind lady for me."

The priest nodded and reached into a drawer for paper and pen.

Angelica wiped the tears from her eyes as she put down the letter from Alicia.

Rafael's mother was dead. The one time in their lives that should be filled with joy was suddenly threatened with pain. She thought of how much she'd suffered at having to tell Rivera about Maya. This was even worse. This was Rafael. Her man. Her love. Her entire life.

"God! Help me be strong," she pleaded silently.

Rafael wiped his forehead. The heat under the shed was scorching as he watched Angelica driving up the road, but he was still filled with joy and amazement at the thought of her becoming his wife.

He leaned into the window and kissed her gently.

"No hug?" he protested when she didn't respond.

She shook her head.

"What is it, Angelica?"

She looked at him but couldn't answer.

"Come on." He opened the door and took her hand to help her down. "Let's get in out of the heat. Besides. I want you to taste something."

Silently, hand in hand, they went into the cool interior of the winery.

Angelica closed her eyes for a moment and let the aroma from the fermented sacramental wine sweep through her.

"I just finished racking the red for the last time." He led her to a barrel of ruby clear wine ultimately destined for a mass or a wedding in a Mexican church.

The cement gutter in the floor was filled with sediment from the dregs of the vat Rafael had emptied into the barrel. Rafael had planned on leaving the wine in the vat a little longer to let a little more of the sediment filter down to the bottom. But Ferrara, with the wisdom of years of experience, had advised him to get it into barrels as quickly as possible so it could start aging.

"What's the matter? Couldn't you find the right dress?"

"Yes . . . I mean no. I mean yes, I found the dress." She felt warm at the thought of it. It was lacy, a golden cream color. "Rafael, I had a surprise planned for you as a wedding gift but . . ."

"But you changed your mind about getting married." He grinned. "Well, my little love, I'm afraid it's too late. You can't change your mind now."

She threw her arms around his neck, and he felt her crying.

"Angelica . . . what is it?"

"Rivera and the crew and I were going to send for your mother and sister so they could be here for the wedding. He said they owed you more than money and that might help repay a little of it. But when I wrote . . ."

Rafael felt the hair on the back of his neck tingling.

"Rafael . . . your mother is dead," Angelica said clutching him to her.

Rafael felt as though he'd been gored with the white hot horn of an enraged bull.

"When?" His eyes filled with tears.

"Almost two years ago."

"My God! My God!" He cried as the pain and guilt of not being there swept through him, chilling his soul.

The two of them stood clutching each other in the dim light.

"Alicia?" Rafael asked, dreading what must also have happened to her over the years without him there to protect and care for her.

"Fine. She's fine. She left the same day the letter I got was mailed from the priest."

CHAPTER SEVENTEEN

Angelica stood quietly as Rafael anxiously paced the platform waiting for the train to arrive at the depot in San Francisco.

As the train hissed, belched, and shuddered to a halt, Rafael treaded through the crowd searching the faces for a fawnlike little girl barely in her teens. As the rush of passengers started thinning out, he became panic-stricken that she'd become lost somewhere during her journey from the east coast.

"Alicia?" Angelica said to the beautiful young woman.

"Sî. Angelica?"

"Sî," Angelica answered, and they crushed each other in an embrace.

"Rafael Orsini. May I introduce you to your sister." Angelica grinned as she tapped him on the shoulder.

Spinning around, Rafael was struck speechless.

"My God!" He finally recovered and swept her into his arms. "You're grown . . . and you're beautiful. I wouldn't have recognized you . . ."

As she returned his embrace, she still couldn't believe it. She'd waited for what seemed a dozen lifetimes for this moment.

Angelica cried with joy at the sight of the two in each other's arms. All three clung to one another and hugged and laughed as they made their way down the platform through the crush of travelers toward the baggage department.

A week later Rafael stood like a grinning fool next to the railing that separated the altar from the pews that were jammed with a host of faces—friends from towns and farms throughout the whole county. Old school friends of

241

Angelica's, farm families, Rivera's crew, the Pachecos; even Forsythe was there with a delicate, wispy-haired blonde whom he introduced as his fiancée.

The small frame church seemed filled with a din that totally engulfed Rafael's senses. Suddenly the din ceased as the organist sitting in the choir loft started playing the prelude to the wedding march. In unison, all the heads turned to watch the procession that headed up the steps toward the aisle.

Rivera saw his friend's face turn ashen as Alicia came into view. His sister, Angelica's maid of honor, was radiant. She was absolutely beautiful as she floated toward him in a soft, flowery gown she'd insisted on buying herself.

Rivera placed a supporting hand on Rafael's elbow. Rafael tried to smile thanks to his best friend, his best man, dressed for the first time in Rafael's recollection in a baggy suit and a white shirt whose collar had been starched and ironed to stonelike perfection by Muriella.

As Alicia turned toward the side of the altar, she smiled at her brother, and the joy of years surged between them.

There was a blur of motion and Angelica, on the arm of her father, started up the aisle, a delicate picture of lace and flowers. Smiling faces and tear-filled eyes followed her as she moved toward the bridegroom.

Rafael's head pounded. It ached with joy. He'd never seen anything more beautiful.

Her father stopped and nodded to Rafael. After a nudge from Rivera, Rafael extended his arm. She slipped hers through his and they turned toward the waiting priest and the four altar boys.

In his whole life, Rafael had never felt so nervous. So dry-mouthed. He tried to follow the ceremony as the priest read from the ornate little book, but his ears were filled with a ringing and the only identifiable sound he was aware of was of his heart pounding. The priest's vestments, his Latin blessings and benedictions were blurs to Rafael. He spoke his "I do's" after becoming aware of the heads turning toward him waiting for his responses. When it came time for the ring, he was suffocated by sudden terror. Where was it? He felt Rivera nudging him and when he turned, saw the ring in his friend's hand. He was almost afraid to take it; his palms felt as though rivers of sweat were running from them. He locked his fingers around the delicate little band of gold and reached for Angelica's hand.

He was enchanted by the beauty of her fingers as he started to slip it on. He smiled: her hand was trembling nearly as badly as his was. He looked into her eyes and realized she was as nervous as he. But when it came time for her to put a ring on his finger, her hand was warm and firm once again.

Finally, he lifted Angelica's veil, and their lips touched. He felt dizzy, almost as though he was going to lose consciousness. But a burst of organ music filled the church and brought him back to reality. The next thing he knew, he was walking back down the aisle with his new wife.

Rafael was still in a state of shock during the reception that followed, but Rivera took charge of his grinning mute of a friend and led him toward a line of waiting friends who pounded him on the back and crushed his hand in congratulations. But despite the friendly chaos, there were few moments when Rafael wasn't staring at his new wife, in disbelief that his life should be so fulfilled.

Angelica was delighted that Rivera seemed to be hovering around Alicia. But although she was cordial, Alicia seemed strangely unmoved by Rivera's charismatic charm. Perhaps, Angelica thought, it was because everything, everyone was so new, so overwhelming, so strange to her.

"Take care your brother . . . my husband," Angelica pleaded to her in Italian. "Bad men try to take him away . . . get him drunk," she warned.

Alicia smiled and nodded her understanding. She was thankful the days since her arrival had been filled with the preparations for the wedding. That had allowed her to soothe her brother's fears and concerns about her years alone in Montepulciano—given her the chance to distract him with inquiries about Angelica, the farm, his years in America. She had managed to keep the focus off herself.

At first, she had felt confusion, even a certain resentment at her brother's good fortunes. It seemed as though all the family luck had gone to him. But during that week, she had learned what a desperate struggle his own life had been. And she was glad that he had found this lovely, smiling woman who treated her as a true sister. This woman whose language she was determined to learn.

Across the room, everyone, including Ferrara, Forsythe, and the Pachecos, along with dozens of people Rafael barely recognized, kept toasting him until he was barely more than a smiling mummy. He'd concentrated so hard on not letting Rivera and Benito get him drunk that he'd fallen easy prey to all the others. Angelica should have been furious, but she knew his ultimate condition was part of the gift of the day from his friends.

The shadows lengthened and the hour their guests should have departed came and went unnoticed. Rafael wove his way precariously through the blur of figures toward Angelica.

Drunk as he was, he couldn't keep the tears from his eyes as he put his arms around his new wife. His whole body tingled with love and pride. Angelica laughed as he slurred sweet nothings into her ear. Leaning on her for support, Rafael surveyed the assembly of friends and couldn't believe the good fortune that this new country had heaped on him, A wife, whom he held in precious awe, his beloved sister and Rivera and a host of friends. Even Angelica's father seemed resigned to happiness.

"May I have a few words with you Orsi . . . Rafael," Ferrara said taking him by the elbow and guiding him away from Angelica.

Rafael draped his arm around Ferrara as they walked back into the peace and quiet of the church. It was as much for balance as from affection. But it felt comfortable just the same as they slumped down in a pew.

"I haven't been exactly kind over the past year or so," Ferrara said.

Rafael started to protest, but Ferrara held up his hand and stopped him. "It's the habits of an old dog unable or unwilling to learn new tricks."

"It's a natural thing, *Signore*. You didn't know me. Who I was . . . What I was . . . anything."

Rafael had difficulty keeping from slurring. But he didn't want Ferrara to think he couldn't handle a few drinks.

"Whatever the reasons, I want you to know that I realize . . . well . . . that you've brought a whole new world to Angelica. Oh, I know she was happy before in a lot of ways. But you gave her a different kind of happiness. One I could never give. I think that's what frightened me. That someone else could give her something I couldn't."

"But you're the dearest thing to her. You gave her life . . ."

"Quit trying to be so damned philosophical, Orsini. You're just trying to placate me."

"No . . . s'not true." Rafael tried to focus on Ferrara's eyes.

"Then what are you trying to do?"

"Trying to act like I'm not as drunk as I know I must be," Rafael said with a big grin.

"Trust me . . . you are." Ferrara grinned back.

Rafael nodded, as Ferrara looked at him and shook his head. "She loves you . . . damned if I can figure out why."

Rafael looked at the old man and saw a faint smile cross his face.

"And I know you love her," he continued. "So that's good enough for me. I'm going to try to change the old dog. But if for some reason I can't, well . . ."

"Knowing you would try is the greatest gift you could give, *padre mio.*"

"I want the two of you to be able to start out on the right foot. So I want you to have another gift," Ferrara said, taking an envelope from his inside suit pocket.

"This was originally for Angelica. It's been hers for several years now . . . since she came of age. She and I had the county clerk change it. Now it's for both of you."

Rafael slipped the envelope open and took out the heavy document. It was a deed to Ferrara's house and the vineyard that Rafael had rented.

He embraced his new father-in-law and tried to hold back his tears.

"By the time you get back, I'll have my things moved out," Ferrara said.

"You can't do that," Rafael protested. "It would take away some of our joy. If it is our house, it is yours as well."

"Don't be ridiculous, Orsini. The last thing you'll be wanting is someone around to side with your wife when you two start arguing. It's best to be able to have your disagreements in private . . . and solve them alone."

"I can't imagine ever fighting with your daughter."

"Just wait!" Ferrara roared with laughter. "Besides, I'm only moving into the loft over the winery. I won't be that far away. You won't be able to yell and argue that loud."

"This house will ever know joy," Rafael promised.

"I intend to hold you to that. Now . . . I think it's about time you gave some thought to getting out of here," Ferrara said, standing up and stepping into the aisle. "If you stay much longer, a few of your friends are going to make sure you don't have any time together your first night."

Rafael stood unsteadily and nodded.

"Why don't you slip on down to my truck? If you think you can find it, that is. I'll get our girl in gear and have her slip off so you can make a dash for it."

"I think I better wait here." Rafael was afraid to walk very far, at least without help.

Ferrara nodded and made his way back into the crush of smiling, chattering drinkers to Angelica. Rafael watched as he whispered in her ear. She embraced her father, kissed him, and started back through the crowd toward Rafael. Suddenly she veered and stopped in front of where Rivera was talking to Alicia. She whispered something in his ear, and Rafael could see the big toothy grin flash across his face. The grin turned to a frown of disappointment, but finally Rivera nodded agreement and with Alicia in tow, followed Angelica toward where Rafael was waiting, trying to keep from swaying.

"Your friend here and some of your other buddies have some really terrible things planned for you this afternoon," Angelica said as she locked her arms around his waist.

Rivera shrugged sheepishly.

"Especially if they can keep you drunk enough to keep on hanging around. So I figure the best way to escape is with him as an escort. That way, it won't look like we're leaving."

"In that case, what are we waiting for?" Rafael slurred.

Arm in arm, the four of them made their way through the crowd toward the escape offered by Ferrara's truck in the shade of the driveway.

"You sure you don't want to stop by my car and have a little drink of tequila for luck?" Rivera grinned maliciously at Rafael.

"Oh no, you don't, Rivera." Angelica answered for her husband as they reached the truck.

"Just for old times' sake?" Rivera asked innocently.

Rafael embraced his old friend. "One of these days, *hermano mio*, I'm going to slip you something . . . for old times' sake," he warned.

"Rafael," Angelica said, slipping behind the wheel. "If you don't get in, I'm going on our honeymoon without you!"

Rafael grinned sheepishly at Rivera. "I have to go now . . . my wife won't let me stay any longer . . ." He slipped in as Rivera roared in laughter behind him.

"She's already got you trained good," Rivera said.

"And he's going to love it," Angelica said as her and Rafael's hands closed together.

It seemed like an eternity before Rivera could crank the engine to life. As soon as he turned the crank, the crush of guests realized the bride and groom were trying to escape and poured out and surrounded the truck.

As Rafael tried to shield them from the storm of rice thrown through the open windows, Angelica ground the stick into gear and roared down the driveway. Suddenly, she stepped on the brakes. half opened the door, and threw her bouquet to a surprised Alicia standing next to Rivera.

Alicia crushed the flowers to her and threw a kiss and a wave to her new sister. She truly felt now a part of this new life in this new country.

Angelica and Rafael were halfway down the street before they realized the terrible clattering racket that followed them was made by the several hundred cans Benito, Rivera, and Angelica's father spent hours attaching to the rear bumper.

BOOK
FOUR

CHAPTER EIGHTEEN

"Mr. Orsini's here to see you, sir," the secretary said into the shiny new intercom, which was Forsythe's newest toy. In less than a beat, Forsythe threw open his office door and with arms extended, embraced Rafael.

"Come in . . . come in," Forsythe beamed at his young partner. "How's little Pietro? And the twins? And where's your beautiful wife? I thought you promised to bring her with you the next time you came down to the Bay."

"Pietro's already learning the alphabet and to count," Rafael said proudly, always ready to brag about his chubby, already spoiled son. "And the twins will be out of diapers soon. Angelica's here, of course. Alicia stayed with the children so we could spend some time alone."

"Then where is Angelica?" Forsythe asked as they headed into his inner office.

"Shopping. Where else?"

"Amazing how women seem to come down with that fever the minute they cross the city limits. How was your trip down?"

"Hot! And of course we had our allotment of two flat tires."

"You should invest in a new car. As a matter of fact, I happen to know where you can get a hell of a deal on a slightly used Oldsmobile," Forsythe half joked. He'd just bought a new Cadillac convertible and hadn't sold his old Oldsmobile yet.

"I don't need a car like that. I probably couldn't even haul a ton of grapes in that thing of yours. Much less three wild kids," Rafael said as they went through Forsythe's office into a conference room where the secretary had set up a small buffet for them.

"I thought we could eat while we go over the accounts,"

Forsythe said. "And while I tell you what I think we can expect now that the country's finally come to its senses."

"It's true then?"

Forsythe nodded. "It'll take awhile for all the states to ratify the Amendment, of course." Forsythe spread hot mustard on sourdough bread to enhance the thinly sliced beef. As they ate they sipped beer that Forsythe always seemed to have on hand, despite the Treasury department. "But in the meantime, growers can go ahead with plans for beer . . . whiskey . . . gin . . . and wine! Good wine! Real wine! Not this foul concoction we've been peddling."

"We've improved it each year," Rafael protested as he bit into a juicy peach he'd been eyeing all through lunch.

"Of course. I don't mean to take away from what you and Angelica accomplished. But it would have sold regardless of whether it was good or not. People wanted to drink. They needed to drink. Especially after the '29 crash. And they're sure going to go on needing to drink as long as this damn Depression lasts. They may settle for Angel Butter. But they want the real thing."

Forsythe looked at the strong young man sitting across from him. He envied him his youth. Contemporaries had often warned Forsythe to marry and raise a family, but he never had. Oh, well! It wasn't so bad He had already become surrogate grandfather to Rafael's and Angelica's three children. Especially to Pietro. Every time the boy saw his car, he ran to it, eyes ablaze, and usually out of breath.

"You've dreamed about it for a long time," he said. "Your own wine . . . your own label."

Rafael nodded.

"I wish I could tell you the joy I've received being able to share your dreams."

"Without your help, they would all still be just dreams."

"Bullshit, Orsini!" Forsythe said. Rafael looked at him. It was unlike the man to swear. "You'd have found a way."

They smiled quietly at each other.

"I assume you want to file for a winery permit from the Treasury department and the state. Even though the states haven't ratified, they'll allow crops in the ground or on the vine to be harvested for future production."

"I want to, of course. But first I'm going to have to talk it over with Angelica."

"There is something you should consider," Forsythe said. "For the next year . . . maybe two . . . maybe longer, everyone's going to get in on the craze Every company, large and small, will be putting liquor, beer, and wine on the market. This has never been a big wine-drinking country. Wine could be a loser."

"It's about time we changed all that."

"You could be wiped out in the process of trying," Forsythe warned. "Or end up selling your wine for whatever you could get. Cheap jug wine more than likely."

"And you could be wrong and we could make a killing," Rafael said confidently.

Forsythe nodded. "Then you could take time off to enjoy some of that money you have squirreled away."

"Do we have money squirreled away?" Rafael asked. "I'll have to talk to Angelica about that. I think maybe she's been holding out on me."

Forsythe shook his head. No matter how much money they ever saved, he doubted that Rafael would ever take time off.

He remembered going over the accounts with Rafael just after their first season. He could still see Rafael's face as he opened the brown manila file and slid it across the desk to the young man.

Attached to the top of the statement was a check made out to Rafael for eleven thousand dollars. Rafael's hand had trembled as he held it.

"If you added together all the money my father and his father before him and his father befcre him made in their lifetimes, it wouldn't come to this much," he said quietly, almost sadly. Even after paying Ferrara, the Pachecos, and the other farmers, Rafael would have almost a third of it left as profit.

"A small . . . but significant success," Forsythe had said. "The first thing you're going to do is feel guilty. But just remember. You and Angelica slaved for this money. The second thing you'll do is decide that you want to make a lot more. So you can protect what you've already earned."

"Thanks for telling me. It'll save me a lot of time." Rafael paused for a moment then looked up and smiled. "Now that I'm through with the guilt, let's get on with the making more."

Forsythe smiled.

"As long as the two of you have to discuss it, why don't you do it over dinner?" Forsythe asked. "Be my guest. That'll make up for the shopping bills this trip cost you."

"That's a deal."

"Good. I'll make reservations for you. I know just the spot."

Angelica put her knife and fork down and wiped her mouth carefully on the linen napkin. It was the first time she'd worn lipstick. The saleswoman had warned her that some women smeared it over half their faces when they ate.

She glanced down at the napkin and saw the impression the lipstick left on the cloth. She was delighted she wouldn't have to wash it.

"Is madam finished?" the waiter who was hovering close by asked.

"Yes." She nodded self-consciously. She wasn't accustomed to such service. Nor was Rafael. But Forsythe had not only made the reservations for them, but had preordered their dinner as well.

Rafael picked and pushed and rearranged the food from one side of his plate to the other.

"Rafael!" Angelica said sternly as though talking to one of the children.

He looked up with a start.

"You finished?" Angelica asked, folding her hands and leaning her chin on them.

"Yes. I guess so," he said, and the waiter promptly picked up his plate and disappeared across the room which sparkled with light from the candles and crystal chandeliers.

Angelica moved a bud vase filled with fresh flowers so she could look directly at her husband.

The waiter returned with a chafing dish in a copper pan. He placed it on a cart at the side of their table, and with a flourish, poured several ounces of liquid into the dessert he was preparing.

He struck a match and the flames from the liquid ignited into a beautiful flame. He spooned the flames over the cherries and smiled at Angelica, who was wondering where he got the brandy to burn so needlessly.

"Monsieur," the waiter held the dish close to Rafael for approval.

"Oh . . . no, thanks. I've already had plenty."

Angelica giggled at the man who indignantly looked to her for approval.

"What's so funny?" Rafael asked innocently, as the waiter ladled out the sweet-smelling concoction.

"A little preoccupied?" she asked.

"Does it show?"

"It shows," the waiter said under his breath but loud enough for them both to hear as he placed the dessert on another dish in front of them.

"What's the matter with him?" Rafael asked when he was gone.

"He's just upset you didn't enjoy the meal."

"Well, he's wrong. I enjoyed every bite of it."

"Oh, really?" She raised her eyebrows as he dug into the dessert. "What was it?"

"What was what?"

"What was it you ate for dinner?"

"When?"

"Just now."

"You mean just now . . . tonight?" he asked, searching around to see if he could spot his plate for a clue.

"Yes . . . just now . . . tonight."

"Well, I don't know what they call it. Here, I mean . . . in this restaurant." He grinned as he squirmed uneasily. "But it was definitely the best I ever had fixed that way."

Several people looked up as Angelica's giggle echoed through the quiet restaurant.

"Okay, Rafael," Angelica said as they walked arm in arm down the street. "Out with it. What's bothering you?"

"What makes you think something's bothering me?"

A cable car came toward them and they ran toward it.

They hopped on just as it slipped over the crown of the hill and started down the other side. Rafael handed the conductor the fare and hung precariously out the side as the fire-engine red car jolted and rumbled down the hill.

"This is the year," he said, swinging back in and looking at Angelica who was still patiently waiting for his explanation. He swung back out, then ducked inside as another cable car going the opposite direction clanged past. "At least it is . . . if you think it is."

"It's true then," she said as she threw her arms around him. He held them both on by hanging onto the brass railing.

"Forsythe thinks so. He's going to apply for a winery license for us. But I told him I had to talk to you first."

"About what?"

"Well, you know. Our own wine . . . our own label."

"Of course. We've talked about it. If you want to do it, I want to do it. And I want you to do it."

Rafael let go of the brass rail with one hand and hugged her, "I know. But I still wanted to talk to you first. Because it's got to be us. You and me together. And if you had any doubts . . . I mean because of the kids or anything . . ."

"Rafael, I haven't got any doubts. At least I don't now. So quit trying to give me some. You don't have to convince me. I'm your wife . . ."

"We'll have to watch our step for a while. Forsythe said the market could be flooded with cheap wine for the first couple of years."

"So? We pinch our pennies for a while. We've done that before. If things go wrong, they still won't be as bad as they already are for a lot of people."

"It could be very bad. We could lose it all."

"We'd still have each other," she said snuggling into his arms. "And our family."

The cable car jerked to a halt in front of their hotel and they hopped off.

"I do love you," he said as it clanged into the night.

She looked up at her husband. She had never felt so happy.

* * *

256

Rafael nursed his overheated truck through the traffic that clogged San Francisco's hilly streets and northward out of town toward the ferry. His mind was a whirlwind as he tried to organize his plan for the harvest.

He could feel his heart beating faster at the thought of their own wine, their own label.

"Wine!" he said to Angelica sitting next to him. "Not Angel Butter!"

She smiled back and took his hand until he had to shift again.

Rafael drove over the double set of railroad tracks where the passenger train from the east had just pulled into the depot.

"First thing next week, I should look for another truck," he said, expecting an argument.

"Of course" She had barely looked up.

Rafael shook his head, knowing she was lost in her own dreams and plans. What he didn't realize was that she'd been trying to convince him of the need for a new truck for months now.

As the truck bucked and groaned over the tracks, he could see the red warning lights from the rear of the train that was easing into the station.

On the train, a huge man with close-cropped gray hair stared out a window. He was watching the porters pulling heavy carts along the caisson toward the baggage cars. He was still amazed by the size of the cities the train had passed through on its way west. This truly was an enormous country. An easy country to get lost in.

It had taken more than a week to cross from New York on the Atlantic to San Francisco on the Pacific. His body ached from the endless hours in the hard seat. He stretched his cramped legs, anxious to be off the train.

He stood and picked up a rumpled paper sack and a small suitcase and made his way toward the rear of the car. Other passengers moved aside for the tall Italian. Those who had made the trip in the same car knew him to be silent and unfriendly. At the various scheduled stops, when they'd gotten off to eat and stretch, he'd remained in his seat, alone and aloof. Actually, he had been afraid to leave the train, afraid it might pull out without him. Besides, he had come to this country because he had a job to do. And he'd been warned to do it as quickly as possible.

Now for the first time since his voyage had started three weeks before, he felt a sense of relief. He was close to the place where the man he was seeking was known to be.

It had taken a bishop to coerce the priest into telling where Alicia Orsini had gone. The bishop understood what the loss of financial support would mean to the church had not the information been made available to Carlo Gianini.

As soon as he could locate Orsini, Dominic would cable the Padrone who would join him. He swung down onto the concrete platform and headed toward the ornate Spanish-style station.

CHAPTER NINETEEN

As the harvest approached, Rafael was worse than an expectant father. Even Angelica found it easier to stay out of his way.

All over the valley, gondolas were hitched behind chugging three-wheel tractors and pulled to waiting crushers at a dozen wineries that had reopened. When the gondolas returned empty, the tattered army of migrant pickers filled them with fruit piled in apple baskets, lugs, burlap sacks, lettuce crates, and even dishpans.

Some of the fruit was going to the scales at Italian Swiss in the northern end of Sonoma, an hour above Santa Rosa. That was the largest winery in the counties of Napa and Sonoma; its giant concrete fermenting vats held hundreds of thousands of gallons of the newly crushed grapes.

In his vineyard, Rafael held a cluster of grapes to his nose. The aroma was deep, almost like that of the heavy preserves Angelica made each year with the grapes that ripened after the Angel Butter harvest. He pulled several of the grapes from the stem and popped them in his mouth.

He smiled. Tomorrow would be his time to harvest. Returning toward the house along the irrigation ditch, he went over his plans for the hundredth time. He would deliver and crush all the grapes at the winery Ferrara had deeded to them. When they fermented, he would transport half of them to the Crystal Rock winery, which he still leased from the Pachecos, for storage and aging.

They were crushing a lot of grapes. Making a lot of wine. But it would be special. It would be pampered, looked after, nurtured until that magical time when he put it in a bottle that bore their own label.

Before dawn, Rafael was already stalking the rows that

were to be picked. By lantern and headlights, he set out the wood lugs that Rivera's crew would fill with fifty to sixty pounds of grapes. He filled five-gallon cans with fresh water to quench their thirst and covered each one with cheesecloth to keep out the dust and insects. As the crew straggled into the rows, bundled in layers of clothing to protect against the early-morning chill, he positioned empty gondolas every few rows so the lugs could be emptied into them and the two-horse team could pull them to the winery with little loss of time.

As the gray dawn crept into the sky, and the crescent-shaped, razor-sharp blades flashed, cluster after cluster of purple, sunburned fruit fell into the lugs and were rushed to the gondola. A few hours later, the sun burned off the fog and the heat of the day descended from the tops of the burned hills to the valley floor below.

The crew stripped off their extra layers of clothes until they were down to thin shirts, pants, and sandals. By halfway through the morning, their faces and hands were covered with a sticky layer of dust and juice that left them looking as though they'd been attacked by some bizarre growth of mold.

"Hey . . . what's the matter?" Rafael yelled driving up with an empty gondola he'd just emptied. "You missed a dozen vines down at the end of that row."

"Bees!" Benito croaked, grimacing at the thought of how he'd almost picked his way into their hive before a swarm of the angry little creatures forced him into a hasty retreat.

"Oh!" Rafael said dejectedly. He'd have to get a fire going to smoke them out long enough to pick the vines around their nesting place.

Unhitching the empty gondola, he backed the team up to a full one, filled with grapes that looked like clusters of dust-covered marbles.

He started to complain that there were too many leaves in the pick, but he knew if they were careful for anyone, it was for him. He was determined to make a sweet, rich wine, though. And leaves and stems would make it bitter.

He clucked and slapped the lead horse on the flanks and rolled toward the winery. The jangle of his harness warned Angelica and Alicia that he was coming back with another load. They fixed the bandanas around their hair and stuffed their pants back into their rubber boots and went out to the dock to meet him as he positioned the wagon so that he could dump it almost on its side and spill the grapes into a big wood hopper that led to a new type of crusher he'd designed and built during the last months before the harvest. Stripping the tired engine out of the old convertible that had brought him into the valley, he had mounted it on two railroad ties and connected the shaft to a galvanized worm gear at the botom of the hopper. When he cranked the engine to life, it turned the gear and fed the grapes into a basket that not only crushed them but also separated out the stems and leaves.

Up and down the valley, wineries and growers were talking about his new invention. Men from all over Napa and Mendicino and as far away as Modesto had taken time off to come by and look at this new type of crusher.

"You could make more money building crushers than from making wine," Ferrara had said.

"Anyone can make money. But very few can make good wine," Rafael had answered.

"Very poetic," Angelica had said. "Did you make that up?"

"No. I can make machinery. But not poetry. I read it somewhere."

Now as the engine shuddered to life, Rafael could see the sediment-filled juice, the "must," flowing from the bottom of the crusher pan into the thick hose that led to one of his ten foot high redwood fermenting tanks. Some of the other vintners used concrete tanks. But he didn't like the idea. He felt the wine liked the cradling effects of the soft wood.

When the hopper was empty, Rafael switched off the engine and walked inside the winery to talk to Ferrara.

"How's it look?" he asked. Ferrara stood on a ladder leaning against one of the open-topped tanks staring down into the cap, the shriveled raisiny-looking mass of skins, seeds, and pulp that floated on the top of the liquid.

Rafael dragged another ladder over and climbed up next to him to look down into the tank.

Ferrara had a hose that was connected to a giant tap just above the bottom of the tank. He was pumping the fermenting juice from the bottom of the tank, back over the cap. It was necessary to pump the new wine back over the cap twice a day so that the color from the skins would dissolve, giving the new wine the deep burgundy color they wanted.

"Looks like a batch of crushed grapes to me," Ferrara said playing the spewing nozzle back and forth over the mushy cap. "Let's just pray the weather holds. So it won't get too hot and kill off the fermentation."

At this stage of the winemaking process, heat was their worst enemy. As the wine fermented, it produced both alcohol and carbon dioxide. From the top it sounded like someone delicately dropping sand on a canvas tarp as the bubbles broke out of the surface below the cap. But it was a deceptive sound because the process created heat that had to be dissipated.

Ferrara leaned a little too far over the lip of the tank and almost lost his balance. Rafael grabbed his sleeve and pulled him back.

"Thanks! You saved my life," Ferrara said, sticking the hose through the thick cap so it couldn't whip around. He wiped the sweat off his forehead and rested his elbows on the tank for a few minutes.

"Little dizzy, huh?" Rafael asked.

"It's that gas the new wine gives off," he said. "Couple of fellas over to Napa were out on a plank breaking up the cap on one of those giant tanks one day . . . gas got to them . . . both of them fell into the tank without a sound."

"What happened?"

"To the men or the wine?"

"Both."

"Killed the men . . . but it added extra body to the wine." Ferrara howled.

Rafael shook his head at being set up for the man's joke so easily. It *was* funny. But he knew more than one man had died from the effects of the carbon dioxide.

Rafael climbed down and was out the door while Ferrara was still laughing.

"What happened?" Angelica asked, as he came into the sunlight. She was hosing down the crusher's worm gear with fresh water.

"You father set me up," he said sheepishly.

"Not the extra body added to the wine?"

" 'Fraid so."

"Do you know how long he's been trying to get someone to bite on that joke?" She giggled.

"I was just trying to make him feel good."

"Oh sure you were!" she said, turning the spray from the hose on him.

As a soaked Rafael slapped the team back up the hill, a cooling breeze fluttered across the vineyard, making the leaves ripple like green waves on a miniature ocean.

He dropped the empty gondola and looked around for some sign of life in the vineyard, but no one was in sight. It was time for the noon meal and everyone had gone back to camp to eat in the shade of the eucalyptus grove.

He looked at the half empty lugs. The temptation was too great. Rivera's crew was paid by volume picked. Rafael picked up an empty lug and started picking for them in their absence. As he worked, he could see in the distance the smoke from the campfire where Rivera and his crew lay exhausted, waiting for Muriella to dish up her mouth-watering creations.

Every day, they allowed themselves the luxury of cold soda pop. Today it was Benito's turn to drive into Healdsburg to pick up the cases of bottled drinks from the little store that smelled of sawdust, coal oil, and leather.

On the way back, he would stop at the ice house and buy a fifty-pound block and chop it over the bottles and head back before lunch was over so they could quench their thirst with something cold before having to go back into the gruesome afternoon sun.

"Damn!" Benito swore under his breath. His radiator was spewing water like a geyser. As he rounded the curve that led up the hill there was a bridge where he knew a running creek was still flowing. He crossed the bridge and pulled off into the dirt.

As he stepped off the running board, he noticed a dust-covered little coupe parked in the shade on the other side of the road.

A large man, with his suit coat off and his shirt-sleeves rolled up, was eating from a rumpled sack as he cooled off in the shade. Benito nodded to the man as he dropped down the bank toward the rocky stream. He'd just about filled the rusty gallon can when a shadow fell next to where he was stooped. He turned and looked back up into the sun. All he could see was the man's huge form as he smiled down at him.

"Hola, señor," Benito said, turning back to his can as it filled.

"Your car have hot," the man said with a thick accent.

Benito nodded. *"Sí* . . . yer, she is *muy viejo* . . . old. All the time she gets very hot," he said slowly using almost pidgin English.

The man nodded and folded his arms across his chest. "You need for I can help," he offered.

"Gracias," Benito said handing him up the can and clambering up the slippery path.

Benito unscrewed the radiator cap and started pouring the water in as the big man watched.

"You worker for here?" the man asked.

"Sí," Benito smiled. "Here and *muchas otras* places." He motioned north and south with his arm.

The man nodded. "I work . . . same as you." The man made chopping motions at the dirt with his arms and held up his hands so Benito could see that they were as cracked and calloused as his.

"You want work with me?" Benito asked. "This time of year, many strong men are needed."

"No . . . *grazie.* I be here on vacation. Am just here for to rest and eat."

"You very lucky man," Benito said as the water gushed back out, overflowing from the radiator. He threw the can back in the car and screwed the cap back on. *"Peones* here . . . much work. Never vacations."

"There are families *Italianos* what live close by here?" the man asked, sweeping his arm in a circle in the direction Benito was going.

"Sí. Many farmers. Many winemakers."

"Any named Pignatelli . . . Cimone . . . Orsini . . . or maybe Bruzzi or Pacegrande?"

Benito thought for a moment and shrugged before shaking his head. "I no think so. Maybe . . . how you say . . . Bruzzi. But others, I no think I ever hear of. Is possible.

But I only work in fields. Hardly ever know names of families unless they work in fields alongside us."

Out of all the names, Benito knew only Rafael's. He'd been in the valley many times: none of the other people the man named lived in this valley. Benito felt that for some reason the man was just throwing out the first names that came to mind, except Rafael's. Whatever it was that made Benito suspicious, he wasn't going to give the man any information.

"You looking for some of your family in this valley?" Benito asked.

"No. Just *paisanos*. Old friends."

"*Bien.* I have bad day ahead." Benito shrugged, wiping his hands on his pants and climbing back behind the wheel. "*Buena suerte!*" he said as he forced the truck in gear and chugged off.

"You never saw him before?" Rivera asked as they worked side by side down the dusty row. "You sure?"

"I'm positive," Benito answered. "I'd remember this one for sure. He smiles but his eyes are dead. And he's big. Bigger than me."

Rivera nodded as he worked down the row remembering the time Rafael had told him about why he'd left Italy. "You think maybe we should talk to him? See what he really wants?"

"His little coupe was covered with dust. So I doubt if he's sitting back there waiting for me to come back. You going to tell Rafael?"

"We have to. It might be nothing. Or a friend that's trying to look him up. But if he isn't . . . then we're close by."

"*Si.* That's for sure." Benito said. No matter what, if it was in their power, Rafael and his family would always be safe.

"What's the matter?" Alicia asked Rafael as he stared down at the tank of newly crushed must. The fermentation had started, but the cap hadn't started to form yet. From where he stood, it looked like a frothy strawberry frappe served up by the local soda fountain. But this one moved. And as he watched it, the liquid looked as if someone was rowing it from below the surface to make it swirl back and forth.

"Nothing." He smiled, trying to hide his concern.

"Rafael, I'm your sister. You can tell that to Rivera. Maybe even your wife. But not me."

He climbed down the ladder and walked with her to the cool of the aging room.

"Benito met a man today. An Italian who was asking if he knew us."

"*Dio!*" She whispered as her heart surged in fear. Carlo Gianini's smiling warning that he'd always find them rang in her head.

"Alicia," he said, taking her in his arms, "Alicia it could be anybody. I've been here a long time. It could be one of a dozen men I've worked with who I invited to look me up." He could feel her trembling.

"It's the Padrone," she said in a near panic.

"No," he said holding her. "There's no way he could know where we are. And even if he knows that it was California, California's one of the biggest states in the country."

"It's the Padrone!" she said, refusing to be calmed.

"If it is, then let's welcome him," he said grimly. "I'm tired of feeling my heart jump every time I look over my shoulder and see a stranger staring at me. If it's the Padrone, he's a long way from the safety of Montepulciano."

Alicia nodded. But her heart was filled with dread.

From then on, she refused to be away from her brother's side. At first Rafael was irritated by her rabbitlike fear. But as the days passed, he realized she was drawing strength from him. He represented her safety and security.

The weeks were filled with searing heat and backbreaking labor as Rivera and his crew worked along with Rafael, Angelica, Alicia, and occasionally Ferrara. Far into each night they could be seen trying to finish the harvest and crush while the grapes were at their peak.

Finally, the vineyards were stripped clean.

The only thing left to do was to pump the new wine into the settling tanks, press the cap to wring out the last precious few gallons of wine before discarding the pomace, the almost dry skins, seeds, and residue left over after the final pressing.

It was the last grueling part of the work. After they drained the wine from the fermenting tanks, Rafael had to climb down inside the tanks and shovel the pomace out into a wheelbarrow before pushing each load to the press. It was hot, sweaty, smelly, gnat-filled work at the bottom of the Burgundy-stained redwood tank.

By now the gnats had taken over every nook and cranny in the winery. Even the walls looked as though they'd been sprayed with a film of tiny gray specks. When disturbed, they hovered in a cloud over the tanks and piles of already discarded pomace like a foggy mist. The gnats were the only thing about winemaking Rafael hated. As soon as he had some time, he'd try to figure out a device to get rid of them.

Rivera volunteered to leave Benito behind until the fermenting tanks were shoveled clean and scrubbed out to await the next season. Rafael knew his friend was being overly kind, and only wanted someone near Rafael in case the Italian turned out to be some kind of threat.

"You sure you don't want him to stay?" Rivera said, not daring to push it, lest Rafael know of their concern.

"My friend, it would only be a luxury."

"So . . . you can afford a few luxuries now."

"Not at someone else's expense. I know how much work you have lined up."

"I could come back in a couple of days and pick him up . . ."

"No. Thanks, I appreciate the offer. But if you left him, within a week people would know it was Benito and not you that did all the work."

"How'd you get so smart?" Rivera protested. "Well . . . *hermano mio,* we'll be back through in a month or so. If you need us before then, just holler."

"The light's always burning in our windows for you," Angelica said.

"*Gracias, hermana mía.*" Rivera smiled. "*Señorita,*" he turned to Alicia. "It has warmed my heart to spend this little time with you."

Alicia blushed from the unexpected compliment.

"When I return, will you do me the honor of taking dinner with me?" he asked.

Before Alicia could answer for herself, Rafael said, "She accepts."

"That was mean," Angelica said as Rivera's flickering taillights disappeared down the highway into the darkness.

"What was mean? Accepting dinner for my sister?"

"No. Not letting him leave Benito."

"Mean? I'm the one who ends up doing the work instead of Benito. How do you figure I'm the one being mean?"

"He only offered so he could come back and pick him up."

"Why would he do something like that?"

"So he could see Alicia again," she said shaking her head. "I swear Rafael. You get married and the first thing you do is forget all about romance."

"I never thought about that," he said meekly. "You think maybe he's sort of sparking a little over Alicia?"

"If you have to ask . . ."

Rafael was delighted. He couldn't wait for Rivera to return so he could ride him as unmercifully as Rivera had teased him before his marriage.

Rafael turned off the lights in the winery after pumping the fermenting wine over the cap the last time. Finally his long day was done. As he neared the barn, he heard a car approaching. It passed the lane that led up to their house and slowed. He could tell by the sound of the engine that it was new, well-tuned, and powerful.

He heard the driver shift into reverse and the whine of the gearbox as the car backed toward their driveway.

Standing in the shadows at the side of the house, he watched as it slowed and cautiously made its way up the bumpy ruts and stopped just out of the light from the porch light.

It was a big sedan and in the darkness it appeared threatening. It sat there idling for several moments. Suddenly he heard the window being cranked down and he could see the shadow of a head leaning out.

"Rafael Orsini?" He was bathed in the beam of a flashlight.

He spun toward the light and faced a man in a rumpled suit and battered felt hat who stood in the darkness near the winery.

"I'm Agent Ames. That's Agent Thompson." He nodded toward the sedan as the other man stepped out toward them.

"What can I do for you?" Rafael asked.

"We're here to investigate a complaint against you. About the illegal production of wine in violation of the Volstead Act," Ames said.

"I'm afraid you're investigating the wrong winery," Rafael said, still not taking his eyes off the two men.

"This is your place, isn't it?" the other agent asked as he stepped between Rafael and the house.

"Yes, but there's no illegal wine here."

A knowing look passed between the two agents.

"All right. There is wine here," Rafael admitted. "This is a winery. And we just finished harvesting. But none of it's illegal."

"Hear that, Harry?" Ames said to his partner. "There's wine here, but it's not illegal."

"I'm telling the truth," Rafael said as his apprehension turned to anger. "We've got a temporary permit for it until this 'Repeal' is ratified."

"Well that's wonderful," Thompson said. "That'll sure solve the problem then. As long as you have a permit."

"Speaking of permits, I wonder if you'd show me your identification."

"Good thinking, Mr. Orsini." Ames smiled, reaching into his coat pocket. He took out a wallet from next to a heavy shoulder holster and flipped it open for Rafael to see. Even in the dark, Rafael could see the shiny brass badge.

"Now," Agent Ames said, "if you'll be so kind as to return the courtesy and show us this permit of yours in return, then we'll be able to call it a night."

"Of course," Rafael said, turning toward the house. "It's inside. If you'll just wait a minute."

"I'm afraid one of us'll have to go with you," Ames said blocking his way.

"Why? There's no one inside other than my wife, my sister, and my children."

"Well, that could be a fact. But every now and then, well, people go in and never come back out."

"This is ridiculous." Rafael's voice betrayed his growing anger. "What are you being so hardheaded about? You know it's only a matter of time before wine and everything else is legal again."

"That's a good point," Ames said. "I'm sure you're right. But until Repeal's a fact, we've got to do what we're paid to do. Now you'll either get that permit or have someone bring it out."

"Angelica!" Rafael called toward the house.

Inside the living room, Alicia heard his voice. Angelica was tucking the children in bed, so Alicia went to the door to answer.

In the darkness, all she could see was Rafael cornered between two men standing next to an expensive-looking, moss-green sedan. Her mind exploded in panic.

"Rafael!" she screamed, trembling. In panic, she flung open the hall closet and grabbed Ferrara's old shotgun from the corner.

Whirling, she crashed through the screen door toward where her brother stood. She leaped off the porch toward the car with the dark-green color that was nearly the same as Carlo Gianini's Bugatti.

"Holy shit!" Ames yelled a warning. Fumbling for his revolver, Agent Thompson felt frozen in his tracks in horror.

Rafael whirled and stepped between the men and Alicia. As she rushed toward them, he grabbed her around the waist, spinning her around. He grabbed the shotgun with one hand and smothered her against his chest with the other.

"Drop it! Drop it, lady!" the terrified Ames was screaming as he finally freed his long-nosed thirty-eight-caliber revolver.

"Alicia . . . Alicia! It's all right!" Rafael shouted.

"*Il Padrone!*" she said struggling to break free and grabbing at the shotgun.

"No, Alicia. It's all right. It's just some men . . . some authorities from the government."

"Rafael!" Angelica cried as she rushed out onto the front porch after hearing the commotion from the twins' room.

"*Dio . . . Dio!*" Alicia sobbed, sinking to her knees as her terror turned to nausea.

Angelica hurried down to them, still not knowing what was happening.

"Okay, lady. You hold it right there!" Ames yelled stopping her in her tracks as he tried to regain a measure of control over the situation. "All of you. Hold it and put your hands over your heads."

"What is it?" Angelica asked Rafael as she stared at the menacing revolver pointing at them.

"Alicia thought it was someone from the past," Rafael said as he lifted his sister and guided her into Angelica's arms. "But they're just agents from the Treasury department."

"What do you want?" Angelica asked.

"Your permit for your wine. Orsini here says you got one."

"You've got to be kidding!" She was suddenly angry. "You mean to say you come out in the dead of night and scare people half to death for a damn permit for something that probably won't be illegal by the time you get back to your office?"

"Lady, you may be right," Ames said almost embarrassed. He hated his thankless job. It wasn't like working in the Midwest where they got to bust in on the mob's breweries. Out here, most of the time all they did was shuffle paper and try to stem the flow of illegal sacramental wine. They'd known about the Orsini place for a long time. Especially since the Orsinis had started making a fortune selling their "Angel Butter" stuff and getting away with it. They'd been waiting for them to make a wrong move or step out of line. And they were sure this was that time. "But until it's all nice and legal, you'll have to have a permit same as everybody else. Now Orsini here tells me you do have one. So if you'll just be so kind as to let us have a look at it, we'll be on our way."

"It's at Forsythe's," she said quietly.

"Who's Forsythe?"

"Our attorney," Angelica said.

"I see. It's at your attorney's." Ames was suddenly relieved that they weren't on a wild goose chase. Their patience with the Orsinis was going to pay off. "And where may we find this attorney, ma'am? I mean, he is close by, of course."

"I'm afraid not. San Francisco."

"San Francisco!" both men said almost together as they grinned at each other. Ames turned away, flipped on his flashlight, and signaled into the night.

Up the road, three more trucks roared to life and shot toward the house. They skidded to a halt, and a dozen more men jumped to the ground like a squad of assault troops. They raced to the winery and with fire axes started battering the heavy wooden doors.

"Wait a minute!" Rafael shouted, running toward them. "What the hell do you think you're doing?"

"Hold it, Orsini!" Ames brought the wicked-looking revolver back up and pointed it at Rafael.

Angelica screamed.

"Okay, greaseball . . . get your hands up! Quick, dammit! You're under arrest!"

"For what?" Rafael shouted furiously.

"For bootlegging. And if you don't get your hands up, the other one's going in too for assaulting a federal officer." He nodded toward Alicia. "All the wine on this property is hereby confiscated," Ames said, spinning Rafael around and spread-eagling him over the hood of one of the trucks.

"Stupido!" Rafael shouted. "It's not illegal. We have a permit, a license . . ."

"That's what everyone says," Ames said pulling out his handcuffs.

Angelica bolted past the agent toward the winery where men were hacking away at the doors.

She charged on through them, screaming as she pushed her way past.

Bewildered, they momentarily backed away.

Tears flooded her eyes at the sight of the splintered doors. Disgusted, she turned the bolt and swung one of the doors open.

"It wasn't locked," she cried angrily. "It wasn't locked."

Sheepishly, the men lowered their axes.

Handcuffed in the backseat of the agent's sedan, Rafael sat in shock and bewilderment as he heard the sounds of the agents shattering the wooden vats and the equipment

272

inside. The last thing he saw before they roared off into the night was Angelica standing in front of the devasted winery like an orphan.

It took Angelica, her father, and the outraged Pachecos until late the next morning to reach Forsythe. And it took him until the following morning to get Rafael released. Even after he personally presented their permits and licenses to the Treasury department at the Federal Building in San Francisco, it was almost two weeks before the wine that had been confiscated was released back to them.

And then they were responsible for getting it back to their winery or they'd have to pay the government warehouse and storage fees.

Six hours after it had been picked up, the wine was back at the Orsinis. But it was too late. Moved from the cool of the winery, stored in the shedlike warehouse during the heat of the day for two weeks, the young wine had given up.

His heart growing heavier and heavier, Rafael knocked the bung out of barrel after barrel to insert a long glass tube known as a wine thief. He sniffed and sampled the few drops he had taken from each barrel and sadly shook his head.

The wine had all turned to vinegar.

Rafael was furious.

Angelica was heartbroken.

But Ferrara was philosophical. "That's the reason I always raise other crops," he said that afternoon. "There's a lot of security in having a truck farm. Sure, I dreamed about my own wine too. But even without Prohibition, it can turn into nothing but expensive vinegar. And for no reason. Let this be a lesson. Grow more than grapes . . . make your money from more than one thing."

"You might be right," Rafael said, staring out the screen door toward fields that now looked barren without their greenery. "After they're out of the ground, all you have to do is sit back and count the money."

Angelica looked up from the counter next to the sink where Pietro was pouring pitchers of milk into a cream separator for her. She knew how much the last few days had taken out of Rafael physically. And as she helped her son crank the handle, she was aware of how costly it had been to his spirit.

"Of course I'm right," Ferrara said pontifically, pleased that Rafael was so receptive to his advice. "You just spent a year in the fields and saw what it's like to lose it all. With truck farming, you get more than one crop a year . . . you got more than one chance not to go bust."

"Yep. I can understand truck farming," Rafael said again.

Angelica stared down at the drops of milk that were splattered over the counter. Pietro absentmindedly painted them into swirls with his fingers before she wiped them away with a damp dishcloth. Wringing out the cloth, she looked at Rafael.

A smile had crept across his face as their eyes met.

"I'm just not sure I could ever do it, though . . . truck farming that is."

Ferrara's head shot up in disbelief.

"Seems to me it would be sort of like getting pregnant and never having a child," Rafael said.

Angelica felt herself smiling back at him.

"You're a fool," Ferrara said, shaking his head. But damned if his son-in-law didn't have pluck, he thought.

"You might be right. But in a couple of years, the wine from this crush is going to end up in bottles with our name on it."

Angelica looked at Rafael and then at her father, not understanding.

"Sounds like the mush in your brain turned as sour as the vinegar in those barrels out back." Ferrara snorted. "Unless you're going to sell 'premium' vinegar."

"Might do that too." Rafael grinned. "But the wine I'm talking about bottling is in the barrels we still got stored down at Crystal Rock."

"I'll be damned." Ferrara shook his head. "They forgot about the wine you already hauled down there. How much is there?"

"I'd say close to a hundred barrels," Rafael tried to act nonchalant. "I'll save the first bottle for you. After that, if you still think so, then you can call me a fool . . . and I won't argue with you."

* * *

After putting Pietro and the twins to bed, Angelica and Rafael spent dinner laughing and toasting and talking of the future. Even Ferrara was caught up in the fantasy-making. He was proud that his son-in-law was a man who didn't know how to give up.

As they finished eating, someone slipped away from the side of their yard. The large man trotted back down to the road where a dust-covered coupe was parked. He coasted slowly down the road before turning on the headlights and heading back toward Healdsberg.

From where he'd been standing in the yard, he hadn't been able to see everyone in the kitchen, but he'd seen Alicia. And he'd heard her talking to two men and another woman. It was enough for him. One of them had to be Orsini. He'd found the man he was looking for.

CHAPTER TWENTY

Carlo Gianini looked at the cable from San Francisco. "Your cousin sister wife children awaiting your visit Stop Dominic. Harbor View Motor Court. San Francisco."

He folded the tissuelike paper and placed it back in its envelope before slipping it under another letter next to his demitasse of espresso. It was Sunday afternoon and he sat in the seat once occupied by his father on the veranda of the Hotel Montepulciano.

He was delighted with Dominic's success. Rafael was married, had a family, and Alicia was with him. A tidy package waiting for him.

Unfortunately, he would have to let them wait a bit longer. Christmas was near and he was the central figure in Montepulciano's festivities during the holidays. The townspeople bowed and scraped to him as though he were their god. He was determined that no one would ever share his limelight. He would remain here.

Of course he could have Dominic destroy Orsini for him, but there would be no pleasure in that. This was his revenge, no one else's. Besides, now that he had a family, Orsini wouldn't be going anyplace.

He'd cable Dominic that there was no rush. The rooster will stay close to the hens on the nest, he thought, composing the reply for his man waiting patiently in the little California room. It won't be long, though; he smiled as his thoughts focused on Alicia.

The thought of her smooth olive skin sent his pulse racing. He was amazed at how much he missed her. He wondered whether or not she'd told her brother of her means of surviving in his city.

"Padrone." Several men on the sidewalk below were

doffing their hats to him as they strolled by with their families.

He smiled and raised his hand in a blessing. He loved this power over his people. And he thirsted more and more for it. He silently thanked Maxmillian for showing him that it was his for the taking.

The first season after Prohibition proved Forsythe a visionary about the liquor market.

True, people were swarming to places to drink. But what they asked for was bourbon, gin, or beer. Harsh and numbing. Wine was big, of course, in ethnic communities or around religious holidays. But the winemaker's market was really that of the exceptionally poor and the exceptionally rich, with no middle class.

Fortunately, Rafael and Angelica hadn't entered the marketplace yet. With what they had earned from Angel Butter, they were able to be patient. Their first harvest salvaged from the marauding Treasury agents was aging, waiting for the day when they could bottle and ship it.

Forsythe had been grateful for the invitation to escape the crowded city by driving up to the Orsini farm. He arrived with a flaxen-haired young woman who could easily be mistaken for his daughter. Forsythe had promised the young women a quiet weekend away from the hustle and bustle.

To his chagrin, it was a far from quiet scene they found themselves in. They were comfortably seated at one of the long picnic tables under a shade tree near the winery, but a wriggling, cooing Rita was in Forsythe's lap, while his blond companion tried to hold her twin brother, Rafael, Jr. And around them was a sea of people.

The young woman was amazed at the variety of guests the Orsinis had invited. Some, like Paolo Pacheco and his new wife, were evidently educated and well-bred, she thought. And she understood that as the Orsinis were Catholic, they had invited their parish priest. But the presence of some of the others confused her. Frenchy and Sue were loud, boisterous, and never without a beer in hand. And she didn't know what to make of Rivera and his crew. She couldn't follow their rapid-fire conversations. Laughing and joking, they switched back and forth between heavily accented English and Spanish without notice. And their children were like locusts. They were everywhere. They were in the fields playing chase or hide-and-seek. They were in the winery climbing perilously over and under and on top of equipment. She had even found them inside the bathroom playing with the water taps and the flush toilet.

Alicia had been watching the nervous young woman from inside the screen door of the kitchen. She couldn't understand Forsythe's infatuation with this city-bred person who wore a martyrlike smile on her face to hide her discomfort at being among the unsophisticated.

Alicia loved the constantly moving mass of humanity. It was a symbol to her of belonging. Of family. Warmth. Sharing. All the things denied her in Montepulciano.

"I think everything's finally ready," Angelica said from behind her where she was unloading the oven filled with large casseroles of lasagna and sauce-covered spaghetti.

The screen door banged open and Rivera came in. "You need someone to lend a hand?" he asked.

"What perfect timing," Alicia teased. "As soon as all the work's done, you show up."

"A little trick I learned from your brother."

Angelica couldn't remember Rivera's ever offering to help before. "You better not let Benito hear about you offering to help," she warned, handing him a heavy tray filled with the baskets of hot bread, garlic butter, and huge pitchers of iced tea.

"You won't tell him, will you?" he asked sheepishly, backing out the door carefully to keep all the baskets balanced.

Little Pietro followed with a heavy bucket of ice as he tried to catch up with his favorite uncle.

"My . . . my . . . my!" Angelica's singsong voice crackled as she started to tease her sister-in-law about Rivera's never-ending attention. But she saw Alicia blush and bit her tongue.

The children looked up expectantly and even the adults greeted the food with excitement. Angelica had a growing reputation as one of the best cooks in the county. Everyone wanted to be invited to what was becoming her ritual Sunday dinner.

Smiling at Forsythe and his companion, Alicia rescued them from the twins as a hush fell.

"Bless us, oh Lord, for these thy gifts . . ." the priest said before he reached for the narrow pointed end of one of the home-baked loaves dripping with cloudy yellow butter.

Just as they all started to eat, a noise from the road below caused them to stop and look up. It was a car, but it sounded as if it were ready to explode from its whistles, wheezes, and backfires. It was a strange mixture of car, wagon, and truck. It reminded Rafael of the kind he and Rivera had once crisscrossed the country in.

As it approached, they saw it was overflowing with what must have been two or three families and all their belongings. Suitcases and cardboard boxes were tied precariously everywhere. And there were mattresses, a large cage of chickens, and three-old-tires on the roof.

The driver and a young boy barely in his teens got out and with hats in hand came halfway up the drive toward them. Rafael and Angelica, each holding one of the twins, went down to meet the man and boy.

"Afternoon, good sir, ma'am." He was a scarecrow of a man, dressed in tattered overalls. The overalls of the boy alongside him had been cut down to fit.

"Afternoon," Rafael answered.

"Was wondering . . . maybe . . . if you had need of a few strong backs? Work real cheap." The man spoke with a thick southern accent.

"Sorry," Rafael answered, shaking his head. He was truly sorry for the man and his family. The last couple of years the Depression had seemed to worsen. Then drought had hit the midwest and the refugees from starvation had started flooding into the promised land of California.

Almost daily, cars, caravans, even families pushing their belongings ahead of them in wheelbarrows stopped to ask for work. This man was just one of many Rafael was becoming more and more used to seeing.

"I'm afraid I can't even think of anybody who does," Rafael added.

The man nodded as he put his arm around his barefoot

son. The license hanging from his car by a piece of bailing wire said their search for someplace they could earn a living had started in Oklahoma.

"You've come a long way," Angelica said. She wished they could help. In the beginning, they had. But now there were just too many.

"Seems the road gets longer each day," the man answered, putting his straw hat back on. A piece of green cellophane was sewn where once a brim had acted as a shade.

"Could you use some food?" she asked.

A smile brightened his face. "Ma'am . . . you must be an angel from heaven."

"I'm sure we've got more than enough. Why don't you and your friends come join us?"

"No friends in that car, ma'am." He smiled proudly. "Just family." He turned and called to them.

"They're all yours?" Rafael asked in astonishment as nine children and a woman piled out of the car and lined up behind the man in anticipation.

Forsythe's young woman had never seen anything like it. Here were Rafael and Angelica taking in another busload of strangers!

Little Pietro loved it. Here was a whole new bunch of children to play with. Unfortunately for him, they were more interested in eating than in playing. He'd have to wait until later to share their string and marbles, and tin cans pounded into toy cars.

"We was down to this place near Bakersfield . . . down south of here. Called it Weedpatch, we did. They's work now and then. But you have to pay a fellow ten dollars for a job that only pays fourteen. Tried to for a while. But . . ." the man nodded toward his brood of youngsters. "They's just too many youngins . . ."

"Weedpatch! Charming name!" Forsythe's girl friend said, a little haughtily.

"Oh, they ain't really no weeds no more," the man's hollow-eyed wife said as she smiled at the pretty young woman across from her. She shifted the bare-bottomed infant she'd been breast-feeding discreetly to the other breast as she ate. "Weeds're all chopped down so's to make room for the cardboard shacks."

"My God!" Paolo Pacheco said.

"Well . . . Mr. Orsini, sir," the tall man said after his oldest son had rounded up his brothers and sisters and had headed them toward their car. "I can't begin to thank you for your hospitality. It was truly Christian of you . . . and we'll remember you in our prayers, sir."

"Who could ask for more?" Rafael said, taking his hand.

"God bless you, ma'am . . . sir! God truly bless you," the woman said through her tears as Angelica forced them to take sacks of sugar and flour and some of the vegetables she'd canned from her garden.

"God has blessed me," Angelica replied, taking the woman's dry, bony hand. "May He bless you and your family as well."

She and Rafael stood next to the road and watched as the family drove out of sight. Angelica looked at her husband. The shoulder of his new shirt was covered with grease from fixing their engine enough so at least it wouldn't explode.

CHAPTER TWENTY-ONE

Dominic put his hand up to catch his balance as he made his way along the narrow corridor of the Pullman. He found the compartment he was looking for and knocked lightly.

"*Avanti!*" a shrill voice called out.

He opened the door and the Padrone's old housekeeper motioned him in and closed the door behind him.

"Has the Padrone risen yet?"

"Of course he's awake," she said. "He and his friend are eating breakfast in the dining car."

Dominic surveyed the opulence. The Padrone had taken four of the stateroomlike compartments, plus a Pullmanette for his housekeeper. One of the compartments was for Maxmillian who had come along with Carlo to make a holiday of this first visit to America.

The Padrone's cousins, Ricco and Alvino Gianini, were still sleeping. Dominic didn't know why the Padrone had wasted the money to bring these two. Dominic needed no other men to help do the Padrone's bidding. And if others were needed, they could easily be recruited from the slums around the docks where Dominic had lived quietly in San Francisco while waiting for the cable that summoned him to New York to meet and guide his Padrone to Orsini.

"These two will do my bidding without question," his Padrone had informed him soon after they boarded the westbound train in New York City's massive Grand Central Station. "Others might fail to do that bidding. Or become a problem afterward."

"Afterward, I would solve that problem," Dominic assured him.

"No. We only want Orsini. This way, it's kept within the

family. It's my father we're avenging. I want no outsiders involved."

"*Sí*, Padrone," he had reluctantly agreed.

"Well . . . well . . . well! What do we have here?" Rafael asked the embarrassed Rivera who stood in the doorway dressed in the rumpled suit he'd worn at Rafael's and Angelica's wedding. He was holding a bouquet of flowers. "Flowers! For me? You shouldn't have," Rafael teased. "Of course knowing you, you probably picked them out of someone's front yard."

"No . . . backyard. Yours." Rivera grinned trying to hide his embarrassment.

"Listen, Rivera. This is the third time this week. What's going on? You got something up your sleeve with my sister?"

"Me?" Rivera protested. "No! I just feel sorry she has to eat at a poor farmer's every night. I think she's too skinny and needs something to help her grow. So I've been taking her to town for dinner. Besides . . . my crew and I go north to Oregon for next month . . . and I want to make sure she's fat enough to keep from starving while I'm gone."

"That my food you're complaining about?" Angelica asked as she came in from the kitchen.

Rivera's face turned flame red.

"*Hola,* Guillermo," Alicia said, saving him from explanation.

Rivera was speechless. She was more beautiful than he had ever seen her. With her jet black hair pulled straight back against her scalp, she reminded him of one of the Aztec women he'd seen in a mural on a wall in Guadalajara.

"*Lista?*" he asked.

"Yes. I'm ready," she answered as he pushed past Rafael to help her with her lace shawl.

"Don't forget!" Rafael warned, pointing to the clock on the mantel over the fireplace. "You have my sister home at a decent hour."

"I jus' *pobre* old *Mexicano peón, señor*. I no for able tell time," Rivera said.

Muriella was drying the last of the big iron skillets when she heard a noise just beyond the campfire lights. She peered into the blackness but couldn't see anything. Earlier in the evening she'd seen the glow from another campfire glimmering through the trees of a distant hill. But she had thought nothing of it. There were many families on the road competing for jobs.

She lay the dishcloth over the side of the camp table to dry and set the skillet on one corner so it wouldn't blow away. She glanced around at the half-dozen children sleeping under the old flatbed truck.

Over the past couple of years, their crew had grown. Maya's brother and his pretty young wife had joined them six months earlier, along with two of Rivera's cousins with their wives. All in all there were now twelve adults and an equal number of children.

Not a bad-sized crew. Big enough and well enough known that they didn't have to compete with most of the other itinerants. They were better off than most of the gringos they met on the road nowadays.

She looked at her husband. He was roaring with delight at winning a hand of cards. Maya's brother and Enrique accused him of cheating.

"Of course I cheat," Benito croaked. "But if you don't have the brains to catch me, I'll just keep on winning."

Once again Muriella heard the noise and looked into the shadows.

She wasn't sure, but she thought she saw the outline of two men. "Benito," she said, going to her husband and bending to whisper in his ear.

"That's it!" Enrique yelled. "Muriella stands behind us and signals what cards we have."

"I thought of that. And I've been watching. But I'm afraid she wasn't even close." Maya's brother shook his head.

"I think someone's watching us," Muriella whispered to Benito.

"Why would anyone waste his time doing that?" he asked. "All are welcome at our fire."

She shrugged and had started to walk back to the truck

when she heard the noise again. She whirled and saw two men standing on the road above them.

"*Hola!*" the tall skinny one called.

Benito looked up from his cards and waved them down.

"Hey! What you standing out in the dark for? Come on down by the fire and have a cup of coffee . . . or a drink."

"*Scusi . . . non capisco inglese.*" The shorter one smiled as they ambled cautiously down into the firelight.

"What did he say?" Maya's brother asked. He was from the interior of Mexico and had never heard Italian.

Benito shrugged.

"*Italianos . . .*" the skinny man said as they stopped next to the fire. "No speka . . . *inglese.*"

"Oh . . . *sí . . . sí,*" Benito said. "You *Italianos!* We have many *Italianos amigos*. You want a drink?" he asked, forming a cup with his hand and kicking his head back.

"Ah, *sì. Sì, grazie.*" Both men beamed.

Maya's brother called to his wife, who hurried over with a wicker-covered jug of tequila.

Benito's eyes narrowed as he saw both men eyeing the fawnlike girl as she poured the drinks.

"*Grazie, bella signorina,*" the short one said, leering at her.

"You here for work?" Benito acted out his question.

"No . . . come America *vacanze,*" the tall one replied.

"Ah . . . *sí. Sì.*" Benito nodded, understanding the word.

After a few more drinks, they all looked up as a shiny, four-door sedan purred to a stop on the road above them. The driver's door flew open and Benito recognized the giant, gray-headed Italian who got out.

"Alvino . . . Ricco!" the man yelled angrily. "The Padrone gave instructions that you were to remain with the cars."

"*Sì* . . . but it was hot and we were thirsty," the skinny one explained. "These kind friends offered us something to help quench . . ."

"Fools!" the man spat, as he walked uninvited into Rivera's camp. "You will give thanks to these people for their hospitality and pay them for your drinks."

He was about to turn and leave when he saw Benito.

"*Hola* again," he said quietly. "Forgive my friends and their thoughtlessness for inviting themselves to your hospitality."

"They were welcome. Did you ever find any of the families you were looking for?" he added.

"*Sì, grazie.*"

"Which one?" Benito persisted.

The man stared at Benito. Why was this any of his business? But this was America. Maybe they had strange customs.

"I think the one for whom you were working earlier this week," Dominic said, nodding toward their flatbed. "I saw your truck parked next to his field."

"Could be." Benito shrugged.

"Then you remember his name?" Dominic asked as he silently cursed the Padrone's two cousins. This man would remember who they were and where they were from once something happened to Orsini.

"Could be . . . but I not think so," Benito said.

"You work for a man and don't know his name?"

"It's not important in our business to know a man's name. Only if his money is good."

Dominic stared at the burly Mexican field hand. He couldn't tell if he was telling the truth or not. But this man was smart enough to be a witness. And the Padrone had warned him of the consequences of leaving anyone who could point a finger at them.

"The Padrone for whom I speak might have work for you and some of your men," he said. "He has asked me to look for men like you. And I can assure you, his money is good."

"What kind of work?" Benito asked.

"Easy work . . . but I cannot tell you about it here. You will have to talk to the Padrone in person."

"Good money? For little work?" Benito smiled in disbelief.

"*Sì* . . . trust me, I speak the truth."

"Where will I find you and this Padrone of yours?"

"Do you know the road next to the river that runs down from the steam geysers near the town called Healdsberg?"

"*Sì.*"

"We are in a grove of trees along there."

"If your Padrone is a wealthy man like you say, why is he living in a grove of trees in the wilderness like those of us who are poor?"

A moment of confusion flashed across the Italian's face. This Mexican is too observant for his own good, he thought, as he struggled to come up with a believable reason. "He has been sick . . . in the chest. His doctors have given him instructions to take fresh air . . . stay away from the dampness and crowds of the city."

Benito nodded his understanding, but could tell that the man had lied. "When can I see this Padrone of yours?"

"Now if you like." Dominic smiled warmly.

Benito smiled back and thought to himself for a few moments. "No . . . I can't tonight. But tomorrow I can for sure."

"Good," Dominic said, though he was disappointed by the delay. "Then until tomorrow."

"He's one bad *hombre*." Enrique breathed a sigh of relief as the sedan disappeared into the night with Ricco and Alvino riding on the running board.

"You stupid pigs . . ." Carlo Gianini screamed as his hand slashed across Ricco's mouth. "Get out of my sight." Carlo whirled and walked back to stand next to their campfire.

Ricco and Alvino disappeared into one of the tents which sat in a semicircle across from the campfire.

"What about these Mexicans?" Carlo demanded. "Will they go to Orsini?"

"I don't think so, Padrone."

"But they work for him . . ."

"*Sì*. But it is not the same here, Padrone. Men like these work in many provinces for many *padroni* . . ."

"You had better be sure, Dominic."

"I am sure of all but one, Padrone. And I have asked him here to meet you. I used the promise of money. When he arrives, I will make sure he talks to no one again."

"If he warns Orsini and Orsini escapes, then my cousins are to suffer what I had planned for him," Carlo said angrily, loud enough and intended for his cousins to hear.

"*Sì*, Padrone," Dominic said.

Inside the tent, the two men looked at each other in terror.

"Did you hear that, you stupid bastard?" Alvino whispered angrily.

"Orsini won't learn. You heard Dominic. The Mexicans probably won't say anything."

"But what if they do?"

"Maybe we can make sure Orsini won't run."

"How?" We can't stop him without killing him. And Carlo would kill us for that."

"There is another way," Ricco said.

Rivera and Alicia had walked hand in hand down the sidewalk of the little town of Geyserville, window-shopping. They had walked the few short blocks off Main Street past the clusters of tiny frame houses. Little patches of carefully watered lawns were outlined by lush light green vines that covered stumps, garages, the sides of tool sheds, even outhouses.

They had returned to Main Street and stopped in front of a store to watch a group of old men slapping dominoes down on a board atop a flour barrel. The store's clutter, lanterns, horse collars, scrub boards, catalog pages, and Coca-Cola signs almost hid a little gray-haired man with a leather-billed hat who had looked up from the game and smiled at Alicia.

She smiled back as the little man and several of his cronies, dressed in bib overalls, turned around.

"Evening, Miss Orsini," one of them, with a pipe wedged where his teeth had been, said.

She was proud they knew her through her brother. She was filled with admiration that in so few years, he'd become known, respected, and prosperous.

After the man with the leather cap had won the game, Rivera and Alicia had walked arm in arm to dinner at Cisco's, a small cafe run by an old friend of Rivera's who'd left the fields and was struggling to earn a living.

When Alicia had asked him to order for her, Rivera had ordered *cabecito*.

It was the head of a lamb. The whole head. Without fur, but with everything else intact from the eyeballs inward.

Rivera had wanted to yell with delight and throw his

arms around her at her bravery. Not only did she try it, after closing her eyes, but she found that once over her repulsion it was delicately delicious.

They were on the way home now and Rivera's heart was bursting like a schoolboy's as they drove along under a sky lit by the gauzy Milky Way.

At first it had made him feel uneasy, almost guilty to think of Alicia. And every time he did, he had thoughts of Maya. But slowly, the guilt had ebbed. It was almost as if Maya were telling him she understood his need for companionship and love.

He pulled off the narrow, winding road that snaked through the valley into a grove of oak trees. He switched off the lights and engine and turned to her. For a few quiet moments he looked at her, and when she smiled at him, he put his arms around her and drew her to him. She responded with the warmth and affection he had long dreamed of. He was lost in the delicate softness of her touch when she tensed and pulled away.

"Please," she whispered.

"Qué pasa?"

"Nothing." Suddenly she turned away from him. "No. That's not true. Everything."

"Por qué? Why?" he asked, putting his hand under her chin and turning it back toward him.

She shook her head. In the dim glow, he could see tears on her cheeks and felt her body trembling.

"Alicia . . . Alicia," he whispered. *"Está bien. Lo sciento.* I'm sorry . . . I didn't mean . . ."

She put her palms on the sides of his cheeks. "It's not you, Guillermo."

"Then what?"

She sat staring out the window for a long time.

"You are a trap, Guillermo. These last few months, I have grown to adore you."

"Fantástico!" he beamed.

"No!" Alicia cried in frustration. "It must stop now. Please! Now . . . this night. Before it becomes a nightmare."

"A nightmare? I don't understand. How can something that is so good become that?"

"Please . . . please don't ask me to explain. Just trust me."

"You ask me to join you in killing something before it has had a chance to live and you say not to ask why. I *have* to ask why, Alicia."

"It's just too late."

"Too late? I'm not an old man," he said indignantly.

She smiled at his uncomplicated innocence. She took his hands to her breast and drew him close.

"Dear Guillermo. How I've dreamed of the thrill of being loved by you."

"And I have dreamed also of the thought of loving you. You've seen me standing around like a grinning jackass. Watching you. Why not share the dream?"

"No."

"Por qué?"

"Please," she almost screamed. "Just don't ask anymore. Stop asking . . . please . . ."

"I have to."

"Because of life." She struggled for an explanation she could give without having to deal with the truth. "Because of what life has made of us."

"This moment . . . now, here together, is what life has made of us," he said trying to pull her to him to soothe her. "Nothing in life that has passed can hurt us now."

"You're wrong," she said, her tears suddenly drying. "Everything from my life can hurt us."

He started to protest, but she placed her fingertips over his lips so he couldn't speak.

"No," she said quietly. "It's too late."

"No! It can't be!" He yelled angrily as a familiar dread settled in his chest. It was almost the same as when Maya died. He pounded the steering wheel in frustration and anger. "Why are you doing this to us . . . to our future?"

"Please, Guillermo, please," she pleaded. "Don't make me tell you . . ."

"You have to."

"In the end, you will hate me."

"What?" He said in disbelief. "There is nothing on this earth that could cause that to happen."

She looked at this man who had filled her with such

love. Such yearning. Such warmth. Such caring. She had never known such a craving to be held, loved, cared for. But she knew she had to tell him the truth, for his own sake. She couldn't let him go on hoping.

"Dear Guillermo, I can never have a life together with any man."

He stared at her uncomprehending, dumbfounded, until she slowly unfolded the story of her existence since Rafael left Montepulciano.

"In the end," she said after there was no more to tell, "it would destroy us."

"*Dios!*" he whispered softly. "You are wrong. And with time I could prove it to you."

"No," she said, holding him to her. "It would destroy us. I could never hold you, give you my love, without fearing that someday I would see a look in your eye, and you would be wondering . . ."

Rivera recognized the finality in her voice. And he wept. And Alicia couldn't help soothe his pain.

As the zigzag tar lines of the patched road passed beneath the car, they rode home in silence. Less than a mile from Rafael and Angelica's vineyard, they rounded a curve that crossed over a bridge. Suddenly out of the darkness, Rivera's headlights picked up the black form of a large sedan parked in the middle of the road without lights and with the passenger door open.

As Rivera swerved to avoid colliding with it, a spray of gravel kicked up and they broadsided off the pavement onto the road's shoulder.

"Stupid asses! You trying to kill somebody?" he yelled angrily into the black night. Probably a couple of lovers who'd left the car to stretch out on a blanket under the stars, he decided, when no one answered.

That last mile to Rafael's was the longest he'd ever driven. It seemed to grow longer with each passing second, as though he were driving toward an endless abyss. Finally, he turned into the rutted lane that led up to the house. His headlights suddenly caught two men running down the lane toward the car.

As he braked, the two figures skidded to a stop and

stared into his headlights like nocturnal animals hypnotized by the glare. One of the men shifted something in a blanket from one hip to another. As he did, the muffled screams of a panic-filled child pierced the night.

"Ricco . . . Alvino!" Alicia cried in stunned disbelief.

Almost before the words escaped her throat, Rivera had the door open and was racing down the gravel-filled ruts toward the two men. As if by slight of hand, a long shadow appeared in the short man's hands. Rivera dove into the gravel as the blast from the shotgun whistled past his head and through his coat. As the thunderous noise faded, both men lunged down a row of grapevines into the darkness.

A child's screams could be heard echoing across the field as Rivera pushed himself up and felt inside his collar. One of the pellets had torn through a muscle between his neck and shoulder.

Good, he thought, knowing he was lucky to have survived. But before he could push himself to his feet, a shadow raced toward him from out of the darkness. His heart thundered. Had the man with the shotgun come back to finish him?

As the figure came into the headlights, Rivera felt himself weak with relief. Outlined in the dimming glow from the car's rapidly depleting battery was old man Ferrara. Even in the poor light, Rivera could see the old man was ashen.

"You okay?" Ferrara asked kneeling next to him.

"Yeah . . . I think so."

"Sorry. Tried to yell a warning . . . I saw them from the winery. I thought they were just burglars and went back in for my shotgun. Then I heard Pietro crying . . . Damn near shot you too, when I saw 'em running toward your headlights. Thought you were probably the getaway car."

The lights went on in the house and a screen door banged open, then slammed shut as a shirtless Rafael charged out into the cool night air.

In the distance, he saw a figure lying in the gravel dressed in the familiar suit of his best friend. Next to him, raising his shotgun and pointing it toward the dark vineyard, was his father-in-law.

Barefooted and barechested, Rafael raced down the lane toward them.

Ferrara sighted down the barrel to the brass bead welded on the gun's tip. The fleeing figures, trying to stay below the vines were rapidly disappearing as they raced away from the glare of the headlights.

Ferrara swung the gun ahead of one of the figures and started to squeeze the trigger. He stopped. Dammit! He couldn't tell which one was carrying Pietro and didn't dare risk a shot.

"You okay?" Rafael asked as he knelt next to Rivera.

"*Sí*. It's just a little scratch." Rivera tried not to show his pain. "I'm sorry I couldn't stop them for you."

"You shouldn't have tried," Rafael said, still thinking they must have been burglars. "Is Alicia okay?"

"*Sí* . . . in the car." Rivera nodded.

"The cousins," she said zombielike as she stepped out of the car and knelt down next to them.

"What are you talking about?" Rafael asked, but his concern was still focused on Rivera.

"Rafael . . . Rafael!" Angelica screamed from the porch. "Someone's taken Pietro!"

"*Il Padrone*," Alicia whispered, her eyes saucerlike black pools of fear.

"Impossible!" Rafael said in shock.

"No!" she cried. "I saw them . . . Ricco and Alvino. They are the ones who ran into the field."

Rafael saw Ferrara disappearing into the vineyard and scrambled to his feet to race after him.

"Wait!" Rivera yelled, struggling to get up. "Help me . . . into the car. I know where they will be heading."

"Where?" Rafael demanded, grabbing him and pulling him to his feet. He jumped into the driver's seat and ground the car into reverse as Rivera clambered in next to him. Alicia tried to squeeze in but Rafael stopped her. "Tell Angelica I'm going after my son. Stay with the twins," he said as he roared out the narrow drive toward the road like a madman.

"This side of the bridge. Someone left a car in the middle of the road. I almost hit it coming off the bridge. It has to be theirs."

As they raced down the road, in the distance they could see the coal oil lamps glowing from Rivera's camp.

"Let me off . . . I'll get Benito and the others," Rivera said through the pain that had seeped down his shoulder and into his chest.

Benito had been buttoning on his denim shirt when the car had raced past and a man had hurtled off it, tumbling over and over before coming to rest in a heap.

Struggling painfully to his feet, Rivera yelled to Benito and the others almost before he stopped rolling.

"I heard the shotgun," Benito said. "What is it?"

"Someone's taken Pietro!"

"Los Italianos," Muriella said, as she made the sign of the cross.

"You saw them again?" Rivera asked, rushing to another one of their cars.

"Si. They were here earlier," Benito said.

"Then we will make sure they don't come back again."

Benito nodded his full understanding. He reached into the cab of his truck and slid a leather scabbard from behind a blanket-covered seat. In it was the machete he'd had since childhood. He'd used it for chopping cane, corn, and brush in Mexico. Now, it was used only to chop kindling for the cookfire, but its razor-sharp blade still glistened in the soft orange light from the coal oil lamps. He dropped the scabbard back onto the seat.

Next to him, Ramon loaded an ancient revolver with half of the grip missing. Across from them, Enrique hefted the long curved blade from a rusty scythe and stuck it through one of his belt loops, while Maya's brother nervously rubbed an old cracked baseball bat and took an imaginary swing at their unseen enemy.

Rivera dragged the single barrel shotgun he used for rabbit-hunting from the back of a car. He tore off the cardboard top of a yellow box of shells and half-emptied it into his suit coat pocket.

Rafael gunned the engine and sped toward the curve. It was a mile by road. Shorter through the vineyard. The rods in the engine clattered at the feverish pitch he demanded from the old car.

In the distance he could see his headlights reflecting off something in the road. It was the chrome bumper of the boxy sedan parked halfway in the middle of the road.

He saw a figure burst out of the vineyard struggling with a thrashing bundle. A moment later, another man carrying a shotgun burst out of the darkness trying to keep up with the figure ahead as they both ran toward the distant sedan.

Rafael's first instinct was to swerve and run them down. But they were carrying his son. He roared past them forcing them to dive back into the dark safety of the vineyard.

God in heaven, what can I do? He thought momentarily of taking his foot off the accelerator. They had his son, a car, and a shotgun. How could he stop them? By taking their car away from them, he thought, flooring the accelerator once again.

He bore down on the sedan parked by the side of the road. At the last second, he locked his brakes. The shattering impact spun both cars around like partners in a square dance and tore the open door off the sedan.

Rafael's head slammed against the dashboard and blood rolled down his face. As soon as the cars stopped spinning, Rafael forced his steam-clouded wreck into reverse to back away so he could ram the sedan once again. But both cars were locked together.

With Rivera's old relic shuddering as though it would come apart, Rafael inched the two vehicles out of the road toward the bank. He jumped as they slid over the shalelike rocks and hurtled down into the creek that ran under the bridge.

From the shadows, Ricco and Alvino watched in horror. They were stranded . . . marooned.

"*Stupido . . . swine!*" Alvino hissed. He had his hand over Pietro's mouth to hold in the handkerchief that muffled the child's screams.

"*Silenzio!*" Ricco hissed, leaning heavily on the shotgun.

Behind them they tried to hear whoever it was who had chased them by foot through the vineyard. They knew he

295

was still stalking them. And farther down the road, they could see a line of lanterns approaching.

In the vineyard, Ferrara knelt in the darkness. He leaned against one of the gnarled grape spikes that pointed like a withered hand toward the dark sky. He could smell the moss-covered bark as he tried to see through the blackness.

He was out of breath and sweating heavily from the sprint through the vineyard, but he knew he had to stifle his pained breathing.

No noise now, he thought, as he peered over the row of spikes that ran symmetrically into the night. He knew exactly where he was, even in the dark. He knew every inch of this vineyard. He'd laid it out, set out every new cutting, and worked each row more than twenty years. At one time, he'd even considered giving each spike an individual name.

He grabbed hold of one of the spikes to pull himself up. The brittle vine snapped under his weight. He fell back on his hip and his shotgun went off.

In the still night air, the explosion sounded to Alvino and Ricco as though it were next to them.

"Gesù Cristo!" Alvino squealed and ran like a stampeded bull toward the bridge at the end of the vineyard.

As the cousins crashed through the vineyard, a shadow suddenly loomed up out of the darkness in front of them. Ricco screamed and veered to avoid colliding with the shadowy threat but lost his footing and tumbled head first down the bank toward the stream.

A few steps behind, struggling to keep a grip on the thrashing, terror-filled Pietro, Alvino identified the menacing shadow as the Mexican they'd drunk with earlier in the evening. He didn't know how the Mexican got here, but he knew he had to get away from him.

Clutching Pietro to his chest, Alvino veered toward where Ricco had disappeared down a slope that ended in a streambed twenty feet below. He was certain he could make it down the slope to safety. He was smiling to himself when he felt a sting across the back of his neck. His smile froze permanently and he felt incapable of keeping his head from hanging at a crazy angle, an angle he'd never known in his life. His legs turned to jelly and he somer-saulted toward the stream below.

The involuntary clutch action of death kept Pietro pressed to the chest of the decapitated young Italian as he pinwheeled down the slope.

Glancing over his shoulder, Ricco froze in horror at the sight of his cousin's headless body sliding over the rim of the bank.

Ricco flew out of the water up the bank on the far side of the stream. In total panic, he crawled along the bank to the bridge. Hanging upside down, he shinnied across on one of the spans underneath the bridge and disappeared into the night.

Ferrara saw the shadow disappearing across the span. Passing silently behind everyone, he slipped across the stream after him.

Benito was staring at the shadow of the disappearing kidnapper and the pursuing Ferrara when Rafael and Rivera raced up.

"Where are they? Which way did they go?" Rafael demanded.

"One just crossed under the bridge . . . but, don't worry, *Señor* Ferrara is after him. The other one is in the water." He pointed to the body with the machete that had separated body from head.

"Pietro!" Rafael said anxiously. "Where's my son?"

"The one that crossed the bridge couldn't have him . . ." Benito was suddenly filled with panic. *"Dios! Jesús Cristo!"* he cried as he slid down the bank toward the headless body bobbing gently in the water's current. "I thought the other man must have Pietro," he yelled as the three of them skidded down the bank where the body still shuddered with an occasional spasm. *"Jesús Cristo,* Rafael, I swear, I didn't see that the man had Pietro."

Plunging into the shallow water that barely covered the streambed, they yanked the body onto its back.

"Oh dear God . . . dear God . . . dear God," Rafael said. Clutched to the dead Italian's chest, a handkerchief still stuffed in his mouth, was Pietro. "Help me . . . help me," he whispered to Benito as he tried to break his son free of the man's death grip.

Rafael felt his heart pounding with dread. His tiny son wasn't breathing. In panic, the two men broke the corpse's elbow and dragged Pietro out of the rigid grasp.

"Dear God . . . Dear God . . . Please!" he prayed silently as he lifted his son.

"Rafael . . . Pietro!" he heard Angelica screaming as she raced toward the edge of the bank. She had left Alicia with the twins and streaked through the vineyard after them. She started to slide over the rim but Muriella grabbed her and held her back.

"*Espera! Espera!* Please wait," Muriella pleaded as she struggled to keep her from sliding down the bank. "Is better for you to wait here."

But Angelica already saw Rafael zigzagging up the slope, clutching their son's limp body to his chest. It was a long time before she was aware that the sobs that filled the night were from her own throat.

The doctor at the tiny clinic overlooking the river near the outskirts of Healdsberg spent a long time talking to them. Through it all, Angelica and Rafael listened, nodded, even responded now and then. But they hardly understood a word that came out of the doctor's mouth.

"Lucky little fellow's still alive. Maybe we'll stay lucky. Few little tykes that age survive a drowning . . . but . . ."

Angelica had looked down at the pitiful little figure on the white sheet under the clear plastic tent that housed the oxygen the doctor had ordered to help Pietro's labored breathing.

There was a trace of blood oozing from the bottom of one of his ears.

"Doctor?" Angelica asked, reaching under the bottom of the tent and wiping it gently with her handkerchief.

The old man shook his head. "Seems like a little concussion. We'll just have to wait."

She nodded, and before folding the blanket back over the edge of the tent to keep the oxygen from escaping, ran her fingers through the curly black hair that made Pietro look like an angelic miniature of his father. His hair was still wet from the stream.

* * *

Alicia pulled into the driveway of the old house that had been converted into a clinic. On the porch she could see Rivera, Benito, Muriella, and others from their crew leaning against the wall next to the door staring into space.

The feeling of dread swept through her again as she remembered the almost emotionless call from Angelica telling her what had happened and to meet them at the clinic. Alicia made sure the twins, asleep in the backseat, were covered with their blanket before she locked the car doors and went up to the porch.

In silence they all waited, each lost in pain. Finally the door opened and Rafael and Angelica stepped out onto the flagstone-covered porch. But all Rafael could do was shake his head and shrug. "We don't know anything yet," he said.

"Why has this happened to us?" Angelica's voice was hollow, defeated. "Why would someone take our child? We're not rich . . . we couldn't have paid much."

Alicia stared at her brother, then at Rivera. Only the three of them knew. Her pain was compounded by not being able to tell the woman she'd grown to love so deeply.

"Why would someone be so cruel? Who could hate us enough to do this to our son . . . a child? Any child?"

Rafael stared at the ground and shook his head.

They all looked up at the sound of Ferrara's truck. Parking, he hurried over to the porch.

"How's the boy?" an exhausted Ferrara asked. He was covered with sweat, caked with mud and foxtails.

"We just have to wait, Papa," Angelica answered.

"I found their camp," Ferrara said quietly to Rafael and Rivera. "The fat one led me right to it. I could have brought him down a dozen times. But I'm glad I didn't. He hightailed it right back to his head man."

"Thank you, Papa." Angelica felt relief that the kidnappers would be caught. "Now the police . . ."

"No!" Rafael said, a hostile sound in his voice Angelica had never heard. "No police. Where are they?"

"Camped in that meadow on the road up to the geysers," Ferrara said.

Angelica watched her husband, not comprehending why they weren't rushing off for the authorities.

"Near the river?" Rivera asked.

Ferrara nodded.

"We camped there once." He remembered the peaceful little meadow at the bottom of a dirt road.

"It's time this business was finished then. Once and for all," Rafael said heading for his father-in-law's truck.

"*Sí. Es tiempo,*" Benito echoed blackly.

"Wait a minute! My God! What are you all talking about? What do you think you men can do?" Angelica pleaded, not believing what she'd heard. "Rafael, this is something for the police . . . the FBI."

"This is personal. Something I have to handle myself. No police!" He said adamantly.

"Personal? No police?" She looked to Alicia for help, support. But there was none. She could see from the look that passed between brother and sister that there was full agreement. When they reached the doctor's with Pietro, she had thought their nightmare was nearing its end. Now she realized it wasn't. "That's why the doctor thinks he's only treating some poor child who nearly drowned. That's why you didn't tell him the truth . . . that someone tried to steal our son, isn't it?" She grew angry as a sudden realization swept through her. "You know them, don't you. You know who did this?"

Without answering, Rafael turned back toward the truck. But Ferrara grabbed him by the shoulder.

"You better stay," Ferrara said. "Angelica needs to know what this is all about. And you need to be close to your son."

"You should know too," Rafael said.

"It's my grandson they hurt. I don't need to know anything other than that." Ferrara's bitterness was clear.

"Dear God!" Angelica moaned. This nightmare was even engulfing her father. "Please! We're not living in a jungle. You're not savages . . . thugs . . ." But Rivera, Benito, and the rest of their crew climbed into Ferrara's truck.

"*Hermano mio,*" Rafael said to Rivera.

"*Sí.*"

"Everyone should know the reasons for this night."

"*Sí.*" Years earlier the two friends had shared the painful secrets of their pasts. "I will tell them. But even if they didn't know, they would do this for you."

"Years ago . . . when I was still a boy and when the echoes of the war could still be heard, I came back home to visit my mother, brother, and Alicia. I used to dream of the moment when I could sneak up . . . surprise them . . . see their faces . . . their smiles. That time, though, instead of smiles, I found my brother on the side of a hill . . . alone . . . dead . . . beaten to death. A man . . . very powerful, very rich, was responsible . . ."

Though the night was fair, Angelica had her arms wrapped around her trying to keep the chill from settling into her soul as Rafael unfolded the story of his brother, sister, and the Padrone.

Rafael knelt between his wife and Alicia, who was sitting on the running board of the sedan where the twins were still sleeping peacefully.

"There were hundreds of times when I wanted to tell you. But when Alicia finally came, I thought for sure it was over. I thought there was no reason for you to know . . . to be hurt . . . afraid."

"No reason? I'm your wife. I belong to you. I had a right to know. Since we've been married, and before, there's been an ugly threat hanging over us. And over the head of our family." She looked at Rafael. He was the same strong, black-haired, smiling man she'd married. Yet the hands that had held her, caressed her, made love to her had known such brutality, done such violence.

"None of this would have happened were it not for me," Alicia said. "It began . . . and still goes on . . . because of me."

"That's not true," Rafael said. "I was the one who made a maniac out of Carlo Gianini by taking vengence on his father."

"But I am the one who first went to the Padrone's. The one who became his lover. And I am the one Carlo Gianini used to find you and Angelica." The realization that she had been used as a Judas Goat to find her brother and his family filled her with rage. "It wasn't enough that he had to use me while you were gone. But to use me to find you . . ."

Rafael looked at his sister. In the years since she had come to America, he had never been able to get her to talk about her life in Montepulciano after he'd left. She had always smiled and assured him that she'd been more than comfortable on the money he'd sent.

Now as she started telling the truth to them, the weight of what she'd endured was almost more than he could bear.

They sat in silence a long time after she finished.

"Maybe I was wrong," Angelica said to Rafael.

He looked at her.

"Maybe you really are a savage . . . a thug."

Rafael had known physical pain many times in his lifetime. But nothing like this. It felt as though a million barbs had pierced his body.

"You mangled and maimed a man in the name of your sister's honor. And what did it accomplish? It filled her life with even more suffering and left my son inside there on a bed more dead than alive. You're not the man I married. The man I loved . . . married . . . would have told me. Warned me! Let me know . . ." She sobbed into her palms.

"If you had known, would it have changed anything?" he asked.

"I don't know. All I know is that I trusted you. In everything. In every way. Our money . . . future . . . lives. Now I'm not sure I ever can again."

302

CHAPTER TWENTY-TWO

Approaching the crest, Ferrara pushed the throttle to the floor. When he had enough speed built up, he switched off the engine and coasted over the crown of the hill. As they surveyed the dark valley below, there was no sign that anyone was camped below. But Benito put his finger alongside his nose. There was the smell of smoke in the air that could only have come from a campfire. Ferrara nodded and set the hand brake, and they all spilled out on the road.

"How should we do this, *señor?*" Rivera asked, deferring to Ferrara.

"Give us a half hour," Ferrara said. "Then have Benito and Ramon drive down into their camp."

Benito looked at the old man. He didn't like subtle plans. He preferred to charge in and get on with it.

"One of the men asked you to come," Ferrara continued the explanation. "You're just coming early. When they see you, keep their attention while the rest of us . . ."

"Ah . . . *sí. Sí.*" Benito suddenly liked the plan.

They made their way off the road and down the slope toward the grove that sheltered the fire. Moving through the rocks and briars on calloused feet used to burning fields, the ragtag army followed their ancient leader. But when they were halfway down the slope, a scream pierced the night air.

Ferrara's army broke into a trot toward the sound.

Through the trees, they could see the camp. It was illuminated by headlights from two cars parked across from tents pitched near a huge stone pit in which red hot coals glowed. The men stopped in the shadows of the trees. A few scant yards away, a man was standing, his back to them. Across the camp from him, near the fire pit, a huge

Italian stood over a man on his knees in the dirt. Ferrara recognized the frightened man as the animal he'd tracked through the countryside.

"Is he one of the men who was in our camp earlier?" Rivera whispered, nodding toward the big man.

"*Sí.*" Maya's brother said close to his ear. "He's the one you must beware of."

"The one with his back to us must be the young Padrone," Rivera pointed to the slightly built, immaculately dressed young man.

The others nodded, mistaking Maxmillian for Carlo.

Behind the lights of one of the sedans, a figure slid off a fender and came toward the man in the dirt. Rivera could see that he was also a young man. Even more handsome than the dandy a few yards from them, but with an arrogant, menacing look in his face.

Carlo Gianini stood for a moment over Ricco as he knelt in the dirt. Suddenly his booted foot flashed and he caught his cousin full in the face. "Stupid son of a whore!" Carlo screamed.

"No, *prego!*" The man pleaded. "Alvino . . . it was Alvino's plan. He said if we took the child, Orsini would surely remain. We were only trying to please you."

Carlo nodded to Dominic and in a flash the big Italian's elbow caught the cherubic man in the side of the head leaving his ear a ruby red where it struck. The dapper young man standing near them spun around to shield himself from the brutal sight. He probably would have seen Ferrara and Rivera had a noise not attracted his attention. A truck was coasting down the grade behind where Carlo and Dominic stood.

"Carlo!" he yelled a warning.

Instantly Carlo and Dominic jerked around. Before they could react, a smiling Benito leaned out of his cab.

"*Buenos noches.*" He doffed his hat.

"You are early," Dominic said as he recognized the Mexican.

"We leave *mañana* at sunup," Benito shrugged. "But maybe we can stay if your Padrone has need of what you spoke of earlier."

Dominic looked into the cab. There was someone else sitting there. He recognized the macabre scar slashed through the man's right eye. It was one of the men he'd seen in camp earlier drinking with the big Mexican.

"Shut off your engine and come out." Carlo smiled to the two Mexicans. "You are welcome here."

Enrique and Maya's brother slipped out of the shadows and under the edge of the canvas into one of the tents. From inside they waited for a signal from Benito or Rivera.

"Gracias," Benito declined Carlo's offer. "It is late. And we only need for to know how to earn this money . . . and not have to work hard."

Carlo looked at Dominic for an explanation. "I told them that our Padrone has use for strong men who are willing to work hard and keep their mouths closed," Dominic explained.

"Our Padrone has use for such men, it is true." Carlo smiled.

Dominic walked over to the running board and leaned on the edge of the window. "It will be better if I can discuss the matter with you in private."

"The pay is as you promised?" Benito insisted.

"Of course. And our Padrone pays in gold."

"Qué dice?" Ramon asked, shifting around so he could hear better.

"Dice pagaran en oro." Benito croaked, reaching up to take his hat off and scratch his matted hair.

"Chihuahua!" Ramon whistled to show how impressed he was.

There was a blur of motion and Dominic quickly jerked back out of the window. He had caught a glimpse of something in the dim light that rang a warning in his brain. In shifting around, Ramon's leg had moved off the old, single action revolver.

"Padrone . . . *pericolo!*" Dominic yelled as he whirled toward one of their sedans that had a shotgun in the back.

As Carlo turned, he saw Dominic abruptly stop in his tracks. It seemed for a vivid moment that he was caught in midstride. Then the dark shadow that looked like a bright red tie under his collar became a stream of blood. When Benito had taken off his hat to scratch his head, he'd closed his fingers around the handle of the machete stuck in the overhead. The blade had plunged through Dominic's back just above the shoulder blades and protruded out of the top of his chest like a silver diving platform.

The giant Italian seemed frozen, amazed that he'd allowed himself and his Padrone to be ambushed so easily. The dapper young man screamed in panic and whirled to make a dash toward the darkness that promised safety among the trees. But a smiling, dark-haired man in a blood-stained, ill-fitting suit stepped out from behind one of the trees with a shotgun in his hands.

Maxmillian's mind felt as though it had a short circuit in it. He tried to speak, but couldn't. He tried to smile, to show he was harmless, but couldn't. His mind babbled and his mouth frothed at the nightmare. This wasn't happening. He couldn't believe that anything so horrible was actually happening and that he was caught in it.

He whirled back toward the fire and saw Dominic toppling rigidly into the dirt, almost like a tree that had been felled. He didn't know who these men were or what they wanted. But it was evident they were killers. Bandits probably, who'd come to rob and kill them all. He had read that such things happened in America's Wild West.

The Mexican . . . the one who'd killed Dominic . . . surely he was their leader. Maybe the man could be reasoned with . . . bribed. He started to run toward him.

A sudden noise . . . a shattering noise erupted behind him.

My God! Maxmillian thought. *He's shooting at me.*

"Goddamn!" Rivera cursed himself, not believing he'd missed a target as big as the man, or as close.

But he hadn't missed. The blast had sheared the back fringe of Maxmillian's hair off and blown it forward across his crown. The shock and panic had kept him from feeling any pain as he stumbled toward Benito.

As Maxmillian lunged across the camp, his babbling sounded like the shrieking of a crazy man to Benito.

"Please . . . you must listen. I will give you anything. I will help you . . ." he screamed, shaking his hand in an animated gesture toward Benito to emphasize his plea.

Benito's blade flashed.

Maxmillian's eyes widened in horror at the frayed edge of his jacket and the stump where once his arm had been.

He sank to his knees in total shock as his life pumped out into the dirt.

As Maxmillian fell, Carlo dove toward the darkness between the tents. The young Italian's movement caught both Ferrara's and Rivera's eye. Rivera was the quicker and fired through the tent where the man's momentum would have carried him.

Two screams pierced the night. One he knew was the Italian's. The other he recognized as Enrique's. Rivera felt sick with anxiety as Enrique staggered out of the tent and fell next to the fire pit.

Racing to his friend, Rivera knelt and rolled him on his back. Enrique's eyes fluttered open. Two furrows had cut across the top of his head as though he had been split with a skinning knife. But they weren't serious.

Still waiting in the shadows near the tree line, Ferrara saw the man between the tents rise to his knees. He looked like a blood-covered giant spider as he tried to scurry off. Rivera's blast had caught the man full in the hip.

With any luck it's broken, Ferrara thought. He raised his shotgun until the bright brass sight bead on the end of the barrel was centered on the man's back and pulled the trigger.

Nothing happened.

"Damn!" The hammer hadn't been cocked.

Quickly he cocked it. The click seemed magnified in the still night. In terror the figure between the tents looked back over his shoulder at the sound and saw the barrel pointing at him.

"No . . . Please! No." The man's screams seemed to echo off the surrounding hillsides as Ferrara pulled the trigger.

This time the hammer fell on an empty chamber. He'd forgotten to reload after accidentally firing in the vineyard. He quickly broke open the breech and pulled a shell out of his pocket. By the time he reloaded, the Italian had worked his way almost to the bottom of the hill.

Ferrara raised the gun and fired. He could hear the pellets smacking into the man's flesh. The impact threw the man farther down the slope and into the river. Ferrara re-

loaded and fired again down the dark slope. But he could
tell by the sound of the pellets splattering that what he'd
hit was most likely a boulder.

No matter, he thought calmly. The man's thigh was
probably broken by Rivera's first shot. If he wasn't dead,
he soon would be. For his daughter's and grandson's sakes,
he hoped the man suffered a long time before dying.

He turned back to the camp.

Maya's brother was wrapping Enrique's head with a
sleeveless undershirt rifled from a suitcase in one of the
tents. Benito was standing watch over the man in the dirt
who had taken Pietro.

The man's face was wet from tears. He was still half
dazed from the beating he'd taken. And he was confused as
to whether he'd been rescued or doomed.

"This one?" Benito asked barely above a whisper.

"It's already been decided," Rivera said without a trace
of emotion.

For a moment Rivera hesitated about killing a man so
nearly helpless. Then his mind numbed in rage. This was
one of the men who'd come from Italy and who was responsible for what Alicia had suffered.

Rivera put his shotgun to the man's temple. The echo
from the blast seemed to take forever before it stopped rat-
tling back from the distant hills.

"*Los Italianos?*" Rafael asked quietly when Rivera and
his band drove up and parked outside the tiny clinic.

"They will trouble you no more," Rivera said.

Rafael nodded grimly but felt a tremendous sense of relief.

Alicia walked slowly off the porch and stood silently
next to her brother, staring at Rivera whose eyes were
locked onto hers. The look that passed from Alicia was
filled with gratitude. But it was her brother she embraced
first.

"*Gracias,* my brothers," Rafael said releasing her and
hugging each one of the sweat-stained Mexicans.

From the porch, Angelica watched in silence. She
crossed her arms against the chill that again shivered
through her. She was numb with horror. The man she

loved, and his sweet sister who cried at the death of wild birds, were embracing a band of friends who had been turned into a pack of assassins, vigilantes. She looked around at the men she no longer knew. Rivera . . . once a warm, gentle man. Benito . . . the big, snuggly bear. Even her father had been dragged into this horror. And all of it brought on by the man she'd committed her life to.

"Where is my father?" she asked, suddenly filled with dread.

"He sent us ahead," Rivera assured her calmly. "To make sure you knew you would never have to fear shadows in the night again."

"I never did before." Angelica turned abruptly and went back inside where she could maintain a vigil next to Pietro.

"*El señor?*" Rafael asked after Angelica disappeared through the door.

"One of the *Italianos* fell into the river," Rivera explained. "*Señor* Ferrara told us to take care of the dead ones and their cars and then return here and not wait for him."

Carlo's eyes came to focus on the water rushing over his knuckles like a miniature rapids. Lying half in and half out of the chilly water, his body was numb both from the cold and his great loss of blood.

His ears still rang from the second shotgun blast that had cartwheeled him into the water. At least the waters took most of the weight off his pain-racked body and brought some relief. And it hid him from the cold-blooded assassins who'd come out of the night. He'd heard Ricco's scream of terror just before the final blast blew his head off.

Everyone else in his camp was dead. Now they would come looking for him. Floating spread-eagled in the shallow water, he strained to push himself into deeper water. Pain erupted through his body. But he fought the bursting stars that shot through his head knowing that if he lost consciousness, he'd never regain it. He bit down on his tongue and clamped his jaw shut to stifle a scream as the current finally caught his mangled leg and allowed him to float into the middle of the stream.

As he floated away, he had to use his hand to fend off the rocks that jutted out of the shallow water. Fifteen minutes later, he was giggling in near hysteria. And feeling a strange euphoria. It came from the thought that he just might survive.

Carlo Gianini felt his body banging helplessly down a small rush of rapids, but he was past pain. A mantle of protective shock gripped him. The banging stopped and he felt the bottom dropping away from his groping hand. He was in deep water. As he treaded water, he saw a shack built out on a dock less than fifty yards downstream. When he grabbed one of the moss-covered pilings of the rickety dock, he could see that it was a summer canoe rental. On the shore between the trees and the bank were dozens of canoes in racks used by annual vacationers to the area.

He tried to ease over the side of one of them that bobbed alongside the dock. But the more weight he put on it, the more it tipped. Finally, with a gurgling hiss, it capsized and sank.

He realized the only way he was going to be able to get into one was to pull himself out of the water onto the dock and roll in. But the minute he pulled himself up onto the splintery dock, his whole body seemed to catch on fire.

Shivering uncontrollably and gasping for every breath, he lay there for almost an hour before he could muster enough strength to roll into one of the tethered canoes. He untied the hemp knot and pushed away from the dock. Within seconds, the canoe carried him downstream into the darkness.

The gentle rocking motion made him drowsy. In the distance he could see lights outlining the steel trestles of a bridge rising out of the water. He didn't dare drift into the beckoning exhausted sleep until he cleared the bridge: he didn't want to bang into one of the pilings and capsize. He struggled to a sitting position and flopped over the bow to fend off in case the canoe came close to the pilings. And then his heart began to pound.

On a little knoll behind the bridge, he saw a half-dozen men standing near a white frame house bathed in lights. Parked next to the house was the delapidated car the smiling Mexicans had coasted down into his camp in.

310

Ferrara knelt at the end of the dock. He couldn't believe it. Not only was the Italian still alive, but he'd taken a canoe and was heading downstream. He put a finger to the edge of a dark smear of blood. Barely dried round the edge. The man wasn't too far ahead.

He set his shotgun down and sloshed water out of the river onto the dock to wash away the blood. They didn't want questions. Then he crept up to the shack that sat on the back of the dock. He could see the kid in charge of the canoe rentals asleep on a cot. Ferrara lifted one of the canoes out of its wood cradle and set it in the water, pulled a paddle off a nail on the side of the shack, propped his shotgun on one of the seats, and pushed off.

Pressed into the shadow at the bottom of the canoe, Carlo felt an eternity pass before his canoe drifted past the huddle of men. He prayed they couldn't hear his heart beating like a trip-hammer. His body felt numb. The black nightmarish shadows had finally disappeared and the river's current carried him toward safety. Exhaustion swept over him. His last reserve of energy was gone. But still, his mind refused to allow him the luxury of rest.

Another hour passed before he saw lights twinkling in the distance on both sides of the river marking an approaching town. As the river made a switchback before running under another bridge, he leaned once again over the bow and with his hand paddled out of the current toward the shore. The nose of the canoe stuck in the muddy bank, and he lost control of his emotions and broke into muffled sobs. He had accomplished the most important feat in life. He had survived. When the sun came up, someway he'd find someone to help him back to the tiny motor court in the little town of Sebastepol where he'd left his old housekeeper. He couldn't keep his eyes open any longer as exhaustion started to strangle his body and he finally lost consciousness.

Lying on his stomach, he felt his whole body throb. His eyes ached when he tried to open them. It took a moment before he could focus on the ribs of the canoe that met at the spruce keel like a spiny skeleton. The fear started sweeping over him again. His body begged for more sleep. But the sweat around his collar told him the sun had been up for hours and he'd already slept longer than he dared. Licking his parched lips, he pushed himself up on one elbow and looked over the side toward where the town should be.

He couldn't believe his eyes.

"Dio!" His heart pounded. He was twenty or thirty yards from shore in the middle of the river. Over the bow, he could see rough water ahead where the river ran past a long reed-covered sandbar and emptied into the ocean swells. While he slept, the canoe must have slipped off the mud bank and into the current. If the little craft drifted into the open sea, he'd never survive.

"Buon giorno!" a voice behind him said, snapping him around in panic. His mind screamed in horror as he stared into the end of the old man's double-barrel shotgun. With the blade of his paddle, the old man had kept the two canoes side by side with one hand while he kept the shotgun trained on the young Italian with the other.

"Hope you don't mind," Ferrara spoke in Italian. "Seems like you were stuck on the mud bank back there. So I took the liberty of pulling you off."

The water was muddy and except for the swirling flocks of sea gulls floating overhead, both banks were deserted.

Carlo Gianini knew there was no escape. The old man had him. He closed his eyes, praying it wouldn't be too painful.

"Some nice sea air . . . a voyage might help heal your wounds," Ferrara said.

"Please, *signore*," Gianini said. "I beg you. Show mercy to a . . ."

"Of course," the old man interrupted. "I will show you mercy." The old man sounded almost fatherly. But there was no such emotion in his eyes. "I will show you the same mercy you showed the child."

"Signore . . . prego! I am not responsible for the child. I swear to you. Please. I can pay you a fortune. I can make you a rich man. No one need ever know you found me. I promise I'll never be seen here again. Rafael Orsini need never fear again . . . if only you . . ."

"You are the Padrone?" Ferrara said, realizing the mistake he and the others had made. He looked across at the blubbering, sniveling man and wondered how he'd ever posed such a threat to his son-in-law's family.

"Sì . . . sì. I am Carlo Gianini. So you see, I can keep my word. You can be rich . . . beyond your wildest dreams. If only you . . ."

He stopped as the old man's face filled with contempt and rage. "What about the child?" Ferrara's voice trembled, barely above a whisper.

"By now he is back with his mama."

"True. But he is near death."

"What?" Gianini said, truly shocked. "But it wasn't any of my doing. Besides, what is all this to do with us?"

"He is my grandson."

Gianini felt numb with dread.

Ferrara looked around. The river's flow was perfect. The Italian's body would be swept miles out to sea before floating to the surface. By then, no one would be able to identify him.

Ferrara tightened his finger around the trigger and then stopped himself. Had he reloaded after firing at the young Italian back on the bank? He let go of Gianini's canoe and quickly broke open the breech. Sure enough, both shells had been fired.

Ferrara never saw the blade of the paddle he'd dropped into Gianini's canoe as it whistled into his face, crushing his nose and part of his forehead. Involuntarily, he dropped his shotgun and clutched at the pain that exploded through his face and head. Half blinded, he saw the shadowy figure of the Padrone pulling the shotgun out of the bottom of the canoe where he'd dropped it. It didn't matter. The Italian might have the shotgun. But he had the shells.

He lunged across the canoe toward the blurred image of the Padrone. He missed and felt himself falling head first into Carlo Gianini's canoe, causing it to pitch violently. He heard the young Padrone's curses when both hammers fell on empty chambers.

He heard the clatter of metal against wood as Gianini dropped the gun into the bottom of the boat, and grabbed

313

the paddle again. A faint whistling sound rushed toward him. He instinctively tried to dodge, but brilliant flashes of light exploded through his head. When the flashes stopped, he was on the edge of a black abyss.

He pawed the air, trying to grab the Padrone's throat. If he could just grab hold, the devil himself wouldn't break his grip. But blood closed out most of his vision: he grabbed nothing but air. Then he felt himself being pushed over the side of the canoe by the Italian's foot. He tried to grab the side, to turn the boat over as he slid into the water, but he was too late. For a few minutes he thrashed and gulped water as he fought to stay afloat.

Gianini watched as Ferrara finally slipped below the surface. He slumped back exhausted, out of breath, and waited until the old man's movements stopped. As Ferrara floated face down, Gianini reached over with the paddle and pulled him toward the canoe. The old man could now help him escape from the rest of those demons. Carlo's passport and papers were in his coat pocket. He would slip his coat on to the old man before setting him loose in the current. When the body was finally discovered, they would think it was his.

He was bent over the old man when suddenly Ferrara returned to life. With a sound like the bellow of a bull elephant, his face broke out of the water and Ferrara grabbed Gianini by the coat and pulled him half out of the canoe.

Carlo's screams of terror were echoed back by the sea gulls as they circled overhead.

The canoe capsized. Carlo felt his body sinking under the weight of the old man. In a crazed panic, he tore away from the old man's grasp, flipped over, and with his good leg kicked as hard as he could. But the harder he thrashed, the nearer the old man's hands seemed to be. Clutching . . . grasping . . . at him.

He felt a surge of power catch his body. He had swum into the river's current: it swept him away from Ferrara toward safety. When he thrashed back onto his stomach, he banged into something. It was the swamped canoe, also caught in the current with him.

* * *

From the still waters near the shore, Ferrara could barely make out the Padrone's head next to the canoe as it bobbed toward the choppy water where the river flowed into the ocean. Finally he saw the swamped canoe start to pitch and buck. Ferrara rose as far out of the water as he could. The last thing he could make out was the canoe thrashing like a mortally wounded animal as it disappeared into the ocean.

Paralyzed with pain and nearly too exhausted to move, Ferrara dog-paddled toward the muddy bank. He finally felt the bottom under him and managed to crawl partway up a mud flat. He was unconscious by the time the logging truck screeched to a halt along the deserted coastal road and its driver leaped out and raced toward him.

Ferrara remembered nothing but the pain throbbing through his body as the truck which smelled of diesel fuel and cigar smoke thundered down the narrow road toward help. He nodded numbly as the doctor tried to stitch up his face after giving him a pain-killer that sent him to a dark, warm pleasant place. He smiled as the last thing he heard the trucker say to the nurse was that it was an accident. And how lucky the old man was because his boat must have been caught in the rip where the fresh water met the salt.

"Happens to lots of guys fishing round there," the man said. "Damn near caught me half-dozen times."

The next thing Ferrara remembered was opening his eyes and seeing Rafael standing over him.

"What happened to your face?" Rafael leaned close to his father-in-law's bed. "Boy, oh boy! I'd sure hate to see the other guy."

"Don't make me laugh," Ferrara warned as he felt his stitches erupt in pain. "Tried to push my boat out of the rapids with my head."

Rafael stood and stared down at the old man's mutilated face. "Can I get you something? Anything?"

"Maybe some ice cream," Ferrara said without moving his jaw. "Mouth feels like the bottom of a saloon toilet."

"Vanilla okay?" He started for the door.

"How's the boy?" Ferrara's question stopped him.

"He still hasn't come around yet," Rafael said quietly.

"Angelica's with him. She won't leave his side. The doctor says there's nothing anyone can do but wait."

Ferrara nodded as he once again drifted off into the soothing depths of unconsciousness.

CHAPTER TWENTY-THREE

Angelica had barely dozed and hadn't been out of her clothes for more than a week as she kept a bedside vigil over her son. She was past the point of exhaustion. Her eyes were hollow fiery holes that seared everyone, including Rafael, who came into Pietro's room.

The only time she'd back away from the bed was when the doctor came to check his pulse and temperature. Or when the nurse came to change the bed and clean up after he'd wet the bed. Or to call Alicia to check on the twins.

The rest of the time, Angelica stood guard like an avenging angel. Rafael brought her coffee. He brought her soup. He brought her sandwiches. But she rarely ate more than a mouthful. Even when her father was finally strong enough to shuffle in to visit them, she barely acknowledged his wounds and apparent pain.

"We have to do something," she said, barely above a whisper, as she stared down at the body of her son. He was wasting away before her eyes, his body curled up into a fetal position.

"The doctor's trying his best," Rafael answered.

"But he isn't getting any better," Angelica said as her eyes lined with tears.

"Do you want to have him moved somewhere else?"

"Yes . . ." Angelica looked up. "No . . . I mean . . . Oh, God! I don't know what I mean." She cried softly. "I only want things to go back to the way they were." She lay her head on the edge of Pietro's bed.

Rafael looked away, his eyes filled with tears. He felt guilt for their pain and for this terrible thing that had happened to their son.

"No cry . . . Mommy." The little voice brought them both up with a start.

317

Staring at Angelica through big blinking black eyes was Pietro.

"No cry . . . Mommy," he said again softly. "Pietro be good boy . . . no cry mommy!"

"Oh, dear God!" she sobbed as she pressed her son into her arms. "Oh, my God! Yes, Pietro is a good boy and Mommy won't cry anymore."

For several weeks after Pietro was released from the little clinic, things more or less returned to normal. There was an unspoken and uneasy truce between Angelica and Rafael as they each spent as much time as possible with Pietro, leaving the twins to Alicia's care.

Alicia buried herself in caring for the squiggly, delightfully rambunctious twins who seemed all arms, legs, drools, and wet diapers. But despite the peace that seemed to have settled over the Orsini family and farm, Alicia still sensed the storm smoldering within Angelica. At first, Alicia hadn't understood and was hurt by her sister-in-law's coldness. In Italy, right or wrong, your bloodline dictates your loyalty. But now that the twins had become her charges, Alicia realized how violently she would react if one of them was threatened. She also could understand how hurt . . . betrayed . . . she'd feel if the reason for that threat came from some private war or feud she should have known about. But no matter what, she knew afterward she'd stand by her man. She prayed that Angelica could understand and forgive. And that Angelica would come to see what she was doing to Rafael and to her—how guilty she had made them both feel. Now that Pietro is home and well God's will and time will erase the past for all of us, she thought.

But as the weeks drifted into months, little things about Pietro started bothering them all. Outwardly, he seemed a happy child, and he was certainly growing. He had Rafael's smile and looked more like his father with every passing day. But he had trouble remembering things. Things that he'd always known before. And he rarely spoke and seemed confused when faced with learning anything new.

When it appeared he was getting worse, instead of better, they finally drove him into San Francisco to see a specialist. They sat in silent dread as the specialist tapped his black pen on the top of Pietro's manila medical file.

"I'm afraid," Dr. Irving Proznin said, "that your son's head injury was more serious than anyone imagined at the time."

"But the doctor said . . ." Angelica started.

Dr. Proznin held up his hands and nodded. "You must understand there's no way anyone could have known under the circumstances. The injury in the simplest of terms was like . . . well, a blood vessel rupturing beneath the skin. The pressure from it caused your son's coma. The pressure also caused damage to the surrounding areas. If it was in, say, the arm, or leg, it would result in a rather unimportant bruise. But in the confines of the skull . . ."

"So what does it mean?" Rafael asked.

"It means a part of your son's brain has been permanently damaged."

"Oh, God." Angelica's eyes filled with tears.

"I'm afraid," Proznin dropped his eyes away from the handsome couple, "that Pietro will be fortunate . . . fortunate indeed . . . if he ever progresses mentally beyond the intellectual age of a six or seven year old."

Instinctively, Angelica reached over to grasp Rafael's hand. But as soon as hers met his, she recoiled.

"What do you recommend?" Rafael asked.

"That you give serious thought to the child's future," Proznin answered.

"Which means what?" Rafael asked.

"As Pietro grows older, he's going to become more and more dependent on the two of you. He'll look absolutely normal. Especially to the other children around him who won't know of his problem. He'll even seem normal to the two of you at times. As the years go by, he'll develop a deep voice, be sexually mature, shave . . . but he'll remain a child. A child in a man's body. He won't be able to function in society, especially our society, without you. So I would seriously suggest you give consideration to placing him in a home."

"No!" Angelica said, the pain magnified in her voice.

"No!" Rafael added without looking at her. "He's my son . . ."

The doctor nodded sadly. He'd expected their reaction.

"Take some time. Don't rush into any decisions one way or another," he advised. "You're both reasonably young. You have other children. As a matter of fact, Mrs. Orsini, you should give serious thought to how little time you'll have left for your other children. And how they may be affected by Pietro's growing needs."

"It's like a curse," Angelica said as they jerked along in the traffic that led them back out of the city. "It's like we're being punished for that night. I never knew life could go from being so bright and beautiful to being so . . . ugly and gray." She tried to hide her anger and pain from Pietro who was sitting in her lap. "And so much of it is because you didn't tell me about the things that happened to you . . . and Alicia."

"I wish to God now that I had. I don't see what difference it would have made . . . what it would have changed . . . but I wish to God I had."

"We'll never know now, will we?"

As the traffic thinned, their speed picked up. But the hours that lay between them and home were spent in silence. Angelica promised herself that she would prove the doctor wrong: someway, someday, her son would be normal. Rafael tried to concentrate on the road, but all he could think of was that everything had happened because of him.

CHAPTER TWENTY-FOUR

Summer in the vineyards is the worst time of year for the growers. The heat is stifling. It scorches the hills, parches throats, and dulls the mind as men tend their vines, waiting like expectant fathers for the sugar to build up in the fruit so they can harvest.

Since winter, when the vines looked like gnarled hands from some weathered corpse reaching out of the brown earth, the growers have waited.

Through the spring, when the vines started showing tender shoots and lush green leaves, they have waited.

While the tiny, delicate, almost invisible blossoms changed magically into tiny hard clusters of buckshot-sized fruit, they waited. Some spent their waiting time worrying about bees and starlings ravaging their grapes. Others kept busy thinning, pruning, irrigating, and weeding. They spent tedious hours cleaning and recleaning fermenting and storage tanks and counting barrels and gondolas, worrying whether they had enough or too many.

From one of his rows, as he fidgeted and waited, Rafael looked up as Angelica's car rattled down the road toward him. Even with the windows down, the interior of Angelica's coupe was still like an oven. It had been parked in the sun all morning.

The wind whipped the ends of her long hair as she drove Alicia, Pietro, and the twins down the freshly tarred road. She slowed and pulled onto the dusty shoulder next to the drainage ditch where Rafael was working on the vines near the road.

"Hello, Papa," Pietro yelled with a big smile as he half hung out the window. He loved to ride with his head and shoulders draped so the wind blew in his face.

"Hello, Pietro," Rafael yelled back as he opened the door and dragged his son out in a growling bear hug. He set the boy back onto the running board.

Rafael felt a tug at his heart. A little over a year had passed since they had seen the specialist in San Francisco. The man had been right. Pietro was growing like a weed. But his mind was lagging farther and farther behind. He looked in the backseat where the usually chattering twins were on the verge of falling asleep.

"Where's this gang off to?" he asked as he wiped the sweat from his forehead with his oversized bandana and pulled his straw hat back on.

"Just into town. The post office . . . department store . . . and bank," Angelica answered mechanically, almost coldly.

Rafael ignored the coolness. By now he was almost used to it.

"We're going to stop in River Park and have a picnic before we start back."

Rafael nodded, aware he wasn't invited.

"Why don't you meet us?" Alicia asked.

"No, but thanks," Rafael said, smiling at his sister.

"There's food on the stove. All you have to do is heat it," Angelica said as she tried to put the car into gear. The grinding of metal against metal sent shivers up her spine.

"I have a couple of pounds of coffee you can grind for me later." Rafael looked down at her with a grin on his face.

"Very funny," she said, unamused as her face turned red.

Rafael shook his head as the car disappeared down the shimmering blacktop while Pietro waved back at him as he hung precariously out the window while Alicia held him by his belt.

Later that evening, Rafael was working in the winery when a voice brought him around.

"You need some help around here, mister?"

Rafael looked down from where he was hosing out one of his fermenting tanks. The raw-boned boy was dressed in a plaid shirt. His hair was cut short and showed the traces of an unsure hand.

"I don't know. Maybe. What can you do?" Rafael asked.

"Just about anything. And iffin I can't, I can sure learn." The boy's grin had a challenge in it.

"What's your name, boy?"

"Joe Anthony, sir."

"Where you from Joe Anthony?"

"All over, sir. My folks'r pickers. So we gets around lots."

Rafael nodded and held out his hand. "My name's Rafael Orsini."

"Yes, sir. I know." Joe Anthony, took his hand and shook it. "We met afore," the boy said in his slow methodical drawl. "I was through this neck of the woods afore."

Rafael looked at him closely.

The boy smiled. "My folks and me stopped off looking for work. You and your missus were having a fancy picnic under them trees you got out yonder and asked us to join in. Treated us like we was part of it . . . invited like."

Rafael smiled, remembering the boy who'd stayed so close to his father. And the sad-eyed woman breast-feeding a scrawny baby.

"We heard 'bout that bad night of yours a year or so ago."

Rafael looked at the boy with narrowing eyes.

"What night was that?" he asked warily.

" 'Bout the night your boy near drowned. Terrible thing. We's all sorry to hear 'bout it." Joe Anthony said, innocent of anything other than what had been reported. "My folks said to tell ya'll they still remembered you in their prayers. Specially now . . ."

"Thanks," Rafael said after a pause. Stupid to be so suspicious, he thought. "How are your folks?"

"They's fine, thanks. Still together and still on the road." He smiled, sensing Rafael's mood shift.

"What kind of work you looking for?"

"Mostly any kind. Course making wine's sorta my specialty. Learned it from my daddy. We make a batch every year out of wild grapes. Pick 'em up in the mountains near the Oregon border on our way back into California."

Rafael raised his eyebrows and nodded to show he was impressed.

"Time I was striking out on my own, though. So my daddy says I should come on down to this neck of the woods and learn more about how to make good wine."

"Rafael . . ." He heard Alicia calling him from the back porch.

"*Sí?*" he called back, walking to the open double doors.

"Dinner!" she said before turning and going back in.

Rafael looked up at the mountains that surrounded their valley. They were starting to play hide and seek through low-lying thunderheads. A cool, moisture-filled breeze blew down from the mountains. The heat was breaking. That meant the crush wouldn't be far behind.

Where the hell's Rivera, he thought, automatically checking the road.

"By the way," Rafael said without looking back as he headed toward the house, "you had dinner?"

"Thank you, sir, I already ate."

Rafael stopped and turned.

"When?"

"This morning," Joe said, after an embarrassed pause.

"Come on," Rafael said, turning back toward the house. "Let's eat. That'll give me time to see if I can come up with something for you to do around here so you can learn a few tricks about how to make good wine."

The boy almost broke into a run as he attempted to catch up to Rafael and match his long strides.

"Angelica . . . Alicia. You remember this young man? He was here a few years back with his family from Oklahoma. This is Joe Anthony, Jr." Rafael said as Angelica passed behind them on her way to the table with steaming bowls of green beans and mashed potatoes.

"Hello, Joe," Angelica said as she set the bowls on folded napkins that served as hot pads. "Good to see you again. How's your mother?"

"Howdy, ma'am. She's fine, thank you. Just like always." He was thrilled the tall, dark-haired woman remembered.

"Joe'll be joining us for dinner," Rafael said as he washed his hands in the sink. He grabbed a towel hung next to the window and left the water running for Joe.

"You live around here now, Joe Anthony?" Alicia asked

from the stove where she was adding flour to the rich, dark gravy.

"No, ma'am . . . yes, ma'am. Well, sort of." He stammered as his heart pounded with just-born love for the black-haired vision at the stove.

"Where's your father?" Rafael asked Angelica as he pulled out his chair and sat down.

Angelica just shrugged and busied herself with the dinner. Her father's physical wounds had healed, but he could never forget or forgive the Padrone who had invaded their lives and destroyed his grandson's future.

Joe ate quietly trying to remember the manners his mother had taught him. He avoided looking at the dark-haired boy sitting next to Rafael at the head of the table. He had spoken to the boy when he first came in, and had shaken hands at Rafael's urging. The boy seemed okay. It was hard to believe that anything was wrong with a little kid like that. He sure looked okay. Not as good though as the young woman who worked alongside Mrs. Orsini. Although she was definitely a lot older than he was, he couldn't keep his eyes off her.

As casually as he could, he tried to look her way without anyone noticing. But Alicia caught him staring at her and he blushed flame red and quickly turned back to his plate.

Rafael chuckled as Alicia coughed pitifully to attract Joe's attention. When the love-struck boy looked back at her, she winked. Once again, Joe turned crimson.

Rafael was delighted. Anything that could help lighten the pall that hung over their farm and lives was a godsend.

What Rafael didn't understand was that Alicia's increasing good mood was tied to the approaching harvest. For with the harvest came Rivera and his crew. Rivera had been on her mind a great deal lately. She had been constantly amazed at how often she found herself thinking about him. The sound of his voice. His laugh His kidding. His warmth. His tenderness. More than once the thought had entered her mind that with Carlo Gianini and the nightmare he represented dead, there might be room in her life for love.

* * *

Rafael walked back down the row of vines toward the house where Alicia was helping Angelica take clothes from the clothesline. They folded the stiff sheets, working as a team. When the last sheet was done, Alicia took it out of Angelica's hand, dropped it on top of the basket, and went toward the back porch.

Rafael stood there, half watching them and half in a trance.

"Troubles?" Angelica asked, pulling the wood clothespins off the wire line and dropping them into the bag attached to the line.

"Nothing more than usual." He half smiled.

"Something's bothering you," she said, finishing and coming toward him.

"No. Really. Nothing."

She stopped in front of him and took a cluster of grapes he had been holding in his hand. She took a couple off the stem, wiped them on her apron to make sure the dust was off, and slipped them into her mouth. Since her childhood, her father had brought clusters into the house to test them for sugar and taste. Some years they were sweeter than others . . . some years harder. It all depended on the weather.

Over the years she had learned to tell how far along the grapes were in the season, when they were approaching their peak, and usually within a week, when they should be picked.

"I don't think I can remember them ever being sweeter this time of year."

"I tried to treat each one a little better this year." He nodded toward the row after row of beautifully tended spikes that blossomed like a virtual garden of Eden.

"It shows," she said as she turned back to the house.

"I think I'm going to go ahead and clean out the storeroom next to the cellar . . ." he said.

"It's about time." She thought of the mass of junk stacked behind the thick walls of the wine cellar's storeroom. Rafael, by nature of his childhood, threw away nothing. He was a packrat.

Over the past few years, Angelica had tried to sneak things out to the trash pile or stack them on the truck to haul to the dump. But invariably Rafael had found whatever it was, and it had ended up back in a closet, a box, on a shelf, or stacked under a dusty pile of something in the winery. He knew in his mind at least a hundred things he could do with every stick, bolt, string, paper, broken tool. Bounty was something they enjoyed. But something he subconsciously never believed would last.

"And I think I'm going to go ahead and bottle a few cases before the crush. See if we can't find someone to take them off our hands."

"Only a few?" she asked knowing her husband's talent for understatement.

"Well . . . maybe more than a few," he reluctantly admitted. "Maybe fifty or sixty barrels." He thought of the tiers of barrels that had been aging behind the stone cellar walls since the Treasury department "raid."

"You're going to need some help then."

"Not from you or Alicia. You both already do too much. I'll use Joe. He's a good boy . . ."

"Bottling's not that hard." She shrugged.

"True. But well . . ."

"But well . . . what?" she asked, her eyebrows raising.

"I got a bottler coming."

"I see." She nodded.

"It wasn't much," he quickly explained. "It needs a little work. But I got it used at an auction in Napa. It fills . . . lines up the bottles for inspection. Only thing it doesn't do is cork them and label them."

He waited for her to comment. But she stayed silent.

"So what do you think?" he asked.

"Does it matter?"

"Of course it matters. I just work the fields. You're the boss . . . the brains. Remember?"

"No." She shook her head. "From the moment you kept my father from pulling up those twenty rows of vines that first summer after Maya died, you were the boss. Even the land knew it belonged to you."

"I'd be willing to give it all up . . . to have my wife back," he said turning and leaving her standing alone.

Joe Anthony worked from sunup to sunset every day clearing out the cellar, hauling out old boxes, old tools, things that had been stacked, stored, and forgotten. For days he sneezed as the dust flew when the things were finally moved to make room for Rafael's bottler.

Ferrara was even caught up in the fervor.

"Damn Frenchman!" Joe heard him cursing one morning. He looked out of the winery and saw that Frenchy was trying to back his trailer down the long narrow drive into the winery so that he could get back out without having to turn around.

"Stop! Damn it, don't you move that rig another foot," Ferrara screamed as the trailer slipped into one of the rows and bent three of the grape spikes onto their sides.

Frenchy put the chugging diesel in neutral and hopped out. He grimaced and quickly wiped his face on his shirttail as he looked at the fruit-laden spikes lying on their sides in the dirt.

"Sure am sorry, Mr. Ferrara," he said, truly pained as the old man and boy ran up. "I never was very good at backing these things up."

"You'll have to wait then till Rafael gets back and does it for you," Ferrara said as he surveyed the spikes.

"I can't!" Frenchy moaned. "I gotta unload this bottler and make a pickup this afternoon at Trentedues. If I don't get there, the old man's promised to have my balls. And I'm already late."

"You move an inch and I'll flatten them tires," Ferrara threatened.

"Mr. Ferrara, the Trentedues is already picked. Their grapes are sitting in the sun already rotting. If they was your grapes, you'd kill me."

"I can't be worrying about the Trentedues' grapes. You ain't fit to drive this thing," Ferrara said, kicking the tractor's mudflap. Ferrara had sympathy for the Trentedues. But this incompetent could knock out a whole row of their vines with his rig and not even know it. He was that kind of driver. And that could be their profit. "You'll just have to wait for my son-in-law."

"If you don't want to wait, I can move it for you," Joe said.

Neither man looked his way or responded.

"I ain't kidding. I drove my paw's rig up in Oregon . . . lugged down with apples."

"Your paw has a rig?" Frenchy asked.

"Sure does," Joe said proudly. "My maw drives it too. When Paw needs us to work a field or an orchard, then Maw does the driving. Matter of fact, she's better'n Paw. Course we wouldn't dare tell him that. But she taught me to drive 'n I'm better'n both of them."

"Well . . . okay," Ferrara said. "If it's okay with Frenchy, that is."

"It's okay with me," Frenchy said, willing to try anything to get his truck offloaded and back on the road.

"But if I say stop . . . you stop! You hear, boy?" Ferrara said sternly.

The black smoke poured from the exhaust that ran up alongside the cab, as Joe pulled slowly ahead out of the vineyard and lined up the trailer as he eased onto the drive.

Without so much as a complaint from the engine and gearbox, he double-clutched and revved the engine so it would shift easily into reverse. His eyes darting as they shifted from one mirror to another, Joe, his head barely showing above the door window, guided the tractor and trailer as straight as an arrow. As he backed past the house, he curved around the yard and eased up to the dock.

"You better let this boy give you a few lessons," Ferrara said as Joe switched off the diesel.

"Lessons, hell!" Frenchy said, acknowledging the boy's skill, "you finish up here, boy, you got a full-time job with me."

"Thanks. But I'm going to be a winemaker," Joe said as he slipped a hook from the winch to the cable that circled the machinery and started cranking the handle that lifted them off the floor of the trailer so they could swing over to the dock.

"Winemaking . . ." Frenchy grinned. "Anyone can make wine. I make fifty . . . sixty gallons every year. Don't cost nothing. Just pick what's left on the vines after the pickers move on . . . throw it in a barrel. Knock a plug in it an' bury it till it's ready."

"Probably tastes like you buried it too," Ferrara said disgustedly.

"Wine's wine," Frenchy said. "Besides, there's no future

in wine. Beer maybe. Whiskey for sure. But nobody drinks much wine over here. Truckin'. Now that's where the future is. That's where the big bucks are," Frenchy said jumping up into the cab.

"You sure you can steer this thing out of here now?" Ferrara asked.

"Oh, I can go forward. That's a breeze! Trucks were made to go straight ahead. If God wanted them to back up, he'd a put the steering wheel in the back." He grinned as he pulled slowly away and carefully eased down the drive between the vines.

CHAPTER TWENTY-FIVE

Ferrara was sitting on a wide-armed redwood picnic chair under his favorite tree at the far end of the vineyard, away from the house. It was peaceful here. He could hear nothing but sounds of nature. Birds. The buzzing of insects. The water in the creek below. The gentle breeze.

Now, on the breeze, he could hear the sound of clothes scraping against the leaves and branches of the vines. Someone was coming through the vineyard toward him.

His daughter slowly made her way toward him, the thick bushy vines all but hiding her tall frame.

"What brings you out to my little part of the world?" he asked, as she sat down on the arm of his chair.

"I could use a little of your shade. A little of your peacefulness. And a whole lot of your quiet," she said referring to the constant clanking and rattle of Rafael's new bottler.

"Glad to share it. I know how hard it is keeping up with those two little rug rats of yours. Not to mention Pietro." He rested his head against the wood back. "Hard, hard work."

"Work never killed a wife yet."

"Glad to hear you using that word."

"Which one?"

"Wife."

She unscrewed the top off a thermos of iced tea she had brought him. "What do you mean?"

"You know what I mean. You're treating your husband like he's anything but one. It wasn't his doing, Angelica. You think he wouldn't do anything to change it all if he could?"

"Please, Papa. Not now!" She cut him off as she handed him the metal cup filled with tea.

It was strong, sweet, and ice cold. Almost as he watched, the moisture formed on the outside of the shiny metal.

"I been thinking about taking a little trip," he said.

"Really?"

"Yep. With all this new-fangled machinery, there's not much left for a man to do around here."

"You've never taken a vacation that I can remember."

"Farmer can't afford to take a lot of time away from his land. But my vegetables done petered out on me for the summer. So . . . I just don't feel like sitting around."

"Where are you thinking of going?"

There was a long pause.

"Oh, I been thinking about a little trip back home maybe. It'll probably be the last chance I get, what between old age and this war thing brewing with that Hitler fellow."

"Italy?"

He nodded.

"That's wonderful, Papa," she said, suddenly thrilled by the reward he was going to allow himself. He had always scrimped, saved, and hoarded for their future. She was delighted he was finally going to take time for enjoyment. "When . . . I mean, what are your plans?"

"Hold on. Hold on now, girl. I can't do anything till the work's all done around here. Your grape harvest has to be got in . . ."

"Oh no, you don't. You can't make your plans around that. Rivera will be here for that. And Rafael has Joe."

He nodded and stared at the ground.

Angelica took his hand. She knew he was feeling the effects of being passed by lately. Every time he mentioned that something needed doing, Rafael either had it done or Joe was working on it. "This vacation is going to do you a world of good," she said.

Ferrara nodded, glad he had made her happy. He didn't want her ever to know how filled he was with frustration and hatred. The two emotions welled up inside him every time he thought of his grandson, a beautiful boy who should be on the verge of a wonderful life and who had become barely more than a grinning, two-legged cocker spaniel.

The memory of the Padrone's face bobbing into the open sea had been with him constantly since he had happened on the article in one of the old yellowed newspapers hauled out of the storeroom to make room for Rafael's new bottler.

BRUSH WITH SHARK BRINGS DEATH TO TOURISTS FROM FOREIGN SHORES

San Francisco . . . Fishing normally holds few hazards, except for the inexperienced. That lesson was vividly learned by Mr. Carlo Gianini, an Italian tourist, as he and four others in his party fished near the mouth of the Russian River.

After hooking a large shark, one of Gianini's party, a Mr. Maxmillian Buntz, took it upon himself to dispatch the creature with a shotgun brought along to shoot at seals and gulls.

The rough waters caused Mr. Buntz to lose his balance as he tried to stand in their tiny craft. When he fell, his weapon discharged.

Mr. Gianini was struck by the errant blast as the craft capsized, spilling his party of nonswimmers into the sea. Hanging onto the side of the craft, Mr. Gianini watched helplessly as, one by one, his friends were swept to their watery graves.

Fortunately, before succumbing to exhaustion and exposure, Gianini was sighted and picked up by a fisherman working south of Mendicino.

As of this writing, Mr. Gianini is off the Mercy Hospital's critical list and has scheduled his return to Italy via the Panama Canal.

Finding that the animal responsible for their pain had survived was a tremendous shock. The newspaper article burned through his mind every hour of the day. The nights were worse. Like an addict, he would draw his curtains and take it out of the little compartment at the back of his wallet and read it over and over. Despite the pain, it was a secret he knew he must bear alone. If the others found out, it would start their nightmare all over. The only time Ferrara felt any relief was when he fantasized about destroying the man himself. That was when he finally made the decision to take his "Italian vacation." He realized he wouldn't survive. But the peace and security it would give his daughter and her family made the price worth it.

"You all right, Papa?" Angelica interrupted his thoughts.

"Of course." He hoped his smile could hid his smoldering feelings. "Just getting old, I guess."

"So am I," she sighed.

The sound of one of the twins bawling drifted up and brought their moments alone to an end.

"Sounds like trouble only a Mama can help soothe," he said.

"Yeah, guess I better get back and keep the world from coming to an end. You coming?"

"Pretty soon. I want to sit and think for a while longer."

"I'll call you when supper's ready." She squeezed his hand. "Then we can talk some more about your trip. Everybody will be thrilled."

He nodded and leaned back and watched his daughter make her way down the row of vines toward the house. He thought again of how precious she was to him.

He looked around at the farm. It was particularly beautiful at this time of year. He reached down to take a handful of the soil. It was one of the things he loved about his life. Being able to hold the rich, dark earth that seemed to smell of life itself.

He had started to put it to his nose when he was struck with another of his attacks of indigestion. He grimaced as tears of pain came to his eyes.

He'd have to go into town later to the drugstore and get some of that stuff he'd heard about that was supposed to bring instant relief.

God! he thought, as the burning pain seemed to explode through his whole chest. He felt the dirt slowly slipping out of his palm. His vision of the farm started getting blurry.

"Please, God! Not now. There's too much left to do." His head felt too heavy to hold up any longer. He let it fall back against the picnic chair.

"Angelica . . ." But she was too far back toward the house to hear. The words faded silently on the gentle breeze and his arm knocked the metal cup of tea off the arm of the chair into the grass.

"Dinner's about ready," Angelica said behind Rafael as he fed empty green bottles into the bottler that looked like a mad scientist's concoction made from equal parts of a printing press, a milking machine, and the wheel-covered metal tracks that were used to unload trucks at markets.

He nodded and pulled the lever that shut off the electric current, and the clanking and rattle of the machine ground to a halt.

"Papa's down at his tree. I told him I'd call him when we were ready to eat."

"Joe . . ." Rafael called as they came out onto the winery dock.

"Yes, sir?"

"Run down to the end of the vineyard and tell Mr. Ferrara supper's on."

"Yessir," Joe said jumping down from the concrete caisson and jogging into the leafy forest of the vineyard.

Minutes later Rafael heard Joe screaming his name. In less than a second, he was out the door, off the porch, and running toward the boy.

"What is it?" Rafael yelled as he and the boy met.

"I think he's dead," the boy cried.

"What is it, Rafael?" Angelica yelled, frightened, from the back porch. She jumped to the ground and started running toward where they were standing.

Rafael grabbed her before she could barge past.

"Angelica . . . stay here! Something's happened. I'll see what it is."

"I'm going with you," she screamed after him.

"No . . ." he yelled without looking back.

Angelica sat in the overstuffed chair and stared off in space in the dimly lit room, totally unaware of the music from her father's old Zenith console. She felt a blast of chilly air and looked up as Rafael opened the door.

"Hi," he said quietly.

She looked at him but couldn't speak.

He came over and sat down on the edge of the bed next to her chair. He turned on the lamp that sat on a maple, hand-carved table next to his window. As he sat there in the soft glow of the lamp, he took in the world that represented the man's life. The things he kept around him. The things he valued. The things that made him unique as a human being. From the bureau with peeling veneer, Rafael picked up a bottle of unopened after shave . . . a Christmas gift from the twins. He set it down and toyed with several pipes lying in a neat row.

He opened a cigar box and glanced through it. There were a few old coins, a quote torn out of a newspaper, a half-dozen packs of hard Doublemint gum, a couple of used shotgun shells, a stale bar of chaw tobacco, some lint-covered pipe stems, and a chain made out of paper clips that Pietro had joined together.

On the nightstand next to his bed, Rafael saw a pair of cracked steel-framed glasses and his old, well-worn wallet. He reached for the wallet and slowly flipped it open. Under one of the scratched plastic windows was a picture of a smiling, pigtailed Angelica. She was probably no more than ten or eleven. The other yellowing, scratched window framed the driver's license that had expired years before. Angelica had warned her father for years to renew it. "Why should I?" he'd asked. "Still have the same address . . . still the same height and weight . . . and can still drive."

Inside the money compartment was a well-worn two-dollar bill. Rafael could see outlined inside the "secret compartment" the lucky penny Angelica had put in the wallet when she gave it to her father for his birthday when she first entered high school. He slipped his finger under the flap and pulled it back, revealing the secret compartment. He ran the tip of his finger across the still shiny penny nestled in the corner next to a worn, folded newspaper article. He started to pull it out.

"Won't it ever end?" Angelica asked blackly from the depths of the overstuffed chair.

"Won't what ever end?" he asked looking up from the wallet.

"This curse. This damn Orsini curse!"

Rafael knew she was in pain. But blaming him for her father's death was too much of a burden to bear. Without another word, he refolded the wallet back in order, lay it on the bureau, and walked out the door into the night.

After he'd gone, the tears streamed down her cheeks.

She was suddenly afraid. For the first time she realized she was the last of her family. Her mother had been dead for years. Now her father was gone. And she'd finally succeeded in driving her husband away.

The next weeks were a blur for Angelica. It seemed as though her father had taken summer with him with his death. The weather turned as gray and as miserable as her life had become.

As the days passed, she found herself staying close to the house praying for the phone to ring and bring Rafael's voice to her. Or she would stand in the driveway, hoping to hear his car. But there was nothing but silence. Even Pietro and the twins seemed to sense the change, and their big old house that was once filled with laughter and joy was like a silent tomb.

On the outside, Alicia seemed supportive and unworried about her brother's absence. But she was masking her emotions. Alicia had seen Rafael disappear out of her life once before. It had been the beginning of a painful nightmare. She prayed this was different.

They loved each other. They needed each other. And there was no reason Rafael wouldn't soon reappear at the back door wondering when dinner was going to be ready, Alicia reasoned.

When Angelica was forced by necessity to go into town, she found herself searching every face, every distant figure, every shadow. The nights were the worst. Searching for relief, she'd walk around the yard . . . through the quiet rows of vines . . . or check the children for the umpteenth time. Even in sleep, they were their father's children. His dark looks, fiery even in sleep, lay there before her.

She knew what Rafael had done that violent night hadn't been right. But she also knew she could no longer place the blame on his shoulders any more than she could place it on her father . . . or on Rivera . . . or Alicia or the others. But it might be too late for her to tell him that.

CHAPTER TWENTY-SIX

Angelica shivered under two of Rafael's heavy winter coats as she slogged through the mud toward where Joe was tending one of the smudge fires in the vineyard.

The boy's face was covered with soot as she emerged from the darkness. "Howdy, ma'am!" he said, trying not to sound tired.

"You 'bout ready to get some sleep?" she asked as she slumped down on the box he'd just vacated.

"Naw! I'm okay. No need for you to be down here. Waste of time. One can more than handle it."

Angelica looked around the vineyard, outlined by the flickering glow from the burning tires. "How's the kerosene holding out?"

"Getting a little low down toward the creek end," Joe said through his muffler tied around the bottom half of his face. "But I 'spect we'll be able to last out the night."

She looked down toward the rows that ended in the creek where Rafael and Rivera had carried Pietro up the slope that terrible night. She squeezed her eyes shut to erase the shadows that became real faces, but when she opened them again, the shadows were still there . . . only closer.

The hair on the back of her neck bristled and her nerves rang a warning as she watched the figures moving toward them from out of the mist. She put her hand on Joe's back to push him into the safety of the darkness.

"You trying to burn the place down?" a voice called to them out of the darkness.

Angelica's fear evaporated.

"Rivera!" she shouted back, almost delirious with joy and relief.

"*Si* . . . we are here at last." He ran down the row toward her.

"I was about ready to hire on a crew tomorrow that knew how to do some real picking," she said laughing.

Rivera appeared in the yellow light and embraced her.

A half-dozen other men filtered in from the blackness as quietly as the fog.

"Smelled your cookfire." Benito leered down at Angelica. "Hey . . . where is your husband? Sleeping while his poor wife takes care of his grapes for him?"

"No. He's not sleeping. He's . . . well . . . he's not here."

"When will he be back?" the big man asked.

"I don't know," she said quietly. "Oh . . . this is Joe Anthony, Jr." she said to change the subject when she realized no one was talking.

"This the picker that's going to take our place?" Another familiar face, one with a horrible scar through his eye, asked as he bent close to stare in Joe's face.

"Goodness, no!" Angelica said as she put her arm around Joe. "I offered him the job but he turned it down. Said he didn't want to embarrass you."

Joe was relieved to see a grin flood over the skinny man's face.

"*Hola,* José," Benito croaked and took the boy's hand in his immense paw and shook it heartily. "*Bueno* . . . *Bueno. Manos de un paisano.*" The boy's calloused hands signaled that he was no stranger to hard work.

"Says he can outpick any man two to one . . . and any wetback four to one," Angelica joked, while Benito still held the boy's hand.

Joe's heart pounded as the huge gorilla leaned down and squinted at him.

"José . . . you say that?"

"No, sir!" Joe said pulling his hand free from Benito's and taking his muffler away from his face. "Actually what I said was ten to one."

The men and women in the crew hooted and jeered at Benito for being caught.

Benito beamed. This was his kind of young boy.

"Joe, run up to the house and tell Alicia that the crew's here, will you?" Angelica asked.

"Yes, ma'am," he said, slipping into the darkness.

"Where have you all been?" Angelica asked Rivera. "I thought maybe the law was after you or something."

"Our stake bed truck broke down up near the Oregon border. So we pulled it with one of the cars for a little while. Then the car overheated . . . well, it was always overheated. But this time she finally quit. So that put us down to one truck and one car. And as you see, there are many of us now. So we had to leave the others behind and come down to get Frenchy in Healdsberg to pick us up and bring us here. He just dropped us off in the grove where we always camp when we pick for you."

"The one by the road?"

"Sí."

"You can't camp down there now. It must be knee deep in mud. You have everyone bring your stuff up to the house. There's an extra bed in Pietro's room and what we . . . I . . . can't fit in the house, I can set up in the winery."

"Gracias," Rivera said. "Angelica, Frenchy told us about your papa."

She nodded and tried to smile.

"We are more than sorry. He was always a friend to us. He always treated us with dignity."

"Thank you, Rivera," she said as tears lit her eyes. "Well now. Let's get your stuff over to the house. Then maybe you can help with the smudge fires."

"Before we do that, I have to ask if I can use your tractor?"

"Of course you can. But why do you need the tractor?" She already knew the answer before she finished the question. "Frenchy?"

"Sí. Frenchy." Benito grinned. "He pulled in the grove to drop our things off. We warned him. He has his shiny truck stuck in the mud up to the axles."

Angelica was still chuckling in disbelief as she turned at the sound of footsteps running toward them from the house. She expected to see Joe returning. Instead, she saw Alicia.

She had on one of the new dresses she'd just bought in town.

Angelica smiled at her sister-in-law's attempted nonchalance. Alicia was trying to hold a coat over her head to keep her hair from being soaked in the mist that was turning to a soft rain. But her sparkling eyes and broad smile suddenly melted into a shy frightened look when she encountered Rivera.

A silence fell over Rivera's crew as the two of them stood and stared at each other, both almost afraid to speak.

Rivera finally moved to her and held out his hand.

"Hola, Alicia!" He smiled. *"Como está?"*

"Bien!" An answering smile burst across her face. "It's been a long time."

"Sí . . ." He said almost sadly. "A very long time."

The two stood there hand in hand until the crew became embarrassed. Finally Benito slipped away to get the tractor to pull Frenchy out of the mud while the others disappeared back toward the grove to wait for him to return.

"If I'm not mistaken, there's a pot of coffee on the stove," Angelica said, abandoned with two people who needed to be alone. They didn't respond as she turned and walked slowly toward the lights from the house.

As Alicia came into Rivera's arms, he could feel her shivering.

"I will keep you warm," he said, nearly crushing her in his arms.

"I need more than your warmth," Alicia said returning his embrace. "I need you, Guillermo."

Rivera couldn't believe his ears. His heart pounded with love and confusion. He had almost decided not to come this year. The pain of seeing her and not being able to hold her, love her was too much of a burden.

"And I need you, Alicia Orsini. I have even been lonely among my friends. And I promise you . . . I will spend my life convincing you that our love is the only thing that matters."

Alicia reached up and put her fingers over his lips to silence him. "I know . . . I was wrong."

"Someone's in the winery!" they heard someone say as a figure hurtled out of the darkness toward Angelica who was halfway between them and the winery. It was Joe, wide-eyed and frightened.

"It's probably the crew," Angelica said, putting her hand on his shoulder to calm him as Rivera and Alicia hurried up.

Angelica could see that the door into the wine cellar was half open. And a faint light shone from the inside.

"No. *No es mi familia*," Rivera said. "They all went back to the grove."

"Burglars maybe?" said the wide-eyed Joe.

"My God! The children!" Angelica's heart suddenly pounded as memories swept into her mind.

She was about to break into a run when Rivera grabbed her. She looked at his grinning face in confusion.

"It is not burglars, Angelica. It is not even the men from the Treasury department. I'm sorry, ' he whispered as they moved toward the door. "I'm not very good at keeping secrets."

Angelica spun around.

"Rafael?" she cried as tears rolled down her cheeks once again.

"*Sí*," Rivera said sheepishly. "We found him alone on the road walking home."

Before he could finish explaining, she threw open the winery door and bolted down the aisle through a tunnel formed by the tiers of aging fifty-gallon oak wine barrels. But the room was empty. She heard a sound behind the door that led into the limestone cellar. She jerked the door open and flicked a switch that flooded the cellar with glaring bright light.

The figure in the corduroy coat whirled and faced her.

Angelica's heart exploded. "Rafael!" she said, racing across the stone floor and into his arms.

"Holy Christ! You damn near scared me to death."

"*Hola, hermano mio.*" Rivera smiled from the door.

"*Hola.*" Rafael grinned back, delighted to see his friend's arm locked around his sister's waist.

"I'm sorry I wasn't able to keep your secret."

"I'm glad you couldn't," Rafael said, holding Angelica as close to him as he could.

Rivera raised his hand and waved as he closed the door, leaving Rafael and Angelica alone.

* * *

342

"Hey . . . hey . . . hey!" Rafael whispered in Angelica's ear as her whole body was trembling. "It's okay. Everything's okay."

"You came back." She buried her face in his coat.

"You know I couldn't stay away from you very long."

"Thank God. Thank God," she whispered, almost afraid to let go for fear that it might be a dream. "I was so afraid, Rafael. I hurt all over . . . inside and out."

"I know. Me too," he said, feeling her warmth through the layers of clothes. "I tried to drive somewhere that would take me away . . . and I couldn't. I tried to think of a life without you because I thought if I stayed it'd destroy us . . . but I couldn't. I just couldn't. I just couldn't think of any kind of life without you."

"God! Rafael . . . please forgive . . ."

He pulled her even closer.

"I was so mean to you . . ."

"No . . . It was just life. It was mean to us." He reached down and pressed his lips softly over her eyes.

She pulled him down to her and kissed him. All the loneliness and love and joy were felt in that one moment.

"It's finally over," she cried with joy and relief as they walked toward the door to let in the crowd waiting for them.

"No . . ." He smiled. "It's finally starting."

The crew had set up their pallets and cots between the tiers of barrels that lined the cellar. The place looked like a refugee center with the children huddled sleepily, shielding their eyes from the glow of the lanterns and candles stuck in little nooks and crannies. It was chilly in the cellar, and it had to be kept that way for the wine's sake.

On the worktable in the middle of the room, Rafael set out a dozen bottles of wine. He looked up as Rivera led Alicia in from the bottling room where he'd been inspecting the new machinery.

"Pretty fancy," Rivera teased good-naturedly.

"Thank you," Rafael answered.

"What are you going to do with such a big machine as that?" Benito asked. "You can bottle a whole valley full of wine with a thing like that."

"Someday . . . someday," Angelica promised. "He will someday!"

A chorus of cheers echoed off the stone walls.

"I'm glad you are all here tonight, my friend," Rafael said to Rivera. "And you, Benito . . . Muriella, Enrique, Ramon . . . all my true friends . . . old and new who travel with the men who have been like brothers to me over these years."

There was another burst of applause and cheers.

"Tonight I want to share something special with all of you. It's the birth of a dream. A dream that my wife and I shared for a long time. It's our own wine . . . in our own bottle . . . with our own label on it."

He took one of the bottles and blew a layer of dust off it. There was a picture of the winery on the label copied from an original drawn by Angelica in pencil, crayon, and her father's leaky fountain pen.

"Tonight I also want to share something special with you and Angelica," Rivera said. "Alicia and I . . . your sister . . . I mean . . ."

"He means we're getting married," Alicia said for him.

Amid yet another burst of applause and cheers, Rafael crushed his sister and Rivera to him, delirious with the joy of their lives being fulfilled.

"Then the first glass out of this first bottle goes to my brother, Guillermo Rivera."

"At last!" Rivera said, pulling Alicia closer to him, afraid he might wake up and find it all a dream. "This is the night we find out what Orsini wine is made of."

Rafael looked around the room at the smiling faces. Some were sunburned. Some brown from nationality. But each face, young or old, was etched with lines from sun, smiles, and suffering. He felt tremendous love for this small group of men and their families.

"*Vasos, mujer!*" Rivera barked, and in a flash Muriella produced a tray which held an unmatched assortment of everything from heavy shot glasses to jelly glasses. With swelling pride, Rivera saw Alicia take the tray from Muriella and head through the throng toward them with the glasses.

Rafael's and Rivera's eyes met as the command seemed still to echo off the stone walls. Both men felt a simultaneous tug at their hearts at the memory of Maya hurrying to fill the command.

With great ceremony, Rafael uncorked the first bottle. Then he held it up to the light so he could study its clarity.

"Sure looks like wine to me," Benito chuckled.

Rafael picked up a glass and filled it to the brim, then pushed the glass across the heavy wood table to Rivera.

Looking at Rafael and Angelica, Rivera raised the glass to them. "May your wine be as rich as your friendship to us. May they know your name for a thousand years. May your children always know full stomachs and warm beds. And someday . . . may your winery grow until all others seem small."

"Thank you, my friend," Rafael said, genuinely touched.

Rivera sipped slowly and swirled the Burgundy liquid around in his mouth before swallowing.

Rafael, Angelica, Alicia, and the others waited silently for his verdict.

"Sunshine, earth . . . vine. You have captured them all and put them in a little bottle." He smiled.

A chorus of cheers and applause echoed off the stone walls as Angelica proudly slipped her arm around Rafael's waist. The atmosphere was festive as Rivera poured the rest of the bottle into Alicia's glass.

"To you, my love," he said as his glass touched hers.

After toasting everything that came to mind with the first dozen bottles, Rafael set out another dozen bottles. The sound of corks popping was almost like a melody.

As the children started nodding in their mother's arms, Rivera slipped his hand out of Alicia's and went over to Rafael who was helping Angelica stack the glasses on the tray so she could take them back in the house and wash them for Muriella.

"It is fine wine, my brother. But it's a good thing you don't make tequila. We would never get any work done . . . only sit in the shade and talk of old times, eh?"

"That's true, my friend . . . which reminds me." He turned and winked to Angelica and Alicia so Rivera couldn't see. "There is one more bottle—the first bottle. I have saved it especially until now. It is for you . . . and you alone. We've been through much." He took the bottle from a wicker cradle under the bench and carefully stripped the metal foil from the cork. "I owe you more than I can ever repay. And as a token of my love and respect, Angelica and I . . . and Alicia . . . decided to make this bottle our gift to you."

Tears came to Rivera's eyes as he reached out and with an unsteady hand took a glass as Rafael poured.

"My dear friends. I don't know what to say . . . or where to begin."

"Begin by talking less . . . and drinking more wine," Angelica teased.

"Would you join me?" Rivera asked, offering the glass to Alicia.

She demurely shook her head. "This is too special. Rafael indeed meant that for you and you alone."

"It is a great honor . . ."

At Alicia's urging, Rivera lifted up the glass over his head to toast them all and, as if it were a shot of tequila, downed it in one gulp. Suddenly Rivera's face turned red. He hissed . . . he gasped . . . he gulped . . . he wheezed. He thrashed around pounding the top of the work bench with his palm as the Burgundy liquid burned from mouth to stomach.

Tequila would have been mother's milk compared to this. He'd never had chili so devastating. But when he saw Rafael, Angelica, and Alicia hysterical with laughter, he knew he'd been had.

His forehead exploded in little puffy rivulets of perspiration. His face seemed to ripple with waves of red, but he wiped the perspiration off his face, picked up the bottle, and in a voice that sounded like that of a man being strangled, he said, "Not bad! Needs a little more aging."

They couldn't stop laughing and Alicia thought her sides were going to burst in pain. Rafael and Angelica were doubly delighted. They had never seen her laugh so hard.

"You do this to your poor old Rivera?" he asked Alicia.

"Don't blame her," Angelica said when Alicia couldn't stop laughing long enough to defend herself. "Rafael's been planning this for years. He told me what you did to him the first time he had tequila. He's been waiting to get even with you ever since."

"Phew!" Rivera exhaled, wiping his forehead again. "What is this stuff anyway?"

"I wasn't lying." Rafael said innocently. "It was the first bottle we bottled . . . from one of our first barrels of wine."

"This is from the grape?" Rivera asked, increduously.

"It was. It's from one of the barrels that turned to vinegar that year they confiscated our wine."

"Someday . . . my friend," Rivera warned Rafael, "someday Rivera will have his revenge."

Angelica looked at her husband and sister-in-law. Seeing them smiling, happy, clowning, and free made it almost like old times. The pain that she had felt seemed to have disappeared. She prayed that the storm was over.

CHAPTER TWENTY-SEVEN

The months drifted into seasons, the seasons into years, and the healing effects of time returned the magic to their lives.

The year after that first bottle of wine was shared with Rivera, Alicia's and Rivera's wedding filled the town's tiny church with grins, tears, hope, and love. As she came down the aisle dressed in a gown made for her by Angelica and Muriella, Alicia was aware of only one thing. The Mexican standing at the altar waiting for her. Waiting for her to become his wife.

It seemed like no sooner were their vows exchanged then they were on the road. Harvest time was at its peak and the crew was needed. Their honeymoon and first days together were spent side by side in a field forty miles east of Rafael's and Angelica's farm. It was hot, dusty, and sweaty. But to Alicia, it was a fairy tale. There was no heat for her. No thirst, other than for her husband. And the sweat was given so their future could be built. It was as if heaven had heard of her torture and rewarded her with a man . . . a strong man and his son who was already working alongside them. And a family provided by his raucous, loyal crew.

Rafael missed his sister. As did Pietro and the twins. But rallying around Pietro, who was rapidly growing into a strapping young man, Rafael, Angelica, and the twins, Rita and Rafael Jr., grew closer and stronger in their family unit. Whether it was exploring tidal pools during a day at the beach or a trip to the Redwoods or waiting in a snarled line of traffic to pass over the Golden Gate Bridge the first day it opened, they shared everything

Rafael could see the most change in the twins. Not only were they not identical; their natures were as different as night and day. Rita, the oldest by seven minutes, was precocious, inquisitive, good-natured, filled with energy and always on the go. Rafael, Jr. was introspective and frequently seemed on the verge of tears. He was possessive of his toys, his mother, his territory. And his brooding personality tended to irritate Rafael who constantly teased and prodded, trying to bring a smile to his son's face.

As still another decade neared its end, radio broadcasts and newspaper articles occupied much of everyone's attention. The end of the thirties brought ominous black clouds of war drifting out from Europe. Gabriel Heatter, Louis Kaltenborn, Ed Murrow brought names to their listeners that seemed alien . . . far away. Axis . . . Luftwaffe . . . Fuhrer . . . Czechoslovakia . . . Cracow . . . Blitzkrieg . . . California was far removed from the Europe that spawned these ugly images.

Still the strange names continued to flood out of what must be a nightmare in Europe. Yugoslavia . . . Belgium . . . Warsaw . . . Lithuania . . . Rumania . . . Maginot Line . . . U-Boat . . . Panzers . . . North Africa.

President Roosevelt assured in his Fireside Chats that no American boys would shed their blood on foreign soil for any cause that wasn't one of our own.

As Rafael read the papers filled with articles and photographs of the European war, his thoughts filtered back to the smell of cordite . . . the concussion from artillery explosions . . . the cold . . . the hunger . . . the heat . . . the fear. And he knew in his heart that there was no way the United States could keep from being drawn into it. It was inevitable.

Two and a half weeks before Christmas, the Japanese attacked Pearl Harbor.

Rafael wanted to do more than conserve gas, save tin cans, and buy War Bonds to help in their war effort. But even though he was a naturalized citizen, he was classified far down for the draft. He was a farmer. And crops were critically needed. And he was a father and the sole proprietor of a small business.

He could best serve, he was informed by the Marine Corps and his draft board, by going home and turning his energies to growing badly needed food crops.

So, he left his vineyards untended for the first time since he had walked onto the land, and he turned his extra acreage into crops his father-in-law would have been proud of. He was finally a truck farmer.

Angelica was relieved. Too many families in Healdsberg and Santa Rosa had received telegrams from the war department informing them the loss of a son or husband . . . or father. She wanted her husband safely at home. They'd already paid a heavy enough price for the peace they had on this tiny strip of land in the picturesque little valley north of San Francisco Bay.

Two years after Pearl Harbor, Rafael was still slaving to increase his vegetable crops. It was late summer and he had stopped for a moment to fan himself with his broad-brimmed straw hat. They were in the midst of a murderous heat wave. It would have been wonderful for his grape vines. But most of the shoots had been pruned back after they budded since they weren't to be harvested.

In the distance, Rita, tall and fawnlike but every inch a tomboy, was furiously hoeing the long fingers of weeds that had crept into the field from the irrigation ditch. Near her, Raf was hacking the earth ineffectively, hitting more of the crop than the weeds.

It was still hard to think of the two as twins. In addition to having her mother's beauty, Rita had a brain. She had finished her second year in school and the teacher thought she should skip a grade. But it would have created a problem for Rafael, Jr. Although not stupid, he didn't do well in school. His moodiness made him a target for the older kids and he spent more time brooding about how to get even than on his lessons.

Rafael looked around the sun-drenched field. Through the shimmering heat waves, he could see Rivera working beside Rita, coaxing, cajoling, and joking with her as if she were one of his own workers. Rivera's crew had dwindled to Benito and a couple of others. Most of the rest, their sons and relatives, had been lost to the Army. Even though they all had come from Mexico, those that were able wanted to help protect the country that had given them a home.

"Rafael!" Alicia called from the back porch. "Lunch is ready."

He raised his hand to signal he'd heard and then leaned his hoe against one of the stakes and headed down the row toward Rivera and Rita.

"Rita."

"Sí, Papa?" Rita answered.

"Ask your mother if she minds if we eat in the wine cellar. It's too hot to eat out here or in the kitchen on a day like this."

"Sí, Papa." She rushed over and propped her hoe on the stake next to his before darting down the row toward the house. She caught up with her brother who had dropped his hoe in the middle of the row and started for the house as soon as his aunt's call echoed through the vineyard.

There was easily a fifty-degree difference in temperature between the aging cellars and the fields. Rivera moaned from the pleasure of the coolness and the fruity smell that permeated their senses.

"What you got there, hermana?" Benito said from one of the oak benches as Angelica came in with two pitchers of iced tea.

"Something cold." She smiled.

"I sure hope this doesn't get out," Benito teased.

"What do you mean?"

"Your husband's supposed to be a winemaker," he said getting up from the bench and taking the pitchers out of her hand. "How's it going to look if someone sees you carrying around pitchers of this stuff? Could ruin his reputation."

"Sí, that's true," Ramon said. "They'll think if Rafael won't drink his wine, why should anyone else?"

"I take it you'd rather have wine."

"Well . . ." Benito shrugged innocently.

"You give them wine and they'll start taking the afternoons off," Rafael warned.

"With the wages we're getting we shouldn't even be working afternoons." Rivera grinned as Alicia and Rita brought in a tray filled with their food.

Between the food, the wine that Rafael finally reluctantly opened, and the cool air, a half hour later there was hardly an open eye in the cellar. One by one, the men found a comfortable spot as eyes grew heavy.

While the others dozed, Rafael leaned against one of the barrels and opened the newspaper Angelica had brought in.

"Are we winning or losing?" Rivera asked from behind tired eyes as he lay next to one of the tiers of barrels.

"We have to be winning," Rafael said skimming the columns. "Whenever the war's in someone else's country, they have to be the ones losing."

Rivera nodded and turned on his side trying to find a more comfortable position on the flagstone floor. Something on a ledge behind one of barrels caught his attention. He reached into the darkness and pulled out the cigar box that had been hidden on the ledge. "This where you keep your money hidden?" he asked sliding it out into the light.

Rafael looked at the box but didn't recognize it.

Rivera flipped open the lid and inside could see a treasure trove of baseball cards, Monopoly money, a yo-yo, a wood top, and a half-empty sack of chewing tobacco.

"Uh, oh!" Rivera said. "I think I have found the secret hiding place of someone's son. He held up the half-empty bag of chewing tobacco. Under the tobacco was the tattered wallet that had belonged to Ferrara. Rivera picked it up and opened it. Inside, in place of the driver's licence, was a grinning Tom Mix cut off the back of a cereal carton. A newspaper article next to a stack of Monopoly money caught his attention. Carefully he unfolded the yellow, fragile paper.

A slow burning sensation seeped into his stomach and he sat up and quickly reread the article.

Rafael looked up from his paper. His friend's face was filled with a terrible combination of disbelief, pain, and hatred.

"*Hermano?*" Rafael asked.

"It was all for nothing," Rivera said, barely above a whisper.

"What are you talking about?"

"*Los Italianos* . . . that night. Pietro. They were all for nothing," he said, handing the article to Rafael.

"My dear God!" Rafael said. He felt numb. The heavy lunch in his stomach suddenly churned making him feel nauseated. The article became a blur before him as its meaning swept through him. "He knew," he finally said.

"Who knew?"

"Angelica's father. He knew the Padrone was still alive. This is how he knew. He told Angelica he was going to take a vacation. After all those years, he was going to go home. That wasn't like him. He didn't have any relatives left there. No old friends. I never thought about it . . . but this is why."

They both sat silently.

"I will have to go for him," he said, tearing the article into tiny bits.

"Rafael, my old friend. My brother. There's a war from one end of the earth to the other. If it doesn't kill Carlo, it could you."

"No. He'll survive." Rafael angrily threw the tiny bits of paper. "He's like a cockroach. And as soon as the shooting stops, he'll come crawling back out of some sewer."

"Even if he survives the war, he is no longer a threat to you."

"He came halfway round the world once. I can't take the chance he won't try again."

"But how . . ."

"I will find a way," he said, heading toward the heat of the afternoon. "Angelica and Alicia can't ever know . . ."

"We will find a way together," Rivera said hurrying to catch him.

"No," Rafael said. "If I don't succeed, someone has to protect my family from him. And you can be sure, if I don't succeed, he'll be coming for them."

Rivera nodded. He would forfeit his soul, if need be, to keep them safe.

CHAPTER TWENTY-EIGHT

"Pardon me, ma'am. Is Mr. Orsini at home?" The well-dressed stranger at the front door smiled warmly at Angelica.

"Yes, just a minute, please." She tried to smile. "He's upstairs getting ready."

She knew who the man was. Harry Clemmons from Washington, D.C. The smiling, polite-mannered man had come to take her husband off to war.

"Not the real war," Rafael had tried to explain when he broke the news that he'd been accepted by the government's new intelligence organization. "Just a job . . . a desk job with a new organization called the OSS. I'll be working on breaking codes and translating messages. Even providing a few pieces of useful information now and then about what I remember from when I was growing up in Italy. And during the last war."

"Why?" she pleaded. "That was years ago. And there must be men . . . hundreds of men who could do the same thing."

"Angelica," he said taking her in his arms. "This is my country now. They can use what few talents I have. And besides, there won't be any danger. How could there be? Sitting in some dreary little hole in the wall office in some basement in Washington."

She nodded as he wiped away her tears.

"He's here," Angelica said after climbing the stairs to their bedroom. Rafael was snapping shut his battered suitcase. He looked up, aware that her voice was already filled with loneliness. He took her in his arms.

"Hey . . . no tears now. It's only for a little while. I'm told my biggest danger will probably be finding a place to live. With the housing shortage in Washington, I might be sleeping on one of those park benches."

She tried to smile.

Rivera and Alicia were standing outside while Benito held the car door open.

"You take care of yourself," Rivera said, slipping his arm from around Alicia and crushing Rafael's hand between his.

Rafael nodded, acknowledging the thing that had meaning only to the two men.

"I would think that within a week . . . maybe two, we should be hearing the good news," Alicia said to Clemmons.

"What's that, Mrs. Rivera?"

"That the war's over. With my brother joining, I wouldn't think the Germans could last much longer."

"I hope not." Clemmons smiled as Alicia pulled her brother to her.

Finally, everyone stepped away as Angelica and Rafael embraced.

"Rafael . . . please take care of yourself," she whispered. "If anything happened to you . . ."

He crushed her into his arms and held her until he could feel her shaking subside.

"Vaya con dios, amigo mio," Benito said softly as Rafael stooped and slid into the sedan.

"Gracias, hermano mio," Rafael said as the big Mexican shut the door.

"Nice meeting you, Mrs. Orsini. And don't you worry now. We're going to take real good care of your husband for you."

Angelica stood there with her arms wrapped around her shoulders after the car disappeared down the shimmering road that led toward Healdsberg. She finally turned, put her arm around a crying Rita and a quivering-mouthed Rafael, Jr., and headed for the house.

It was almost two weeks before Angelica opened the mailbox and saw Rafael's first letter. Her heart raced with excitement and she felt herself crying before she was even able to tear it open.

She sank down in the grass at the edge of the irrigation

ditch. He was all right! He missed her desperately. He missed the kids being in his hair. They'd found a small room for him at a tiny hotel within walking distance of where he worked. The work was boring . . . but important. The weather was getting cold. He missed her more than their vines missed sunshine. Love to the children, Alicia, Rivera. He prayed to see her soon!

"God!" she cried, shading her eyes from the sun as she read and reread and felt and smelled the letter a dozen times before folding it and returning it to the envelope. "Please . . . take care of him."

She sat up and looked around their tiny domain. The farm and her children's future would depend on her until her husband returned. Slowly she walked back toward their house. She would read Rafael's letter to Pietro. Then to Rita and Raf when they came home from school.

Alicia and Rivera and Benito had been gone a week, eastward into Napa. But they called every night to see if she had any word from him. When they called tonight, she'd read the letter a final time for them.

Rafael looked up the passageway toward the red glow of the cockpit. He could see the silhouettes of the pilot and copilot as they sipped coffee. He leaned back against the bulkhead and shifted around, trying to find a comfortable position in the bucket seat.

As he listened to the engine's drone, his thoughts were filled with Angelica, Rita and Raf, Pietro, Alicia . . . and Rivera. If anything were to happen to him, he was grateful for the knowledge that his family would be in his friend's strong hands.

He thought of the stack of letters he'd left behind. Angelica would get one every two or three weeks. What she'd never know was that they had been written at Clemmons's suggestion before Rafael left the country. And they would be mailed routinely for him. There were enough to send for quite a while. Then the job of corresponding would fall to Clemmons, who would write in his place.

The drone of the airplane finally caused Rafael to doze. An hour later he and six other men were waiting for a signal from the navigator, a signal to jump into the moonless night on missions known only to the individuals.

Some of the men in the plane were native Italians like Rafael. Others were sons of immigrants anxious to vindicate the Italian–American community back home. All of them had been recruited by Clemmons.

Occasionally they looked down the bucket seat to the dark-headed man they referred to as the "old man." Rafael had to be in his late thirties. God knows! Maybe even in his forties.

But they had discovered during the rigors of their intense combat training that he was their equal physically. More than once during night exercises, they'd felt a cold blade at their throats, raised their arms, and surrendered to the silent giant who'd successfully penetrated their defenses.

They had taken off from a bleak, almost deserted base in North Africa and were now approaching the coast of Italy. The plane would fly a large sweeping circle and drop off human cargo before returning to the strip of desert that served as its home base.

Rafael was the fourth man in the jump. The team he was joining had been operating almost eight months. He was the replacement for their radio operator who'd been captured and executed by the Germans.

His main responsibility was to transmit a steady stream of intelligence reports to tiny planes that shuttled back and forth from North Africa especially equipped to pick up their weak transmissions.

"Standby!" he heard as the copilot turned and barked the warning that their target drop zone was approaching.

A few moments later, Rafael was hurtling toward the ground in the chilly predawn air.

As the ground rushed up, he tumbled and rolled, then quickly gathered up the camouflaged silk parachute. He knelt on it to keep any breeze from carrying it away while he shoveled out a shallow hole in the field where it would be buried. He finished and brushed the dirt off his clothes. He bent back down and picked up a handful of the soil from the land of his birth. He put it to his nose and smelled as he let it slip out of his hand back to the ground. Then he made his way across the field toward the forest that bordered the highway leading toward Milan.

His forged papers were there in Ferrara's battered old

wallet along with pictures of his family printed on Italian paper. He had money also. Not too much. Only what a man identified as a mechanic would have. His clothes, covered with sweat and grease, proved his identity as much as his native tongue and papers did.

His specialty was heavy equipment. Since the Germans were short of mechanics, he would likely be conscripted into their labor force. That would give him access to the armored columns moving in and out of the country from the north.

The next morning, on a side street in Milan, he found the tiny cafe he was looking for and ordered breakfast. The waiter acknowledged his coded conversation and quickly introduced him to the members of his underground team.

There were four men and one woman. All Italian nationals. All young. All bright-eyed. All daring. Two of the men were from the country. Two were from the city. One claimed to be a Communist. One, the youngest, was a Jew. The girl, like Alicia, had been an orphan forced into prostitution.

As they made their way through the morning traffic of pedestrians on their way to work, Rafael saw few vehicles on the street. Most of the people were unsmiling. Rafael's group blended in effortlessly as they made their way out of the city toward the small farm near the Swiss border from which they'd operate.

One of the first things Rafael observed was that the Germans in evidence through his sector were mostly very old or very young. Their equipment was worn, suffering from lack of maintenance. And the uniforms looked like second- or third-generation hand-me-downs on the soldiers who straggled up and down the highways of this land that belonged to their ally.

Rafael befriended as many of the Germans as he could, sipping wine and brandy with the older men and listening to their boasts. He acted as a father to the younger soldiers, listening to them complain about commanding officers and where they were going or had been.

Though his main responsibility was to forward information back to Clemmons in the States, Rafael found himself becoming the leader of his team, under his tutelage, the team members became experts at sabotage, disruption, terror.

One week they might simply replace road signs at a dozen major highway intersections so that the Germans would become totally disoriented. Another week, in the predawn shadows, his team would slip in and dump molasses, wine, kerosene, anything else they could carry, into the Germans' fuel tanks.

One of the simplest of Rafael's ideas had one of the costliest effects on the supply convoys destined for the German mess tents. He had packets printed with labels warning that they contained poison. Over the months, as supply columns rumbled south, Rafael's team would slip into the back of the German trucks, puncture as many cans and cartons as time allowed, strew the white powder over everything, and leave the empty packets behind. When the supply officer found the contamination, he would be forced to scrap the entire shipment for fear of the poison. But if he had checked, he would have found the fine white powder was nothing more than cream of tartar.

As the months passed, the team dealt in more and more serious sabotage. Rafael taught his group to use the thing feared by every living creature. Fire.

Many a staff car gas tank erupted into a funeral pyre. And many a grinding collision occurred when brakes failed after throttles stuck open.

Once Patton and Montgomery were on the march and the Americans and British pushing north, the small band had to change their method of operation. They were now dealing with German troops who had seen Poland . . . France . . . some had even seen Russia. These troops wouldn't trust the smiling faces of their Italian allies any more than they would a man in a trench across from them.

Rafael's group learned that with terrible finality when Rosanna, the girl member of their team, came face to face with a sentry on a road in a restricted area deep within an encampment. Without giving her a chance to talk her way out of the situation, the sentry lifted his rifle and blew part of her head away.

The Jewish boy, Aaron, the youngest member of the team, almost went berserk. Rafael locked his arm around Aaron's neck, squeezed his breath out of him until he collapsed unconscious, and carried him back to their camp, saving not only his life but that of the rest of the team.

After two years in Italy, Rafael could see the end of the war in the eyes of the men sitting atop the rumbling armored columns. They'd seen battles . . . death . . . hunger . . . victory. Now they were experiencing defeat and for the first time, Rafael could think once again about his personal war.

He knew Carlo Gianini might well be dead. He could live with that if he had proof. But he had to be sure the Padrone wouldn't disappear again. At least alive.

Clemmons finally ordered Rafael and his team south to provide information about the retreating Germans. With their papers identifying them as mechanics, Rafael's group had no trouble heading south. As a matter of fact, they were conscripted and put on the first available train. Most of the German technicians and non-combatants were heading north, leaving behind their retreating army desperate for supplies and equipment.

"I'm not going all the way," Rafael said to the young members of his team as the ancient coach rattled on.

They looked at him not understanding.

"You have been ordered somewhere without us?" Aaron asked.

"The team's to split up?" Guido, the boy who no longer claimed to be a Communist, asked.

Rafael shook his head as he looked around the tiny, smoke-filled cubicle at each of the four young men to whom he'd become so attached these last two years.

Were it not for the German guards in the corridors, they might have been taken for college boys on vacation as they smoked, drank from unlabeled bottles of wine, munched on thick pieces of sausage, and broke huge hunks off the hard loaves of bread.

"No. There is something that I must do. For myself. For my family. Something that I've waited a long time for the chance to do."

"A vendetta!" Rudolfo, the Sicilian boy named after an American movie star, said almost excitedly.

"Let's just say it's my own personal war."

"Then we will go with you," Luigi, the young man from

the country, said, leaning forward and staring into Rafael's eyes. "We will help you end this war of yours as you have helped us end this war of ours."

"No. You can't. Italy . . . the Allies still need you to help finish the work we already started."

"Forgive me, but that is ridiculous, Rafael," Rudolfo said. "The war is almost over. I mean, if we were all killed today, the war would still end soon and the Allies would still win."

"*Sì*, that's true," Aaron nodded. "It is decided then . . . we will help."

"I can't ask for your help. You all know that."

"And you also can't order us not to." Luigi shrugged.

"Okay." Rafael slowly shook his head when their grinning faces told him of the futily of argument. "I'm getting off at the next water stop. You'll have to follow after the train starts up again. Otherwise, the guards will miss us."

As the train slowed, Rafael picked up his knapsack and strolled out onto the platform between the cars and lit a cigarette. When the train screeched to a halt at a water tower near a tiny village, he slipped off near the train crew and joined them in refilling the train's water tank. When the engine's whistle shrieked its warning, he stayed with the local crew who remained mute as the train rumbled off. They were Italians. They weren't about to betray a fellow countryman escaping the Germans. Rafael searched the compartments as they fluttered past. He couldn't see his team and knew they were waiting to jump before the train gathered speed.

As the whistle's shriek faded, Rafael turned and surveyed the village. After two days on the train, he was less than thirty miles from Montepulciano. He set off toward the coast on a road now seldom used. He smiled a half hour later when a noise attracted his attention. Behind him, his four team members were hurrying to catch up, whistling, laughing, and acting more like children on a picnic than the professionals they were.

The weather was sunny and mild and nothing seemed to have changed as they walked through the fields near his birthplace. Time seemed to have stood still in this little corner of the world.

He turned onto the path that headed toward a little valley. A crystal clear stream still ran over a little rock dam amidst boulders that seemed strewn by some unthinking giant.

Rafael looked over at the green hillside where he'd found his brother lying dead. The valley seemed the same, but there were no sheep.

The members of his team dropped down next to the stream and waited as Rafael walked into the field and knelt down next to a small, grass-covered mound.

He could still see his brother's face . . . so young . . . the sheep dogs . . . his mother. Tears filled his eyes as he picked up his knapsack and turned away from the place that held such pain. The young members in his team quickly scurried to put back on shoes, wring out handkerchiefs dipped in the cool waters, and rush after him.

They reached Montepulciano at sunset.

The only vehicles on the street were painted with camouflage and bore the German insignia. The market was deserted. The population seemed to have disappeared.

They walked past the cafe on the veranda of the hotel. It was also deserted. Occupied only by layers of dirt and unraked leaves.

Suddenly he was afraid. Would the Padrone's villa be deserted like the rest of the city? But when he turned the corner, he found the hated fortress ablaze with lights.

In the front courtyard, a dozen cars sat. Most were German, with drivers waiting. Inside, through the French windows, Rafael could see that some kind of reception was in full swing.

Rafael felt his pulse rise. He had reached the end of his journey. Followed at various distances by the others, he walked along the street, ignoring the bored stares of the drivers.

Near the end of the block, out of their view, he leaned into the thick vines and located the door that opened into the overgrown, untended garden. When he put his shoulder against it, he could feel the rotten wood giving way. As the other members of his team gathered, he pressed his weight against it harder.

They heard the rusted screws pulling out of the rotted wood. But the sound was covered by the noises from the reception a dozen yards away.

"Find yourselves a window you can see what's going on through. If the man I'm looking for is here, I have to be the one to finish the business I have with him. If I miss . . . fail . . . make sure the man is dead. Then save yourselves."

He stepped through the wall and into the courtyard. It too was weed-filled and overgrown. He circled to the back door that led down into the kitchen.

Pulling his hat down and shoving his hands into his pockets, he sauntered down into the kitchen crowded with cooks, scullery workers and maids and waiters serving the assemblage upstairs.

"*Sí?*" An obese man in a wrinkled white jacket asked, looking up from a tray of food he was arranging. "What do you want?"

"Someone called for some extra help." Rafael leaned lazily against the worktable without bothering to take his hands out of his pockets.

"Who?" the chef asked sullenly.

Rafael shrugged as he took his hands out and arrogantly picked over the scraps that littered the table.

"Someone upstairs, I guess." He shrugged again, starting to back toward the stairs. "Look . . . if you don't want any more help, it's okay with me."

"Come back here," the man said wiping his forehead with a folded dish towel. "Have you any other clothes?"

"I didn't come as a guest. My wife has enough trouble keeping my children fed without having to worry whether or not I'm pleasing to some kitchen help . . ."

"You are talking to the head chef . . . not to some kitchen help," the man said dismissing him with a wave.

Rafael shrugged and started up the stairs.

"Wait . . ." the chef called him back. Despite the man's attitude, he could use another set of hands. "Get an apron out of the pantry. You will help clear tables. Glasses . . . plates. And try not to embarrass anyone."

Rafael ducked into the alcove beneath the stairs where the workers had left their coats and handbags. He dropped his knapsack over one of the pegs in the wall and grabbed a linen apron from the shelf and tied it around his waist.

He felt around in his knapsack until he found the oil-covered jacket that his weapon was wrapped in. It was a Luger he had taken from the debris of one of the staff cars his team had destroyed. He slid the magazine out of the butt of the beautifully balanced weapon. It was full. He slammed it back and slowly pulled back the breech to muffle the noise as he cocked it.

He slipped it into his belt under the apron and readjusted the apron so no matter how he moved, it was hidden in the folds. He grabbed an empty tray and headed up the stairs and into the activity.

It was clear that this was an important function. Most of those in attendence were fashionably dressed or German staff officers in tunics and riding boots. There was no way he could confront Carlo Gianini in this setting and come out the winner.

He worked his way across the main room to where a group of men were engaged in animated conversation near the double doors that led into the library.

Rafael felt his temple throbbing. There was a man in a well-tailored gray suit standing with his back to him, a man surrounded by Germans.

The man's glass was empty and he looked around for someone to relieve him of it. As he turned, Rafael approached him and extended his tray. Without a glance, Carlo Gianini placed the glass on Rafael's tray.

As Rafael turned and started to melt back into the throng, Carlo whirled again, his face ashen, and began screaming orders in guttural German. There was no doubt Gianini had recognized the face that inhabited his own personal nightmares.

Rafael spun and hurled the tray with its heavy load at the men surrounding Gianini. Two of the officers, one old and fat, the other lean and strong, were drawing weapons out of shiny patent leather holsters. In terror, the fat one dropped his gun clumsily to the floor when he saw Rafael's weapon appear from beneath the apron.

The panicking crowd hid the younger officer from Rafael's view. In an almost reflex action, the young officer had his weapon out, cocked and aimed. Out of the corner of his eye, Rafael caught a glimpse of the young officer and the gun pointed at him. His heart stopped as he waited to be carried into the blackness of death.

His mind screamed with anger and disappointment that he had failed. The explosion he awaited came. But instead of death, it brought life.

The French windows shattered and sent deadly shards of glass into the shrieking crowd. Rafael threw himself to the ground as the chatter of Aaron's automatic submachine gun reverberated through the room.

Rafael dropped to the floor and rolled toward a protective wall. He could see the windows were gone. The fat German officer was still staring at his fallen weapon when a second burst from the automatic tore into his chest. The young officer was writhing in agony, his back shattered, part of his leg missing.

Expended shells from the automatic weapons spewed into the room and clattered across the polished stone floor as burst after burst of fire filled the night while the wounded moaned and the escaping guests and servants screamed with panic.

Rafael expected reinforcements from the German drivers at any moment. But one of his team had positioned himself outside the entryway and caught them in a burst of fire as they rushed blindly into the reception.

Rafael searched the room for Carlo Gianini.

He spotted him and a half dozen others pushing through the doorway into the library.

As Rafael crawled across the floor toward the library, he heard someone yell his name. When he turned, Aaron slid a grenade across the floor to him.

He picked it up just as he reached the library wall. He stood, flattened himself against the wall and cautiously turned the handle. A hail of bullets splintered the door, knocking it partway off its hinges.

Rafael pulled the pin from the hand grenade and lobbed it through the sagging door. The explosion splintered the door and it disappeared in a shower of kindling.

As flames licked the library furniture, Rafael threw himself into the room and rolled toward the safety of a heavy leather sofa. He peered around the smoke and flame-filled room for Carlo.

Two of the Germans lay like discarded rag dolls against the wall. A third man's face was half gone from shrapnel, The windows into the courtyard had been blown out. And Gianini wasn't anywhere in the room Nor were the others who had been with him.

Rafael heard a car roar to life. He leaped through the window and pounded up the flagstones toward the car sound. As he reached the circular driveway, the car roared past, spewing gravel at him like grapeshot. He shielded his face while emptying the clip of his Luger into the back of the car. But it continued toward the end of the block.

Suddenly, the others in his team were at his side, their faces lit up by the muzzle flashes of their automatics as they blazed away at the fleeing car. As it neared the end of the block, it suddenly erupted into a volcano of fire. One of the bullets had punctured the gas tank and the explosion had turned the interior of the car into an inferno.

"You're even," Aaron said, as they dragged him away from the blazing pyre. "Your war is finally over."

Carlo Gianini stood shaking as he watched Rafael and his band of assassins disappear into the darkness from which they had come. He stared back at the burning car which held the Germans who had pushed past him and abandoned him in their panic to escape.

The rage that he had felt at their betrayal was replaced now with elation. He could just as easily have been inside the charred, smoldering wreckage.

He glanced back at the spot where Rafael Orsini had disappeared. He had all but forgotten about the man and his family . . . even Alicia. He had decided their mutual revenges had been satisfied. But now . . . he knew he would have to destroy this man. This enemy. Once and for all.

CHAPTER TWENTY-NINE

Rafael felt his excitement growing as one of Healdsberg's two taxis dodged the chuckholes in the road as it carried him home.

He'd spent the past five days in a hard, lumpy seat in a coach on a troop train clattering and swaying toward the Pacific Coast. Overcrowded and smoke filled, the train carried swarms of men singing, playing cards, drinking from bottles hidden beneath their uniforms, telling war stories, showing off tattoos and scars, or sitting in stony silence, unable to believe they would soon be back home.

During those five days that seemed to stretch into an eternity, Rafael had laughed, smiled, and cried as he read and reread two years of letters from Angelica and the children. That treasure from his family was the first thing Clemmons had handed him when he got off the Liberty ship at the Brooklyn Navy Yard.

He shook his head at the evidence of Clemmons's ingenuity and attention to detail. The man had obviously never forgotten a birthday, had pleased everyone's tastes at Christmas, and had aroused no suspicions with his advice and suggestions about the farm. The only times he had come close to a problem were when Angelica had suggested taking the train to visit Rafael. One of those times, Clemmons had him being sent to a Caribbean secret base, and another, to interrogating Italian POWs in Canada.

Rafael felt his nerves clanging like church bells as the taxi sped down the road that had been unrepaired since the war began. It was early afternoon, a beautiful balmy day during the first week in October. The air was warm, clear, and free from the heat of summer already passed.

Rafael had the driver leave him across from the vineyards. For a few minutes he stood in silence and stared beyond the beautiful rolling fields to his house where Angelica and his family would be. This was the picture he had kept in his dreams.

But the fields were different from when he'd gone off to war. When he'd left, there had been tiny rows of vegetables growing between the rows of his precious vines. Now, as he stood on the decaying asphalt in the sunny afternoon, he could see rows of tiny seedlings across the slopes of one of the fields. They were new grapes. Just planted, they looked delicate and frail, unlike their older cousins on the slopes above them.

He picked up his battered suitcase and started down the lane toward the house. As he walked, he could see that a small section of the vines had just been harvested. He dropped his bags on the porch and went in. The house was cool.

He walked into the kitchen and looked out the open back door. Across the yard, he could see the doors of the winery standing open. He could hear voices . . . some laughing . . . some demanding . . . and the sound of the little electric pump used to pump their wine from one tank to another.

Rafael dropped his coat over the back of the kitchen chair and walked out the screen door. He rolled his sleeves up and pulled his tie off as he crossed to the winery. He was ready to get to work, he said to himself.

He entered the winery and the sweet fruity smell brought him to a halt, as it washed out of the cold shadows over him.

He walked silently down the row of fermenting tanks toward the voices.

He could see Rita between two of the tanks at the top of a rickety ladder, spraying a hose back and forth across the thick, crusty cap at the top of the tank. At the bottom of the ladder, Raf stood next to the pump. A steady barrage of banter shot back and forth between them.

Rafael, Jr. wanted to do what Rita was doing, he complained. Rita ignored him and kept the hose playing back and forth, breaking up the cap to give the wine the Burgundy color it would carry the rest of its life.

Rafael felt his heart pouding with pride. His two children were absolutely beautiful. His eyes started to water.

Angelica appeared at their side from behind another one of the tanks.

"I'm getting tired of your bickering, young man," she warned.

"But, Mama," Raf complained. "Rita always gets to do the best parts . . ."

"Last week you were complaining that she never helped you pump the wine over the cap," Angelica said impatiently.

"You don't even like working in the winery. You're always up in your room reading comics and listening to your radio." Rita half-turned on the ladder. As she did, she spotted the figure watching them.

For a moment, she stood there stunned.

"Daddy . . . Daddy!" she screamed as the recognition swept through her. She dropped the hose and it spewed wine around the winery like a berserk snake.

Angelica whirled toward him, ashen-faced. Her knees went rubbery and she grabbed the ladder for support.

From a dimension not unlike a dream, Rafael watched the blur of motion as Rita grabbed the hose, buried it back in the cap of grape skins, and leaped off the ladder. With grace beyond her years, she raced across the concrete floor and leaped into his arms. He buried his head in his ten year old's hair, reveling in her feel, smell.

Looking up, he saw his son standing shyly, but when he held out his free arm, the boy flew into it.

Angelica, her face still drained of color, crossed her arms as she stood without moving toward her husband.

It was the last pose Rafael remembered her in as he drove off in Clemmons's car what seemed almost a lifetime ago.

"You didn't call," she said quietly.

"No," he said, still crushing the twins to him. "I wasn't sure when I would be able to get in, what with all the servicemen on their way home. Besides . . . I wanted to surprise you." He freed himself gently from his children and reached out to Angelica.

She was suddenly in his arms. Crying . . . laughing . . . squeezing him. Rafael thought if there were a heaven this was surely how it felt. His emotions burst and he joined her tears.

"Pietro?" he asked, when he was able to talk.

"He left this morning with Auntie Alicia and Uncle Rivera," Angelica assured him, her arms still tight around his neck, her head buried in his chest.

"Uncle Rivera?"

"Yes. It's what Pietro calls him. He can't say Guillermo. So he became Uncle Rivera. The other kids even call him that now."

"I'm sorry he's not here."

"He's been hounding me to go with Aunt Alicia and Uncle Rivera for weeks. So they picked him up just after sunup. He's going to be on the rest of the harvest with them, probably two weeks . . . maybe three. He loves the adventure of being with them. And they love having him. Especially Benito and Muriella."

That night he watched as the twins opened presents he'd bought for them and hidden in the bottom of his suitcase.

Finally, it was late . . . past their bedtimes.

"Upstairs . . . the both of you." Angelica snapped an order like any one of a dozen sergeants he'd come to know on the train home.

They moaned. But they shuffled off after giving Rafael a suffocating hug.

Husband and wife sat at the kitchen table across from each other, holding hands, staring, talking, and laughing.

"I still can't believe you're really home," Angelica said, squeezing him.

"I can't either," he said as they stood and walked up the stairs to their bedroom. "It's like a dream."

"Maybe we don't have to wake up then," she said, quickly undressing.

"My God! My God!" he whispered as she slid across the bed into his arms. "I haven't thought of anything but this moment since I left."

"I know," she said and tears filled her eyes. She found herself sobbing with joy. She and her children had survived until he returned. Now, at last, she could breath without fear.

"Hey . . . hey!" he whispered. "It's all right."

"I'm sorry. It's just that . . . well . . . my whole life seemed to have stopped when you drove away." She crushed herself into his warmth. "I don't know why . . . but I was sure when you left . . . we'd never see you again."

"It'll take more than a war for you to get rid of me." He ran his hands across her body. "You are more wonderful and beautiful than I could ever remember."

"It better be exactly as you remember it," she warned, "or I'm going to make you tell me who could make you forget."

He laughed, squeezing her to him.

BOOK
FIVE

CHAPTER THIRTY

The little red-and-white twin-engine Beechcraft buzzed over the blue of San Francisco Bay. The pilot smiled as the man seated next to him shifted nervously as they headed straight for the orange strands of the Golden Gate Bridge.

At a more than completely safe distance, the pilot banked and climbed and headed north toward the tiny strip that serviced the growing town of Healdsberg and the Orsini Winery.

The pilot pulled back on the throttles, easing off the airspeed, and his action brought the expected look of panic to the face of Peter Murphy.

"Are we all right?" Murphy asked, pulling his seat belt tighter.

"Couldn't be safer," the pilot said, pointing the nose toward the distant rolling hills that joined the two valleys of Napa and Sonoma just a few miles east of Healdsberg.

"We're not going to crash or anything?" Murphy grinned sheepishly.

"Trust me," the pilot said as he spotted the tiny airfield where a car would be waiting to take Murphy to the main Orsini offices.

"You, I trust. It's this damn little toy plane I'm not sure of. And if we're going to crash, I'll be late for my appointment with Mr. Orsini. And you know how he feels about being punctual."

The pilot shook his head. His passenger had a strange sense of humor. He could never tell if he was kidding or not.

The plane descended into the mountain pass that led from the old Pacheco farm west toward Orsini's. The treetops were close to the undercarriage of the plane. Murphy grinned at the pilot and raised his feet off the floor.

The plane swooped over the beautiful knoll where Rafael and Angelica's house nestled. The countryside surrounding the house had grown almost unrecognizable. It was rapidly approaching the look of a small petroleum refinery rather than a winery.

The pilot gently dropped the plane onto the runway and taxied toward the chain link fence where a station wagon was waiting to take Murphy to his meeting with Rafael.

"See ya in a little bit," the pilot grinned as he took off his yellow-tinted glasses and watched Murphy clamber out of the plane.

"Thanks, I can't wait." Murphy rushed toward the waiting station wagon with the Orsini logo on its side.

As Murphy was driven toward the winery, he could see that the crush was in full progress. On the access road next to the highway, almost two dozen giant tractor trailers waited to make their way toward the giant mechanized crushers Rafael had updated and manufactured from his original design. They could crush so many tons of grapes that for the past five years Rafael had been buying grapes from dozens of growers in the valley who didn't make wine of their own.

The trucks' huge exhausts rumbled like angry volcanoes in the heat of the late morning sun as they waited for the Orsini Winery dispatcher to guide them toward the scales where they would weigh the entire rig, load and all, before heading off toward the crusher.

Before they reached the crusher, a few pounds of the grapes would be tested for sugar content. Once the grapes were dumped into the worm gear of the crusher, the trucks would head back to the scales and be reweighed. The difference from their original weight and the sugar content from the tested grapes determined the price paid for the grapes.

The asphalt shimmered in the growing heat as Murphy passed across the access road where the trailers snaked toward the scales.

Murphy was constantly amazed at the lack of serenity of this giant winery. To him, a winery meant stone cellars, oak casks, peasants in berets stomping grapes, dusty bottles aging in dim light, and a hushed atmosphere.

He was aware the Orsini Winery had started out like

that. But now, instead of redwood fermenting tanks, they used stainless steel. Instead of small oak-aging casks, they stored their wine in metal tanks that looked as though they'd been purchased from Standard Oil. Even the new buildings were stark and functional. Not vine-covered and hand-hewn stone.

It had all come about because located within this tiny valley, a great deal of which now belonged to Rafael and his family, was a section of earth that produced some of the finest wines in the world. The valley itself always reminded Murphy of the Bordeaux region he'd visited in France. But this stretch of land seemed more fertile and the wine even sweeter.

As the station wagon approached the three-story office complex, Murphy shook his head. A massive pile driver was huffing and steaming as it drove concrete caissons deep into the newly excavated earth: yet another building was going up.

The car pulled into the shade of the trellised arbor under the entryway, and Murphy got out and headed into the air-conditioned building.

"Hello, Murph," a cheerful voice called out, as a young woman passed him in the hall.

"Hello, Rita . . . Miss Orsini . . ." he mumbled embarrassed. She was gorgeous . . . tall . . . black hair and black eyes. She could have been a model with her sultry looks and sensuous body. But instead she was on the road to becoming chief winemaker for the Orsini Winery and the only woman winemaker in the entire United States.

Murphy knew that Orsini's confidence in his daughter was well deserved. She had slaved and busted her tail over every phase of the business. From the vineyards where she sweated and broke her back helping to irrigate, prune, fertilize, and baby the vines all year, to the laboratory, aging cellars, blending rooms, the bottling and packaging lines. And she'd mastered the technological aspects of winemaking at California's university at Davis.

Murphy knew her biggest problem was that she was a woman in a man's world. Her second problem was her twin brother, Raf, Jr. But as far as Murphy could tell, it was Rita and not her brother who took to the business.

Murphy pushed the elevator button and waited impatiently. The light above the door seemed stuck on the basement floor where the laboratory was. Finally the light flickered and the stainless steel doors parted. Murphy smiled. There standing at the back of the elevator in a work shirt with the sleeves rolled up was Rafael Orsini.

Murphy remembered the first time he'd met the old man. He'd been sent up by his advertising agency to salvage an account that Raf, Jr. had literally destroyed. The previous account executive had let the young man influence the campaign for one of the red jug wines that were stacked in tiers in every supermarket in the southwest. As a result, the wine was probably still stacked in the supermarkets, and the agency had taken the brunt of the failure.

The agency had sent Murphy as their sacrifice. Murphy had been young and inexperienced, but it hadn't taken him long to figure out that something wasn't completely right. He had spent almost ten days waiting in the anteroom for the appointment he was supposed to have with the elder Orsini.

Finally Murphy had caught Rafael at his favorite restaurant, a little diner run by a family of ex-migrants. Murphy had paid one of the sons twenty dollars to let him wait on Orsini.

"Don't I know you?" Rafael had asked.

"Yes, Mr. Orsini."

"From where?"

"The waiting room outside your office."

Rafael nodded. "And what are you doing here?"

"Practicing."

"For what?"

"For the job I'm going to have if I don't get in to see you soon."

Rafael looked at the young, red-faced Irishman and grinned.

"Well . . . maybe you'd better come back by my office this afternoon. The service's pretty good here, and I'd hate to see it get screwed up."

"Thank you, sir. Will two . . . I mean . . .what time is good for you?"

"Depends on when you get off here. By the way, what will I be seeing you about?"

378

"Advertising, sir."

"That L.A. outfit send you down?"

"Well . . . actually, the San Francisco office."

"Then maybe it might not be a bad idea for you to practice up for a waiter's job like this full time," Rafael said, pushing his empty salad plate toward Murphy.

Murphy never did know if he was kidding or not.

"Hello, Murph," Rafael said now as Murphy hopped on the elevator.

"Hello, Mr. Orsini."

"You just get in?"

"Yes, sir."

"Come in on the company plane?"

"Yes, sir."

"How do you like flying around in that little thing?"

"Oh, fine sir. It's convenient. And quick," he lied, dreading the thought of having to fly back later the same afternoon.

"Beats me how anyone can stand them." Rafael grinned. "Those little things scare the hell out of me. Fact of the matter is, you couldn't get me in one on a bet."

The elevator stopped on the top floor and he headed down the corridor to his small office at the end of the hall, little more than a cubbyhole.

"Pull up a chair," Rafael said, clicking on the tiny black-and-white television on a shelf cluttered with books on grapevine growing techniques and theories. "Today's the day, is it?"

"Yes, sir. I think you'll be pleased." Since that day in the Mexican restaurant nearly three years ago, Murphy had become the account exec for all of the Orsini labels that had once been spread among four major advertising houses.

Now, this afternoon the first Orsini Winery television commercials were to air. Murphy was as nervous as a new father. It had been his baby: the creation of an image the American public was going to become familiar with. Hopefully, through his talents, the winery would become as familiar as Coca-Cola or Kleenex. The test markets had sent back reports that said they were brilliant.

He was ecstatic. In a few brief minutes the public was going to learn of a new strain of grapes developed by the Orsini Winery that experts couldn't tell from the high-priced French wines. At least his ads said so. As long as they didn't want to know the names of the experts, he'd be okay. And the fact they were using Raf in the ads should help with the old man.

"Just a few minutes now, sir," he said, glancing at his watch. "We've explained why we're using the soap opera shows to air them . . ."

Rafael nodded. He never would have imagined so many people watched those terrible daytime programs. But as long as they were wine buyers, it was all right with him.

Murphy looked across at the man who'd become the father of the American wine industry in the few short years since World War II and Korea.

The program faded, the music swelled . . . and Murphy's commercials were rolling in front of their eyes.

"What do you think?" Murphy asked after Rafael flipped off the program and sat there staring out the window toward the line of tractor trailers still winding toward the crusher.

"Kind of cute." Rafael shrugged without looking away from the window.

"Kind of cute?" It was as close to a compliment as he was going to get from the old man. "In that case . . . we've probably got a smash hit campaign." He picked up his briefcase. "But I was hoping for a little more than 'cute.' "

"Listen, Murph, you tell me the TV commercials will sell our wine. And whether or not I like them, I trust you. On the other hand, if I liked them and they didn't sell wine, your replacement probably wouldn't be able to bribe you with twenty dollars to let him wait on me."

Murphy smiled as he shook Rafael's hand and headed toward the door and the waiting airplane.

"How's the campaign coming for Rita's new wine?" Rafael asked, going with him to the elevator.

"Fine. I should have the layouts and storyboards by next week."

"Good. You call me and I'll send the plane."

"You don't have to bother with that, sir. The way the weather is, maybe I'll just drive up."

"No bother, Murph. It'll save you time. That's what I got the thing for."

Rafael heard Rita laughing hysterically as he walked into his son's office. But Raf was far from amused.

"What's so funny?"

"Did you get a chance to see those new television commercials?" Rita shook her head.

"Yes, I saw them. Is that why you're howling?"

"When I saw my dear brother, the TV star, leaning against the back end of that horse hooked up to that cute little cart, I thought I'd die. And that big boobied blonde! Where did you get her?"

"I still fail to see the humor," Raf said angrily.

"For one thing, there hasn't been a cart like that within ten thousand miles of this winery. And you hate horses. And another thing. I couldn't figure out if you were selling wine . . . or brassieres—what with that girl playing peek-aboo in the vines behind you."

"She wasn't playing peekaboo. She was picking grapes. And that's the message we're trying to convey, sister dear. Open skies. Sunny days. Satisfied big thirsts by drinking our wine."

"Looked more like open blouses . . . sunny smiles . . . and big tits."

"Rita . . ."

"Sorry, Papa." She giggled. "Look, I know we're fighting Italian Swiss's 'Little Old Winemaker.' But I'm not sure big blondes and horses are the image we're after."

"We're after selling wine. That's the image we're after. And if you'll remember, I'm responsible for the sales and the images. Not you. And with that girl's smile . . . and sure, maybe even her boobs, you can bet we're going to create more of a thirst than we have wine for," Raf said haughtily.

"Better watch out then, TV star. Or the next commercial she might be in front of the camera and you might be the one smiling out from behind the vines with an open-peasant blouse."

"Well . . . at least she has boobs," Raf smiled. The

only thing that gave his sister any feeling of inferiority were her small breasts. "What did you think of the commercials, Papa?"

"Doesn't matter what I thought. It only matters if they sell our wine or not." Rafael directed his last sentence to Rita.

"Thank you, Papa." Raf said.

"Now . . . what's going on with your European negotiations?" Rafael asked.

Raf looked at his sister for a moment before answering. "If you'll excuse us, I'd like to talk to Papa alone. Don't you have some fertilizer or something else to spread?"

"Is there some reason I can't stay?" she asked.

"Yes . . . there is, sister dear. This is my project. And it's in my department. If you'll remember, you picked the fields and the grapes. I picked sales and promotion. I stay out of your fields and cellars. You stay out of my sales and promotions."

"That won't be hard for you. You don't have the faintest idea where the fields are. As far as you're concerned, wine just magically appears already bottled, labeled, and boxed."

"And you think it disappears out of those warehouses and onto a buyer's table the same way," he shot back.

"Stop it, the both of you," Rafael interrupted. For tax purposes, he had made each of the family a full and equal partner in the winery. Pietro's share was in a trust administered and voted on by Alicia. It had seemed a good idea at the time. And certainly profitable from a tax-savings standpoint. But it was also the reason Raf had so many confrontations with Rita. Since becoming a partner, she had become a tempest, attacking anything planned, proposed, or suggested by her brother. "If I want to see a good fight, I'll go over to the wrestling matches at the fairgrounds."

Rita nodded and stormed out. She knew that by virtue of his being a male, her brother was being prepared to take over the winery when their father stepped down. But he was damn well going to have a battle on his hands.

"Sorry, Papa," Raf said as he looked across at his father and nervously shuffled the papers on his desk.

He hated getting in these cat fights with Rita when his father was around. She was so glib, she always made him

382

feel he was losing even before he knew where the argument was going. It irritated him that she was in the business in the first place. It was a man's business and a man's world. And his father was grooming him to head it. He shoved a paper filled with the itinerary for his upcoming trip across the desk to his father.

"Looks pretty good," Rafael said after looking at it. "O'Hara tells me he thinks you might just pull it off."

"He's pretty excited about it," Raf nodded enthusiastically. "Just think, Papa, if my idea works out . . . we'll be the first American wine in Europe . . . France . . . Germany."

Rafael grinned at his son. He knew how important this project was to him. It was a way for him to make his own mark, and not just follow in a father's footprints.

"You don't have to convince me. But it isn't going to be easy for you in Europe. Those Frenchmen have their market locked up tighter than a drum. They've got a wine curtain that's harder to get through than the Iron Curtain."

"I know, Papa, but I still think Europe's a natural for us. I mean we've got glamour . . . glitter . . . television . . . Hollywood . . . Clark Gable . . . Elizabeth Taylor. In the next few years anything American is going to sell over there."

"Son, you and James Pike O'Hara have convinced me. That's proof enough for me."

O'Hara was their chief operating officer. He'd been hired at Angelica's suggestion to keep Rafael from having to take sides between Rita and Raf. The young, high-powered executive had the responsibility of running the day-to-day operations of the winery. Everyone knew Rafael was still the master. But if he needed to dodge a decision that would make one of the twins a loser, it was better to have someone front for him.

"And I'm going to convince the Europeans too," Raf said as he shoved another small folder across to his father. "These are the confirmations. Vin Franco—Italo Et Cie, the Swiss company—the largest in all of Europe—will be there. And another company, owned by a German family in the steel business, is sending one of their sons. We've even got a half-dozen chateau owners slated to sit in."

"So . . . next week, is it? Paris . . . Cannes . . .

Monaco." Rafael grinned mischievously. "Sounds more like a vacation . . ."

"I thought you'd want me to get a little culture to bring back to our out of the way valley." Raf grinned back.

"Just stay out of that casino in Monte Carlo. I don't want you breaking the bank there." Rafael stood and came around Raf's desk and embraced him. "I think it's a great plan . . . a great adventure. And if anybody can pull it off . . . you can."

"Thank you, Papa." Raf's heart swelled with pride as his father walked out. He'd never had such a feeling of accomplishment before. He'd made his father proud of him. And knowing how it would upset Rita thrilled him.

Rafael wanted to talk to Jim O'Hara about his son's upcoming junket. And he knew he would catch the man in one of their fields, poking around to learn first hand about the business he'd been drafted into little less than a year earlier.

Driving into the emerald-green field, he located O'Hara's shiny jeep parked next to the beat-up truck that belonged to Juan Griego, one of their full-time vineyard workers.

Rafael honked and waved as he crossed in front of the line of idling trucks waiting on the access road for their turn to move closer to the scales. A couple of the trucks that bore the "Anything . . . Anyplace . . . Anytime" motto honked and waved back.

Rafael pulled off onto the shoulder of dirt and watched as O'Hara and Griego worked their way through the vines toward him, testing the sugar content of the fruit to determine the ideal day to harvest.

Unlike Raf, O'Hara seemed not afraid to roll up his sleeves, loosen his tie, and sweat alongside the field workers. The six-footer had graduated number one in his class from Harvard Law School, and he'd had the pick of opportunities. He'd accepted a position in the legal department of an international division of Vin Franco–Italo Et Cie, the parent company of an extensive European business empire.

After he proved himself by reorganizing the archaic structures within the parent company, he had been given the presidency of one of the smaller divisions. So it came as a shock to the elitist European business community when he left them for the wilds of California at the behest of an American winemaker.

To those who knew him, though, it was a natural move. Jim O'Hara was ambitious. True, Vin Franco–Italo had prestige. But it was controlled with an iron fist. And chances for advancement were small. Orsini, he felt, offered him a direct line to the top. It was true that the Orsini Winery was a family-controlled corporation. But Jim O'Hara felt he held the key to becoming an indispensible part of that family. A key so valuable that without it the family and winery might collapse.

O'Hara walked to Griego's pickup and held several bunches of grapes under the water cooler on the tailgate. He popped a few of the berries in his mouth before coming over to Rafael and offering him some. Rafael sampled the fruit. The grapes were sweet . . . but not sweet enough. If they were going to ship them back east for home winemaking, they'd be perfect. But since they were going less than a mile to the winery, they could wait until they matured and contained as much liquid sugar as nature allowed.

"What's up, boss?" O'Hara asked.

"What do you think?" Rafael nodded toward the field.

"I'd say three to four weeks at the earliest. If this heat holds, a little sooner."

Rafael nodded.

"You didn't come out here to ask me that. You could tell me the exact day . . . the exact time. I can only guess the week."

"I want to talk about my son's trip."

O'Hara came around and got in next to Rafael. "As I've said before, I think it's a good idea. A little ambitious maybe, but not impossible."

"But that's really playing in the big leagues over there."

"Hell, you're the biggest in this country. That's not exactly the minor leagues."

"But what does that mean to the winemakers in France? Their whole economy . . . and arrogance . . . is based on wine. What with the tariffs, and shipping costs, we could lose our shirts."

"Rumor around here says you started with less. Besides,

the prestige of being the only U.S. wine distributed in Europe would be an incredible accomplishment. Not to mention what it would do to help increase our domestic sales."

"If he can pull it off," Rafael said studying the dirt between the rows still wet from the recent irrigation.

"Do you want me to go over with him? I could make it work. I've played in their ball park before. I can make sure they don't put anything over on him."

"That would be the safest way. But . . ." Rafael sighed. "No. It has to be his baby. The negotiations have to be his responsibility totally. I know it was your idea from the start. I know without you there wouldn't be any idea. But it's time for my son to know what it's like to be under the gun. To have the responsibility of a lot of people's futures in his hands. So . . . I don't want you to go with him. This has to be his and his alone. But I do want you to prepare him as much as you can."

O'Hara looked at the powerful, dynamic man who had challenged and conquered all the giants in the wine kingdom. He finally nodded.

"Thank you," Rafael said. "Do what you can to see to it they don't rough him up too bad."

"They might bloody him a bit . . . but he comes from hearty stock. He'll survive."

"And Jim, I want you to get our advertising people on this. I would think this warrants some kind of news coverage."

O'Hara nodded as Rafael started the engine signaling that the meeting was at an end.

CHAPTER THIRTY-ONE

The Pan Am Clipper dipped through the clouds and dropped toward the airport outside Paris. Raf felt a rush of excitement as the emerald-green patchworklike countryside flashed by outside his tiny port. He snapped his briefcase shut and handed the flight attendant his linen napkin and champagne glass as he searched under his seat for his shoes.

As soon as he cleared customs, he started down the ramp into the main terminal, searching for the person who was to meet him.

"*Monsieur* Orsini?" A young woman wearing oversized sunglasses, her blond hair hanging down over the collar of her tan trench coat, pushed her way through the crowd and held out her hand to him.

He felt his face flush. He'd never expected to be met by a gorgeous creature like this.

"Welcome to Paris, *Monsieur*. I am Michelle Renaud." She smiled as she took his arm and guided him toward the Rolls-Royce limousine waiting in front of a row of Peugeot taxis. "I understand this is your first trip to France."

"Yes . . ." he mumbled, ducking into the door held open by a gray-capped chauffeur with a white mustache. "But I guarantee, not the last."

Sipping champagne in a crystal goblet from the hand-carved bar built into the credenza in back of the chauffeur, Raf was overwhelmed by the sights outside the window and the woman next to him.

"I must say, this is a pleasant surprise," he said as umbrella-filled cafes, crowded boulevards, and the outline of the Eiffel Tower flashed past. "I mean, I certainly wasn't expecting a woman."

"Your Mr. O'Hara requested that someone meet you

and make you feel comfortable. It's depressing to arrive in a new place without a friendly face to greet you."

"That's for sure. And I do hope we can get to be friends." He leaned against her slightly.

"*Oui*, I hope so as well, *monsieur*. But I'm afraid I will only be able to accompany and assist you until you fly on to Cannes tomorrow."

"That's terrible. My first friend in France and we'll be parting so soon."

"Well, luck has helped avoid a total tragedy. I have business that takes me to Monaco at the end of next week. I understand you will be there also. Possibly we can meet again." Her smile filled Raf with a rush of warmth.

"Wonderful. You can count on it." He smiled as he inhaled the aroma from her perfume. "Where are you from, Michelle? Your accent doesn't sound French."

"I'm French Tunisian. But my mother was Italian. So half the time in our house we spoke French, the other half Italian."

"But your English is excellent. I'm very impressed meeting not only my first friend but one who speaks three languages."

"Five, *monsieur*. I also speak Arabic. And as I finished my education in Spain, I speak Spanish as well."

Raf shook his head in amazement. The way Europeans seemed to assimilate languages amazed him. And the thought that she had traveled so extensively impressed him.

He'd rarely been out of California. He'd been to New York on business several times with his father. And the family had spent one Christmas in Acapulco. Even college had been a California affair. Though he didn't have the required grades, a liberal grant to Stanford by his father had provided him admission to the prestigious school.

"*Yo hablo poquito español, tambien.*" He smiled.

She raised her eyes. "Very good. I didn't know you spoke any Spanish." She had a difficult time understanding through his American accent the little Spanish he'd learned from the times he'd spent on the road with Alicia and Rivera.

"Would you care for more champagne?" Raf asked, taking the heavy, dark green bottle out of the ice bucket and refilling her glass without waiting for a reply.

"I shouldn't," she smiled coyly, watching him over the rim of her glass as she sipped.

"Me neither," he flushed. "But after that flight, if I don't, I'm afraid I'm going to be totally bushed."

"Would you like me to cancel dinner this evening then?"

"I didn't know we had dinner planned."

"It's unimportant." She shrugged. "I just felt that if the flight hadn't totally destroyed your senses, I'd show you some of the delights Paris can offer."

"I wouldn't miss it for the world. It'll be my pleasure. What time?"

"How will ten o'clock be? I'll meet you in the lobby."

Raf nodded as the chauffeur turned into the courtyard of his hotel. He was thankful they wouldn't be eating until late. That would give him time for a few hours' sleep.

The following afternoon he stood in the train station that led from Paris as the porter loaded their luggage into the private compartment he'd booked to Cannes. He'd decided to take the train instead of the plane. He wanted more time alone with Michelle. Another night like the one she'd just given him. He'd never seen such a city. From the Moulin Rouge to the Left Bank . . . to crowded cabarets . . . to the elegant four-star restaurant where they'd finally eaten. Topping it off, she'd suggested a dawn swim in the palatial pool in the hotel's gardens. She'd taken his breath away when she came out of the bathhouse in a tiny, flame-red bikini. He'd seen an occasional two-piece on the beaches near San Francisco. But he'd never seen anyone in a bikini before. He was speechless as she dove into the mirrorlike water.

An hour later, in a small dressing cubicle in the ladies' section of the bathhouse, they were making a kind of passionate love Raf had never imagined in his most erotic daydreams. He intended to have as much time as possible with this enchanting creature who had dropped into his life compliments of O'Hara.

As the train rumbled out into the French countryside, Raf closed the blinds, locked the compartment door, and pulled Michelle to him. She was a willing lover. There was no doubt, he thought vainly, that she'd fallen for him in the worst way.

* * *

"Well, well, well," Rita smiled as Jim O'Hara strolled into her brightly lit laboratory. "What brings the bossman down here?"

"Rumors have it you're creating some Frankenstein kind of monster down here in the basement." He nodded toward the equipment, both chemical and electronic, that lined the work benches around her. "Thought maybe I'd better come down here to the dungeon and check them out."

Leaning against her lab table, he pinioned her between his arms as he looked over her shoulder to see what she was engrossed in. She swiveled her stool around and looked up into his eyes.

"I've got him curing in one of the fermenting vats. So you can't see him yet." She closed her arms around his neck and kissed him lightly.

"Then . . . in that case, why don't I take you out of this damp, dismal dungeon up to where the sun's shining and show you what a beautiful day it is over lunch?"

"I've got lots of things to finish," she purred as she ran her hand behind his neck and up into his hair. "I'm supposed to figure out what Carnero Brothers has done to their Burgundy by this afternoon." She nodded toward a tray filled with lab equipment and long-stemmed glasses used to sip, analyze, rate, study sweetness, clarity, and age. She had been analyzing the almost maroon wine to find out what chemicals had been added to enhance its flavor. Once she found that out, she'd test the comparable Orsini wine with the same chemicals to see if it made any difference in its quality.

"I understand," O'Hara sighed his resignation. "I just thought possibly a warm sun . . . a sandy beach . . . a hidden cove . . . a picnic . . . might lure you out of here for a while. But I guess not."

"As long as you put it that way, I accept. After all it does seem you have your heart set . . . and it doesn't make sense to turn the boss down when he asks you to lunch."

While she took off her lab coat, O'Hara bent down and studied the comments in her journal about the wine she'd been testing. Type of grape. Grower. Sugar content. Date of crush. Temperatures during fermentation. She knew everything about it. He shook his head. Not only was she as efficient as a pathologist, but she also had access to secret information that would have been difficult for Mata Hari to come by about their competitor's product.

"Any idea what they're doing?" he asked picking up the Carnero Brothers wine and studying its color in the light.

"I've got a couple of ideas." She smiled. "But until I'm sure, I don't want to say."

O'Hara took the bottle and poured a small amount into one of the long-stemmed glasses. He swirled it around and stuck his nose to the glass to inhale. Whatever they were doing, it was definitely giving their wine a heartier aroma. Whatever they were adding was also filtered out before the wine reached the bottler so that neither competitors nor the authorities could detect anything in an analysis other than pure California wine.

"I'm sure if anyone can unravel the mystery for us, it's the Orsini family brain."

"Oh, sure . . ."

"Sure. As a matter of fact, that's what attracted me to you in the first place . . . your brains." He chuckled as they headed for the elevator.

"Bullshit!" She laughed as she locked her arm around his waist. "It's my body you're after."

The elevator doors opened and her father was standing there. Quickly, she and O'Hara pulled apart.

"Papa!" She half-smiled, embarrassed.

"Rita . . . Jim." He was almost as embarrassed as his daughter.

"Mr. Orsini . . ." O'Hara quickly grabbed the door as it started to close again.

"Your mother and I are having lunch in the cellar," Rafael said, referring to the cool little room in the back of the original winery which held tiers of their best premium wine. Rafael and Angelica often ate there among their creations. "We thought you'd like to join us . . . and you too, Jim."

Rita looked at O'Hara, who was nodding without a glance her way. She sighed. So much for a secluded beach and an afternoon picnic in the sun.

"I'd love to, Papa."

"That will be nice," Rafael said as the two got on the

elevator and the door swung shut. "And afterward, maybe I could take Jim up to the house and show him my collection of guns."

Rafael had often teased Rita's dates about his extensive collection of "dangerous" weapons. They'd grin and chuckle and shuffle their feet. But they never failed to bring Rita home on time.

Rafael selected a bottle of wine from a rack, blew off the dust, and slowly pulled out its cork as Angelica and Rita spread out the lunch on the heavy oak table. He poured a small amount into one of the crystal goblets and sipped. He swirled it around the inside of his mouth before finally swallowing. He seemed upset as he poured a little into each of their glasses.

O'Hara took the bottle from Rafael and studied the label. It wasn't the Orsini label.

"Montagne Cache Cellars. Hidden Mountain." He raised his eyebrows at their having wine from a competitor as he handed the bottle back to Rafael. "I don't think I've ever had it before."

"You'd remember if you had," Angelica said as she served heaping portions onto their plates.

Rita almost grimaced as her mother added extra spoonsful of the rich, heavy courses she'd spent the morning preparing. Rita dreaded the heavy lunches her mother prepared. But Angelica was the daughter and wife of farmers. And she was used to preparing the heaviest meal in the middle of the day.

"What do you think of the wine, Jim?" Angelica asked as she nodded toward a plate she had filled for him. "I'd like to get an honest opinion for a change. Rather than one from a grumbly old Italian and his daughter who think they're the foremost authorities."

Rita grinned and squeezed her father's hand as O'Hara sipped. The wine was almost black red, rich, and had a distinctly different taste.

"I like it," he said setting his glass down and squeezing onto the bench next to Rita. "It's a little young. But I'd say it has one of the most distinctive tastes I've come across since working in France."

"And unfortunately, it gets better every year," Rita jokingly complained as she stared, eyes half glazed, at the abundance she knew she couldn't escape eating. There was linguini with fresh clams, a giant red snapper baked and covered with a buttery lemon sauce, a mushroom-filled salad and enough dessert for a dozen diners.

"As distinctive as it is, maybe Rita should do an analysis on it. Find out what their secret is," O'Hara said digging in.

"She already knows," Rafael said.

"It's some of Joe Anthony Jr.'s private stock," Angelica said picking at her plate which had only a dab of the dishes she'd prepared. She was on a diet.

"Isn't he our local politician?" O'Hara asked.

"Our congressman," Angelica said proudly. "He grew up here on our farm. Until the war, that is. Then he lied about his age and joined the Marines. They didn't find out how young he was until after he was wounded on Iwo Jima."

"Sounds like an exceptional man."

"Youngest congressman California's ever had," Rafael said proudly.

"I don't know how he is as a politician. But he's a good winemaker," O'Hara acknowledged.

"He ought to be. He learned how to make it here," Rita said. "Papa taught him everything he knows."

"He always warned us he was going to be the best winemaker in the country," Angelica said. "After the war he used his G.I. Bill to help open his winery."

"And . . ." Rita held up her glass. "*Voilà!*"

"How much of this does he produce a year?" O'Hara asked.

"Fortunately for us all, only a few thousand cases a year," Rita answered.

"But he never forgets to send us a dozen or so of those cases," Angelica said. "He's still a dear and appreciates everything he got here."

"Bull, Mama!" Rita shook her head. "He's just showing off. Reminding us he's keeping his promise."

"Does he raise his own grapes?"

"No. They're native grapes," Rafael answered.

"Native . . . you mean wild?"

Rafael nodded.

"I'll be damned."

"Every year, Joe and his family get together at a big reunion. And let me tell you, he comes from a big family. They spend the week covering the countryside up north in the mountains. Like a swarm of locusts . . . they strip every berry and tote it back down to his place. He uses them as the base for his wine."

"You must be proud of him," O'Hara said. "It sounds like he's almost one of the family."

"He is," Rafael said with a gleam of pride.

"Speaking about one of the family, has Raf called today?" Angelica asked. She knew her son was to call daily about the progress of his negotiations.

"I talked to him just after breakfast," Rafael said. "He said he'd been going full steam from sunup to sundown."

"Yeah, but is he getting any work done?" Rita asked.

"Rita . . ." Angelica said putting her palm on her daughter's hand.

"Sorry, Mama."

The rest of the luncheon was filled with a closeness O'Hara still felt strained and awkward about. He was at a loss as to how to react to the warm, close relationship displayed among father, mother, and daughter. He was a stranger to such emotion and intimidated by it. He'd spent his entire childhood either in the care of a nanny or in a private school, seeing his mother occasionally and father only once in thirty years after his parents were divorced.

"Well . . ." O'Hara said when he was afraid his uneasiness might start to show. He pushed his chair back and patted his stomach. "I think it's time I headed back to the mill."

"How about a ride back?" Rita said standing and taking both their plates to the little sink.

"I don't know," he hesitated. "I'd like to see your father's famous gun collection first. That way I'll know if I'm going to take the long way or the short way back."

Rafael grinned as the two of them disappeared into the sunlight.

"They certainly make a handsome couple," Angelica mused as the door closed behind them.

"Don't go getting any ideas," Rafael warned. "We've got enough troubles without having to worry about a romance between those two."

"What kind of trouble could that possibly cause?"

"What's Raf going to think if those two become involved? O'Hara's supposed to be neutral. Rita can gang up on her brother without any help. I hate to think what she'd do if she had some."

"How about walking instead of driving?" Rita asked, taking O'Hara's hand and heading toward the edge of the vineyard that lay between her parents' house and the winery complex.

"Long way . . ." O'Hara complained. "In this heat and after that lunch, I may end up carrying you."

"Are you kidding? I used to walk it a dozen times a day. Every morning I'd cut through this very row to catch the school bus. Then every afternoon, I'd take food out to where Papa, Aunt Alicia, and Uncle Rivera and their crew were working."

O'Hara dropped her hand and slipped his arm around her as they disappeared into the green rows. He smiled as the thought of her as a little girl, with braces probably, racing back and forth between the vineyards and the house.

"This was our favorite spot," Rita said, as they came to the stand of eucalyptus trees at the end of the row. "It was always coolest here. Everybody would stagger in and flop down to cool off, eat, and complain. It was almost like another world. Sometimes they'd only speak Spanish. Or a bastardized Mexican Indian. Sometimes Italian. Sometimes the crew would have a Portuguese family . . . or a Japanese family with them."

"Don't tell me your family speaks Portuguese and Japanese too," O'Hara said as he flopped down in the cool grass.

"No . . . a little Portuguese," she said dropping next to him. "But we used sign language with the Japanese."

They lay back and for a few minutes stared up into the blue of the cloudless sky. He sat up on one elbow and looked down at her. Like her mother, she was beautiful, exciting. She had the kind of wonderful olive complexion and the kind of long legs that drove him crazy. He bent down and kissed her. She looked at him and smiled.

"I think it's about time I got back to my dungeon," she said rising.

While she brushed the grass off the back of her skirt, he went through a series of exaggerated gestures begging her to stay.

"Is that supposed to be sign language?"

He nodded.

"Funny . . . you don't look Japanese." She laughed and disappeared toward the winery leaving him alone.

CHAPTER THIRTY-TWO

Raf's eyes felt as though they had sand in them as he tried to focus on the cards across the green felt table of the casino at Monte Carlo. He felt Michelle's hand on the back of his neck and turned.

"How about a break?" she asked. "Maybe get something to eat. You do have a breakfast meeting with Paul Buntz. Remember? And it's late."

He nodded, numbly picking up the few remaining chips in front of his seat.

"Good night, *Monsieur*," one of the casino managers said as the young American swayed toward the entrance.

"I'll be back," he warned.

"*Oui, monsieur*. It will be our pleasure to see you again," the man smiled politely.

Raf didn't know if he was being sarcastic or challenging him to return. It didn't matter. He would return. He had to. He had to try to regain some of his losses. He'd gone through his entire expense advance plus enough checks to ruin his bank account back home. Normally his checks would not have been accepted. But Michelle had arranged it for him through the casino manager.

Thank God for Michelle, he thought as he slumped into the back of the tiny taxi. Everything else about Monaco and the conference O'Hara had set up was awful. A nightmare.

The men he was dealing with had made it clear how much power they had. From their first meeting Raf had felt inadequate.

One of the men, Gustav Scheneblin, was a grandson of the man who had manufactured much of the armament for Hitler. He was humorless, unsmiling, and seemed irritated at having to tolerate this boorish American. Of all the men at the conference, Raf felt this man might be unwilling to come to an agreement.

At least Paul Buntz, the Swiss head of Vin Franco–Italo was cordial to him. Raf felt comfortable with the ever-smiling man despite his unbending position during their negotiations. Several times Buntz had taken him for a stroll through the palatial grounds of Vin Franco–Italo's European headquarters. Raf found it easy to confide in Buntz. And it was through Buntz that Michelle had gotten his checks guaranteed at the casino.

The contingent of chateau owners from France was headed by Jacques Chantellier. Raf thought the rotund Frenchman was a joke: he looked like a bad actor playing the villain in a B movie. And he didn't even attempt to be polite or cordial. But as much a pain in the ass as he was, Raf knew the Frenchman was the key to his success or failure. Without the French market, there would be no deal.

The meetings were torture for Raf. He felt as though he was being squeezed through one wringer after another. Whenever he thought they'd agreed on something concrete, someone would nitpick. Any solution he came up with seemed to upset something else. During the lunch break, Raf would rush back to his hotel and collapse. On more than one occasion he came close to bolting. But each time, Paul Buntz would seem to sense his impending panic, and suggest a break, a rest, time to reflect.

Raf's nerves sent him plunging into the depths of depression. He knew his father would have been able to handle these men with ease. Goddamn! he thought, as a vision of Rita's laughing face flittered across his mind.

The more frustrated he became with the meetings, the more he took it out on Michelle. He didn't try to control his temper anymore with her. But Michelle would smile and take it.

Then he had discovered his power over the managers at the casino. Though he was still losing heavily, they willingly approved his ever-increasing line of credit. It seemed the more he lost, the more money he had access to. They must have come to realize how important he really was, he reasoned.

At one session, Gustav Scheneblin blew up, stormed out

of the room, vowing to be on the first plane back to Munich.

Raf was shaken and gladly agreed to the lunchtime recess suggested by Paul Buntz. The Swiss had walked him through the gardens toward a table set up under a massive tree and suggested they dine alone.

"There's no doubt that the concept you've proposed is unique and offers an opportunity for all of us," Buntz said, cutting into a soft cheese. "The problem is that as you've presented it now, all the benefits accrue to your company."

"I don't know if I would agree," Raf replied exasperated. "It's changed so damned much, minute by minute, I'm not even sure who's who . . . and what's what."

"That often happens during the course of delicate negotiations."

"That asshole, that goddamn German. I should have just kicked his ass and got it over with. He's had it in for me ever since we started."

"Quite possibly," Buntz said as they were served a delicate veal by a white-jacketed steward. "It's as Churchill said . . . they're either at your throat or at your heels."

"I'd like to get him at my heels."

"I'm afraid that won't be possible if you continue your rather extraordinary activities at night."

Raf looked down at his plate. Paul Buntz sounded amazingly like his father, and he could no more respond to him than he could to his father.

"In addition, I'm afraid there's another problem that might interfere . . ." he waited until the steward left with the serving cart.

"Great! Just what I need. More problems!"

"Yes. They are unpleasant. But nevertheless, I'm afraid we must discuss them." He slid a folder across the linen tablecloth.

Raf opened it and felt his blood pressure soaring. It was a balance sheet, submitted by the casino to Vin Franco—Italo Et Cie. The line of credit to date was one hundred and fourteen thousand dollars.

His face felt prickly as if he'd received a bad sunburn. And he had to fight desperately to keep from bursting into tears.

"Our Chairman of course has already submitted payment for you. I must tell you, though, he was more than a little taken aback . . . shocked by the amount. But as he vouched for your integrity, he personally paid the casino."

Raf carefully set the folder back on the table, fighting the nausea that coursed up from his stomach.

"You seem to have gotten a little out of control. How do you say . . . gone a little overboard," Buntz said.

Raf was still speechless. He remembered signing a series of vouchers, but between his bouts of depression and his heights of elation, he'd lost track of how many. Still, the folder contained the individual vouchers which he indeed had signed.

"You can tell your Chairman that he'll get his money. He doesn't have to worry if that's what's bothering him. If he'll just wait a few days, I'll get in touch with my father . . ." he tried to muster as much indignation as he could.

"Raf, my young friend, I think you must take a moment and examine this attitude. Your benefactor . . . our Chairman . . . is a gentleman. And I must admit a rather remarkable man with extraordinary talents. He's been following our efforts almost since the offset."

Raf was thankful that someone was interested.

"He has proposed a number of alternatives that might offer a solution to the stalemate we seem to have arrived at with Scheneblin and Chantellier's group." Buntz folded his palms together as though in prayer as he leaned back in the comfortable lounge chair. "The problem as he sees it seems to be basically one of egos with respect to the German and French wine interests. You want to send wine into their marketplace. In return they can send wine into your marketplace. The problem is that they can and already do that. So the only thing you offer is to act as a more effective sales agent for them via your newly adopted advertising program through the television media."

"It certainly couldn't hurt their sales," Raf said, leaning his elbows on the table.

"The problem is of course one of trust. The German won't trust the French, the French won't trust the German, and neither will trust the American. It's as simple as that."

"You of course trust us all," Raf said pointedly.

"Of course," Buntz held up his hands and smiled. "The Swiss are always neutral. When you are historically neutral, you can afford the luxury of trusting."

"I don't know what they're afraid of. I don't know what they don't trust." Raf shook his head. "We've talked these things to death for almost two weeks. We've come up with dozens of ways to protect everybody."

"But none foolproof for the skeptic. Wherein lies that which will ultimately send you home emptyhanded. And I might add, with an empty pocketbook." He tapped the folder from the casino.

"So? What's your Chairman's bright idea?"

"Very simple. A unilateral merger of all parties in the negotiations into one giant, invincible company."

Raf looked at him, not certain he understood.

"The Chairman proposes very simply that we merge our individual companies into one corporation. We would maintain, of course, our individual identities within the countries of origin. But proprietorship would be under an international banner. An international corporation."

"I'm afraid I didn't come over looking to sell out."

"It's not that at all," Buntz said. "It's a merger. Four companies, each with equal representation on a governing board of directors. Two members each. One of the members from your company I assume would be you," Buntz said throwing out bait.

"Why would this Chairman of yours, if he's as successful as he appears to be, want to do something like this?"

"Simple. To gain an interest in your winery. But he gives up an equal interest in his company as well. There's future value to both that can't be anticipated now. He's a visionary. He looks to the future. It would give all the companies involved a powerful base from which to operate."

The wheels started turning in Raf's brain. The idea of his holding a seat on the board of directors on an international conglomerate staggered his senses. He found himself already going over the sales pitch to his family about the merits of the merger he'd instituted in Europe during the negotiations.

"I believe you had indicated on several occasions that

you have the authority to conclude an agreement between the parties currently involved in our negotiations."

Raf nodded, wishing he hadn't been so arrogant about his position within his father's company.

"I'm afraid," he finally sighed, "that this is beyond my authority. It's so far afield of my original idea that I'll have to present it to my family."

"Can you anticipate their response?"

Raf shook his head.

Buntz placed his hand on Raf's arm to emphasize a possibility. "Possibly they might be more receptive if they thought it was an evolving part . . . a logical progression of your original idea."

Raf looked at him, his eyes narrowing in suspicion. "But it's not my idea."

"The Chairman is a generous man."

"I tend to be a little suspicious when someone all of a sudden gets generous like that."

"You are very perceptive."

"Thanks. So maybe you'll level with me and tell my why this guy's so willing to let my family think this great idea is one of mine?"

"I would think it would be simple to comprehend," Buntz slid the folder back across the table. "He's a practical man. You have incurred a sizable obligation in his name . . ."

"I might have known it would come to this. A squeeze."

Buntz looked puzzled by the expression, but understood its meaning. "Not at all. If we successfully conclude this merger, the individual owners of each company reap a significant gain by the increased value of their shares of stock. That stock could easily be pledged for a small amount of money such as this. Say until such time as profits from that stock repay a kind man who was charitable to a young man in a difficult situation. No one else need ever know of his problem."

The hook was set. Buntz was providing him a way out. A way for him to eliminate the debt and all its traces without having to be confronted with it by his father.

"It will take some time. And some good old-fashioned American salesmanship, no?" Buntz smiled. "But I'm sure in the end, you have the talent to consummate this rather remarkable project."

Raf nodded at the man's well-placed opinion of his talent.

Within hours after they reconvened, Raf was delighted to see the progress they suddenly seemed to make in hurtling previous stumbling blocks. Scheneblin, who'd reluctantly returned, and Chantellier, with his group of chateau owners, seemed excited by Raf's revamped proposal. Like Raf, they would have to make proposals to their respective families. But it looked good!

Raf swaggered back into his hotel suite, ready to share his kill with Michelle. A note on the pillow apologized. Her mother had taken ill in Tunis and desperately needed to be with her, she loved him madly and would call when she arrived later in the evening.

He didn't have time to grieve her departure. No sooner had he finished her note than the phone rang. It was Paul Buntz with an invitation to join him and his wife at a small intimate dinner party. Raf was delighted. Things suddenly seemed to be going right for him. He had a deal for his family that would make their fortunes immensely larger, he no longer had the threat of his gambling debt hanging over his head, and he was suddenly being invited into the cream of Europe's society.

For half the evening, Raf stood with his mouth agape. Small and intimate to Buntz meant nearly forty people. And among those were some of the most famous names in Europe.

A top French fashion designer sat next to an Italian movie star who was equally as famous. A top name in English banking chatted with a shipping magnate who'd just purchased an island to shelter his warship-sized yacht.

The rest of the week, as the negotiations rushed toward their conclusion, Paul Buntz tantalized Raf with a royal life-style few Europeans knew to exist. And Raf developed a burning passion to be a part of that life. Its glamour and sophistication lifted him to heights he'd never dreamed of back in the little California valley that was his home. He had to convince his family of the wisdom of this merger!

After the tentative agreements were finalized and the letters of intent signed, Raf had a few moments alone in his suite to finish packing for his flight home. He looked around the suite. It would always be special for him. He'd more or less been born in this cluster of handsomely decorated rooms. He thought of how immature he'd been those first days. Now he was a new man. He smiled at the thought of his affair with Michelle and felt a tug of disappointment that he hadn't heard from her again.

Paul Buntz was sitting in his expansive office overlooking the gardens when his secretary signaled that his call to the Chairman in Zurich had come through.

Smiling confidently to himself, he lifted the receiver. *"Signore . . . come stai?* I'm pleased to be able to bring you good news. The boy took to the idea immediately. Yes, *signore,* he was more than enthusiastic. No . . . the girl was given instructions to leave before I made the proposal. *Sì, signore,* it was a simple, yet masterful concept. The boy was terrified of the prospects of having to confess to his father his rather distressing losses. *Sì, signore.* He literally leaped at the opportunity of taking the idea as his own. I don't know, *signore.* I would say the chances of his family accepting are slim. They certainly don't need this alliance. The father won't be tempted by the wealth alone. But we have the tools to keep pressure on his son. The original notes from the casino should be leverage enough. If not, then the girl is available if we need her again. *Sì . . . sì, grazie,* Padrone. *Arrivederci."*

In the office of his chateau on the slopes overlooking the city, Carlo Gianini hung up and walked to the leaded glass windows that opened onto the panoramic view. He smiled at the success of the plan born on a night so many years earlier. He had vowed then, as the flames of the German staff car died, to be patient. To bide his time and seek Orsini's jugular.

He was delighted to have found such a clever tool. If Rafael Orsini was foolish enough to accept his son's negotiated proposal, Gianini would end up controlling the winery that Rafael and his wife had spent their lives building. True, they would have two seats on the board of the internationally owned company. But three of the four were owned by an umbrella company of which he was sole proprietor. And if the family refused, he'd turn Rafael Orsini's son ever so slowly on a spit over the bed of coals he'd fired himself.

Rafael reached into the woven mat of brittle canes that led up from the treelike spike. He clipped off a heavy cluster of grapes hidden within the depths of the lush green vines and held it up to the sky to inspect. The velvety fruit was packed together in a hard knot like drone bees clinging to their queen. Pulling several of the berries from the stem, he popped them into his mouth. The musky flavor literally burst in his mouth.

He slowly surveyed the new vineyards that surrounded the gnarled vines Ferrara had planted. The spikes were the same. But now, thanks to the technology he'd helped bring about, the canes were leading from the plant to wire trellises where grapes matured quicker and were easier to harvest.

He turned as the sound of an approaching truck kicked up gravel. The pickup swerved off the asphalt into the dirt and skidded to a halt. Smiling out from the truck were Alicia and Rivera. While the dust still swirled, Alicia leaped out and dashed into her brother's arms.

"Just get in?" Rafael said crushing her as he twirled her around gleefully.

"We dropped off some stuff at the house and had lunch with Roberto first. We found Pietro asleep in the grove by the river on the way out," she grinned. "Thought we better give him a ride home."

Years ago, true to the doctor's prediction, they were forced to take Pietro out of school. His learning capacity had reached its maximum. The doctors suggested they think about putting him someplace where "he'd be happy." But thanks to Angelica's patience—and Alicia's when she and Rivera were around—he was happy at home. They had taught him the basics of everyday life. And he was a familiar figure pedaling around the countryside in their little valley. Everyone in the small community of Healdsberg knew him, and they all looked after the man with the child's mind and innocence.

"Hello, *hermano*!" Rivera said, stepping out of the truck

and embracing his brother-in-law who was still embracing his wife.

"How are you, you old bandit?" Rafael said, delighted to see his old friend.

"How do you think?" Rivera asked, sweeping his hand to bring attention to their new truck.

Rafael stepped back to inspect it. It wasn't new by any stretch of the imagination. But it was new considering the truck Rafael had seen them in the previous year. Over the years, as he prospered, he'd offered Rivera and Alicia innumerable chances to stay in Healdsberg and become part of their rapidly growing business. But Rivera and Alicia were happy on the road. Together. And no matter the temptation offered by Rafael, they resisted.

"Not too bad." Rafael whistled. "Not too bad! Alicia must have finally got you off your fanny and made you do some pretty fancy picking to be able to afford this."

Rafael stared at his old friend. He hadn't changed a bit through all the years. After a lifetime of stooping . . . picking . . . weeding . . . harvesting . . . driving endless roads . . . he still had his ready smile and marvelous sense of humor. And over the years, Rivera and Alicia had attracted a steadily growing army of migrants to them. Whether they wanted advice, support, solace, food, or a warm blanket, they knew they could rely on Rivera and his wife. Without realizing it, Rivera had more and more become the unofficial spokesman for the itinerant.

Last year men had turned to him for more than support. A group of hollow-eyed, sun-blackened migrants had asked him to help organize a work boycott . . . a strike against a large farm in one of California's central valleys. The farm, owned by an absentee corporation, was one of the largest in the area and was known to abuse and underpay their laborers.

The strike, though hastily organized, had remarkable results. Especially when the corporation realized it was risking an entire harvest if it didn't negotiate with this ragtag band led by Rivera.

The corporation tried force at first, intimidation, the power of the press. But Rivera kept his workers above the chaos and out of the violence the corporation hoped to trick them into. By the time the corporation finally issued orders to its foremen and managers to cooperate, Rivera had won the migrants' undying gratitude and the animosity of most of the growers in the West.

That hostility flourished when, after the success they'd won from one of the agricultural giants, this band of dusty revolutionaries announced the establishment of a fledgling labor union. A union especially for that forgotten man, the migrant.

Despite his reluctance, after a night of worrying, arguing, and debating with Alicia, Rivera had accepted their draft to be their leader.

"Hear you're having trouble rounding up a crew," Rivera teased now.

"Wouldn't if I wasn't stuck with you every year. If it wasn't for you, I could probably get into that bracero program." Rafael referred to the Mexican peasants who flooded into California under a Federal program to pick crops. They were paid slave wages. But they lived on nothing and sent their money back to their families in Mexico's interior.

"No way," Alicia said. "Put too many of my husband's people out of work. Besides, you try that and I'll sic Roberto on you."

Rivera's son Roberto was the attorney for their young union.

"Speaking of the devil, where is Roberto? I haven't seen him since you've been gone."

"He's back at the office drawing up a contract for you," Alicia said ominously. "You want your grapes picked, mister, you're going to need a contract."

"I didn't think I needed one with you."

"You don't," Rivera said. "But for your own protection, it's about time you got one. We thought you might like to sign one that gives your workers a little bigger bite of the apple."

"You guys get any more of a bite and I'm going to have to get a rabies shot," Rafael grinned.

"Well, we'll be easy on you this year then," Rivera said. "But there is something in the works that I'd like to . . . we'd like to talk to you and the family about."

407

"Go ahead . . ."

"Not without Angelica." Alicia shook her head. "And the kids as well. Rita and Raf."

"Sounds very mysterious," Rafael said as he walked around to the back of the pickup where Pietro was still sleeping off the effects of his giant daily lunch. Angelica's passion was overfeeding him. For a moment Rafael looked at the handsome features nearly hidden by his growing girth. Then he reached down and gently tousled Pietro's hair.

Pietro opened his big brown eyes and instantly broke into a smile. "Hello, Papa!" He yawned through his grin. "Oh . . . hello, Auntie and Uncle Rivera." He looked around the back of the truck confused. The last thing he remembered was yielding to the inviting soft green grass under the shade of the trees next to the road.

"How about tonight, then?" Rafael said, turning to Alicia and Rivera. "Everyone should be home. Except Raf. He's still in Europe. But I expect he'll be back any day now."

"How about tomorrow?" Rivera replied. "You think we'd miss one of Angelica's Sunday dinners?"

"Oh . . . come tonight!" Pietro pleaded.

"How about tonight *and* tomorrow then?" Rafael said.

"You got a deal." Alicia said. "Besides I'm dying to give my sister-in-law a hand. It's been a while since I've had a chance to try my hand in a new kitchen like hers."

"Great! You want to stay with Papa or go with Aunt Alicia and Uncle Rivera?" Rafael said, turning to Pietro,

Pietro looked at them as he struggled to make a decision. "I want to ride some more." He looked around at his bike.

Rafael nodded and reached in the back of the truck and lifted out the Schwinn Flyer, the fanciest bike available at the Western Auto in Healdsberg. It had lights, a horn, and mud flaps behind the overinflated whitewall tires. It had cowboy grips and a chrome basket filled with the treasures Pietro found along the road.

Rivera slipped his arm around Alicia's waist and watched as Rafael helped his son start off into the afternoon. He felt a strange mixture of joy and sadness. Joy that such love could exist between a father and a son. Sadness that the young man had been robbed of his future. But maybe, he thought, it was a blessing to remain eternally a child.

CHAPTER THIRTY-THREE

Sunday was cause for celebration at the Orsini household. Raf had called the afternoon before from New York's La Guardia Airport to tell them he'd just flown in and would be home by midnight.

It was apparent when he got off the little company plane Rafael sent to meet him in San Francisco that he was past exhaustion, nearer a zombie than a son. But zombie or not, he was greeted like a returning hero by the whole family.

Rita, as much as the others, was anxious to find out whether or not he'd had any success. But he evaded her questions.

"Tomorrow!" he promised as, arm in arm with Pietro who was carrying his briefcase, he was led away from the plane.

"You seem more smug than tired," Rita said trying to provoke him into revealing something about his trip.

"With good reason, sister dear. With good reason." He knew he'd arouse her curiosity to the point where she probably wouldn't sleep that night.

The next morning, a pounding at his door brought Raf stumbling out of bed. As he opened the door, a smiling Rita barged past his still half-asleep figure with a white paper bag filled with coffee, doughnuts, and a Sunday paper picked up on her way over.

"Morning!" she said cheerfully. "Hope I didn't wake you." Before he could answer, she swept past and into his kitchen where she poured the coffee into mugs and put the doughnuts on a plate. "Your place really looks different," she said. "Guess your being gone gave the maid time to catch up on shoveling out the debris."

"Very funny . . . very funny," he moaned as he stretched.

Rita handed him the mug and headed into his palatial-sized bedroom. She could never get used to his canopied bed. She went through into the bath and turned on the shower, adjusting the water.

"What do you think you're doing?" he asked, following after her. It was bad enough she had wakened him. But she'd done it in the middle of a dream about Michelle.

"Just trying to help my little brother," she shrugged innocently.

"I get a little tense when you start hanging around helping," He nodded toward the door. "So if you'll excuse me." He set the mug of coffee on his bureau and pulled the silk pajama top over his head.

Rita sat down on the couch and studied her brother's living room. She still lived at home, but for the sake of his social life, Raf had moved into town almost a year ago. Though his place was still sparsely furnished, the pieces Raf had selected for it were elegant as well as expensive. Most were from the mansions overlooking San Francisco Bay and had been bought by her brother after the decorators gave him their illustrious history.

As she waited, she picked up the Sunday paper and leafed through it until she came to the business section. She'd nearly finished the section when Raf came back in, dressed in tight pants and a sweater he'd bought in Paris.

"Jesus!" Rita said, shaking her head in disbelief.

"What's that supposed to mean?"

"Nothing. I was just wondering how long you think you've been gone. I know it's been a long time, but it's damn near still the middle of the summer. If you keep wearing that fuzzy sweater, I'm not sure you'll make it through the day."

"Cute! Very cute!" he said sitting down to pull on his tight Italian shoes. "But I'll have you know these are designer's originals. They're very expensive and very hard to come by. But I don't see any hope of educating you in finer things . . ."

The sound of their father's pickup coming up the driveway cooled them both off.

Rafael went around to the back of the truck to help Pietro get his bike out while Angelica rushed up the steps with a sack filled with groceries. She set the bag down and crushed her son to her. She'd seen him the previous night, but she still had to make sure he was really home.

"Papa," he said embracing Rafael and then Pietro who followed, a huge grin across his face. "Hello, big brother!"

"You need a good breakfast. You probably haven't had a decent meal since you left," Angelica said, heading directly for the kitchen.

The bag of groceries that Angelica brought seemed bottomless. She made pancakes, with fresh strawberries, thick slices of smoked ham, and fried eggs just the way he loved them.

Throughout breakfast, Raf described the events of his trip, the negotiations, the exhaustion, the personalities, told of the aristocratic German, the group of arrogant Frenchmen, the personable Swiss head of Vin Franco–Italo Et Cie.

Finally, after a well-planned dramatic pause, he handed each of them a folder containing the proposal of the tentative agreement.

He was delighted to see their heads bouncing between documents, agreements, market reports, prospectuses, suggested corporate structures, annual reports from the European companies involved. Most of all he was delighted by the rapt attention they gave him.

Raf smiled, he charmed, he soothed, he wove a fantasy of what he'd accomplished. Of course, he tactfully omitted the unimportant little problem the Chairman of Vin Franco–Italo had handled for him. And he omitted any mention of Michelle.

Almost parrotlike, he presented his family the sales pitch Paul Buntz had poured into him. He told them the proposed stock transfers would bring them valuable shares from the other corporations. He showed them that dollarwise, he had almost doubled their assets by the mere stroke of a pen. He painted the picture for them of how important it was in these troubled times to be visionary, to be aware of the growing international marketplace. Not only in wine, but in other commodities as well.

412

"With the clout an organization like this would have, who knows what products or services we might get involved with in the future? Even now we can profit in small ways. Vin Franco has a virtual monopoly on the cork industry in Spain and the Middle East. The Germans have a half dozen absolutely huge glassworks. They produce, I'd say, about half the wine bottles for all of Western Europe."

Rafael sat there with his hand around Angelica's shoulder, watching and listening to his son in absolute amazement. The concerns he'd felt before his son's trip, the worries he'd discussed with O'Hara had proved groundless. The young son he'd sent to Europe had come home a seasoned businessman. A young man who was able to enter the lion's den and emerge safely after taming the lions. Rafael was proud. He was pleased. With or without this transaction, the future of their winery would be safe in his son's hands.

"Our protection lies in our representation on the board. I would suggest of course that Father head our chair. The second seat I think should be alternated between Rita and myself."

He was very pleased when Rita's head shot up. He knew she'd been totally unprepared for that. But it was an offer he could make easily. She had neither the temperament nor the patience to sit on a board for long. So he'd gladly share that seat with her in the beginning, make himself seem both generous and practical. It should swing her to supporting him.

"What about Mother?" Rita asked, unwilling yet to leap on his bandwagon.

"That's an even better idea," Raf said, throwing up his hands as though he should have thought of it first. "As a matter of fact, that would be a wonderful way for the two of you to have a vacation," he said turning to his father and mother. He knew his mother would not go to Europe. She would never allow anything to take her away from Pietro for an extended period of time.

Rafael nodded, but Angelica was noncommittal.

"How often would this board of directors have to meet?" Angelica asked.

"Normally the board would only have to meet once or twice a month. More often only if there were an emer-

413

gency of some kind. But you have to remember this board would be responsible for more than one major company. Sometimes they'd be called on to make decisions weekly . . . even daily. They're all experts and all professionals. So we'd have to be there."

"Well . . . if we do go ahead with this, I certainly don't think I'd want to be caught in a mess like that," Angelica said as Raf had hoped she would.

"We seem to give up a great deal," Rita said, starting to probe.

"It's more than offset by our gains."

"What about things like production? Who dictates that?"

"The board dictates the quotas they want shipped abroad. We still control the amounts we should produce domestically."

"How about quality control?"

"That's something that very definitely stays here . . . in our hands."

Rita nodded and went back to studying the proposal. She was numb from the astonishment that her brother had come up with such a complex proposal. She'd expected him to come back home whining about being maltreated and armed with nothing but a hangover, V.D., and a huge expense statement. At best, she'd expected an order for a few thousand token cases to each country. But a merger into a corporation that included some of the world's most prestigious companies? She shook her head as she studied the contents of the folder. It was brilliant. There was no denying that. Was she just being a jealous bitch in her negative feelings about it?

No! Godammit! That wasn't it. Something about the deal just didn't ring true. It just wasn't Raf. It was beyond his depth. She became impatient to call Jim O'Hara and talk to him as soon as she could. He'd know what was going on and if it was legitimate or not. He'd worked over there. Even for the same company. If there was a rotten fish hidden in the reams of paperwork, as an attorney Jim would smell it out.

"Well, this isn't going to happen overnight. I've got to get to Mass." Rita stood, closing the folder. "Maybe we can take some time to think about it and get together in a couple of weeks . . ."

414

"Rita, the machinery is all cranked up and moving. I've got those Europeans so excited they can't wait. I told them we'd have an answer for them within a couple of weeks."

"My God! You've got to be kidding! Do you believe that, Papa? Mama! He goes away to sell a little wine and comes back with a grand scheme that says we have to move out of the store in a couple of weeks!"

"It's not *my* grand scheme," Raf said. "It's something that will benefit the whole family. Plus our name. If you agree with Rita that it's just a scheme, Papa, I'm sorry." He rose dramatically and picked up as many papers as he could. "I'll call Herr Buntz first thing in the morning and tell him the deal's off."

"No, I don't agree that it's merely a grand scheme," Rafael said. "I think you have come back with something that is significant . . . important. We are obligated to treat it with the same respect."

Rita felt as though she'd been slapped in the face. Raf saw the look on his sister's face and bit his lip to hide his jubilation.

"Rita, sometimes good things happen fast," Angelica said, sensing her daughter's confusion and pain.

"Yes, Mama," she said as she went through the living room toward the door. Angelica slipped out of her chair and headed after her daughter to comfort her and to assure her nothing would be done without considering everyone's feelings, concerns.

"What do you think, Papa?" Raf asked after the women had disappeared.

"I'm a little numb, to be perfectly frank." Rafael looked at his son's anxious face. "Rita's right, you know."

Raf felt his heart sinking.

"We sent you off looking to sell a few cases of wine . . . you come back with an offer to merge with half of Europe."

His father's proud smile sent his spirits soaring again.

Rafael looked at his son. He was in a dilemma. He and Angelica had all the money they'd need in a dozen lifetimes. They didn't need to expand their market. Surely not to Europe. But his son had come home from his first crusade with a well-devised plan. A plan that gave them the ability to multiply almost by the square.

If he said no to it, from then on Raf would know the weight of his father's hand. It could destroy his spirit, his desire, his initiative. He knew what the impact would be on Rita. But she'd survive. Even if their answer was yes, he knew she'd survive. But could he say yes to it? He honestly didn't know. Life sure didn't get any easier as it went on, he thought. "Your Aunt Alicia got in yesterday," he said. "We'll have to talk to her about it, so she can vote for Pietro."

Raf nodded and slipped another folder out of his briefcase with her name already stenciled on it. He'd thought of her and of her vote. But she usually voted the way his father wanted.

Rafael rose and embraced his son for a job more than well done. "We'll see you at home later then. Your mother's having her usual Sunday dinner. It'll be a good time to talk to your aunt. I'll leave that up to you."

"Fine," Raf smiled. That'll be a piece of cake, he thought as his father stopped in the living room to take Pietro away from the television.

"That asshole! That smug, pompous, son of a bitch!"

Jim O'Hara watched in amused disbelief as Rita stormed around his living room. "I assume you didn't come over here to tell me your opinion of your brother. It's rather well-known."

"He's not going to get away with it. There's something rotten in here and you're going to find it." Rita hit her knuckles against the folder she'd dropped on the table next to his favorite easy chair.

"Yes, ma'am!" he saluted as he picked the folder up and quickly leafed through it. "Whatever you say."

"I'm sorry, Jim." She slumped down in his lap crushing the folder between them. "I guess I sound like a jealous bitch . . . but . . ."

"But what?" he laughed, pulling her to him.

"Well, dammit! The least you could do was to tell me I didn't sound like it."

"Later. Look, it's very simple. You're upset and concerned and you have a right to be. At least from what you tell me. Now if you're right and there's a plot to steal the keys to the kingdom, then you're not a bitch. But, my dear,

416

if you're wrong . . ." He pushed her gently from his lap. "Now let me read this and we'll find out which one you are."

While he poured over the contents of the folder, Rita stalked around his apartment. Occasionally she'd stop behind him and put her arms around his neck and nuzzle his ear. But he was oblivious to her attention. She looked through his collection of reading material. *Wall Street Journal* . . . a dozen old agricultural magazines pilfered from her lab. A couple of books on philosophy . . . quarterly magazines from Harvard. Damn! She was glad he wasn't as dull as his reading material. She glanced around. He didn't own a television set, so she went to the record player. She shook her head. Even that was odd. It only played one record at a time. And his collection of new hi-fi records was all classical.

Finally, he handed the folder back to her.

"Well?" she asked after he went to his bar and returned with a tumbler filled with scotch and soda.

"Well, what?"

"Tell me what the scheme behind the scheme is. Tell me how we're going to come riding in with the cavalry and rescue dear old Ma and Pa from the bad guys so they'll live happily ever after while the villains are banished into the sunset."

"I'm afraid we can't use that scenario."

She looked at him in disbelief. "You're teasing."

He took a sip of his drink and placed it on a coaster next to his hi-fi. He leafed through the albums, selected one, and put it on. The strains of the music drifted in.

"As far as I can see, it's legit. I'm sorry. I truly am. But there's no reason for me to tell your father there's reason to kill the deal. If anything rotten's in Denmark, it's too slick for me to pick up."

Rita stared down at the folder, her spirits drained. She knew Jim O'Hara's legal reputation. If he couldn't find anything, there wasn't anything.

"How about a drink?" he asked.

"Thanks, but we have to be at the house later. Mother's Sunday dinner, remember?"

"Who could forget one of those?"

"Well," she said flipping through the pages of the proposal, "it looks like when this goes through, I'm going to have a lot of time on my hands. Rafael Orsini, Jr., fair-haired young torchbearer is sure not going to have me around raining on his parade . . ."

"Let's hope it doesn't come to that. Because if you have a lot of time on your hands, I'm going to be unemployed too."

That afternoon, in the cool of the grove of huge shade trees that circled Rafael's and Angelica's home, Raf watched Rivera's pickup rattle up the drive and stop next to the old stone winery. His Aunt Alicia, Rivera, and Rivera's son Roberto got out of the front while Benito and Muriella got out of the back. Raf had always felt uncomfortable around his aunt's husband. Now her stepson provided an even larger source of irritation. Roguishly handsome, Roberto Rivera was a real charmer, Raf thought, as the young Mexican walked toward the growing assembly of guests gathered for the Orsini Sunday feast.

After shaking Rafael's hand and hugging Angelicia, Roberto strolled casually toward Raf. As he neared, Raf could almost feel his mood changing. Roberto was a few years older than he and had always been the center of attention, the kind of son every parent hoped for.

He had spent most of his youth in the backseat of his father's jalopies. But when Rivera and Alicia bought a tiny frame house in Healdsberg to spend their winters in, Roberto became the first migrant's child to graduate from high school there. He had been a local hero thanks to his football heroics. Going on to junior college, he had attracted the eye of football scouts at U.S.C. who offered him the sports scholarship that opened the door for him. Working nights and studying afterwards till dawn, he did what few others were capable of doing. He graduated from their pretigious law school.

To add to his growing legend, he had enlisted in the Marines when the Korean War broke out. And he had been awarded the Silver Star and given his Captain's bars when his unit was trapped behind the enemy lines at a place called the Chosun Reservoir.

But now, knowing what he'd accomplished in Europe,

Raf realized how adolescent, how juvenile his feelings of inadequacy around Roberto had always been. He was more than an equal to this local Mexican. Roberto would remain ever tied to the earth while Raf reached for the stars.

"How you doing, Raf?" Roberto held out his hand.

"Can't complain," Raf tried to exert an equal amount of pressure to the handshake. Roberto was a lawyer, but he still had the grip of a man who'd grown up in the fields.

"I hear you just got back from Europe," Roberto said.

Raf grinned and raised his eyebrows. "Yeah. I was over for a few weeks on business."

"Business? Sure you were!" Roberto grinned. "You'll have to give me some of the phone numbers. Knowing you, you probably have an extra dozen you'll never use."

"At least," Raf lied. But he was amazed to think Roberto would believe any of the girls he'd known would go out with a Mexican.

"It never changes, does it?" Roberto said as he looked at the crowd of people passing the picnic table set up buffet style. Since the old days, the number of tables had grown until there were now almost enough to qualify as a small park. It was always a festival during the summer. The conversations, the children playing, people face to face with those of other races, other religions, other political convictions, other economic backgrounds.

As the line moved past the table heaped with fried chicken, potato salad, deep dish Italian dishes laden with sauces and cheeses, and wine, Roberto saw Rita standing next to O'Hara.

"How's your sister?"

"You know Rita. She'll never change."

"Let's hope not," Roberto said. He'd had a crush on her since childhood. "So . . . how'd you make out in Europe? Businesswise, I mean."

"Pretty well. Better than I expected. As a matter of fact, that's why I'm glad to see your dad and my aunt here. I'll need to talk to Aunt Alicia. There's a family meeting coming up where we'll all have to vote. I'd like to make sure she knows what it's all about before then."

"Sounds pretty big."

"There's a possibility that once we conclude the negotiations I started, the entire complexion of the wine business in this country will change."

"Phew!" Roberto exhaled, as if impressed. He wished he could figure an easy way to end this uncomfortable bullshit he and Raf always seemed to indulge in.

They stood for a few moments in silence.

"So, what brings you back out to the farm?" Raf finally asked. "I thought this new union thing kept you stuck in town in an office job or something."

"Like they say, you can take the boy out of the country . . . But you're right. I have been stuck in town too long. In a way I guess my father and I are here for more or less the same kind of thing you just mentioned. Nothing so earthshaking of course. But we're getting ready to try something that could also change the face of our industry. Our world's a lot smaller than yours," he smiled humbly. "But it will mean a lot to us."

"Sounds exciting," Raf smiled, unimpressed. "Tell me about it."

"I will. But I have to wait for the elder statesman." Roberto nodded toward his father and Alicia who were sitting at a table with Rafael and Angelica. "My father and Alicia want to ask your folks about it first."

"Well, I'm sure whatever it is, if it's something we can do, you know you can count on us."

"That's great," Roberto nodded. "It's nice to know we have friends like you to count on."

"Why don't we grab something to eat before everything disappears." Raf walked off toward the food, feeling magnanimous about the forthcoming help that would be extended Roberto and his family.

As could be clocked with almost scientific regularity, a half hour after Angelica's meal, the activity had approached a snail's pace. The conversations had died and eyelids fluttered shut as the heat of the afternoon and the full stomachs brought on blissful naps. It looked like a plague of sleeping sickness had struck: bodies were strewn on every available chair, bench, and soft green patch of grass.

Sitting on a bench that his grandfather had built, Raf

poked a toothpick between his teeth as he listened to Rivera tell his parents and a small cluster of intent listeners what had happened to them during the strike against the corporation down south. Rivera was a master storyteller and clearly in his element now.

Raf looked at the squat Mexican leaning against the arms of his wife like an overgrown child. Thanks to television he had become almost a Don Quixote hero: The news programs had made him a celebrity. It amused Raf to think of how unsophisticated the American public was. Not at all like his new friends in Europe.

Their advertising man, Murphy, had been right on the money. If TV was responsible for making this simple man a hero, think what it could do for them.

"Sounds like the old days," Rafael said, reaching over and slapping his friend on the shoulder. "I wish I could have been there."

"Well, that's sort of what I had in mind." Rivera grinned.

"You want Papa to carry one of your picket signs?" Raf asked, as he slipped down in the grass next to them. "That ought to be a pretty dramatic sight."

"If that's what my brother and sister want . . . that's what I'll do." Rafael shrugged.

"No. I don't want you to do something like that. In this sun, an old office man like you couldn't last half the day," Rivera teased.

"What we have in mind is something better," Alicia said.

"What do I have to do?"

"Let us strike your winery." Rivera grinned, the wrinkles around his eyes turning white against his sunburned skin.

"What?" Raf Jr. almost swallowed his toothpick. Then he laughed, thinking he'd been caught in a practical joke. Rivera and his father were always pulling them on each other. But when he saw the two men hadn't stopped looking at each other, he knew it wasn't a joke. "You're not serious?"

"We're very serious," Roberto said from the redwood bench behind his father and Alicia.

"But why? What would it prove? You already know you

could get anything you wanted by just asking." Raf fought to control his anger.

"What are you getting so upset about?" Rita asked as she watched his unexpected outburst. She looked at O'Hara to alert him to listen in case her brother revealed something he shouldn't about his big deal. But O'Hara hadn't taken his eyes off the two men in the center of their little circle.

"For one thing," Raf groped for reasons, "we're too close to harvest. Something . . . or someone screws that up and we're the big losers."

"You don't have to worry about that," the giant Benito said from where he leaned against a tree fanning himself. "I'll pick your grapes myself if I have to. No little pain in the butt union man is going to stop me. I promise you."

"That's the big mystery you two waited until now to spring?" Rafael asked as he sipped on a glass of melting ice left from the tea.

Alicia and Rivera nodded almost in unison.

"It won't be a real strike, Rafael," Alicia explained.

"But you want it to look like a real thing, right?" Rafael asked his sister as he set his glass in the grass."

"Harvest is close," Rivera said. "Within a month, if I miss my guess."

"Who should know better than you?" Rafael asked.

"So, let's say if someone were to strike your big winery, say a little band of farm laborers, it might put you in a bad spot. You might have to deal with them, come to some kind of agreement or else lose your harvest."

Rafael shook his head and let out a low whistle.

"Sure sounds like you . . . I mean that little band of workers would have us over a barrel."

"I thought so." Rivera nodded enthusiastically. "It's a pretty good plan, *sí*?"

"*Sí*, a pretty damn good plan," Rafael conceded.

"It should be," Rivera said, drawing Alicia to him. "Your sister thought of it."

Alicia blushed.

"What's all this supposed to accomplish?" Angelica asked.

"Maybe . . . just maybe afterward," Alicia explained, "the other growers would be easier to deal with. Especially if we . . . my husband's association forced the Orsini Winery to come to terms."

"It could give us the key to our future," Roberto interrupted. "The other unions in the A.F.L. and C.I.O. would recognize us. It would sort of shirttail us into legitimacy."

"Pretty smart pair I got working for me, *sí*?" Rivera beamed proudly.

Rafael grinned and shook his head.

"But you know you can write your own ticket. I mean even before your crew wants or needs a raise, you get it from us without having to ask," Raf said. "You already use us as a wedge against the other growers as it is. So it seems to me you could accomplish the same thing without calling this phony strike."

"That could take years, longer," Roberto said. "This way you help us save those years. You're the biggest in the business. If we take on the biggest, it'll look like David and Goliath. Our tiny movement against your giant company."

"Very touching. But it sounds like we're the ones that will come out on the short end of the stick. We end up the bad guys."

"Not in the end. In the end, you are the ones given credit for recognizing that the workers in the field are men and women. It's time they had their share of dignity. Just because they work in dirt, mud, and rain doesn't mean they can't enjoy some respect as human beings. The public knows that and will respect you for showing it after the strike's over."

Benito and several others applauded Roberto's passionate plea. "Your father understands," Alicia said quietly. "He came out of the same fields we're still working."

"That's partly true, Aunt Alicia. But part of it's bull also. You're still in the fields because you want to be. You . . . none of you have to be. Papa's told you a hundred times . . ."

"We chose to do what made us happiest," Alicia explained.

"And now striking us makes you happy?"

"That's not true," Roberto said. "We come to you . . . and your father and mother out of friendship . . ."

"Friendship?" Raf laughed sarcastically. "You're planning a strike out of friendship?"

"That's right." There was a deadly calm to Roberto's voice. "We could do it without your permission."

"No! You're wrong," Rivera said, silencing his son. "My friendship with Rafael Orsini runs deeper than this. If he said no, for any reason, we would go somewhere else."

"You know you don't have to do that," Rafael said.

Raf felt his face burning. For all intents and purposes, his father had approved the proposition.

"Raf is right though," Rivera said turning to him. "We are using our friendship . . . and family to further our goals. Without your help, our little baby organization would be eaten alive. We'd never be able to take on a giant like the Orsini Winery. It would be a war we could never win. It would be suicide."

"Don't you think the public's going to be smart enough to spot that for what it is?" Raf asked. "Especially when they find out that your wife . . . Roberto's stepmother . . . is an Orsini."

"Some of our friends and neighbors inside the valley might be a little suspicious. But just imagine how it sounds to the press," Roberto said. "Rafael Orsini's sister takes sides against her own brother and supports the strike against the family winery. It'll give us the national news coverage we need. And I guarantee, to those watching outside this valley, it'll look genuine."

"That could cause problems for us," Raf warned. "It seems to me that strikes go hand in hand with fires . . . crop damage . . . outsiders who come in to agitate."

"We guarantee there won't be any problems. My father, all of us, are committed to nonviolence. To prove that to the public, we'll set up around the clock vigils. Our people will be up and down the road in front of the winery around vigil fires. It'll look great on TV. A great symbol for people to identify with. At the same time, it'll be a place from which our people can watch over everything, everyone. Besides, in the end, the national publicity that helps us also helps you. The Orsinis will look to the public like truly great people when they sign their history-making contract with us."

"If something happened to the harvest," Raf warned, "it could make those truly great people bleed to death."

"There will be no problems," Rivera said to Rafael. "After all, in the end, you will see the light, *sí*?"

"I can't see how it could hurt us then," Angelica said, sliding closer to Rafael and putting her arm over his shoulder.

Rita looked to O'Hara who almost imperceptively nodded his agreement. "Neither can I," she added.

"How about you, son?" Rafael asked.

Raf stood there without committing himself. He knew there was no way to deny Rivera his strike now. But he dreaded the thought that it might somehow affect his recent negotiations.

"Your father spent a lot of years slaving in fields like ours," Angelica said. "Some people were fair . . . like your grandfather. Most weren't. And still aren't. If we can help the same men he worked alongside, we should. We've been blessed with abundance. It won't hurt to share a little of it by helping friends. Especially when we have so much."

"I couldn't have said it better, Mama," Raf tried to grin. "I just wanted us to be sure of all the aspects. Know what the limits were . . . things like that."

"When it comes to Guillermo Rivera and his wife," Rafael said quietly to his son, "there are no limits."

CHAPTER THIRTY-FOUR

Murphy watched in disbelief as a battery of television mobile units followed the small army of tattered migrants as they walked back and forth peacefully picketing. All up and down the road, there were tiny fires dotting the roadside. There was a spirit, a unity about the migrants Murphy hadn't expected to see when he was hastily called by Rafael to handle press support for the winery's point of view.

When the migrants first announced their strike plans at the tiny frame house that served as their headquarters, less than a half-dozen reporters bothered to cover them. And when those reporters heard what the Mexicans planned to do, they shook their heads in disbelief.

The strike was timed for the height of the harvest season. Almost magically, the trucks that had been rumbling into the Orsini crushers suddenly stopped in their tracks. A quick call from Rafael to Frenchy, who handled all Orsini trucking, had reminded him that as a member of the Teamsters Union, his local shouldn't cross the picket line.

What the press failed to observe was that many of the trucks weren't filled with grapes. With Rafael's help, Roberto had the trucks filled with cull apples, green grapes, hay, leaves, anything they could pile grapes on to make the giant gondolas on the trucks look full. The first pictures of the long line of giant diesel trucks, loaded to the brim with a perishable cargo, giving way to the little band of weather-beaten men and women, brought the television newsmen running.

Revolution was in the air and they wanted to be on hand to bring it live into the nation's living rooms.

* * *

426

Rafael looked over the series of photographs on his desk. Murphy had chosen those that focused on Rafael and the winery's positive qualities. Rafael quickly overruled him and authorized only those which showed him menacing or berating his friend Rivera or his workers.

"You really want these to go out?" Murphy asked.

Rafael nodded.

Murphy looked at him for a moment. The old man was far too smart not to realize what he was doing. "You really intend to play the heavy in this?"

Rafael smiled. "Yeah. As a matter of fact, I've been thinking of buying a black hat. What do you think?"

"That I just walked into a setup."

"Murphy, I'm more than happy to find that my confidence and trust in you are justified."

"I've heard you two were closer than friends. I didn't think it added up. Especially with him married to your sister. But these days, who can tell?"

"I want you to do an all-time job on this, Murph. I don't want a day to go by when it doesn't look like we might grind those poor old migrants into the dirt. I want every guy sitting home reading his newspaper or watching his television to start rooting for Rivera. The little guy. The underdog."

"This could backfire, you know."

Rafael shook his head. "The deck's been pretty well stacked. And by both players."

"Okay," Murphy sighed. "It won't be easy. But I guess I can paint a scowl over this beautiful, sensitive, Irish face and go amongst them preaching the gospel according to Orsini."

"Good," Rafael said enthusiastically.

During the following days, the press grew to love the strike. There wasn't much news that week anyway, so this was a natural. Especially since they had an identifiable good guy . . . and an identifiable bad guy.

It came to be known as the "Cain and Abel Affair." It seemed like the wealth of California against the Grapes of Wrath.

Amid the pickets, Rivera stood out like a messiah. He smiled gently, spoke softly, and pleaded innocence as to why the mighty Orsini, his brother-in-law and once his

427

friend, refused to allow his few workers, members of his tiny union, the basics of life every American was entitled to. Home, hearth, family, and a pot of beans.

Pictures captured the pickets roasting in the sun, while Rafael glowered down at them from the comfort of his air-conditioned office. All attempts to interview him brought a negative response. Members of his family were unavailable and, except for longtime employees, the winery was closed to all outsiders.

The late news was fed pictures as the strikers huddled around the tiny campfires. "Huddling together in small masses of determination," one newsman said. The cameramen did superb jobs of catching the faces of the workers.

Between Murphy and Roberto, the choreography of events was perfect. They had their national audience and each side its supporters. The little man in the living room watching the black-and-white box he owed monthly payments on rooted for Rivera. The corporations and executives backed Rafael.

Many called Rafael to offer assistance in any way they could. Rafael thanked them but declined. To accept their offers, he told them, merely emphasized the existence of this nuisance. He was determined to go it alone. They applauded his stand, wished him luck, and thanked their corporate lucky stars it was him and not them.

"An overseas call for you," Raf's secretary announced over his intercom.

His hand darted for the phone. "Paul, how are you? Sorry we haven't talked sooner . . ."

"Your father seems to be generating some rather unfavorable press. I just got off the phone with both Scheneblin and Chantellier. They are both understandably concerned."

"No problem, Paul, I can assure you."

"Possibly we're being misinformed as to the seriousness of this labor dispute. But I must tell you that it is receiving more coverage here than I would expect. Especially in light of your assurance and apparent lack of concern."

"Listen, Paul." Raf carefully explained what his father and Rivera had conspired to do.

"I see," Buntz said. "Then your father feels that this warrants jeopardizing our initial agreement?"

"Not at all. As a matter of fact, he's quite excited by our progress."

"Excellent. Then I can inform our other associates to proceed?"

"Well . . ." Raf was seized with panic. "I think it would be advisable to wait a few days . . . a week at most. Until my father and this Mexican finish their little charade."

"I'm a little confused." Buntz sounded irritated. "If it is indeed no more than a simple game to gain a measure of respect for this group, then why should we delay? After all, on the basis of your assurances, we've committed ourselves heavily to getting started. Everything on this end is going ahead full steam. If I call Scheneblin and Chantellier and suddenly tell them to forestall any further activity, we chance losing them again."

"Yes . . . of course."

"And if that happens, of course there is the rather unpleasant problem that exists between you and the Chairman."

Raf felt his heart pumping laboriously and his forehead suddenly perspiring. "Yes . . . of course. As I said a few minutes ago, Paul, I can assure you there're no problems. I don't see any reason for you having to call them back. I'll take care of things on this end and get back to you."

"Good, Raf. I'm counting on you." Buntz's confidence relieved Raf as they severed the connection.

A half hour later Raf caught up to his father in the middle of one of the rows. Rafael was taking samples of grapes to test for their sugar content. Standing at the head of the row was a television reporter, microphone in hand, trying to yell questions to Rafael over the jeering from the band of pickets led by Benito and Rivera.

"Do you see a possible settlement in the works?" the reporter shouted.

"Not with that band of bandits," Rafael answered sullenly without looking up.

"In the event that you can't reach a settlement, sir, and seeing as how no one will cross their picket line, how do you expect to harvest your grapes?"

"I'll pick them myself if I have to. Done it before. Can

do it again." Rafael raised his fists at the jeering band of pickets.

Benito was walking along the road next to the vineyard taunting the "gringo" to come out to the road and settle the strike between them.

"Wouldn't waste my breath . . . or my sweat. Besides, I don't want to have to beat up on an old man," Rafael said, turning away to keep from breaking up at Benito's reaction.

"Don't you think this is getting a little out of hand, Papa?" Raf asked as he walked down the row, trying to keep out of the mud of the recently irrigated vineyard.

"I'm just starting to have fun." Rafael turned and raised his fist once more for the cameraman.

"Papa, to the public, those people out there who buy our wine, you're anything but fun. I can guarantee you, they believe you. Right now I'm not sure you could win a popularity contest against Adolph Hitler."

Rafael knew his son was right. He was walking a dangerous tightrope. Even some of his closest neighbors were beginning to wonder whether he was serious.

"Please, Papa, I just got a call from Paul Buntz in Switzerland. He says his group is worried about what's happening. And he needs to know if we've given any serious thought to their proposal . . . my proposal. It's been almost two weeks."

Rafael nodded and looked at his son. He was in a quandary. His oldest and dearest friend needed support at the same time his son did. But despite what Raf thought, the offer and negotiations for the merger had rarely been off his mind. He'd spent hours going over the proposal, the stockholders' reports of the individual companies, their profit and loss statements which showed impressive profits and growth. Rafael's inclination was still to veto the merger. But he knew his son would never present them a more important opportunity. He sighed.

"Raf, I've been giving this thing of yours more time than you realize. Your mother and I both have. As a matter of fact, we both seem to find more things for than against . . ."

Raf's face beamed with relief.

430

"The only thing is . . . well, I can't see the harm in waiting a few more weeks before we come to a definite decision."

Raf's smile faded. He didn't have a few weeks. "We could risk the whole thing," he said almost weakly.

"Son, with the kind of money everyone seems to be talking, I can't imagine they'd walk out because of something like this. They're businessmen. I know you're anxious. I know you need this. And I'm determined to help if it's good for the family. But they have labor problems, too. They might well be having one this minute. You call this Buntz fellow back. He seems to be your friend. Tell him it looks good but we can't move until your father's through with his little game. We both know it won't be more than a couple of weeks. It can't go longer than that. Rivera and his crew have to get to work harvesting for us." Rafael smiled.

Rafael watched as his son headed back toward his car and made his way through the camera crews and pickets as though they weren't there.

Paul Buntz waited in the heavily upholstered chair in the main salon of the white yacht docked at Malaga on Spain's Mediterranean coast. Out of dark-tinted windows of thick-tempered glass, he could see gaily dressed couples bidding good-bye to the Chairman after an afternoon of sunbathing.

Buntz stared at the collection of paintings hanging in the cabin. He identified a Renoir, a Monet, three Picassos, and a Dali. He'd heard that ocean air destroyed art. But either the Chairman was unaware of it or unconcerned.

Buntz was used to luxury, but not on this scale. The wood-carved walls, the antiques, and the large staff clearing away leftovers from the day's feast left no doubt that he was in the presence of corporate monarchy.

The yacht was preparing to get underway. The Chairman was going to cruise eastward, first to Barcelona, then on to the Greek Isles. So Buntz would only have an hour at most to report on his progress with the Americans. He walked out onto the deck and leaned against the heavily varnished caprail.

431

The captain nodded pleasantly from the bridge above as he directed a host of seamen in their preparations. Buntz squinted into the sun as he caught sight of the Chairman's newest toy neatly secured on the top deck with cable. Shrouded under a bright canvas cover with the Chairman's coat of arms was his helicopter.

"Paul?" the Chairman called from the hatchway.

"Mr. Gianini." Buntz quickly held out his hand to the Padrone who took it warmly between both of his and led him back into the comfortable interior of the salon.

"So, how are you progressing with your project?" Gianini asked as he accepted a scotch and soda from a silver tray held by a butler.

Buntz smiled. "To be perfectly frank, it's almost like shooting birds in a cage. The boy's terribly immature. He's in over his head and running scared. He's made a series of pledges I'm sure he can't possibly keep. And as luck will have it, their company is embroiled in some sort of dramatic labor dispute that's being given extensive television coverage."

"Marvelous! Is that your doing?"

"I wish I could take the credit," Buntz said, refusing a drink from the tray. "But it seems the boy's father is involved in a scheme that casts him in the role of one who is intent on suppressing labor." Buntz described the strike the winery was involved in and the reasons Raf had given him for it.

"Wonderful. Especially since it keeps the elder Orsini displayed before the American public. Let's tell our man there not to let this opportunity slip away."

"Of course."

"Fortune indeed smiles on those who are patient," Gianini said, raising his glass. He thought back to the days when his violent temper had often brought him close to death. The years had taught him patience. Now he was on the brink of reaping some of the rewards of that patience. He no longer needed to take situations like this into his own hands. There were legions of men like Paul Buntz willing to risk their lives, limbs, families, and futures for money.

Since that night when Rafael had disappeared into the darkness with his faceless butchers, Gianini had prospered beyond all comprehension. Within the European business community, he was a reigning monarch. True, he maintained anonymity. But his reputation, his power was consummate . . . unquestioned.

"Do you think the boy will be able to persuade his family to accept our offer then?" he asked.

"I have mixed feelings about that. The boy is the natural heir. If the father is wise, he'll let him taste accomplishment . . . victory. My experience tells me this will be too big a bite. In any event, we can keep him roasting if his father feels negative. Ultimately, he'll have to respond to the boy's dilemma."

"If you were a betting man?"

"I can't imagine a parent letting his child suffer. I'm a father . . . I'd help my child. But I wouldn't do it at the cost of destroying the rest of my family."

"So you think he'll try to arrive at something that will be face-saving for his son. And at the same time break the tentative agreement he's reached with you."

"That would be my educated guess."

"Thank you, Paul. I value that educated guess. But under no circumstances do I want you to let the Orsinis, father or son, find a solution that is comfortable. I want you to do whatever is necessary to keep pressure on this young man. And Paul, keep this new public resentment toward their company alive and growing."

Buntz nodded. He'd just been given approval to use any means, coercion, extortion, blackmail, or violence against the Orsinis. He'd been given similar powers before and he hadn't failed his Padrone. His ability to use those means and still keep the Padrone's image spotless, had brought him rapid advancement within Vin Franco–Italo Et Cie. . .

"Should I place a limit on our efforts regarding this labor problem of theirs?" He carefully phrased his question so the Chairman could set whatever restrictions he desired, yet remain protected from any direct knowledge.

"None!" Gianini said with a trace of bitterness Buntz had never heard in his voice before.

"I understand." Buntz smiled as Gianini stood to signal that their time was at an end. "I think I can guarantee you'll be pleased."

Raf sat across from O'Hara, waiting for him to get off the phone.

"What's up, Raf?" O'Hara asked, as soon as he hung up.

"This goddamn strike's the problem," Raf said angrily.

"No calls," O'Hara said into his intercom. "Okay, what's the problem with the strike? As far as I can see. it's coming off pretty well the way your father and Rivera choreographed it."

"That's the problem. It's coming off too damn well."

O'Hara listened while Raf related his phone conversation with Paul Buntz. He nodded, knowing exactly the kind of pressure Buntz had exerted. He'd witnessed it before.

"So what do you think?" Raf asked. "I mean, you've met the man. You set all this up through him."

"Wait a minute, Raf," O'Hara warned. "I didn't set up anything with this man. I only set up a meeting for you in which you could pitch an idea that might mean something for this company . . . and for you in particular."

"Yeah, I know that. That's what I meant," he admitted. Actually he was anxious to find someone to share the blame and responsibility in case his deal went sour. Someone who'd help generate enough smoke so the casino debt could be slipped in the melee.

"I can't tell you whether Buntz was being truthful or not," O'Hara said. "He's tough. Under that suave, refined exterior beats a heart filled with ice water. But I can't think of any reason for him to lie. This deal means a lot to him. Both financially and prestige-wise."

"So you don't think he'd blow the deal?" Raf felt relieved.

"Not if he could help it. But you have to remember, it's not his deal. There are others involved. I can guarantee you one thing. If Scheneblin and you don't get along, he might blow the deal just for spite. So, if he doesn't need it, watch out. Meanwhile, maybe I can help. As they say . . . two heads and all that."

Raf smiled, grateful for an ally.

"Now, we know where Buntz stands. And we know your father has to play it out because of your uncle and aunt. So maybe you should talk to them. Do they know what's going on?"

Raf shook his head.

"It might help if they knew."

Raf felt a sense of discomfort as he and O'Hara drove through the older part of Healdsberg. The buildings looked as though they were decaying remnants of a long-dead civilization.

He had always hated it when his father had brought him down to this part of town when he was small. Though Rivera was his uncle as well as his father's closest friend, he'd always felt uneasy around the man. But now he had to see him.

The Riveras' tiny frame house, which also served as strike and union headquarters, sat on a lot beyond where the pavement ended. A dozen trucks and cars in various stages of deterioration were parked around it. On the porch sat the straw-hatted migrants who formed the core of Rivera's advisory council.

"Rivera around?" Raf called out as he pulled into the yard.

"Which one?" asked a man with a faded scar across his eye. Raf knew him as one of the men who'd been with Rivera for years.

"How many you got?" he asked sullenly.

"Maybe a dozen . . . maybe more." The man smiled.

"Guillermo . . . or Roberto."

"Who wants to know?" The man's smile broadened as he sensed Raf's frustration.

"You damn well know who wants to know."

"Oh . . . *sí*. Now I remember. You used to be that little white-bottomed baby I had to help change diapers for."

Inside at a battered desk, Roberto watched in amusement as Ramon had fun at Raf's expense.

"In here, Raf," he finally called from the living room.

Raf walked coldly past the man who'd been his father's friend since before he was born. Inside, the shades were drawn in an attempt to keep out as much heat as possible, but it didn't help much.

"Well . . . well . . . well! This must be pretty serious to bring two of the head honchos out," Roberto said as

O'Hara followed Raf into the cramped room cluttered with piles of strike memorandums, instructions, and banners asking for support, donations, food, clothing for the strikers on the picket line.

"I'd feel better talking about this to your father and my aunt, but O'Hara says that could be a no-no if the press got hold of it."

"He's got a point," Roberto admitted.

For the next half hour, Roberto listened as Raf explained the need to bring the strike to an end. He told him vaguely about the proposed project in Europe, explained that those involved in the deal were getting anxious as the strike was hurting the Orsini image. And, he added, if it continued, it might destroy what they were attempting.

"It all sounds wonderful for your family, Raf. But what do you want us to do?"

"Call off the damn strike."

"I'm afraid I can't help you, Raf." Roberto tilted back in the squeaky chair perched on worn rollers.

"Goddammit!" Raf said, instantly angry. "You've got your exposure. And you know we'll pay you what you want. What the hell else are you after?"

"You know as well as I do that it's not up to me . . . or you for that matter. It's between your father and my father. No one else."

"Well, goddammit! You can talk to him. Tell him what I told you." He felt his heart pounding in rage when Roberto shook his head.

"You know it doesn't work that way."

"How the hell does it work then? What do you want? Money for yourself? Is that it? Something under the table so you can build up a little bank account?"

Roberto felt his face flushing as the anger shot through his body like a current of electricity. "If it's so important to your family, you go to *your* father. He in turn goes to my father. And within the hour, our pickets will be off your ass," he said, barely above a whisper. "It doesn't work the other way around."

"You're going to be sorry for this," Raf warned.

"Why?" Roberto said, his eyes becoming menacing slits.

"If this deal is blown because of this shit of yours, it's going to create something you'll never be able to repay."

"Then go to your father. Unless it means more to the son than to the father. Or maybe the father doesn't know how important it is."

"He knows!"

"He knows? And he still feels no need to bring my father or Alicia into it?"

"It's none of their business, goddammit!" Raf pounded the desk in frustration.

"If it's none of theirs, then it's none of mine. And in that case, what are you doing here abusing our hospitality? Think about what O'Hara said before you got here. How would it look to the press? The rich son of the winery owner comes to the poor migrants' camp and tries to threaten and intimidate them into stopping."

"He's right," O'Hara said. "The press would crucify us."

Raf felt helpless, as though he was in a bad dream.

"Look," O'Hara continued. "You're both right . . . and you're both wrong. Why don't you both back off and give one another a little time to cool off?"

"What do you suggest?" Roberto asked.

"Compromise."

"I'm willing to try," Roberto said.

"How much longer do you think your strike's going to last?" O'Hara asked.

"Ten days . . . two weeks tops," Roberto said. "Which is why I can't see why you can't hold off till then."

"Raf's being more than honest. The men he's dealing with won't wait."

"The problem is," Roberto explained, "we have a big rally planned as the climax to the whole strike. People are coming from all over the southwest to show their support to us. We'll have every television camera in the state on us that day, plus the papers and the magazines. It's to show the unity that truly exists among workers everywhere . . . not just the small group of guys here. It's the big event that's supposed to put so much pressure on your father that he has to give in. The next day we'll have our historic meeting between the two men. Afterward my father will embrace yours and it'll be over."

"Very nice! All neat and clean. And it should work. But can you move the date up any?" O'Hara asked.

"I honestly don't know. But I'll try."

"I think that's all we can ask, an honest effort. Don't you agree?" O'Hara looked at Raf.

Raf nodded, almost from a ɪrance.

"You did well, Roberto," Rivera said after his son explained what had happened while he and Alicia were out.

"I'd be a liar if I said it was easy," Roberto admitted.

Rivera nodded. "You'd probably be the same way if you were in his shoes."

"Maybe."

"You and your brother wouldn't be keeping something from this old Mexican, now would you?" Rivera asked Alicia.

"You know I've never kept anything from you." She shook her head, as upset as her husband and stepson. "Rafael told me about this business thing that Raf wanted to do in Europe right after Raf got back. But he said it was separate and wouldn't have anything to do with us or the strike. But knowing my brother, he wouldn't say anything. Especially if he thought it would hurt what we're doing."

"True. He is probably the most stubborn human being I ever met," Rivera said. "And he would sacrifice for us."

"He's proven that by the strike," Roberto admitted.

"Maybe it's time you stopped by and visited my brother," Alicia said.

"It has been too long. This strike's kept us from at least three of Angelica's Sunday dinners."

An electric pump hummed and rattled on the wall next to the fermenting tank where Rafael stood atop a steel catwalk directing the hose that spewed the must over the cap. He was lost in thought as the heavy stream of juice broke up wedges from the cap before sinking back under the purple mush of skins.

"Better be careful," Rivera warned from the aisle under the catwalk where he waited unobserved by Rafael.

"Damn!" Rafael said breaking into a grin. "You damn near scared me to death."

"Well, I wanted to make sure you didn't fall in and add a little extra body to your wine," Rivera laughed, reminding him of the old joke Ferrara had caught him in. "The way I hear it, if some poor old Mexican falls in, you just leave him so you'll get a few extra gallons out of each tank."

"You know that's a lie," Rafael said climbing down and turning off the pump. "I learned a long time ago that that leaves the wine with a chili-powder taste."

"And the way I hear it, that's how you get the flavor in your wine."

"What the hell are you doing here anyway?" Rafael asked. "You crazy?"

"I had to talk to you," Rivera answered as they walked toward the aging cellar. "And don't worry. I used Griego's truck. They know he still works for you. So no one paid any attention when I drove in. Besides, everybody knows, all Mexicans look alike!"

They sat down at the heavy oak table and Rafael pulled out one of the dust-covered bottles and uncorked it. He poured his friend the first glass and waited, smiling.

Rivera sniffed it to make sure it wasn't bottled vinegar like the night they'd opened the first bottle of Orsini wine. It was wine. He took a gentle sip and let it trickle down his throat. It was aged to perfection and felt as mellow as a piece of satin.

"Alicia and I hear our strike is starting to cause some troubles for you on that deal you're working on in Europe."

Rafael looked up at him mildly surprised.

"Seems like a young son of mine has been talking a little too loudly."

Rivera shrugged. "It's not important who has the big voice. What's important is—are we hurting you?"

Rafael looked across the table at the face he'd known for what seemed like a dozen lifetimes. He reached over and put his hand around the back of Rivera's neck and squeezed. "Nothing that you do could ever hurt me . . . or my family."

Rivera nodded as he took another sip of the Burgundy liquid. "Your wine is as sweet as ever," he said softly.

"It's all in the picking," Rafael said. "So . . . how's your rally coming? It's getting lonely every Sunday not having someone to pick on."

"If you weren't such a hardhearted man . . ." Rivera grinned. "But I think the rally is going to be better than we planned. We might get as many as a thousand workers to show up across the street . . . for your enjoyment, of course."

"Thanks. And for yours, I have a dozen busloads of braceros coming in that same day. That should give your people something to hoot and jeer about."

"They'll be in fine voice."

"They'll be given instructions to start into the fields. Then at the last minute, just when they start to harvest, and when it looks like I've beaten you, one by one they're to start walking off . . . until it looks like a stampede to join you."

"Fantástico!" Rivera whooped. "That ought to make a believer out of you!"

"I'm afraid it will." Rafael emptied the bottle into their glasses. "C.B. De Mille couldn't have planned it better."

Across from the winery where Rafael and Rivera drank and toasted their friendship, a small two-door Ford sedan drove slowly down the road. Inside, a young man smiled, waved, and yelled support to the line of picketers.

"How ya doing? Hey there, you guys keep it up, ya hear?" He steered slowly past the friendly smiles.

"Gracias, amigo!" A couple of the older men said as he passed a pint bottle of tequila out the window to share with them.

"Hey! When's that there rally? I drove near halfway cross the country to get here." It was hard to place his accent. It could have been Texas . . . or Arkansas. Or it could have been faked. He was wearing a worn white T-shirt and he had an ornate chain tattoo circling his left wrist. "I didn't miss it now, did I?"

"No! You can bet you didn't miss it," the man with the scar across his eye called out. "It's next week. And it'll be worth your drive."

"Boy, oh boy! That's really great!" the driver said as he pulled between two of the dust-covered trucks and parked.

The Mexicans smiled. From all over the southwest, families were coming, packed like sardines in battered cars. The roads and highways were filled with migrants flocking to Guillermo Rivera's call.

The man with the tattoo got out of his little Ford and strolled back to the closest group of Mexicans. For a few minutes he smiled and made idle chitchat as he passed the bottle of tequila around. He turned to watch as an old pickup came past the winery's security shack and out the front gate onto the road.

"Hey! Ain't he one of your people?" the man asked.

"*Sí*," Ramon said. "He's one of those strikebreakers."

"A scab?"

"*Sí*. That's the word."

"Hey! You want me to do a little job on him for you?"

"No. *Gracias, señor*. But Guillermo Rivera, the man who leads us, has pledged that we will accomplish what we need to without violence."

"Yeah . . ." The man nodded. "Well, I was just kidding . . . know what I mean?" He noticed that the truck's taillights had gone out after passing the picketers a couple of hundred yards farther down the road. He watched as the bottle made another round. Out of the dark, a man came toward the flickering fires.

A murmur ran through the crowd as the man made his way down the line, stopping occasionally to shake a hand here, embrace a friend there.

"Who's that? One of your biggies?"

"*Sí, señor*. That is Guillermo Rivera," Ramon answered proudly.

The man with the tattoo nodded as the men made their way toward Rivera. He watched Rivera for a while. He'd seen him on the television news, but he was smaller than he expected. And his hair wasn't as black as the television made it look.

The man walked back to his Ford and got in. He reached down and turned on the ignition and pressed the starter button. Emptying the bottle of cheap tequila, he threw it out the window into the weeds across from the winery and slowly drove past the group crowded around Rivera.

He smiled and waved and yelled good luck as he disappeared into the night.

"*Gracias!*" It was as if a chorus had answered him. He drove slowly back toward Healdsberg. He was certain that

441

Rivera was the same man who drove out of the Orsini Winery a few minuters earlier. The information that had been passed on to him had been accurate. As always.

"Well! Don't you look all slickered up!" Rita said from where she'd been working down one of the rows of experimental vines.

O'Hara turned off the ignition of his jeep and swung out. His shiny, wing-tipped shoes made neat, even impressions in the soft dirt as he walked down the row to where she was kneeling.

Pulling his tie loose, he knelt next to her.

"Better watch out, city boy. You might get a little smidge of dirt on that fancy suit."

"It's not my idea," he moaned. "It's your father's newest one."

"Papa?" She looked up, amused. "He wants you in a suit?"

O'Hara nodded. "Until the rally's over. Says it should bring attention to the 'poor old guy' in the field when they see how the people who work for your father are dressed."

"Everyone?" she shook her head. Her father didn't miss a trick. It was a marvelous idea. Well-dressed, affluent-looking executives shown alongside the poor but proud laborers was a picture the press would love exploiting.

"How about some lunch?" he asked.

"You drove all the way out here for that?"

He nodded and shrugged and shuffled like an embarrassed teen-ager asking for his first date.

"That's really sweet of you, Jim."

"I'll have you know I think of you more often when my stomach says it's time for lunch."

Rita felt her face flushing. "I'd love to. But as long as I'm already here, I have to get a lug of these grapes back to the lab."

"Great! I'll give you a hand."

Despite his suit and tie, he knelt and worked alongside her.

She had never felt closer to him. To her the rich loamy smell of the soil, the feel of the leaves on the vines were part of what kept her alive. Now, to have a man working alongside her who seemed to feel as she did made her spirits sing.

"Thank you, kind sir," she said taking her gloves off and giving him a kiss on the cheek when they had loaded her grapes in the back of her pickup. "And where would you like to take me for lunch? Oh, you are buying, aren't you? I mean, you asked me."

He put his arms around her waist and pulled her to him. "I sure did, ma'am. So why don't you hop in your little truck and follow me?"

"Where to?" she asked as he headed toward his jeep.

"Oh, I know a special grove of trees where a little girl used to help her daddy and Rivera with lunch . . ."

"You mean it?" she beamed.

"Sure do," he said reaching in and holding up a picnic basket.

An hour later, Rita sat in the shade feeling the breeze blowing softly. But her mood had changed drastically. O'Hara had described his and Raf's visit with Roberto.

"I shouldn't have told you," O'Hara said after the smile faded from her face and her mood changed.

"I don't know why not. It has to mean something's definitely bothering dear old brother."

"Maybe no. If it was my deal, I'd want to stay on top of it, too."

"Then why the hell did you tell me?" Rita asked angrily.

O'Hara's head shot up and he felt himself getting red. "Certainly not to gossip or tattle, if that's what you're thinking."

"Oh, God! Of course not!" Why do men always have to be such little boys when they think they're being accused of something, she thought. "But you thought it was important for me to know, right?"

He nodded.

"Then you must think something's rotten in Denmark Or Monaco . . . or wherever the hell this goddamn deal of his is supposed to be from."

"I'm not sure."

"What do you mean, you're not sure? Listen, Jim, you've been the absolute tower of neutrality that Papa and

443

Mama were hoping you'd be. So when you start hinting around, out of the blue, and I might add in the middle of a not too unromantic picnic, it does make me just the tiniest bit curious."

"Whatta you say we don't talk business anymore. Okay?"

"Oh no, you don't, buster. You're the one who started it. And I have a feeling it might be for my benefit. Now . . . out with it."

"I just thought it was a little strange for Raf to be so worried about bringing the strike to an end so quickly. I mean, he knows it's just a farce. If he didn't, I could understand his reaction. It seems like he might be getting some pressure from the outside. I guess that's why he tried to go directly to Rivera without your father knowing about it. True, he told me the guy in Switzerland was threatening to blow the deal. But I told him I knew the guy. And to trust me that it was just a smoke screen. A pressure play . . ."

"What'd he say to that?"

"He said to stay out of it. It was his deal and he didn't need any advice. Said it was between him and your father and no one else."

"Goddamn him!" she swore. She knew by the way her father had been treating Raf since he came home that he believed something magical had happened to him in Europe. His son had suddenly become a man . . . grown up all of a sudden. Maybe on the outside he seems different. But I know that son of a bitch, she told herself. On the inside, the same thoughtless, irresponsible old Raf is still hiding. And some way I'm going to prove it to Papa.

"I'm not going to lose," she said.

"Of course you're not." He lay back and looked up into the cloudless sky.

"I'm serious, Jim. I have as much right around here as he does. More, as a matter of fact. I was born first."

"I always liked older women." He pulled her down next to him.

"You feel sensational," she whispered as the anger and churning in her stomach started to ebb.

"You don't feel too bad yourself, lady," he said nuzzling and kissing her ear gently.

"It's just . . . well . . . that son of a . . ." she started to rise again.

"Ah . . . ah . . . ah!" he warned, pulling her back down. "It's too beautiful a day to be thinking of things like your brother."

"You're right," she said, squeezing him until her anger drained. She smiled as the sounds of the union pickets drifted to them from the road. Whatever her brother was up to, there were now two people onto him. She pulled O'Hara closer to her. He felt wonderfully warm and comforting. She could get used to that warmth and comfort, she thought. Raf might not like it. But he might have to learn to live with it.

CHAPTER THIRTY-FIVE

The day of the rally against the Orsini Winery was magnificent. Sunny . . . hot . . . clear blue skies.

And, Rafael thought, it's the day before Rivera and his pack will have to get off their butts and back out in the fields to harvest my grapes.

They would mature under the hot sun on the exact day he'd predicted. Lavender-, purple-, and champagne-colored fruit was bursting with sugary juice as it lay hidden beneath the leaves.

From where he sat in the conference room on the top floor of the office complex, Rafael looked down on the growing crowd outside his front gate. Up and down both sides of the road, cars were parked on the shoulders and in the dirt of the fields next to the road. Still more were looking for a spot to pull off. Television had certainly proved the ideal way to spread Rivera's image and gospel.

Rafael estimated there were more than ten thousand people streaming toward the flatbed truck which had been decorated as the speaker's stand.

Even the winery employees who still crossed the picket lines—secretaries, accountants, bottlers, stenographers— now stood at windows and fences to watch the happenings.

A group of men were setting up the portable P.A. system in front of the speaker's truck. The air of the throng was festive and reminded Rafael of the crowd at the county fair at which he'd asked Angelica to marry him. People had brought lunch baskets, soft drinks. Some sat on blankets, some set up little awnings to shade themselves from the sun. Some roasted hot dogs over the still-burning vigil fires.

The crowd waited with growing excitement for Rivera to

make his appearance. It was planned for high noon. But rumors had it changing from minute to minute.

"Quite a show you're throwing out there," a voice said as the door into the conference room opened.

O'Hara watched as Rafael, Angelica, and Rita leaped up and rushed across the room to greet the gangly young man in the doorway. Dressed in denim pants and plaid shirt, he was literally engulfed by their hugs, handshakes, backslaps, and greetings.

"Jim," Rafael said, leading the young man toward the window. "I'd like you to meet Joe Anthony, Jr., congressman and sometimes winemaker."

"Most of the people think it's the other way around," Joe said, extending his hand to O'Hara.

"I didn't see you come in." Rafael nodded down toward the crowd'

"It's probably a good thing, too!" Angelica said.

"That's for sure. I'm not about to let those people, especially those cameramen, see me coming in there. I've got my future to think about," Joe joked.

"You better take good care of that job you got in Congress," Rafael warned. "I tasted that last batch of wine of yours. As a winemaker, you're a helluva politician!"

Joe's smile beamed. "That's one of the reasons I stopped by. One of the committees I'm on in Washington had a resolution they wanted me to ask you about. They wanted to know if you'd consider changing the name of your winery to 'Italian Swill.'"

Rafael was laughing so hard he had tears in his eyes.

"By the way," Joe added, "when are you going to give up all this wealth and success and come to work for me?"

"Doing what?" Rafael asked.

"Making wine . . . real wine!"

"If you want to make real wine, you've got to get your hands dirty," Rafael said, stroking Joe's shirt. "You can't do it in these fancy duds."

"Fancy duds? Why hell, my mama still makes all my clothes. Or I get 'em from one of my older brothers," he laughed as Rafael pounded him on the back and led him to one of the chairs near the window.

"Damn!" Joe whistled softly. "You and Rivera really put together quite a show! And damn if you don't have the best seats in the house. From here it looks like the Colosseum just before they turned the lions loose on the Christians."

"A show? Are you kidding?" Rafael asked acting indignant. "Why this is serious business."

Benito steered his two-door Chevrolet down the bumpy dirt road toward the highway to the rally. In the backseat, Rivera and Alicia both seemed lost in thought. Rivera looked at his son sitting in front next to Benito and Muriella.

Two strong men, he thought. Like mountains. He was feeling strangely melancholy—had been ever since awakening just before dawn. It was as if he'd suddenly been allowed to see his life in one picture.

He smiled at Benito who was mumbling and complaining as he always did about having to drive. His old friend had added to his girth after more or less retiring with Muriella to a little house with a garden and a string of vines on the outskirts of Healdsberg. Now that their children were out on their own, Benito and Muriella were living in a little more comfort.

Rivera felt Alicia lean against him. He looked at her. She'd grown even more beautiful, despite all her work alongside him in the fields since their marriage. Now there was a maturity about her, a sense of accomplishment. He slipped his hand in hers and they both squeezed in mutual love.

As they turned onto the road that led toward the Orsini Winery, Rivera was overwhelmed by the dimensions of what he had created. There were people everywhere: families precariously perched on trucks, trailers, bumpers, anything they could grab and hang onto as they made their way down the road toward the winery.

"What's the matter? What is it?" Alicia asked as she turned and saw the fear in Rivera's face.

"Nothing," he said shaking his head.

"Probably a little case of the nerves," Benito teased.

"You better believe it," Rivera admitted.

"Do you believe this traffic?" Roberto asked in a state of bliss.

"Yeah! Wonder where they're all going? It sure couldn't

be to hear you speak. You never had anything to say before that I'd drive all the way out here to hear." Benito turned and leered at his old friend who was looking more and more ashen.

"Benito!" Alicia shrieked. He slammed on the brakes, narrowly stopping behind a truckload of grinning, waving children. They were stuck in a long line of cars waiting to snake their way forward.

"Sorry!" Benito called out embarrassed to the driver ahead of him.

"You got your speech all memorized?" Roberto asked.

"Am I supposed to be making a speech?" Rivera asked innocently. As a matter of fact he hadn't really prepared a speech. He had a few things to say. But they all seemed insignificant now that the time was quickly approaching. And the larger the crowd became, the less he seemed to be able to remember what he wanted to say.

"Boy, oh boy!" Benito warned. "I sure hope you say all the things these people came to hear. You make this mob mad and you're on your own."

As the line of traffic slowed to a halt, horns started echoing up and down the line.

"I hope we get there in time to hear Guillermo Rivera," the man driving the truck ahead of them leaned out of the window and called back to Benito.

"You will. I guarantee it!" Benito yelled back.

"You can't be sure." The man lifted his arm in frustration at the traffic that wound toward the winery in the distance.

"Benito . . . please," Rivera started to protest.

"Yes, I can," Benito said to the man. "As long as he's in the back of my car and we're stuck in traffic together, he won't be speaking for a while."

The man's mouth dropped open. His door flew open and he raced back to Benito's car. With mouth still agape, he doffed his hat and reached in to touch Rivera's shoulder. Something he'd be able to tell his grandchildren in the years to come.

Suddenly he was a man of purpose. Abandoning his truck and family, he became a one-man marshaling force. He deputized others in surrounding cars, and they formed a human cordon as they moved traffic and people to allow

Benito's car into the middle of the road and toward the speaker's platform in the distance.

To the television crews baking atop their mobile units in the noonday sun, Rivera's arrival was their salvation. His appearance meant that soon this assignment would be over and they could get back to cold bars and hot baths.

To the man with the chain tattooed around his wrist, it looked like a cordon of secret service men escorting a guerrilla chieftain to a meeting with Federales.

He zipped up the blue windbreaker he wore despite the growing heat of the midday sun, and slid off the hood of his car. By getting there the night before, he'd been able to park facing into one of the tractor rows that led through the vineyard. The vineyard was more than a mile wide, which should give him easy escape from the rally.

Slowly he started threading his way through the applauding crowd toward the speaker's platform.

Benito's Chevrolet rolled to a stop, and hundreds of hands thumped its top in happy welcome to their leader. Benito pushed the door open and pulled the seat forward so Rivera and Alicia could squeeze out. The men who'd escorted the car formed a spearpoint to lead them through the crowd. It wasn't necessary, though. As Rivera and Alicia and Roberto made their way through the crowd, it parted as if for Moses at the Red Sea.

Reaching the steps that led up to the back of the stake-bed truck, Rivera motioned for Alicia and Roberto to preceed him. They shook their heads.

"This belongs to all of us," he said.

They both embraced him and started up to the top of the stairs. Rivera followed behind them, but stopped. Something was missing. Suddenly he smiled and walked into the row of grapevines behind the truck. He took a hat from a man standing near him and quickly filled it with bunches of grapes he stripped off the vine.

Holding the hat as if it were filled with eggs, he made his way back up the steps to the center where a battery of microphones had been set up. He was flushed with embarrassment and tears moistened the edges of his eyes as the thunderous ovation swept over him.

He held up his hand finally, and after a few more minutes of chanting his name, the crowd finally started to quiet down.

"*Hermanos . . . Hermanas . . .*" The words were no sooner out when another thrilling ovation greeted him back.

He held up his hand again and reluctantly the joy-filled crowd hushed.

"Welcome to our cause. Thank you for your sacrifices that brought you here . . ." He had to rush the last half of his sentence as the applause and cheers started to build again.

This time, though, most of the crowd hushed with his signal.

"We have come here . . . to this beautiful part of the world . . . in peace." Applause interrupted again and he joined in it, applauding the determination that had maintained that peace. "We have come here to ask a man I have known a lifetime to help us with our journey toward a better life. A life that can bring us together for the future of our children . . . a journey that gives us all dignity . . . one man to the other . . ."

Even with the knowledge that it was a charade, everyone in the conference room with Rafael and Angelica felt as moved as the crowd.

Rafael looked at Angelica as in the distance a growing sound pierced the roars of the crowd. The sirens of highway patrol cars and those of sheriff's deputies escorting a dozen busloads of braceros to harvest his crop rose above the crowd noise.

"I just hope and pray Rivera can keep control over that crowd when they see what's going on," Angelica said, voicing the concern of both of them.

"If anyone can . . . Rivera can," Joe said in quiet confidence.

A hush fell as the black-and-white patrol cars, red lights flashing, sirens shrieking made their way up a side road to the winery's side gate near the crusher. As the convoy rolled toward the gates, the crowd could see sudden activity inside the winery grounds. Tables filled with food and wine were being set up as a welcome for the braceros.

451

The mood of the crowd changed from euphoria to black anger. The patrol cars were escorting in a work force to destroy everything they'd worked for.

"*Hermanos . . . Hermanas . . .*" Rivera shouted into the microphones as the crowd started to surge toward the busloads of frightened braceros, calling out threats. "Listen to me . . . Listen to me!" he demanded. He held up the clusters of grapes from the hat in his hands. "These . . . these are fruit from the earth . . . gifts from God. They make sweet things to spread on our bread. They make juice for our pleasure and they make wine to soothe our souls. And they make money for our families to live and prosper . . ."

The crowd applauded reluctantly.

"Yet all those things are not worth the shedding of one drop of blood in anger. We have taken a vow to seek our goals by goodwill. By peace. And by the sweat of our brow . . ."

The mood of the crowd seemed to turn again, caught by the words of a simple man who believed in his cause and spoke from his soul.

"Those poor men in those buses whom you curse . . . yell insults at . . . spit at . . . they do not deserve your anger. They are innocent. It is the man who stares down at us from his tower like a Caesar who deserves your scorn . . ."

"Pouring it on pretty thick, isn't he?" Raf said from where he was sitting, his hands fidgeting with a paper stapler.

"Son of a gun should have been an actor," Rafael said.

The man with the blue windbreaker that hid the chain tattooed around his wrist made his way to the steps at the back of the truck. He shouted, whistled, and nodded his support along with everyone else. His eye ticked nervously. From this vantage point he had a clear, unobstructed view of Rivera speaking less than a dozen feet away.

"We must appeal to our brothers," Rivera continued, "who are getting off those buses and heading into the fields to turn their backs on this tyrant and join us. Help us . . ." he pleaded.

452

"When those braceros start coming over to their side," Rita said over the crowd roar that filled the conference room, "that crowd's going to go through the roof. If there was a roof, that is . . ." She smiled at O'Hara who stood looking down at the assembly ignoring her.

At Rivera's request, the crowd turned and started calling out to the braceros.

The man in the blue windbreaker reached into his jacket and pulled the hammer back on the well-oiled automatic concealed in his belt. No one was paying any attention to him. All eyes were turned toward the braceros as he aimed and squeezed the trigger.

Had it not been such a large caliber automatic, the shot would have been lost in the crowd noise. But the sudden explosion echoed through the open microphones.

Screams erupted, heads spun anxiously, frightened . . . shocked . . . surprised. No one knew where the sound had come from as the P.A. speakers had been set up all around the crowd.

Rivera suddenly felt weightless as the velocity threw him over the cab of the truck. Confused, disoriented, he saw Alicia and Roberto rushing toward him with anguish-filled eyes.

He never saw the man in the blue windbreaker nor heard the explosion. He wanted to reach out and lose himself in Alicia's embrace and to take his son's hand and tell him not to be afraid.

Then he was gone.

The man in the blue windbreaker stepped up onto the platform and fired again into Rivera's already dead body. Screams of panic and outrage roared up from the crowd. Roberto tried to hurl himself over his father's body to protect him from further harm.

Alicia sank to her knees, feeling as though her own life had been snuffed out. She was numb, mute with anguish.

Before the crowd could react, the man in the blue windbreaker had leaped off the back of the truck and pounded through the dusty rows of vines toward his car. *I'll knock down half the goddamn vineyard,* he thought, *but at least*

I'll be able to get to the other side of the field. Once there, another car was waiting with a change of clothes.

A soul-chilling scream of anguish spilled out of Rafael as he leaped out of his chair. To his family, it seemed to blend with the screams of terror that filled the sky from the mob in front of their fates.

It was impossible to tell what had happened from this distance, but it didn't matter. Rafael was racing for the door.

"Rafael . . ." Angelica screamed.

He didn't hear her or anything other than the ringing in his ears of the pandemonium outside as he flung the door open. His friend, the man who'd given him and his family their life, had been attacked. Maybe even hurt. Nothing would keep him from going to help him.

Suddenly he felt disconnected from his body and on his knees looking down at Joe's shoe tops. Joe had clubbed him with a crock pitcher filled with coffee. The last thing that flashed through his memory as he dropped into the blackness of unconsciousness was Rivera's face, the smiling face of the man who had lifted his glass and toasted him and Angelica the night they'd opened their first bottle of wine.

Like a hare in front of a pack of hounds, the man with the tattooed wrists huffed and wheezed as he sprinted toward his car. It was almost within reach when suddenly, a huge bear of a man reached him. He grabbed for the gun in his belt, but he felt his hand being squeezed until the bones were crushed. He tried to fight back, but the man was on him like a crazed beast, screaming with pain and rage. The man's calloused hands attacked his throat, cutting off his scream. The last thing he saw were tears streaming down the man's cheeks.

By the time the rest of the pursuers reached the man with the tattooed wrist, he was dead. It took all of Ramon's and Enrique's combined strength to break Benito's hand away from the man's throat. It took another hour before the highway patrol and sheriff's deputies could claw and beat their way through the crowd to where they found what was left of the man. The battered, torn, kicked, and stomped mass was impossible to recognize as having once been a human being.

Once the hysterical crowd was convinced the assassin was dead, they turned their rage on the winery across the road. The sheriff and highway patrol formed a cordon and with their nightsticks, shotguns, and tear gas, they beat back the wailing, grieving crowd.

In the conference room, Rafael and Angelica were crying together, still on the carpet where he'd fallen.

"You can't go down there . . . you can't go down there . . ." she crooned over and over as she clutched him to her. "They don't know the truth . . ."

"Are you okay?"

Rafael looked up as Joe massaged the back of his neck where he'd belted him. Rafael tried to focus through his tears but could only shake his head in pain. "Rivera . . ." he finally managed to squeeze out of his throat.

Joe shook his head. "He's gone, Rafael."

It was after dark before the crowd disbursed and the police could escort the coroner onto the scene. Those who remained stood back silently as a frail, dry-eyed Alicia walked to the ambulance and climbed in to sit next to her husband on his last ride back into town. Ramon and Enrique helped Roberto, Benito, and Muriella into the old Chevrolet and slowly fell in behind the ambulance as it headed back toward Healdsberg.

It was also after dark before the authorities were able to figure out which car had been the assassin's so they could start the process of identifying him. It was an angry, sad nation that sat in front of their televisions and watched in horror as this terrible tragedy was shown over and over to the home audiences.

It was after midnight before the coroner shrugged and gave up. They'd been looking for any clue to the man's identity to take back to their lab. But finger tissue, identifying marks, and even teeth had been ground into the dirt of the vineyard.

* * *

Four days later, under a tree in the mission's little cemetary overlooking the winding road that first brought them into the beautiful valley, Rivera was buried next to Maya.

The governor of the state attended as did the Vice President, sent by the President in respect for his labor support. A Supreme Court justice stood next to sun-blackened migrants. A Mexican girl buried her head on her husband's shoulder as he tried to soothe their infant.

The nation gave Guillermo Rivera a hero's burial. The Vice President handed the folded flag to the black-veiled widow supported by her strong stepson.

When the faded limousine from the mortuary drove back into Rivera's driveway, there was a car parked in front of the house that Roberto and Alicia recognized.

Inside the screen door was Rita.

Coming up the steps, Alicia held out her arms and Rita came into them crying softly. She buried her face in Alicia's shoulder as Benito, Muriella, and the others went on inside.

She cried with Rita. She also realized the terrible irony her brother and his family were trapped in. Rafael, as much in pain as she was, wouldn't allow them to say anything about their friendly conspiracy lest it destroy all Rivera had worked for.

Yet to the world at large, the Orsini Winery and Rafael Orsini in particular were responsible for Rivera's death. There had even been speculation he was connected in some way with the Mafia. After all, wasn't he an Italian?

"What are we going to do?" Rita asked as they followed the others inside.

"Go on . . ." Alicia said as she looked around the tiny living room that had served as her husband's union headquarters. It still was cluttered with placards, posters, and union and strike paraphernalia. "What is life for other than for going on?"

"It's as if it were my own papa," Rita said as she leaned into Roberto's arms. She tried to wipe her tears from the front of his jacket.

"I know," he said, trying to soothe away some of the pain they both felt. "How are your folks doing?"

"Not well," she admitted.

A distant squeaking grew louder and finally stopped outside. Through the screen door, Rita could see her older brother Pietro trying to get the kickstand of his bicycle down with the toe of his shoe. When it wouldn't budge, he bent down and pulled it out with his hands. Slowly, cautiously, he came up the sidewalk toward the porch.

"Hello, Pietro. Come on in," Alicia said, trying to sound as light as she could.

Pietro came in with a puzzled look on his face. As he'd pedaled through the valley, he'd seen many of the people he usually saw. But instead of smiling, waving, and wishing him a good day as they usually did, they had glowered angrily, turned their backs on him, or called him names he didn't understand. They had kept mentioning Uncle Rivera's name so he'd decided to ride over here to see what their unhappiness was all about.

"Hi, Pietro." Rita too tried to sound cheerful.

"Hi," he nodded, half smiling. He looked around the room which somehow seemed sad. He felt sad for their sadness. Usually when he came over, big Benito and Ramon or Enrique laughed and joked with him. Usually they were all smiles and laughter. But now they all looked like they'd been crying.

He searched the room for Rivera but he didn't see his uncle.

"I came to see Uncle Rivera," he said. Surely his uncle could help him understand. He had always taken him in his arms when he was hurt or confused.

Alicia came to Pietro and embraced him. "I'm afraid Uncle is not here, Pietro. He . . . had to go away."

Pietro frowned. "Will he be back soon?" He saw a strange sadness cross his aunt's face. It filled his eyes with tears and he didn't understand why.

"No, Pietro," she explained softly. "You see, your Uncle Rivera had to go back to God . . ."

"Oh! You mean God's house at the mission?"

"No, not in the mission," Alicia explained. "But on the hill in back of the mission. You remember? Where Grandfather went when he had to go back to God."

Pietro stared at the floor. Now he knew why they were sad. His grandfather had never come back when he'd gone to visit God.

"Hey, why don't you come with me and we'll get something to eat?" Rita asked her brother. Whenever they wanted to distract him and get him onto another subject, they'd fill his gentle mind with thoughts of the food he loved so well.

"Okay." He nodded.

"How would you like to go into town to the new drive-in? I bet they have great big juicy hamburgers. And French fries!"

"I don't want to go there anymore!"

"To the drive-in?" She was surprised. It was his favorite place.

He nodded.

"Why not?" Rita asked as she took him in her arms.

"There's some bad men at that hamburger place. They said some bad things to me when I rode by. I don't like them anymore."

"Poor baby!" Alicia put her arms around him also.

"They're probably not mean," Rita tried to explain. "They're probably just sad like we are that your Uncle Rivera had to go to God. Don't you think?"

He shrugged.

"Maybe I can take you someplace else then. Why don't you pick another place and we'll go there instead."

"No. I think I'll just go home. Mama's probably looking for me. I'll get food from her."

Rita and Alicia watched as Pietro pedaled off down the dusty street toward the road that led back toward the winery.

"I better be going too," Rita said heading toward her car.

Roberto walked with her out to the driveway.

"I'm sorry about this crap with Pietro," he said as he opened her door for her.

"I know." She slipped in behind the wheel.

"It's not going to get any better for a long time, Rita."

"I know that, too."

"Why don't you let us help? Alicia and I and the others talked it over. My father wouldn't let you go through what you're going to have to go through. Alicia . . . me . . . all of us think . . ."

"Bullshit! We already talked about it. You know how my father and mother feel. Your father lost his life. None of us will let him lose what he died for. If you tell the press, or anybody, he will have died for nothing."

"You don't understand, Rita. The thing Alicia and I are afraid of is this special investigator the President's appointing. Politicians and people all over the country are trying to get in on this. A lot of people want to make their reputation by destroying whoever's responsible. And if whoever it is can't be found, your father will suit them just fine."

"We've got Joe Anthony on our side," Rita said. "He'll fight for us. He knows how to fight. He'll know how to do it so your father can keep what he died for . . . and we . . . we'll be all right in the end." She tried to sound confident, as though she believed what she was saying.

He watched as she disappeared into the heat of the afternoon. There were many times he wished they weren't family, he thought, turning and heading back into the house. This was one of those times.

CHAPTER THIRTY-SIX

Pietro stopped on the side of the road and looked out over the grassy field to the tiny airport built between town and his father's winery.

It was one of Pietro's favorite places to visit. Especially this last week since his Uncle Rivera went back to the Mission to see God. He liked to watch the mysterious little planes, even though he couldn't figure out how they got off the ground. He'd tried it himself. Putting boards on top of his handlebars, he'd ridden as fast as he could. But he could never get his Schwinn Flyer to fly.

He steered through the weeds alongside the road to the chain link fence that ringed the field. Hopping off, he sat down outside the fence. He watched enthralled as a sleek twin-engined plane settled over the end of the apron and reversed its engines. It was one of the biggest planes Pietro had ever seen land at their little strip.

He leaned forward to watch it more closely as it taxied toward a jeep waiting at the edge of the strip. Pietro suddenly grinned as he recognized the jeep. It belonged to Mr. O'Hara, the man who worked for his papa.

Pietro's heart raced with excitement as the plane stopped next to O'Hara's jeep. Two men got out and went with O'Hara toward one of the hangars.

Pietro hopped back on his bike and pedaled toward the gate where a guard was on duty.

"Hello, Pietro!" The guard smiled as he stopped next to the security shack that sat in the center of the access road to the airfield.

When the airport had opened, there hadn't been a need for security. But recently a guard had been hired to keep out the curious youngsters who passed the field on their way to and from school.

"Hello, Mr. Hank," Pietro said, stopping at the white line behind the stop sign.

"What can I do for you today?" the old man asked.

"I'm here to . . . well . . . I'd like to see Mr. O'Hara if it's okay." He nodded toward the hangar.

"You sure he's here?" the man asked. He knew Pietro had a fascination for planes. He was a familiar sight sitting outside the fence watching them take off and land by the hours. But he was never a problem.

"Yes, sir, Mr. Hank. He's down there talking to the men from that really big plane." Pietro pointed to the plane that sat on the apron with one of its propellers still spinning.

"Okay. But you stay out of trouble, you hear? You go straight in . . . and right straight out again when you're done. Understand?"

"Yes, sir," Pietro said trying to mask his excitement.

Pietro parked his bike between the lines of a marked parking space and peered into the shadows of the hangar. He couldn't see anyone, but he could hear voices. One was soft, another angry. They sounded as if they were coming from the back of the hangar.

Pietro walked in, his hands stuck in the back pockets of his jeans. The hangar was filled with shining airplanes that took his breath away. They were even more shiny than the paint on his bike.

". . . don't have the time . . ."

"Are you out of your goddamn mind?" Pietro recognized the angry voice as O'Hara's. He walked over and ran his hand over one of the smooth fuselages. It was so smooth, it felt almost like one of his mother's china plates. And he could see his reflection in it the same way, too.

"Of course we have time. With the Mexican dead, all we have to do is wait . . ."

Pietro could still hear the voices. And O'Hara's sounded really mad, he thought. Maybe he'd better wait until they finished talking before asking if he could see their plane up close.

". . . unless someone sees you here. Then they might wonder if it was Orsini . . . or some lunatic . . ."

Looking around the hangar, Pietro saw that the door of

one of the planes was slightly ajar. He walked under the wing, pulled it open, and peered inside.

"Don't think that your success with Orsini's daughter gives you an option, O'Hara . . ."

The cockpit took Pietro's breath away. It was just like the inside of a spaceship he'd seen on television taking some men and a woman to Mars. It smelled all fresh and leathery, he thought, slipping up into the upholstered seat.

"I'll be damned if I'll change anything without talking to the Chairman personally, Buntz."

"What?" the voice asked incredulously. "You'll do as you're directed. I'll brook no lack of discipline from you. How dare you question me? I have full authority from the Chairman . . ."

"Then you can tell the Chairman to relay that directly to me . . . I have no intentions of jeopardizing anything just so you can look good . . ."

Pietro was enthralled by the sea of dials, switches, levers, and instruments. He heard the voices coming his way and he was suddenly afraid. Not from the voices or what they'd been saying. He hadn't really paid any attention to them. What he was afraid of was being caught inside the airplane.

He slouched down hoping O'Hara and the other men wouldn't see him.

But it was too late. One of the two strangers spotted him and barked something to O'Hara who spun around. By then Pietro had ducked safely down. But his heart pounded with dread as he heard footsteps rushing toward the plane The door flew open and Pietro grinned up from the seat. In a blur of motion, he felt himself being dragged out of the seat by a man whose face looked really angry.

Pietro screamed in pain as the man bent his arm behind him.

"Please . . . please!" Pietro pleaded to O'Hara who seemed to be staring at him with a look of shock frozen on his face. "Tell him to stop hurting my arm. It hurts bad! I'm sorry . . ." Tears filled his eyes.

"What are you doing here?" O'Hara demanded, barely above a whisper.

"I just wanted to see the planes up close . . ."

"You know this man?" the man standing next to O'Hara demanded.

"Yes. It's Pietro Orsini," O'Hara replied quietly.

Paul Buntz's eyes darted toward Pietro with a mixture of fear and hatred.

Pietro was afraid. The man next to O'Hara really seemed angry. Maybe more angry than the other man hurting his arm. Pietro didn't know why. He hadn't been in their airplane. Their airplane was still parked outside with its engine running.

"Why are they being bad to me, Mr. O'Hara?" he pleaded as the pain in his arm shot up to his shoulder. "Tell them I'm sorry . . . please!"

"Rafael Orsini's son?" Buntz hissed.

"His oldest," O'Hara confirmed.

"Take him to the plane." Buntz nodded to the man holding Pietro's arm in a vise behind him.

"Are you insane?" O'Hara angrily grabbed Pietro's arm out of the man's grasp. "Do you want it all to have been for nothing? If anything happened to him, how could we explain it . . . especially to the Chairman?"

Buntz's eyes showed his confusion. "Do we have any choice?"

"Get out, Buntz! Goddammit, get the hell out of here. Just get back on that goddamn plane of yours and to hell out of here. There was no reason for you to come in the first place. Except to prove your authority. You weren't needed. Things were going according to the agreement . . ."

"I'm sorry, Mr. O'Hara," Pietro tried to interrupt the two men's angry argument, thinking it was over him. "I just wanted to sit in his plane. But I didn't touch anything. I promise . . . honest," he pleaded.

"You see," O'Hara said, suddenly calm, as Buntz looked at Pietro in confusion. "There's no need. He would never be able to figure any of this out. He's retarded."

Pietro's jaw shot out sullenly. He didn't like that word. It was the word kids used when teasing him. "I am not," he said angrily.

O'Hara's face turned crimson, partly from anger, partly from shock.

"Get home!" he yelled as he grabbed Pietro and half dragged, half pushed him out of the hangar into the sunlight. Before Pietro could regain his balance, O'Hara was pushing him toward his bike. "And if I hear a word about this from anyone, I'm going to tell your father I caught you in an airplane. And you know what that would mean, don't you?"

"Yes, sir . . . I won't. I promise," Pietro said, as he hopped on his bike. Without daring to look back, he pedaled toward the guard shack.

"Hey . . . what's the matter?" the guard asked, seeing his tears.

"Nothing . . ." Pietro said, wiping his eyes on his shirttail. "I just have to go now."

"Oh . . . I see," the guard said shaking his head. "You weren't supposed to be inside, were you?"

Pietro shook his head as he stared down at his foot which was on the pedal. He was ashamed about not telling the truth to the guard when he came in.

"You didn't touch anything, did you?" the guard asked.

"No, Mr. Hank . . . Well . . . I sat inside one of the planes. But I didn't touch anything. I promise. And I didn't fly it or anything either."

"Okay. That's good, Pietro." The man smiled.

"I want to make certain Pietro Orsini remains silent," Buntz said as they rushed toward his plane.

"This is America, Paul. Not some medieval backward barony. Pietro Orsini is one step above a blithering idiot. He poses no problem. If one exists, it's your doing."

"Even so, he could say something accidentally. Reveal something," Buntz warned as he slipped into the rear seat of the plane and fastened his seat belt.

"Buntz . . . what did he see? Me talking to a couple of men at the airport. It's not exactly something out of the ordinary."

"But he left afraid and in tears."

"He was caught messing around with an airplane. The owner got pissed. I happened along and came to his rescue. Or I could deny it even occurred. But in any case, there's no need to complicate things any further. He's out of it. Understand?"

464

O'Hara could see Buntz's face turning red. His blood pressure must be soaring, he thought. He was used to getting his way. That's why he'd come. To make demands, exert pressures, change plans that didn't need changing. Mostly he'd flown in to check up on O'Hara's romance with Rita. He wanted to make sure O'Hara wasn't going to use it against them. He wasn't . . . for the moment. But if Buntz kept up his personal involvement, his brutality, he might consider it, even if it risked the Chairman's wrath.

As the plane lifted off, Buntz looked down at the little field nestled at the end of the green valley. He could see O'Hara's jeep pulling out. His eyes narrowed as he saw the figure of a guard talking to Pietro Orsini as he sat on his bike next to the entrance.

As O'Hara approached, the guard waved.

O'Hara was wrong, Buntz thought. There was another witness to Pietro Orsini's story.

"Hi, Mama. What can I do for you?" Raf said into the phone. He'd noticed his light blinking and waited for his secretary to buzz him, but he'd forgotten it was long past quitting time.

"If you see your brother, how about bringing him home?"

"Sure. Is he supposed to be here?"

"Rita said she passed him on the road heading for the winery. He told her he was going there until dinner."

"Okay, Mama. I'll see if I can't round him up."

"How about staying for dinner yourself?"

"What are you having?" He grinned to himself, knowing it would make his mother mad.

"Dinner," she said flatly, onto his little game.

"Sounds good to me. I'll see you as soon as I can round up Pietro."

Raf walked through the sprawling complex toward the building behind the crushers that housed the fermenting tanks. The sun was setting and everyone was gone for the day. That is, those who still showed up, he thought, as he walked inside the building and down the aisle.

The place was ghostly quiet. Sort of prophetic, he thought. Especially if their sales kept falling.

The federal investigation into Rivera's assassination still ground slowly along. But there was nothing to tie the Orsini Winery to it, and nothing to tie Rafael or any of his family to their reputed Mafia connections. None of their income could be traced to anything illegal.

Rafael had always been a stickler about paying his honest share of taxes. This country had been good to him. He didn't intend to dishonor that generosity by cheating the government out of a few dollars. But there were those who wondered why a man would willingly pay his share if there wasn't something in his closet he was trying to hide.

Then when it looked like the hostility, the hatred would finally die, someone suggested the idea of boycotting Orsini Wine. If you wanted them to talk, people said, make it hurt them in their pocketbooks. Then Orsini would talk.

It had started slowly. But without much effort it got worse.

One of the problems grew from an advertising promise they'd made on television to return the full-purchase price of any of their wine if the buyer was dissatisfied. Assholes! Raf thought. People were sure dissatisfied all of a sudden. Financially, it was becoming disastrous. But Rafael felt it was vital to honor their commitment.

As he walked toward the open double doors at the opposite end of the building, hoping to find Pietro on the way, Raf looked down the rows of huge stainless steel fermenting tanks. Thanks to Rafael's mechanical genius, every tank in the building was connected. The maze of pipes and valves and manifolds and gauges looked like a plumber's jigsaw puzzle.

Looking around his father's incredible creation made him feel almost insignificant again. Though never giving up his dedication to making truly fine wine, his father was always tinkering, searching for ways to modernize and improve the process.

Rafael had automated as many things as possible. As massive as the interior of the winery was, and as many hundreds of thousands of gallons of wine as they fermented, blended, aged, and bottled, it took relatively few workers to accomplish all the tasks.

Lucky thing, too, Raf thought. Considering that most of

their workers had slipped back into the job market without ever mentioning that they'd worked for the Orsinis.

Raf jumped over the trough in the floor that led by conveyor belt from the fermenting tanks to the half-dozen modern German presses. Those presses extracted the final precious few drops of juice from out of the skins. Rafael bragged that they were now so efficient that the remaining pomace was dry enough to burn when it was taken by another conveyer belt to a waiting truck to haul off for fertilizer.

The fields, he knew, were a different story. Grapes still required human hands to harvest, and aside from Benito, Ramon, Enrique, and the rest of their crew, no other workers would be seen harvesting Rafael Orsini's crop. Despite the contract that had been signed between the union and the Orsini Winery—despite the urging of Roberto as the new head of the union—no one would pick for them.

The fruit, long past its maturity, was starting to rot on the vine. It was heartbreaking but there was nothing they could do. There were still protesters up and down the road that bordered the winery. Now they weren't pickets but people keeping a vigil and waiting—waiting for the great Orsini Winery to die as atonement for Guillermo Rivera's death.

Those on the vigil watched in silence as Benito and his crew worked a portion of one of the fields. The watchers knew better than to question Benito. Rumor had it he was the one responsible for the death of the unidentified assassin. Benito had never been charged. There had been too much confusion, too much panic, too much violence for any one man to be charged. Besides, Guillermo Rivera's murderer deserved to die, and there wasn't a jury in the state that would convict his killer. But those on the vigil were confused as to why Benito and his crew were harvesting for Orsini. The only conclusion they could come to was that this was a way to contaminate every drop of Orsini wine. Once the grapes were harvested, crushed, blended, there wouldn't be a drop of wine in his winery that wouldn't have the juice of those grapes in it. Grapes that Guillermo had died over. No one would buy or drink that wine.

* * *

467

Raf had checked the entire complex. There was no sign of Pietro. He headed back toward the parking lot and his car.

A few minutes later, he pulled under the shade trees, parked next to Rita's car, and honked. "Hi, Mama," he said as Angelica came out to the porch. "I'm afraid I couldn't find Pietro."

"Well, supper will bring him." She smiled as she walked back into the kitchen with her arm around her son's waist.

"Hello, brother dear," Rita said coming in from the living room.

Raf half smiled, but didn't answer.

Sitting there quietly as his mother and sister finished preparing dinner, Raf looked out the window and across to the fires that flickered along the road in front of their house.

The phone rang and Raf's head darted around to the receiver on the wall by the table. It rang again and he still sat there watching it. Every time the phone rang, he'd been afraid it was Paul Buntz calling to tell him their deal was off. And that he had to pay up the money he owed.

"For God's sakes, Raf," Rita complained as she reached across him for the phone. "Hello!"

Raf waited.

"Oh, hello, Jim. How are you, my love?" She looked down at her brother, knowing her intimacy would irritate him. "You coming over later? Great! Yes . . . he's here."

Raf's heart pounded.

"Papa!" Rita called through the door. "Jim O'Hara returning your call."

"What does O'Hara want?" Raf asked, trying to seem nonchalant.

"If you're interested why don't you go in and ask Papa? He's the one who wanted to talk to him."

Raf nodded and made his way through the door and across the hall to the living room.

"Okay. Yes . . . Great! We'll see you in a little while then. Yes . . . I'll tell him. He's here right now." Rafael hung up and smiled at his son.

"Did I interrupt?" Raf asked apologetically.

"Not at all," Rafael said. "Just thought I'd invite Jim to

join us for dinner. Oh, by the way, he said you had a couple of important calls after you left."

Raf's heart pounded with dread.

"The deal in Europe?" Rafael asked softly, sensing his son's mood.

"Probably," Raf shrugged.

"We've been neglecting them quite a bit, haven't we?"

"Put yourself in their shoes, Papa. The only thing they hear is what's in the news. I finally gave up trying to convince them otherwise."

"Maybe we can call them tomorrow. See if we can't breathe some new life into this thing."

"Do you mean it, Papa?"

Rafael nodded. "There are a few things I need clarified . . . and want changed. But I don't see why we can't work something out. After all, it could be a godsend, given what's happening here."

"I couldn't agree more." Raf beamed. Goddamn! He just might end up saving their collective asses, he thought. If there still was a deal. If that asshole German or Frenchman hadn't already blown it.

Suddenly the thought of calling Paul Buntz was no longer a burden.

O'Hara hung up the telephone and leaned back in his chair to let his favorite Mozart recording soothe his emotions. Earlier he'd received a call from the Chairman aboard his yacht at Cannes. The Chairman had heard about the incident with Pietro Orsini from Buntz and he was furious. He wanted O'Hara to have no doubt that Buntz acted with his complete authority.

"I'm not questioning that authority," O'Hara replied. "I just feel he's overreacting. After all, I don't know if Buntz mentioned that the man's retarded . . ."

"I'm well aware of that."

"Then I'm sure you understand why I suggested Buntz forget the incident. I'm sure Pietro Orsini has."

"And if not?"

"I hadn't given it any further thought," he said honestly.

"Then I suggest you do," Gianini said angrily. "You're being compensated for thinking. Rather well, I trust. In the meantime, until you reestablish your ability to think, I'm authorizing Buntz to handle the situation as he sees fit. It's out of your hands. Do you understand?"

"Yes, sir," O'Hara said, his face stinging.

"I've also instructed Buntz to call the younger Orsini tomorrow to inform him that the merger proposal is off."

"I see."

"And he's to tell the younger Orsini that both you and his father will be informed of the obligation incurred at the tables in Monaco. You are to see to it that the pain and pressure and suffering in the Orsini household continues unabated. Is that understood?"

"Yes, sir. Completely, sir." He said it several times after Gianini had hung up.

As the music swelled, O'Hara's anger died and he closed his eyes. His insides were once again like stone. Cold. He had often wondered about the real purpose of Gianini's interests in the Orsini Winery. There was certainly more to it than the merger. Or recovering the money Raf had blown in Monaco. He'd heard rumors, but discounted them. He'd better take another look at them. Examine them for a clue to what this was all about. It might mean a great deal to him later.

O'Hara checked his watch. He had time for a quick shower and a shave before leaving for dinner at the Orsinis. It certainly was an opportune invitation, he thought. Maybe during the course of the night he could pick up something that tied the two men together.

CHAPTER THIRTY-SEVEN

As the sun set, Pietro peddled his bike slowly toward the little airport. He was tired and hungry, but a man in town had told him his father and mother wanted him to meet them at the guard shack outside the airport.

At first he'd been scared. He was afraid his parents had found out he'd been caught inside one of the airplanes. O'Hara had promised not to tell. But someone else might have.

The man had seen his concern and smiled warmly. "Don't worry," he'd said. "It's not bad. As a matter of fact, it's a surprise for you."

Pietro smiled. Maybe it was going to be a ride in one of the planes. Maybe even a ride in the company plane. That would be great! Usually his father wouldn't let more than one member of the family ride in it at a time. But maybe this was a special time, his birthday maybe. He always forget when that was. But they always surprised him and he loved it.

He saw the guard shack in the distance and pedaled faster until he could lift his feet and coast the rest of the way. The guard saw him coming and waved as Pietro braked to a halt.

"Hello, Pietro. What brings you out here this time of evening?"

"I'm supposed to meet my papa and mama." He knocked the kickstand down with his sneaker.

"Well now, ain't that nice?" the man said looking up from where he was shining the patent leather brim of his uniform hat with a white handkerchief.

"Have you seen them, Mr. Hank? I mean are they here yet?" Pietro asked anxiously.

"Nope. Afraid not. Are you sure you were supposed to meet them tonight?"

"They have a surprise for me."

"In that case, I'm sure they'll be along any minute." The guard pulled his hat on and checked his profile by the reflection in the window.

"I sure hope so. Maybe they're already here and you just didn't see them come in," he said looking anxiously through the fading light toward the cars still parked near the hangar.

" 'Fraid not. I'd know if your papa and mama was here." The guard smiled. "It better be soon, though. I'm just about fixing to lock up and leave."

"It will be," Pietro tried to assure him.

The guard checked his watch. It was later than usual. But one of the airplane owners had been waiting for a part that had just been delivered. As soon as the parts truck left, the guard was going to pull on his coat hanging in the window by the door, grind his aging car to life, and rattle home for a night of television.

"Can I go watch them?" Pietro asked, nodding to where the parts truck was parked on the apron alongside the little Piper Cub.

The guard looked at him for a moment. "Aw, why not?" He smiled at Pietro's delight. "But you stay out of their way now, you hear? You go getting in their way and I won't be able to let you inside anymore . . ."

Pietro trotted down the road toward the airplane that stood with its cowling raised. He felt excited. He'd never seen inside the propeller place before.

The two men looked up as Pietro trotted up and stood a respectable distance away to watch them work. One of them smiled and nodded as he went back to work under the cowling. It looked wonderfully mysterious to Pietro. He wished he could get closer, but he remembered Mr. Hank's warning.

As he watched, the sound of a car coming down the highway toward the airport caught his attention. Maybe it was his father's truck. But it sounded like it was going really fast. And his dad didn't like anyone driving really fast.

From the dust kicking up from the shoulder, Pietro

could tell the car wasn't on the asphalt. The driver shouldn't be driving like that, he thought angrily. Especially if he wasn't going to drive on the road.

Inside the shack, the guard was busy putting his few things back into his lunch pail. He looked up at the approaching headlights. Goddamn! He sure wished they'd move this little pissant of a shack back closer to the fence and farther away from the road. One of these days some idiot was going to drive right through the damn thing.

Suddenly the guard heard the sound of something loud and heartstopping. It was the sound of an agonized scream of terror. It was hysterical, loud, unexpected . . . and his.

To the men standing next to the airplane, the booth suddenly looked as though it had disappeared. To Pietro it looked like a demolition derby he'd seen on television.

The men raced around the plane toward the shattered glass and splintered wood as the car screeched and spun down the road before shuddering to a stop. As Pietro followed, he could hear the driver grinding the starter over and over until it roared back to life. With one headlight missing and the other one shooting into the sky at a crazy angle, the car raced back to the scattered debris lying alongside the road.

The men sprinting toward the road saw the driver roll down his window and stare out at the carnage strewn in the weeds next to the chain link fence, then put the car in gear, and with tires smoking, roar off into the growing darkness.

"You son of a bitch!" one of the men screamed. "Come back here, you murdering bastard!"

They could hear the sound of the engine racing as it disappeared into the night.

"Goddamn! Goddamn motherin' son of a bitch!" The driver of the car screamed angrily to no one but himself.

When he'd demolished the guard shack, he had felt the flush of success pulsing through his body. He knew the guard and the Orsini guy were both inside. He'd seen shadows through the shack windows and the guy's bike parked outside. But when he'd come back, he'd seen only one body. His anger exploded when he saw the Orsini guy running toward him. No question about that. He was the one whose arm he'd twisted inside the hangar.

The car shuddered violently as he raced back down the highway toward where his partner would be waiting to switch cars and abandon this wreck in a ditch.

"Goddamn! Son-of-a-bitching bastard!" He would have to figure a way to finish this job or find himself finished.

Alongside the wreckage of the shack, the man who'd been working on the Piper Cub looked down in horror at what remained of the guard.

"God! Is he . . . I mean, do you think there's any chance . . ." the parts truck driver asked trying not to be sick.

The Piper Cub owner shook his head. "No. But we've got to get help." He broke into a run back toward the hangar. "There's a phone in the office. I'll call the highway patrol."

Pietro looked around and tears suddenly flooded from his eyes. In the shadows he could see the torn, mangled remains of his Schwinn Flyer resting in the strands of the chain link fence. He went over and knelt down in the dirt alongside it. He put his hand on the frame. He was sobbing at the thought of his bicycle and of his friend the guard both lying broken in the weeds alongside the road. He knew deep down inside that neither would be able to be fixed again. He hoped his papa wouldn't be mad that his bike was broken like this.

"Hey, what's the matter, old buddy?" Roberto said, coming out after hearing someone on the front porch. He saw Pietro huddled next to the wall of the house. "What are you doing here at this time of night? Aren't you supposed to be home?"

"I . . . I came to see Uncle Rivera. Then when I got here, I remembered he's gone . . . to the Mission. So I don't know what to do."

"Well . . . come on up here and sit down. Better yet, why don't you come inside where it's light. Then we can talk . . . just you and me. Okay?"

"Okay." Pietro answered as Roberto led him into the living room.

"Pietro!" Alicia said, surprised as they came in.

"Hello, Auntie," he mumbled.

"What's the matter? Are you all right?" she asked.

He nodded as Roberto sat him down on the tattered sofa.

"Why aren't you home? I bet your mother's worried," Alicia said, sitting down next to him. "Have you eaten?"

"No. But I'm not hungry."

"You're not hungry? Now what could keep a big guy like you from being hungry," she asked praying that someone else hadn't taken out their frustration about Rivera's death on him.

"My Schwinn Flyer." He shook his head as the tears came back into his eyes.

"What's wrong with it? Did you have a flat or something?" Alicia asked.

"No. It's wrecked."

"That's too bad. But I bet we can fix it as good as new . . . don't you think?" Roberto asked.

"No, it's too bent. And the tires are broke . . . and the seat came all the way off."

"Wow! That sounds like you had a pretty bad accident," Alicia said. "How about you? Are you all right?"

"Sure," Pietro said showing them his arms and hands.

"That's good. You were pretty lucky then, weren't you?" She smiled.

"I was . . . but Mr. Hank sure wasn't," he said shaking his head.

"What's the matter with Mr. Hank?" Roberto asked.

"He was runned over by the same car that runned over my Schwinn Flyer," Pietro replied.

Alicia looked at Roberto, a fear showing.

"Do your papa and mama know, Pietro?" Roberto asked.

"No. I don't think so." Pietro shook his head dejectedly. "I stopped by to tell them. But Mr. O'Hara was there and . . ."

"I better call and let them know you're here and all right," Alicia interrupted.

She went to the phone and came out a moment later, a look of shock on her face.

"What is it?" Roberto asked.

"There was an accident at the airport. The guard was run over by some hit-and-run driver. Everyone's out looking for Pietro. They were just about to call us. They found his bike there and were worried to death. They thought he might have been in the wreck."

"No . . . I wasn't." Pietro tried to explain how he'd been with the men working on the plane.

"I know. I told them you were perfectly all right." Alicia smiled, relieved that the troubles for once weren't related to their problems. "But they do want you home as quick as a wink."

"Well, we better get you home then," Roberto said standing and holding his arm out to Pietro. "A wink's a pretty fast thing to try to beat, you know."

"Do I have to? They might be mad at me."

"They won't be mad at you," Alicia said hugging him as they walked to the front door. "When someone's worried about you, they're always happy to see you."

"You think so, Auntie?" He half-smiled.

"I know so. Now you go with Roberto. If anybody can get you home faster than a wink, it's Roberto."

"Yeah!" Pietro beamed at the thought, forgetting his confusion and pain and wrecked bike.

The night was dark and traffic nonexistent as Roberto turned onto the road that led to Rafael's and Angelica's valley. In the dim light cast from the dashboard he could see a worried look on Pietro's face.

"You're not still worried about your folks being mad are you?"

"No." Pietro shook his head.

"Okay, then. What is it?"

Pietro looked at him but didn't want to answer.

"Come on. You can tell me," Roberto assured him.

"I don't think I can. I mean, I'm not supposed to."

"Why not?"

"Cuz Mr. O'Hara told me not to tell . . ."

"Oh . . . I'm sure he wouldn't mind you telling me."

"But he was there tonight . . ."

"At the airport?"

"No . . . at my house. After that guy at the airport wrecked Mr. Hank and my bike, I went home. But I saw his jeep there."

"Whose?"

"Mr. O'Hara's. And I thought he might be telling my papa what happened at the airport."

"But if he was at your house, Pietro, he couldn't have known about what happened at the airport to Mr. Hank and your bike."

"No . . . I mean the other day. When I was inside the place where they keep the planes parked. He was in there too, and he saw me inside one of the planes. And I wasn't supposed to be. And his friends . . . the men with him got mad. And he told me he wouldn't tell Papa. And that's why my bike and Mr. Hank got wrecked . . ."

"I don't think that's why they got wrecked." Roberto smiled and slapped Pietro's knee to try to lift his spirits. "But when we get you home we'll talk to your father and Mr. O'Hara about it. Then you'll see everything's okay," Roberto said, not able to make sense of what Pietro was trying to say.

In the distance, Roberto could see the headlights of one car parked in the road alongside the taillights of another. It was as if two people going in opposite directions had stopped in the middle of the road to talk to one another.

"Do you think they might be able to fix Mr. Hank's little house at the airport? It was pretty busted. And Mr. Hank, too?"

"I'm pretty sure they will. And I bet we can find someone to fix your bike, too." Roberto blinked his lights a couple of times. But nothing happened. It looked as though the car they had pulled up behind was empty. He couldn't tell about the one next to it, facing them in the opposite lane, as its lights were shining toward them.

A man in a business suit stepped into the glare of the headlights and walked to Roberto's window.

"Hey . . . I'm sorry," the man apologized. "Fellow in the car in front of you seemed to be sick or something. I stopped to help him."

"He okay?" Roberto asked.

"Yeah . . . looks like he just had a touch too much to drink, if you know what I mean?" The man smiled.

"Maybe we should get him off the road," Roberto said reaching down for the door handle. "We already had someone killed tonight by a hit-and-run driver."

"Yeah, that's what I heard. An old man and a young guy, wasn't it?"

"No. Just the old man. This is the young guy here. I'm getting him home to his folks."

The man's smile faded. He looked into the shadows and nodded.

From the darkness next to Pietro's window, a figure suddenly appeared. Roberto sensed it more than he saw it.

"Hello, Pietro," the man from the shadows said.

"Friend of yours?" Roberto asked, suddenly uneasy.

"No. He's Mr. O'Hara's friend. The one who ran over my bike . . ."

There was a blur of motion and Roberto was suddenly aware of what seemed like a stream of brilliant flashes and the smell of burned sulphur. He'd seen flashes like them before—fired at his company of Marines during the long, cold nights in Korea.

The moment he saw the cars blocking the road, he should have recognized what it was. He'd seen the same thing thousands of miles away during his tour of duty.

It was an ambush. Cold, deadly and as efficient as any professionals could pull off.

And easy. If someone was looking for an Orsini, and he wasn't home, all they had to do was wait along this road. It was the only one that ran past their house.

The ringing in his ears was excruciating, partly from the guns, partly from Pietro's screams of fright and pain. The last thing he felt before falling into darkness was the thousands of tiny shards of glass from the windows splintering from the gunfire.

Rafael and Angelica stood holding onto each other as they stared down at Pietro lying in the tiny cubicle of the brightly lit emergency room. He looked peaceful, as though in the midst of a long night's sleep.

Rafael reached down to touch his son's soft black hair

and began to shake. A month ago his oldest friend had been killed . . . now his son. He lay his head softly on Pietro's still chest and tried to stifle the anguish that spilled out.

Angelica tried to comfort him through her own pain and grief. But all Rafael could do was stare helplessly down at his son. Looking at the young face, all he could remember was his ear-to-ear smile. As warm as sunshine, as innocent as a new fawn. Now it was gone. Why? He choked in fury as his thoughts raged around his mind.

Near them, in a tiny room farther down the corridor from where Pietro lay, a team of doctors was fighting to suture, patch, and pump warmth, blood, and oxygen back into the unconscious Roberto's body.

Outside the tiny operating room, Alicia stood in a silent daze as Benito and a growing host of friends and relatives tried to tend her. Most were stunned beyond words, as reporters who rushed in from the Bay area wandered among them digging for headlines.

"It doesn't take much to figure out who's responsible," one of the young Mexicans said bitterly.

Benito's hand flashed out and dragged the boy close, his breathing suddenly heavy from the anger he felt toward the boy. "The man you talk against is crying over the body of his own son."

The boy stared at the floor ashamed.

The next morning, though, as Roberto still hung to life by a frayed thread, newspapers throughout the country ran front-page stories featuring pictures of a tearful Alicia, Benito, and the army of tattered workers gathered around the hospital. Headlines and lead stories told of how the war between the tiny union and the giant winery had erupted once again in violence.

The stories speculated that both young men, friends since childhood, knew too much about the infiltration of the underworld into the wine industry. There were no reports about where this theory originated. But readers everywhere could read between the lines. The finger pointed to Rafael Orsini.

Rumors the next few days had the two young men on their way to a secret Grand Jury hearing into the inside workings of the winery . . . Both men were working for the FBI. The only thing never mentioned in the stories or rumors was that Pietro was retarded. The view fed to and accepted by the public was that of another martyr in the war against the Orsini Winery.

Pietro was buried in the little cemetery behind the Mission, next to where Rivera and Maya lay.

Despite the presence of Alicia, Benito, Muriella, and a host of their friends at the funeral, the public refused to believe Rafael wasn't somehow responsible. The public couldn't think of Rafael Orsini without thinking of the pictures of the man snarling out from his vineyards at some helpless migrant . . . or staring down from his elegant office just before Rivera was assassinated.

Instead of his and Angelica's grief at the loss of a son being met with sympathy, the weeks following the funeral seemed to magnify the public's determination to boycott anything to do with a family that had such a history of brutality. Sales of Orsini Wine practically ceased.

"Paul Buntz is on the line. He's in New York on business and wants to talk to you," O'Hara said as he came into Raf's office.

Raf nodded as he picked up the phone. "Hello, Paul." He swiveled uncomfortably in his cushioned chair.

"Hello, Raf. I'm terribly sorry about your brother. Please relay my sympathies to your mother and father. Is there anything I can do?"

"I don't think so, Paul. Thank you. Other than having a little more patience, that is."

"I'm afraid patience is the only thing I'm not in a position to offer."

"I see." Raf's chair slipped off the runner onto the carpet.

"We've lost Scheneblin."

"I understand. I'm sorry to hear that," Raf said.

He sounded calm. Too calm, Buntz thought, his mind flashing to O'Hara.

"I realize, of course, this is not an opportune time to be discussing business. However I thought you would want to be informed."

"Thanks, Paul. I appreciate that. But at this particular time I'm not sure what I can do about that. If your Chairman will give me a few days till things start getting back to normal, I'll take it up with my father. Including the . . . you know, the money."

"The Chairman had asked me to propose that in light of your present problems, you might wish to entertain changes that might salvage parts of the proposal."

"That sounds interesting." Raf sat forward in his seat.

"Of course, for all intents and purposes, we must consider that original proposal and its contracts canceled."

"Yes, of course. Without Scheneblin and with what's happened here, I understand."

"Now, if you'll refer to your copy of our original proposal, I'll explain the new terms that the Chairman suggested. I think you'll see the offer does provide a solution for your family's current situation. Including that rather bothersome problem that still exists between you and the Chairman."

Raf dropped half the file from his desk as he frantically tried to arrange the original proposal so they could discuss it.

"I'll be in New York until the end of the week. If these changes are acceptable to you and your family, I can fly out to California. We can then bring everything to a conclusion and eliminate the problems inherent in long-distance negotiations."

"Of course," Raf said smiling to O'Hara and giving him the thumbs up sign.

O'Hara grinned broadly and mouthed, "Fantastic!" at Raf's signal that things between Paul Buntz and him were okay.

Minutes after Raf hung up, they raced toward town and the hospital where Rita and Alicia were keeping their vigil. O'Hara had suggested they go to Rita with the offer first. If she agreed, it would be easier to convince Rafael and Angelica. They would also have to convince Alicia. Before Pietro's death, she was the person Rafael had made responsible for voting his share. Now, under the terms of the trust Rafael had set up for his son, Pietro's share went automatically to her.

"Hello, Jim," Rita said, coming into his arms as they entered the tiny room they'd made their home since Roberto had been brought in. "What's up?" she asked when she saw her brother with him.

"A little business," Raf said as he closed the door so they could talk in private.

"Jesus! You're really something," she said. "How can you think of business when Roberto is still lying in there unconscious?"

"If you two will excuse me." Alicia, hollow-eyed and gaunt from the sleepless hours, struggled to her feet and started for the door. "I'm going to the cafeteria."

"Please, Aunt Alicia. This concerns you too," Raf said.

For the next hour the two women listened as Raf explained the new offer the European company had made . . . the advantages . . . what it would mean to them all . . . especially to their mother and father. Rita leaned against O'Hara for support, too exhausted to move or protest.

Rita tried to look at the papers that Raf kept waving in front of their faces but everything seemed a blur to her.

It all had little or no meaning to Alicia. "Has your father decided it's something he wants to do?" she asked, handing him back some of the papers.

"We haven't had a chance to talk to him about this newest merger yet. When we talked a couple of weeks ago he told me that he was close to saying yes to the first plan. Course that was before . . . Uncle Rivera and Pietro. I came here first because we've got to be practical. Realistic. Our name is not exactly something too many people want to be associated with. Right now the folks might not be thinking too clearly. Believe me, this merger will be good for them . . . for all of us. The folks especially."

"I can't help feeling that as wonderful as all this seems now," Alicia said through her exhaustion, "that you are asking your papa and mama to give up something priceless."

Raf looked at his aunt puzzled. "What's that, Aunt Alicia?"

"Their life's work. The thing they spent their lifetime building. It's true things are bad now. It's a black time. But they gave their love . . . their hopes . . . dreams . . .

even their soul to that land. That business. Now you're asking them to give it up for money."

"That's not true. I'm not asking them to give it up. This is a merger into something bigger. And if we don't take it there might not be anything left later. It might all be taken from them. Then they'd have nothing to show for those hopes and dreams. You have to help me make sure they believe that. Please!"

"No. I won't do that. But I will do whatever your father and mother want to do, Raf. Whatever is good for them, or bad for them . . . I will only do what they want to do," Alicia said.

"Fair enough. Rita?" he said turning to his sister.

"I think it's a sellout, Raf. Pure and simple. Why the hell are you trying to bullshit us and make it look like something else?"

"No, it's still a merger," O'Hara said, interrupting. Alicia was firm, had made her decision and would follow the lead set by the others. But Rita's physical and mental exhaustion were ripe for exploiting. And he didn't dare lose the chance. "If your father and mother are to survive . . ." He took her arm and pulled her up. "Why don't we take a little walk? Just the two of us. Okay?"

She nodded.

"We'll be right back," he said to Raf and Alicia.

"Sure," Raf smiled at his unexpected new ally.

"Let's face it," O'Hara said as they sat on a bench on the lawn across from the hospital. "Right now you can't give your wine away. Besides, what are you losing by this deal? In the end, your father still grows the grapes, you make the wine, and Raf sells it. You still make part of the profits. The Europeans come in . . . give you a new name, different packaging, and it looks like some classy wine from Europe. It sells . . . makes lots of money. You all still get part of the profits. So tell me. What's more important. Surviving . . . or ego?"

Rita looked up into the face of the man she'd come to rely on for strength, support, and love. "You really think it's the only way?"

He looked deep into her eyes and nodded. "I'm sure it is," he said responding to her dilemma. "It leaves your father's pride intact. And it gives his daughter time and money on her hands." He grinned. "And the way I see it, with my tastes, I'm going to need a rich girl with a lot of time on her hands."

Rita smiled and buried her head against his chest.

"Okay," she nodded, eyes closed. It suddenly felt good for the first time in a long time. The weight that seemed to be pressing down around all their lives suddenly seemed to be lifting. "Thanks, Jim."

"Now . . ." he said. "Why don't you get your purse and I'll drive you home. You look like death warmed over. You're about ready to drop. I'll put you to bed and . . ."

She pulled back, shaking her head. "I can't."

"There's nothing you can do here."

"I can be here. It's not much. But it's something I have to do."

"I understand."

"Do you?"

"If it was anyone else, I'd be jealous," he said, holding her close. "But I know Roberto is family to you, almost as much as Alicia is."

"I'm glad you understand," she said standing and heading toward the hospital entrance.

"Okay, brother dear," she said as they came back into the tiny waiting room. "Give Papa and Mama my love. Tell them that as long as you and Jim O'Hara think it's all right, it's all right with me, too."

Raf smiled. His heart pounded with the thrill of success.

Raf and O'Hara found Rafael and Angelica next to the huge, stainless wine press.

"Looks like a posse," Rafael tried to grin at them. He was covered with flecks of purple as the grapes splattered into the basket that would slowly close around the already fermented grapes. Angelica turned a switch and the conveyer rattled to a halt.

"I have something that might help us all out of this," Raf said sitting down on the metal catwalk next to his mother.

Rafael joined them and Raf went over the new proposal Paul Buntz had made.

The main difference was that it was no longer an equal

merger. They would no longer have a vote on the board. But Vin Franco–Italo offered them a face-saving advisory representative's seat.

Rafael looked down the corridor of stainless tanks as his son talked on. It was a magnificent creation he and Angelica had spawned. Now it was all close to escaping them. The proposal meant a great deal of money to them. But it stripped away their proprietorship, the soul, the life they'd breathed into these walls.

He listened to the hum as the massive basket slowly closed around the tons of shriveled grapes. The motor cycled the basket open and shut several times as it squeezed more precious gallons of juice out of the otherwise useless waste.

If he and Angelica agreed to this proposal, he might take the time to design another type of press. One that was more efficient and less expensive than this one, he thought, his mind wandering.

As Raf finally finished, Rafael looked at O'Hara. He knew, by the look on O'Hara's face and the occasional confirming various points, that he was agreeing with the proposal.

Rafael turned to Angelica and put his arm around her shoulders. "What do you think?" he asked her softly. "You about ready to retire? Take some time and relax and get fat?"

Angelica looked into his eyes. She knew how much he was suffering. The death of Rivera and their son would haunt them for the rest of their lives. But the thing that would destroy Rafael Orsini would be having to stand in the midst of everything he'd created and see it destroyed by the hatred that surrounded them. She smiled at him and crushed herself against his chest. She still marveled at his warmth and the muscled body that never seemed to change even after all these years.

"Why not?" she asked. "It's about time we did something for ourselves. It's about time to see if our kids can stand on their own two feet."

Across from them, Raf smiled broadly. He'd saved them all. He'd given them a way out of this nightmare . . . and he'd saved his own ass in the process.

* * *

485

They met the charming Swiss lawyer who'd flown in from New York and initialed the rough draft of the contracts over dinner. The following morning, in a simple ceremony over coffee, they formalized their agreement by signing the contracts hurriedly approved by their attorneys and accountants.

As Paul Buntz wiped his green-tinted prescription lenses, Rafael looked down at the bank drafts, the stock certificates, the signed contracts and agreements that lay before him and Angelica. A lifetime of work and love and sweat represented by a few scraps of paper with typewriting on them.

He put his arm around Angelica.

"How about you and me getting out of here and grabbing a bite of lunch?"

"Sounds wonderful." She smiled. "As long as it's alone. Just the two of us."

"Hey! How about your poor old son?" Raf complained. Now that an envelope containing the Casino notes rested safely in his inside coat pocket, he was jovial, outgoing, the epitome of charm.

"I'm afraid you're on your own," she said taking Rafael's hand and heading toward the door.

Back at his hotel in San Francisco, Paul Buntz placed his call to Carlo Gianini.

"I'm most pleased, Paul. My gratitude to you will be undying," Gianini said. But the Padrone was almost sad. The hunt . . . the chase . . . the game was near its end. All he wanted now was the joy of relating his success to the man he'd won it all from, Rafael Orsini himself.

CHAPTER THIRTY-EIGHT

"Rita! Rita!" Alicia cried happily as she dragged her out of the chair she'd been sleeping in.

More asleep than awake, Rita didn't know where she was or what was happening.

"He's awake! He's awake!" Alicia sobbed joyfully. "He's going to be all right!"

Rita felt a surge of energy rush through her body. As if by magic, the exhaustion and pain were erased from her body.

Hysterical with joy, she followed her aunt and tiptoed into Roberto's room. After seeing him and smiling at him and squeezing his hand and feeling him squeeze it back, Rita called everybody she knew to tell them the wonderful news.

"Jim?" she said as O'Hara finally answered his phone. "It's me . . . Rita."

"Hello, my darling. Are you all right?"

"Yes . . . yes . . . yes!" She laughed and cried and laughed. "I just wanted you to know that Roberto is conscious. The doctors say he still has a long way to go. But it looks like he's out of the woods."

"That's wonderful news," he said, genuinely pleased. He'd always liked the tall Mexican. He was relieved that the list of broken bodies didn't have to include anyone else.

"I've got to go now," Rita laughed, almost intoxicated from the joy and relief. "But I'll see you soon. Okay?"

"I sure hope so, my darling. And give Roberto my best. He's a lucky guy to be waking up to such a pair of beautiful faces."

"Thank you, Jim. You really know how to make a girl feel great."

"She deserves a little happiness. And with luck maybe I can add to it pretty soon."

Rita felt her shoulders tingling.

O'Hara sat back in his favorite chair and stared up at the ceiling. Life was wonderful. His was growing more wonderful by the day.

But it hadn't been the call from Rita that had sent him into his euphoria. Just before she called, he'd received a call from Carlo Gianini.

To show his appreciation and confidence, Gianini was appointing James Pike O'Hara president of the remains of the Orsini Wine empire. The news would be breaking sometime next week, Gianini told him. In the meantime, he already had his battery of PR people working on the changes at the winery. The American public would want to know the good news so they could rejoice over the eradication of the cancer that until now had been growing in their midst.

Rita pushed the door quietly open and looked into the dimly lit room. In the days since he'd recovered consciousness, Roberto had continued to improve. She tiptoed across the shiny tiled floor and looked down at him. He looked so frail, so weak. Not like the strong, robust athlete she'd known all her life. She leaned over him and his eyes opened just a slit. She smiled and the corners of his mouth turned up slightly as he smiled back.

"Still lying around on your butt, I see," she joked softly.

He nodded. She looked around the room where he'd hovered between life and death. There was a metal stand next to him that still supported the bottles of IV, plasma, vitamins, and antibiotics that dripped into his arm.

Monitoring machines stood by the wall at the head of his bed feeding signs to the nurses who came in every half hour to check up on him. Rita studied the apparatus which registered his heart and respiration.

"Hey, looks like you're alive," she grinned as he finally awoke fully.

He started to speak, but his throat still felt as parched as though he'd been marooned on the desert.

"If you don't want to talk, I understand. I can talk enough for both of us."

"You always could," he finally managed to half whisper.

She laughed, delighted that he was improving enough to joke with her again.

"They told me about Pietro this morning," he said.

"Yeah . . ." She nodded. "They thought it best if they waited . . . till you were better."

"I should have known . . ." he whispered, shaking his head slowly in disgust at his stupidity that night.

"Should have known what?"

"That it was a trap."

"How could you have known?" Rita said, putting her fingertips across his lips.

"Pietro knew them, Rita."

"What?" Rita felt herself tingling. "You mean he saw them?"

Roberto nodded. "I did, too." He closed his eyes for a moment as tears started to form as he relived that night. "Rita . . . it was Pietro they were after."

"For God's sakes! Why would anyone be after Pietro? Why would anyone want to hurt him?" She stared at Roberto in disbelief.

"I'm going to find that out as soon as I can get out of here," he promised. "I'm going to get the man who set it up and find out from him before . . ." He clenched his jaw shut before he could allow himself the luxury of telling her he planned to kill the man. As coldly and as brutally as Pietro had been killed.

"Roberto, my God, if this is true the police have been waiting to talk to you. You have to tell them. Please! It's my brother. You have to."

"No!" He shook his head angrily.

"But why?" Rita pleaded. "I don't understand."

"There's no way to prove anything. I've been lying here since I woke up trying to figure the thing out. It doesn't make sense. But I'm going to get the truth."

He looked at her and Rita could see that his eyes were burning with hatred.

"If he was there, your word is enough proof."

"He wasn't there. But I'm sure he sent the men who were. And someway . . . I don't know how . . . but someway it's tied to my dad, too."

"My God, Roberto. Who is it? Do we know him?"

"You don't need to know. I'll take care of it. Afterward, then you'll know."

"If I'll know afterward, then that means I know now."

Roberto stared at her but wouldn't respond.

"Pietro was my brother, Roberto. I have a right to know."

Roberto stared at her for a long, deathly quiet moment. "O'Hara," he finally said, quietly.

Rita felt as though she'd been kicked in the pit of her stomach. "I don't believe you." She choked back the tears that had started streaming down from her eyes.

Roberto remained silent. He didn't have the strength to argue with her.

"Why would he, for God's sakes?" she pleaded.

"I don't know," he said. "But Pietro knew the men . . . one of them anyway. Just before . . . it happened, he said the man was O'Hara's friend."

"But you know how easily Pietro was confused. He might have just thought he knew him."

"No. He knew this man. He was afraid of this man."

"No . . . I don't believe you." But she hadn't convinced herself. With tears streaming down her face, she raced out of the room and down the corridor, past a confused Benito who stared after her.

Heartsick that something might have happened to the man he considered a son, Benito raced into Roberto's room.

Roberto smiled as the big man came over to him. He resolved to say nothing about O'Hara to Benito. Otherwise, his old friend would do the job for him.

Her tires screeching, Rita raced down the highway toward home where O'Hara had promised to meet her and the rest of the family for dinner.

Her mind, usually facile, logical, and clear was deluged by thoughts. She couldn't focus. She could only pray over and over that Roberto was wrong . . . that somehow her brother had been mistaken.

As her car hurtled down the nearly deserted road, her thoughts became darker, more and more muddled. Why would anyone want poor Pietro dead? And who could have ever wanted to kill Rivera? Roberto said he thought the two murders were tied together. But what did her brother and Rivera have in common—other than that their deaths nearly destroyed her family? Dear God! Was it possible all their disasters—Rivera's murder . . . Pietro's . . . the merger . . . the death of their winery—had been orchestrated by one man? And if so, how could it have been? And why? Why would the man she loved even consider such a thing?

As she swerved into the narrow lane that ran past the old winery to her parents' house, she could see O'Hara's jeep. The sight filled her with dread. No! Dammit! Roberto had to be wrong. Jim O'Hara had always been the first to help . . . the first to offer valuable advice. He even let her brother have credit for the idea to sell their wine in Europe. Even helped set up the merger. Oh God! Every part of their lives that was in shambles was a part he'd touched. The pain filled her until she felt like screaming. She didn't know who or what to believe.

"That you, Rita?" Angelica called from the kitchen.

"Yes, Mama." She was standing in the cool of the big living room. She looked around at the heavy, upholstered chairs she'd known since childhood, reminders of another era, with her arms covered with doilies crocheted by her mother. Her father's chair, which had once sat next to the radio so he could listen to the farm report about the next day's weather, was now near the television, though the radio was still on top of the TV.

Hurt and pain and warmth and joy swept through her as she thought of the memories this room held for her. Christmas mornings before dawn . . . birthday parties . . . her first prom date. Now, memories of one disaster after another that had happened to them since Jim O'Hara's arrival.

She walked into the kitchen where her mother and Aunt Alicia were. "Hello, Mama . . . Aunt Alicia," she said embracing them both.

491

"Hello, Rita. Did you talk with Roberto?" Alicia still had dark circles under her eyes from the exhaustion and stress of tending her stepson.

"Yes. He . . . looks great."

"I know." Alicia busied herself helping Angelica. "When I left to come over here, he was already making plans . . . chomping at the bit to get back home . . . back to the union." Now that Roberto was on the road to recovery, Alicia was filled with a new determination. She would help her stepson carry out his father's goals. They would work together in memory of the man she loved.

"Is Jim here? I saw his jeep."

"Yes. He's out with your father and brother in the wine cellar," Angelica said. "Your father insists on opening the last of the special bottles to celebrate Roberto's coming back to us."

Rita nodded and moved toward the back door.

Rita stood on the porch and watched as her father and brother came out of the wine cellar. The old oak doors still showed the marks from the ax attack by the Treasury agents the night they had confiscated Rafael and Angelica's first batch of wine.

A moment later, out of the shadows, came the man she thought she knew so well and loved so much.

O'Hara waved when he saw her and hurried to embrace her.

"Don't touch me!"

The three men were dumbfounded by her sudden hostility. They stood confused as she turned and stormed back through the screen door into the kitchen. She suddenly couldn't stand to look at O'Hara.

"You want to tell me what's the matter?" O'Hara said following her in.

"I don't know if I can," she said flatly, refusing to face him.

"How about a drink first? Then maybe we can . . ."

"It would take more than a drink," she interrupted, "to make me forget that I ever trusted you. That my family trusted you."

He stared at her shocked. She could not have found out

about his involvement with Vin Franco–Italo Et Cie. So far there had been no press releases. No announcements. Like a computer, his mind started formulating excuses, alibis, avenues of escape, and outright denials.

Rita looked around at the sound of wine bottles clinking together. As her father set them down on the kitchen table, he looked at her, confused and worried.

"Rita," Angelica said, "if you and Jim have something to discuss, have the courtesy to spare him and the rest of us embarrassment by doing it alone. Between the two of you."

"It's not between the two of us, Mama," Rita said angrily. "It's between him and the whole goddamn Orsini family."

O'Hara looked at Rafael and Angelica and shrugged his innocence. There was no one who could tie him to anything, he assured himself.

"Then don't beat around the bush, Rita," Rafael said. "If it involves us all . . . and Jim . . . get on with it. Get it out."

"This person . . . this creature . . . this filth, who came to us and pretended to be our friend, is responsible for Pietro's death. Maybe even Rivera's."

"What?" O'Hara said as though he'd been hit. Then he recovered his poise. "Rita, darling. You've been sitting at the hospital for days on end. You're exhausted. You haven't had any rest. And you're not thinking . . . you're talking crazy."

She looked desperately to her father for support, but all he could do was wait for her response. It was up to her to convince them.

Slowly she wove a story for them that she had worked out in the car. It started with Raf's trip to Europe, and his return with a remarkable proposal which O'Hara had supported to the hilt. Especially behind the scenes with her . . . away from her family . . . even in bed. She heard her mother gasp but her father, unflinching as ever, stared, waiting for her to go on. She brought the story through the strike . . . Rivera's death . . . and finished with her brother's and Roberto's ambush. Then she stood there glaring, daring him to refute it.

"It's a hell of a story," O'Hara said. "A masterpiece.

493

And I don't see one thing in it that's not true. But what's the connection? My God! Please, tell me. How does it relate to me? I mean, you could tell a story like that and make anyone look like a goddamn Judas. But you're pointing at me! What, in God's name, is there in all this rambling drivel that points to me killing your brother? It's insane!"

"No," Rita said. "It might be drivel. Insane. But the animals you used to tie the job up in a neat little package for you were sloppy. They left Roberto Rivera alive."

"So? I'm as overjoyed that he's alive as you are." O'Hara searched his memory for something that would tie him to Roberto or Pietro. There was nothing.

"You won't be for long." She had a look that challenged him to ask why.

"Why?" He responded to her challenge, as he would to any challenge proposed to him.

"Because, when's he's well enough to walk out of the hospital, he intends to kill you."

"My dear God!" she heard Alicia gasp. "I don't believe Roberto would do such a thing."

"He would to the creature that had his father shot down like an animal. And my brother."

"How does Roberto know?" Rafael asked quietly.

"Pietro told him. He told Roberto the men who did it were friends of Jim O'Hara's."

"Pietro told this to Roberto?" O'Hara howled with disbelieving laughter. "Rita, for God's sakes! Use your brain! Even at his best, Pietro was a confused child. He rarely made sense. Now all of a sudden, something he tells Roberto Rivera during a tragedy . . . a horror . . . a nightmare that ends with him dying . . . is your proof?"

"It is for Roberto. And it was before they were shot. He told Roberto about seeing you at the airport with them . . . and how angry you were. And how you made him promise not to tell about it. That's probably why the poor guard was killed, too!" She turned away in disgust trying to fight a nausea that boiled inside.

"That's insane!" O'Hara shouted. "Rita. You have to stop this," he yelled angrily as he took her by the shoulders and spun her back around.

"That's enough." Rafael put his hand on O'Hara's shoulder to stop him. Even if his daughter was hysterical, exhausted, he wouldn't tolerate anyone touching her that way.

"Enough?" O'Hara's face was crimson. "Your daughter, the woman I planned to ask to marry me, has just called me a murderer. And you want me to stand here like a beat puppy while she walks over me? No sir! Not me! Some of her other pussy-whipped little boyfriends maybe. But not this cookie! I don't have to stand around here and take shit from her . . . or you either for that matter, or anyone else, buster."

Raf looked at the man in disbelief. He couldn't believe his loss of control.

"Yes, you do," Rita said, furiously jabbing him in the chest with a finger. "You have to take our shit. Like you have to take shit from that guy from Switzerland. What's his name? The guy we signed the papers with? Oh, yeah . . . Buntz. Just like that asshole. You're just a guy going through life with his nose buried up the asshole of some guy at the top. First it was my father's. Now, if I don't miss my guess, it's Buntz's that's next in line."

O'Hara looked like a lobster just hauled out of a cauldron.

"No one . . ." he spat. "No one. I don't have to worry anymore about people like you! Your father, your idiot of a brother . . . and I'm not talking about Pietro." He shot a look at Raf. "After this week, I'll be the one running the remains of this piece of shit you call a winery. Me alone! I'm the one who's going to pick up the pieces and put them all back together again. I'm the one they're giving the keys to the front gate to. I'm the one who'll say who comes in and who goes out. And you . . ." He pointed angrily at Rita, "little Miss Bitch! You're the first piece of garbage I'm flushing down the drain!"

"You have to be kidding!" Rita howled. "Who the hell would be crazy enough to trust you with the keys to the toilet . . . much less the front gate?"

"The one who put all this together. The Chairman of the board of Vin Franco–Italo Et Cie."

"Buntz is not the Chairman of Vin Franco—Italo?" Rafael asked, turning to his son.

The look on his son's face answered the question for him.

"Of course not," O'Hara jeered triumphantly. "Buntz is just an errand boy."

"That shouldn't matter," muttered Raf.

"I think it should matter a great deal," O'Hara grinned arrogantly. "I understand that the Chairman is an old friend of yours, Mr. Orsini. The two of you go back a long time together. At least that's what the Chairman—*Signore* Carlo Gianini—told me. I believe you used to call him the Padrone."

Alicia's scream of disbelief echoed through the room. "My God! My God! My God!" she babbled.

"Yes, he is a God to some." O'Hara could joke now. The power was his. "He thought I was his tool. I prefer to think of him as mine."

There were tears in Rafael's eyes. Angelica looked at her husband and Alicia with the feeling that they were all in the middle of a nightmare that would never end.

"Carlo Gianini died in the war . . . in an attack on his home," Rafael said.

Angelica and Alicia looked at him in shock. Since the night Pietro had been kidnapped, they'd believed Carlo Gianini had died in the river. Why had Rafael not told them what he knew?

"He seemed out of our lives," Rafael said to his wife and sister, sensing their unspoken questions.

"You're wrong," O'Hara smirked. Not only is he in your lives, he's very much in control of them. Through me, of course."

"We took you in . . . made you a part of our family . . . treated you with love, respect . . . and you would do this to us?" Angelica asked in disbelief. "Murder our friend . . . our son?"

"I had nothing to do with their deaths," O'Hara protested. "As a matter of fact, I tried to keep Pietro out of trouble. It's your other son I didn't try to keep out of trouble. Fortunately. If it wasn't for him, none of this would have been possible."

With an agonized howl, Raf lunged for O'Hara. He locked his fingers around his tormentor's throat.

Rafael leaped between the two men, trying to break his son's stranglehold. Angelica, terrified for her husband and son, tried to pull them both away. But her unexpected weight spun Rafael off balance and sent them all crashing against the kitchen table.

"No!" Rafael shouted. "Rita . . . no!"

All eyes turned toward Rita who had the shotgun that stood behind the back door. With blind rage in her eyes, Rita raised and leveled the massive old gun at O'Hara who dropped to his knees with a scream of terror. He felt himself going limp as he tried to crawl across the floor to the safety of Rafael . . . the stove . . . the door . . . anything. But it was as if he were mired in quicksand. He felt his pants suddenly flush with warmth.

The explosion roared through the little kitchen, and the smell of sulphur seared their nostrils. Rita stared in disbelief. Just as she had fired, the gun had been jerked away from O'Hara's head by Alicia. She tried to struggle, but her aunt wrested the gun from her hands and hurled it across the room. It smashed against one of the ice box doors and clattered harmlessly to the floor where O'Hara was blubbering hysterically.

"No . . ." Alicia screamed at the top of her voice. "No! It is enough! It is over! There has been enough death . . . enough killing . . . enough pain! Enough . . . enough . . . enough!" She suddenly started shaking as though she were freezing.

Rafael rose and rushed to take his sister in his arms.

Rita watched almost in a trance as her father crushed Alicia to his chest and tried to soothe away the lifetime of pain.

"You are right, Alicia," he whispered as Angelica came to them and embraced them both. "It's over. At last, it's finally over."

Rafael walked over and picked up the empty shotgun with one hand and pulled O'Hara to his feet. With the barrel, he pushed O'Hara toward the door.

"You want the keys to the front gate, you'll get the keys to the front gate." Rafael forced the blubbering man into his truck.

CHAPTER THIRTY-NINE

"Johnson . . . Ortiz!" Rafael yelled to two men in the guard shack behind the main gate as his truck skidded to a halt. One of the men was the guard, the other the night foreman.

"Yessir!" the guard said, quickly sliding the glass door open and trotting to the gate.

"I want the two of you out of here! Now! Mr. O'Hara's in charge. Go on home . . . spend the night with your families for a change. Come up to the house in the morning and I'll pay you what you've got coming . . . plus enough for a vacation."

The two men glanced at each other, confused.

"Now!" Rafael shouted at them in an uncharacteristic anger that brought response from both men. In a trot, they headed for their cars as Rafael put his truck in gear and sped through the gate.

As they drove toward the center of the winery complex, O'Hara felt a growing fear welling up in his stomach. He'd escaped Rita's wrath. But Rafael still had the shotgun. His eyes darted anxiously as the truck passed the crane and pile driver abandoned by construction crews who had refused to cross the picket lines weeks earlier.

"Out!" Rafael barked, prodding him with the barrel of the shotgun as he braked to a halt in front of one of the main buildings.

"Please . . . you have to believe me!" O'Hara begged. "I swear to you I didn't know anything about Pietro. I knew they were going to do something to Rivera. But they said they were just going to rough him up a little. Please . . . believe me. With Pietro, I tried . . ."

"Out!" Rafael said angrily. He looked up as he heard

another car approaching. It was Rita's car. Angelica, Alicia, and Raf were all crammed into the tiny front seat.

Like a group of prairie townspeople flocking a hanging, they filed out of the tiny Thunderbird.

O'Hara cowered in the grass between the access road and the winery walls. "What are you going to do?" He tried to force himself into the earth as his terror grew.

Rafael prodded him with the barrel of the shotgun and motioned for him to go into the cavernous building. Under this one roof, almost a million gallons of new wine rested in deep pools within stainless steel tanks.

"No," Rafael said to his family as they started to fall in behind him and O'Hara. "I want you to wait outside. This is something that only I can do."

Rafael prodded O'Hara down the concrete corridor toward the interior of the building. As they walked, the only sound was their footsteps echoing back from the walls of the tanks.

"This is far enough," Rafael said, bringing O'Hara to a halt next to one of the tanks. A card holder on the side of the tank described the wine within the cool steel walls: the variety of grape, date of crush, sugar content, alcohol content, and projected bottling date were all logged in Rita's neat handwriting.

For a moment, Rafael stared at the massive tank, its piping, its plumbing, its valves, its manifolds, and its card—and felt a sorrow running through his body at the thought of what he had to do. Then he poked O'Hara with the shotgun and nodded toward the huge valve that jutted out from the bottom of the tank like a giant faucet.

"Open it," Rafael said.

O'Hara looked at him dumbfounded. Using the butt of the shotgun, Rafael viciously pushed him across the pipes that ran between the tanks and walkway.

"I'm not going to tell you again. Open the drain valve."

Trembling, O'Hara put his hands on the spokes of the big wheel and strained. He put his weight into it and grunted, but he couldn't get it to budge.

Rafael pushed him out of the way and wedged the barrel of the shotgun between the wheel and its shaft. Using the barrel as a lever, he strained and pushed until he felt it finally start to turn. He stepped back and motioned for O'Hara to finish the job.

O'Hara twisted the wheel around and around as it slowly unwound along its thick shaft.

There was a sudden hiss of air and a stream of Burgundy liquid gushed from the drain pipe under the valve into the concrete gutter that ran the length of the aisle.

"All the way," Rafael warned. O'Hara wiped the sweat from his forehead and continued to turn the wheel counterclockwise until the wine thundered into the gutter like a raging waterfall.

In shock, O'Hara stepped back away from the tank into the corridor as the wine splattered and stained the front of his clothes. He stared in horror as the tiny drain at the bottom of the gutter quickly filled. The drain was too small for the torrent of Burgundy liquid churning down the trough. In seconds, the gutter had overflowed into the corridor between the tanks.

"The next one," Rafael said without any sign of outward emotion.

Rafael forced O'Hara to bang, strain, and sweat until one row of the giant tanks was cranked open. The inside of the winery sounded like a raging river as thousands of gallons of wine boiled and swirled out of the shallow gutters on to the floor. The aroma spewed out into the night air to where Angelica, Alicia, Rita, and Raf stood.

Things were going too slowly, Rafael thought. It was too painful. If it was to be ended, it had to be quicker.

Slogging toward him through the flood, he saw his family. "Go back!" he pleaded.

"No!" Angelica said adamantly. "Not until I know for sure why you are doing this thing."

He pushed O'Hara away from him into the middle of the flood and walked over to Angelica. "If I don't do this thing, Carlo Gianini will keep on and on until he's destroyed us. If he believes that he's pushed me into doing this, then he'll think he's won. It will be over. Believe me, my love, this is the only way. Afterward . . . it'll finally be over. We'll be free of him."

"I understand," she said embracing him and crushing

herself to him. "But you're wrong about one thing. You can't do it by yourself. We must all help. We must all have a part in this."

He was filled with the strength of her love. Carlo could never defeat him as long as he had her. He looked down at her and nodded.

With Alicia, Rita, and Raf following, she disappeared toward the open doors.

Rafael turned and jabbed O'Hara with the barrel of the shotgun. "Move away from where you're standing and you'll never leave this building alive. Understand?"

O'Hara nodded. It was clear to him that Rafael and the rest of his family had gone insane.

Rafael sprinted down the aisle, his steps kicking up splashes of wine behind him. He leaped into the yellow forklift that sat at the head of one of the rows of tanks. He turned the key, pressed the starter, and the tiny engine chugged to life. Then he pushed a hydraulic lever next to the steering wheel and two steel fork arms started to raise.

Rafael put the forklift in gear and raced it down the aisle toward one of the tanks as the wine sprayed up like water in a rainstorm behind him. As he collided with the tank, the forklift's steel arms pierced its sides like twin harpoons. A torrent of wine thundered out. Rafael backed away and aimed for the next tank. With expert skill, he gouged and ripped the steel sides of one tank after another. Finally the last of the dozens of tanks were ruptured and the aisles resembled a flooded stream racing for a distant ocean. As he backed out of the flooded corridor toward the double doors, he motioned for O'Hara to get on the back of the forklift.

As soon as he hopped on, Rafael gunned the engine and raced toward the next building. Inside the noise of escaping wine already filled the air, and the floor between the tanks was becoming a twin red river to the buildings they'd just abandoned. Rita and Raf, both in tears, stood side by side, forcing the huge valves open with sledgehammers.

Speeding to the next building, he found Angelica and Alicia in the last storage building, covered from head to foot with wine. They'd used Rita's Thunderbird as a battering ram to knock the drain valves out of the sides of the tanks. The rivers of red and white that had poured from the tanks had finally flooded the car's interior, half drowning the two women. As Angelica tried to grind the badly mangled little car back to life, Alicia yelled and screamed encouragement.

Rafael gunned the forklift and backed out into the night. By now the road between the buildings had become a red river.

He roared down the road through the flood toward the executive complex. He braked to a halt beside the pile driver that stood silently across from the offices and turned to O'Hara.

"Off!" he ordered.

O'Hara, looking like a drowned rat, quickly dropped off the soaking forklift.

Rafael hopped down and pointed back up to his seat. "Climb up. That should be the best seat in the house," he said as he hopped up into the cab of the pile driver.

On the highway outside the gate, those manning the vigil fires were starting to gather near the entrance. They didn't know what was happening, but from the noise and the torrent of wine flooding down onto the highway, it was clear the winery was dying. And they wanted to witness its death.

Rafael disengaged the clutch and the mechanical dinosaur started slowly rumbling toward the offices, the asphalt grinding apart like sand under the heavy machine. Rafael guided the diesel pile driver closer and closer toward the heart of his empire. He touched another hydraulic lever, and the huge cranelike arm fell onto the building's roof. The cedar shakes flew off the roof like shingles blown away by the winds of a hurricane.

Rafael leaped off as sparks flew from the electrical wiring that the machine was cutting through like spiderwebs. The huge machine lumbered on without him, through the reception area and toward the core of the building.

Finally it ran into the panels where the power for the plant was routed.

There was an eruption of sparks and the pile driver's fuel tank exploded, showering flames through the rubble. In seconds the complex was an inferno.

Rafael watched the flames consuming the building. Then

he walked slowly back toward the forklift where his family had gathered.

Rafael and his family marched like vigilantes through the night, from building to building, from wine cellar to wine cellar, spreading the fire onto everything in their path.

Outside the gates, the crowd watched in stunned silence at the destruction. Now they felt no hatred, no joy. Only an awe and wonder at all this being done by the Orsini family themselves.

"I believe these are yours, Mr. O'Hara," Rafael said throwing the man his ring of keys. "The keys to the kingdom. I'm sure the key to the front gate is on there somewhere. Give my regards to your master. Tell him that in you, he indeed has a faithful dog."

As O'Hara stood there, unable to move, Rafael led his family up the hill that lay between their house and the winery. It was the same hill on which Rafael had so often sat during that first year he'd leased the vineyard from Ferrara. It was the hill on which he sang and pleaded to the vines from which their empire had grown. It was the hill on which he and Angelica often sat and made love. The hill on which he first told her of his dream.

It was fitting that it should also be the hill from which they would watch those dreams and that empire end.

Standing there, wine-splattered, soot-covered, and silent, they could hear the fire engines wailing toward the flames from the little town of Healdsberg. But the fire was too complete. Its heat too searing.

As one of the buildings collapsed sending ashes and smoke billowing toward the black heavens, Rafael heard someone sobbing gently behind him. He turned and saw Raf trying to hide the tears in his eyes. Rafael reached over and pulled his son to him.

"I'll kill the son of a bitch," Raf said angrily as he watched O'Hara standing alone, desolate, near the front gate.

"No . . . it's over," Rafael said.

"But he killed my brother . . . he was the cause of all this." He tried to control his rage.

"No . . ." Rafael hugged him again to soothe him.

"Another man . . . a lifetime ago . . . killed your brother. But he can't hurt us anymore."

Rafael felt Angelica's arms around his shoulders and made room so Rita and Alicia could join him also.

"You mean to let it end this way?" Raf asked, not understanding.

"There's been enough pain . . . enough hate . . . enough killing," Angelica said, wiping the tears from her son's cheeks. "Your father has said it . . . and I agree . . . it is over." She turned so she could look directly at both her children. "I want you to promise me that."

Raf and Rita stared at her.

"Yes, Mama," Raf finally promised.

"Rita?" Angelica insisted.

"Yes, Mama. I promise, too." She turned and started down the slope.

"Where are you going?" Rafael asked.

"To town." She wiped the purple soot off her forehead. "To sit next to a wonderful man in a hospital bed and convince him that it's all over for him as well."

"Wait for me," Alicia said heading down the hill toward her. "I'll go with you."

"Great! It's not going to be easy, but I think the two of us can convince him how much a waste his plans for Jim O'Hara would be," Rita said waiting for her.

"Give him our love," Rafael said as the two women headed down the hill between rows of grape spikes that looked like dead hands reaching toward the sky in the reflected glow from the fire.

"Raf," Alicia said stopping and calling back to her nephew.

"Yeah?"

"Why don't you come with us? We could use your help."

"Besides," Rita called when he hesitated, "you're the only one with a car that's still running."

Raf looked at his father and mother and shook his head. "She'll never change, will she?"

Rafael and Angelica shook their heads almost in unison.

"I'll see you all later," he sighed trotting after Rita and Alicia.

* * *

504

"Not much left," Rafael said, staring down at the dying flames.

"We've had less."

"At least we've still got the house . . . and the old farm. They may have bought the wine and the winery. But we've still got our vines."

"We never needed more," Angelica said.

"Good time for pruning," Rafael said as he and Angelica started slowly toward the house.

"Too early."

"Yeah, guess you're right," he acknowledged.

"If you're looking for something to do, maybe now you can finally take Joe up on his offer."

"You mean . . . go to work for that little snot-nosed brat that used to hang around here?"

"Not for . . . with. Go to work with. You know he can't spend as much time running his winery now that he's in Washington so much. Besides, you always wanted to make great wine."

"His isn't that great."

"With the two of you working together it could be."

"You always were the one with the great ideas, weren't you?" Rafael took her face between his hands. He still thrilled to the feel of her warmth and softness.

"That's right! I'm the brains . . . you're the brawn. Remember."

He nodded.

She reached over and patted his stomach. "Of course, lately you've gotten a little more brawn here than before."

Despite the chaos and destruction around them, a smile came to his face.

"Are you sure, Rafael? Is it finally really over?"

"Yes, I'm sure."

"You weren't just saying that for Raf's benefit?"

"No, I said it because it was true. Everyone . . . including Carlo Gianini . . . has suffered enough. Both his family and ours have known grief . . . death . . . pain . . . destruction. Only two madmen would want it to go on from here. Maybe there was a time in the past when I was one . . . but no more."

"But Carlo Gianini may still be."

"No. After tonight he'll celebrate a victory. Let him believe it . . . savor it. In time, he'll fade like the darkness . . ."

Thank God, she thought. Their war is over.

"You still think you remember how to make grape butter?" she asked.

"Angel Butter? Sure. Who could ever forget that. Why? You expecting another Prohibition?"

"No. But if it doesn't work out between you and Joe, you're going to have to start somewhere."

He hugged her to him. "I think your father was right. You could always make better tires out of the stuff than wine."

They both laughed. Rafael felt as he had that first night after he'd leased the vineyards from Ferrara. There was a new life before them.

The fire from their holocaust still lit up their fields. But its destruction had to do with their past. Now there was only their future to think of.

The passionate sequel to
the scorching novel of
fierce pride and forbidden love

THE PROUD HUNTER

by Marianne Harvey

Author of *The Dark Horseman* and *The Wild One*

Trefyn Connor—he demanded all that was his—and more—with the arrogance of a man who fought to win . . . with the passion of a man who meant to possess his enemy's daughter and make her pay the price!

Juliet Trevarvas—the beautiful daughter of The Dark Horseman. She would make Trefyn come to her. She would taunt him, shock him, claim him body and soul before she would surrender to THE PROUD HUNTER.

A Dell Book $3.25   (17098-2)

THE WILD ONE

by
MARIANNE HARVEY
bestselling author of *The Dark Horseman*
and *The Proud Hunter*

Proud, beautiful Judith—raised by her stern
grandmother on the savage Cornish coast—
boldly abandoned herself to one man and sought
solace in the arms of another. But only one man
could tame her, could match her fiery spirit,
could fulfill the passionate promise of rapturous,
timeless love.

A Dell Book $2.95   (19207-2)

The

The third chapter in the triumphant saga that began with *The Immigrants* and continued with *Second Generation*

Establishment

The Lavettes—a special breed. A powerful and passionate clan. Swept up in the McCarthy witch-hunts, struggling to help a new-born Israel survive, they would be caught up in a turbulent saga of war, money and politics. All would fulfill their magnificent destinies as their lives became a stunning portrait of their times.

A Dell Book   (12296-1) $3.25

Howard Fast

Dell Bestsellers

- [ ] **RANDOM WINDS** by Belva Plain $3.50 (17158-X)
- [ ] **MEN IN LOVE** by Nancy Friday $3.50 (15404-9)
- [ ] **JAILBIRD** by Kurt Vonnegut $3.25 (15447-2)
- [ ] **LOVE: Poems** by Danielle Steel $2.50 (15377-8)
- [ ] **SHOGUN** by James Clavell $3.50 (17800-2)
- [ ] **WILL** by G. Gordon Liddy $3.50 (09666-9)
- [ ] **THE ESTABLISHMENT** by Howard Fast........$3.25 (12296-1)
- [ ] **LIGHT OF LOVE** by Barbara Cartland $2.50 (15402-2)
- [ ] **SERPENTINE** by Thomas Thompson $3.50 (17611-5)
- [ ] **MY MOTHER/MY SELF** by Nancy Friday $3.25 (15663-7)
- [ ] **EVERGREEN** by Belva Plain $3.50 (13278-9)
- [ ] **THE WINDSOR STORY**
  by J. Bryan III & Charles J.V. Murphy $3.75 (19346-X)
- [ ] **THE PROUD HUNTER** by Marianne Harvey ..$3.25 (17098-2)
- [ ] **HIT ME WITH A RAINBOW**
  by James Kirkwood $3.25 (13622-9)
- [ ] **MIDNIGHT MOVIES** by David Kaufelt $2.75 (15728-5)
- [ ] **THE DEBRIEFING** by Robert Litell $2.75 (01873-5)
- [ ] **SHAMAN'S DAUGHTER** by Nan Salerno
  & Rosamond Vanderburgh $3.25 (17863-0)
- [ ] **WOMAN OF TEXAS** by R.T. Stevens $2.95 (19555-1)
- [ ] **DEVIL'S LOVE** by Lane Harris $2.95 (11915-4)

At your local bookstore or use this handy coupon for ordering:

Dell **DELL BOOKS**
P.O. BOX 1000, PINEBROOK, N.J. 07058

Please send me the books I have checked above. I am enclosing $_____
(please add 75¢ per copy to cover postage and handling). Send check or money order—no cash or C.O.D.'s. Please allow up to 8 weeks for shipment.

Mr/Mrs/Miss _____

Address _____

City _____ State/Zip _____